THE
CRUSHING

THE
CRUSHING

OLIVIA CALLAHAN SUSPENSE

KERRY PERESTA

LEVEL
BEST BOOKS

First edition

ISBN: 978-1-68512-770-1

Cover art by Level Best Designs

This book was professionally typeset on Reedsy.
Find out more at reedsy.com

This book is dedicated to Lynette Phillips. As Meredith from Grey's Anatomy would say: "You're my person." Lynette, you and I have been through some crazy, hard stuff and we get it. We get the sweaty struggle to climb over obstacles...some of our own making and some not. We get the frustration of setbacks as we try to make our worlds a better place...two steps back and one step forward. You've been my rock through it all, and this one's for you, girl.

Praise for The Crushing

"Fans of Frieda McFadden and Lisa Jewell will stay up past their bedtimes devouring the latest thriller from Kerry Peresta. Haunted by her abusive ex-husband, P.I. Olivia Callahan had better keep her friends close and her enemies closer. Now if she could only tell them apart. When one of her best friends goes missing in a Florida swamp, the clock is ticking as the suspense winds tighter on every page."—Kelly Oliver, author of the Jessica James mysteries

"The tension in Kerry Peresta's "The Crushing" is off the chain. *Chilling.* "I can beat this," the captive whispers from her locked room. "I *will* escape." Taut. Gripping. Engrossing. Highly recommended!—Tracy Clark, award-winning author of the Cass Raines Chicago Mystery series and the Det. Harriet Foster series

"Rich details, a strong, character-driven plot, and enough snaky twists and turns to give you vertigo—this fourth entry in Kerry Peresta's Olivia Callahan series will have you sweating bullets and turning pages like a tornado, and leave you breathless as a mile sprinter. There's nothing less simple than a simple missing-persons case, and there are far worse things than gators in the dark, dank Florida boonies. Don't believe me? Read *The Crushing.*" —J.R. Sanders, Shamus Award-winning author of the Nate Ross novels

"Relentlessly paced and unputdownable, *The Crushing* is a thriller with twists, turns, and plenty of heart. Taking the reader from Maryland to the everglades of Florida, Kerry Peresta delivers complex characters and deft plotting in this latest Olivia Callahan suspense. You won't want to miss it!"—K.L. Murphy, author of *Last Girl Missing*, *Her Sister's Death*, and the Detective Cancini Mystery Series

"In *The Crushing*, Peresta manages an exquisite balance between the jagged and the tender edges of humanity. Complex, relatable characters, engaging writing, and a nail-biter of a plot had me hooked from the first page."—Susan Crawford, bestselling author of *The Pocket Wife* and *The Other Widow*

Prologue

Sherry crammed the phone against her ear as she dashed through the thick undergrowth, trudged across boggy marshes, and arrived at a feeder stream.

"*Olivia!* Olivia?"

Nothing.

"Dammit!" she muttered, shoving her cell back into her pocket. She calculated that the nearest town rested fifteen miles down the highway out here in Florida-cracker country, and holing up until the shooter emerged seemed the best option.

She should've known there'd be no service out here.

Where did he go? She scraped mud off her face and rubbed her sunburned cheeks. He actually *fired a weapon*. On no planet had she ever thought this little trek would become a fight for her life, yet here she stood, hands glued to the trunk of a huge palm, eyes darting back and forth across the marshy, pancake-flat wastelands of inland Florida. Behind her lay a wide body of water surrounded by suspicious-looking marsh grass and, she suspected, alligators. In front of her lay miles of marshland and bedraggled palms spearing the sky.

Why had she volunteered for this assignment in the first place?

"I just *had* to get my investigator's license," she muttered. "Maybe I should've stayed put as Olivia's assistant instead of private investigator. This isn't quite how I envisioned the job."

She rubbed her calves. How long had she been running? Fifteen minutes? Twenty? An hour? Where was Olivia?

The distant blast of gunfire reached her ears. A bullet sliced through the air and hit the tree she'd wrapped herself around, missing her hand by inches. Sherry felt her stomach freeze into a block of ice.

Wiping the sweat from her eyes, she slid her hand to the paddle holster on her belt, gripped her Smith & Wesson revolver, and released the safety strap. Another crack of gunfire erupted, closer this time. She swallowed, hard. A whoosh of air zipped past a mere twelve inches in front of her nose. Sherry dropped to the ground like a stone. The spikey bushes on the ground dug into her arms, her chest, her legs. She located a slight rise about ten feet away and hastily low-crawled through the weeds on her stomach, edged to the top of the incline, and threw herself over the top.

Panting, she peeked out above the edge. The crack-crack-crack of shots fired caused her to dive for cover. She took a deep breath, wiped the sweat off her palms, and fired back a volley of her own. When silence fell, she relaxed against the incline and tugged out her phone. A signal!

With fumbling fingers, she pressed in a number. She waited through one ring, then two.

The connection faltered. Static made it impossible to hear, and she despaired of ever reaching Olivia. Her heart started beating again when she could make out the words: "Where are you? Are you okay? Sherry, are you there?"

Tears of relief trailed down her cheeks. She rattled off a description of her location while focusing on best-case origination of shots fired. "I found Hannah. She's exhausted and weak, but I've got her." Sherry crammed the phone against her ear, listening intently to Olivia's instructions. "Okay. I'll meet you at the airport, but...wait. I hear something," she whispered. She stuck the phone back in her pocket and gripped her weapon with both hands.

Minutes passed. Sherry tried to breathe.

Something shuffled through the grass. Her eyes sliced left, right.

The shuffling stopped.

The hum of cicadas intensified. She swatted at mosquitoes. Sweat trickled down her face.

She adjusted her grip on her sidearm.

Only the faint squawk of herons and hoot of owls reached her ears. No footsteps. The setting sun left a red slash on the horizon. Bats dipped and swooped above her.

She lowered her weapon, puzzled. Had one of her prior shots wounded her target?

Taking her time, she rose from her niche behind the incline.

A single shot burst from her adversary's weapon and sizzled through the air.

She cried out in pain. The bullet had nicked her, the sting of a monster wasp. She groped her waist with her free hand and lifted it away wet with blood. Rage rushed through her chest and down her arms. She planted her legs wide and emptied her weapon in the direction of the shooter.

The phone in her pocket vibrated with a text as she reloaded.

Another bullet clipped her in the shoulder.

The sound of sirens wailed in the distance.

She collapsed.

Chapter One

Olivia Callahan

Two months earlier

The tower of crackers that I'd made from the charcuterie on our table at Eddie's Bistro collapsed.

"That proves it, Olivia," my friend and colleague, Sherry, teased. "You are now old." She pointed at the wasteland of crackers scattered across the table. "Your coordination is slipping."

"Stop that," Callie said, with a shake of her head that wagged her ever-present ponytail. "Forty-five isn't old. It's the prime of life. You are at your absolute best, Olivia. Happy birthday."

"Agree," I told her, resting my elbow on the table and taking a sip of wine. "I propose a toast." I lifted my wine glass. "To Sherry, who passed the private investigation exam at the top of her class and graduated from receptionist of Watchdog Investigations to full-fledged PI!"

Callie and Beth applauded. Next, I tilted my glass to Beth. "And cheers to Beth, our new addition as administrative assistant-slash-receptionist. May you ever have our backs." After a pause, I added, "And our paychecks."

Beth's plump cheeks reddened. She smiled and trained her sparkly, brown eyes on Sherry and me. "Don't you worry. I'll take good care of you two."

Sherry's head whipped toward me. "She's doing payroll, too?"

I nodded, acknowledging Sherry's struggle with letting go of the reins as

1

she transitioned into full-time PI work. "She's a retired accountant. It's a good time to keep our payroll in-house."

Beth reached over and patted Sherry's hand in a sweet-auntie way. "I promise not to short you, Sherry."

Sherry chuckled. "Working for us is a funny way to retire," she joked.

Expanding my firm had not been the easiest decision.

Beth had waltzed into my life when I'd been muddling through grieving the death of my mentor, Tom Stark. I'd been on crutches and blurry about life in general as I recovered from two gunshot wounds. At that point, Sherry had expressed interest in becoming a private investigator and working for me in that capacity, and I agreed. She attacked her online courses with zealous fervor, but I wasn't sure what we'd do about a full-time assistant to take care of the day-to-day necessities. When I learned about Beth's past career as an accountant and administrator, I didn't even blink. I hired her on the spot.

My neighbor and best friend, Callie, lifted her glass in my direction. "And to our celebrated Mercy's Miracle and friend, Olivia Rosemary Callahan... happy mid-life birthday!"

I frowned. "Mid-life? "Isn't forty-five the new thirty? Besides, I'm going to surprise everyone and live 'til one hundred. You'll be sick of me."

A pause hovered.

I struggled with what to say. I didn't like being the center of attention, and I certainly didn't like birthdays. A change of subject had become necessary. I cleared my throat. "I hate to talk about business, but..."

"You can't help yourself," Sherry said.

I laughed. Sherry knew me so well. I couldn't stop thinking about our bottom line, and Watchdog Investigations had hit a speed bump. "I'm always thinking about new business." I studied my wine glass. "Remember that phone call we had? The mystery call?"

"The one that came in six months ago? I *do* remember, because it sounded like someone in trouble. The caller stuck with me." She took a sip of wine before continuing and leaned in on her elbows. "I tried to return the call several times. They went straight to voicemail. One of those innocuous ones that only give you the number."

"Do you think that could've been Hannah?"

Sherry shrugged. "Maybe."

Callie pursed her lips. "Hannah made her choice. She got married and moved to Florida without even letting us meet her guy. I, for one, am offended. I mean, I forgive her, but maybe she doesn't have room for the Wine & Whine group in her life anymore."

"It's odd that she wouldn't keep in touch. To be honest, I'm worried about her," I said.

Sherry poured more wine from the bottle for us. We'd chosen to split a Rombauer Cab tonight. "I haven't had time to think about Hannah." She threw me a look. "When I'm not shadowing you on investigations, I'm cold calling for new business. So. Back to Hannah. Do you think she might need us? Maybe her new marriage isn't working out."

I tapped my chin, thinking.

"Could be," Callie said.

We paused our conversation as the server cleared the table.

Beth thanked us for inviting her and told us she needed to get home to her grandkids. With a glance at her watch, she rose from her chair and slung her purse over her shoulder. "See you both at the office in the morning."

Callie watched her walk away from our table and out the door. "Wonder when we'll have grandkids," she mused.

"Don't even *think* about it."

She gave me a wicked grin. "You're right. I need to get re-married, first."

Sherry blanched. "I won't touch that with a ten-foot pole. You're still fresh. How long has the divorce been final?"

Callie reached for her wine glass. "Three months or so."

I remained quiet, my fingers trailing up and down the stem of my glass.

Callie had confided in me that her ex, Graham, had begged her to come back to him, which put me on high alert. We'd both had horrible experiences with our exes...my husband Monty sat in a cell for his part in a homicide, and hers...well, he had his own issues, and in no universe did I believe he wanted her back. Graham and Monty shared similar ambitions...and even

3

remained friends, though Monty had been incarcerated for the last four years. It scared me a little. They fed off each other. Graham didn't want Callie back, he wanted to use her for something. He could *not* be trusted, and she knew this intellectually, because we'd talked about it. Her heart, though, was another matter.

Sherry deftly slid the conversation toward private investigation classes. I exhaled in relief. We didn't need to further explore Callie's thoughts about re-marriage.

"I have to say, it does feel incredible to be done with the courses and the training. I'm trying out how it sounds. She rolled the words off her tongue: 'Sherry Lattimore, Private Investigator.'"

Callie beamed. "So proud of you, girl."

I reached into my cavernous purse and pulled out a box. "Surprise."

I slid the small box across the table. Sherry grabbed for it like a kid reaching for an ice cream cone.

She lifted off the top and gasped. "My business cards!"

"It's official. You and I are now colleagues." I shook my head. "I never realized the lasting impact Tom Stark would have on us." A quick flash of his funeral sped through my mind. I felt moisture gather in my eyes. "He'd be so proud of us, Sherry."

She hugged the little box of cards to her chest, then pulled one out and gave it to Callie. "I know he would; may he rest in peace. I miss him so much." Sherry put the box in her purse. "Very sweet of you."

The sounds of chattering diners and fidgety toddlers curled around us. Eddie's Bistro had been our favorite gathering place for five years. The Wine, Whine & Win group had begun with Hannah, me, Callie, and Sherry. The Hannah-shaped hole in the group still hurt...that she could drop us without a thought didn't sit right. I'd camped out on the question for weeks: could she be in trouble?

"What happened to your therapist, anyway?" Callie asked. "What's her name, again?"

I smiled. "Hazel. She presented me with a certificate for "client that's shown the most progress in therapy" or something—her way of announcing

4

she'd decided to retire and move to the beach. She's in Pensacola, busy decorating her villa. It's been an easy pivot for her. She's now obsessed with flamingos and seagulls and turtles."

Callie's eyebrows rose. "Does she live anywhere close to Niceville? Where Hannah is?"

I blinked in surprise. I'd not made that connection at all. I tugged out my phone and opened the map app. "Wow. It's *so* close. Forty minutes."

"We should take a vacation down there. We could stay with one or the other," Sherry said.

I made a little snorting sound. "If I don't hear from Hannah pretty soon, you can bet we'll be taking a trip down there."

Chapter Two

Sergeant Hunter Faraday

"Looks like you'll be taking a trip to the dark side, Officer," Sergeant Hunter Faraday told the young patrol cop standing at attention in front of his desk at police headquarters in Richmond, Virginia.

The cop grinned. "Do you mean what I think you mean, sir?"

Hunter chuckled. "You hard of hearing, Berkshire?"

"Ohmigod," he whispered, clapping his hands over his mouth. He straightened. "Sorry, sir."

"A celebration is appropriate." Hunter popped a salute. "We'll email the details. Congratulations. Welcome to homicide detective training."

The young man lifted his chin and strode out of the office, his back ramrod-straight.

Hunter smiled and leaned back in his chair, threading his fingers together behind his head. "I was that guy, once," he whispered, thinking about his training at the Richmond Academy, his years on a beat, the laborious testing process before he'd been accepted into the program. How long had that been, anyway? He chuckled. "Longer than I want to think about, that's for sure," he said. His admin, Officer Becker, walked in and stuck out a file. "From Lieutenant Donaldson, sir." Hunter thanked him and flipped through the file.

A sinking feeling rumbled through his chest. As sergeant of the Major Crimes Unit of Richmond PD, he had to be looped into any investigations snaking through his city. This one seemed gift-wrapped and tied with a bow but felt more like a punch to the gut. A major drug heavyweight had set up shop in Richmond.

He cursed when he saw who'd been ordered to travel from her home base in Savannah to coordinate with his office in Richmond. His mind looped itself into emotionally complicated places, and her name, Shiloh McPherson, seemed to expand and contract on the page. He paced back and forth in the small office, then dropped into one of the armchairs in front of his desk and tried not to overthink, but it was hopeless. His focus had evaporated into thin air. He needed a sounding board. He called his buddy, Nick Ramsey, Richmond's assistant DA.

Nick answered on the first ring. "Hey."

"You busy?" Hunter asked.

"Busy? Of course not. I'm staring at a pile of folders that would make you run screaming from the room, and my landline is on fire with three waiting calls because my way-too-legit assistant refuses to tell them I'm unavailable if I'm here, even though I've explained to her AT LENGTH that I'm not lying, just busy. Another bullet point to add to the list: get new assistant." Nick paused to exhale. "What's going on with you?"

Hunter's full-throated laughter lasted an awkward fifteen seconds.

"Okay. Not that funny. What's wrong?" Nick asked.

"You sure you have time to talk?" Hunter asked, rubbing his beard stubble.

"Let me step outside. I could use a break, and it'll be a thrill to watch my assistant glare at me when I don't tell her where I'm going."

Hunter laughed again. "Your brand of stupid humor is just what I needed."

As he waited for Nick to settle somewhere, he listened to steps walking on linoleum, a door squealing open, the sounds of birds.

"Okay, I am now on a bench, enjoying the chilly sunshine of autumn in Richmond."

Hunter closed his office door, then put his feet up on his desk. "I got notified of a new investigation dumped in my town. They requested my team's assistance."

"Okay..."

"*Shiloh's* been the lead on this investigation the last four years."

A heartbeat pause occurred. "Shiloh...the chickie who set you free a year ago? If I remember, she was kind of a bitch about it."

"I wouldn't put it that way..." Hunter began.

"Oh, I *remember* brother. She *was* a bitch about it, and if I understand this right, it's going to get complicated."

Hunter groaned. "You have the gift of understatement."

Nick chuckled. "How can I help?"

"I need perspective; that's why I called. Remember when I proposed to Olivia, and she couldn't commit? What was I going to do, become a hermit? After that, I moved on with Shiloh in a more, uhh...serious way."

"You've gone back and forth with Olivia for years," Nick said. "I get confused. I don't remember a proposal."

"She shot down that brilliant idea about a year ago," Hunter said. "Shiloh and I have a strange relationship to begin with, and now we're going to be thrown together in this work situation, and I have no idea how to handle it. I'm pretty disgusted at my lack of ability to keep work and pleasure separate."

"Whatever, man. That's a myth. It's impossible. If you're attracted to the woman, you're attracted. Period. Are you still attracted to Shiloh, even after she bailed on the relationship?"

Hunter bristled. "Listen. Shi got the raw end of that deal. We dated, and I gave her all the signals that we'd be moving forward. It shocked her when I started backing off because I couldn't get my damn mind off Olivia Callahan. That was it for her, and yeah, she wasn't nice about it, but I don't blame her."

Three seconds of silence shimmered through the airwaves. "Wow, man. You're *defending* her now. I see where this is going." Nick laughed. "This should be so much fun to watch."

Hunter sighed.

"Hey. I'm here for you, buddy," Nick said.

"Do you want to grab a beer tonight?"

"Sure. Meet me at Wonderland. You talk. I'll listen," Nick said. "I'll try to muzzle my jokes and dispense wisdom instead."

Hunter smiled and stuck the cell in his pocket.

Lieutenant Nicholson, Unit Chief of the Criminal Investigation Division, walked into Hunter's office at two p.m. on the dot and stood in front of the desk.

Hunter lifted his head. "Sir?"

"I've had some concerning communication. Is there a conflict of interest between you and Detective Shiloh McPherson, the lead on this case from Savannah?"

"Not in my opinion, sir."

"You have no issues with close, physical contact or dangerous situations with Detective McPherson? Issues that could get one of you killed?"

"Not at all, sir."

The lieutenant frowned. "Then why would she mention it?"

Hunter tapped his fingers on his desk and looked away. "You might say we have history."

"Don't beat around the bush, Faraday," he snapped.

"We saw each other, sir. For a while."

"Serious relationship?"

Hunter nodded.

"It's over?"

"Yes, sir."

Hunter settled into his chair to wait for him to run the information through his analytical brain. When Lieutenant Nicholson mulled something over, it took a few minutes.

That Shi would need his unit's help had never crossed Hunter's mind. If one of her suspects blew through town, she'd handled it on her own, and he'd never even known about her presence unless she reached out. He hadn't talked to her or seen her for a year.

He glanced at the lieutenant. By the look of him, the wheels in his head were still spinning.

Would being with Shi create tension? Stir up feelings? If they landed in an alley with bullets flying, would he fall on his sword to protect her in a moment of crisis and forget about the rest of the team?

9

Lieutenant Nicholson cleared his throat.

Hunter straightened in his chair.

"Look, you can assign a couple of your top investigators to her and not be involved at all if you'd rather, whatever you think. But you know in your gut if a former relationship will get in the way of doing your job." Before he left Hunter's office, he turned. "It might be better to sit this one out. Think about it."

He left.

But Hunter didn't have to think about it. He *knew* it'd be better that way. He could already see the smirk on her face when he sent out two of his investigators to assist instead of diving in on his own. She knew how much he loved undercover...she'd have questions. She'd think he still had feelings for her, that he'd distanced himself for that reason. Why did her thoughts about him matter? Would his pride be wounded if she didn't want to re-connect?

"What the *hell*," Hunter growled at himself.

He shut off the leaky water faucet in his head and attacked the files on his desk.

After work, Hunter parked his four-door Jeep Wrangler in Wonderland's packed parking lot and frowned. He hated crowds. He texted Nick, who replied he'd already gotten a table.

Hunter pushed through a sea of people huddled in the lobby and through a bar area where people waited three-deep for bartenders to take their order. He'd have avoided the chaotic venue at all costs, but he relied on Nick as a good, bottom-line guy for perspective. He didn't want to argue over venue. With a sigh, he walked through rooms decorated like someone had shoved a red-light district into a Walt Disney cartoon. To his great relief, Nick had secured a quiet table in one of the private rooms in the back. Hunter slid into the chair across from him. Outdoor lights crisscrossed a red ceiling, throwing weird shadows across Nick's face.

"I've already started, bro. First round's on me. What'll you have?"

Hunter flagged a server. "Stella."

Nick rolled his eyes. "You should change it up once in a while."

"Why? I like Stella."

"Don't you need a little diversity?"

"I hear that's going around." Hunter chuckled at his joke.

"Speaking of diversity…" Nick took a drink of his Old-Fashioned. "Olivia and Shiloh are about as diverse as two women can get. I think they're claiming what's left of your old fart brain."

Hunter laughed. The server returned with his Stella. Hunter took a deep swallow, then plunked the frosty bottle on the table. "You're catching up with me, and over forty is 'old-fart' territory, by the way."

"Yeah, but 'almost fifty' is a whole 'nother country."

"Shut up," Hunter said. He tapped his fingers on the table. "You're right. They each have a spot in my head."

"Whose is bigger?"

Hunter groaned. "Olivia."

"That's what I thought." Nick smiled, drained his Old-Fashioned, and re-ordered. "So why is working with Shiloh a problem, then? She's not going to take over Olivia's spot, is she? Is that what you're worried about?"

"I'm not worried."

Nick chuckled, leaned back in his chair, and folded his hands across his chest, waiting.

"Okay. I'm worried," Hunter admitted. "Olivia's on a fast track now. I hear that she's hired another investigator. I don't want to distract her."

"How long's it been since you talked to Olivia?"

"A year and four months. Yesterday."

Nick laughed. "You're keeping records, dude. That's sad."

Hunter frowned and slid his fingers the length of his Stella bottle. They came away wet.

"Okay." Nick leaned in, his black eyes shimmering in the crazy lighting. "Here's how I see it. Shiloh comes, you agree to share some of the work onsite, you two get all hot and heavy inside the investigation and one thing leads to another."

Hunter's leg started bouncing. He stared at the menus on the table.

Nick stroked his chin thoughtfully. "If you keep your distance, that all

11

goes away. But, what if it's still on the back burner? It might be worth it to see how you guys gel after the historic dumping. Maybe you guys are better off as friends and colleagues. Working together might solidify that jellyfish in your gut right now."

Hunter cocked his head. "Maybe."

Nick leaned in further, his elbows sliding across the table. "On the other hand, if you stay away from her, Olivia wins, right? If you're still keeping her on your radar, in a way, you're being faithful to Olivia for no reason. She'll never have any idea you made this heroic decision. And I know it's hard to hear, bro, but what if she doesn't care anymore?" Nick slapped the table, then made a little explosion with his fingers. "Boom."

Hunter's leg stopped bouncing. A weird sensation fluttered through his chest. The words hit hard.

Nick studied his friend's face. "Ha!" He pointed. "See? That hurt, didn't it?"

Hunter scowled and slumped in his chair.

Nick shrugged. "And that, my friend, is why I became a lawyer. I dig the truth out of people."

Hunter drained his beer. "Both of them are incredible. If I move forward with either one, it'll be fantastic."

Nick laughed. "Maybe so, but I think you've burned your bridges, man. No more credits left in the ole' account. So why worry about working with Shiloh? At least you'll find out if she's still interested. Simple."

Chapter Three

Hannah Delaney-Somerset

Hannah swept her light-blond hair over her shoulder and stared into the small mirror on the wall over a sink. She scowled at her reflection. How long had it been since she'd had it styled or cut? How long had it been since she'd stopped caring about her appearance? "How long has it been, Patrick..." she whispered to her reflection. "...since you've given me *permission* to go to a salon?" She lifted her thin arms and laughed a mirthless laugh at the sight of them and muttered to herself, "To think that you used to put a finger down your throat and make yourself throw up to lose weight." She dropped her arms to her sides. "All you had to do was marry a *monster*. I should do an Insta reel. Guaranteed weight loss," she spoke into the room, her voice crackly and hoarse, her eyes red with exhaustion. She backed away from the mirror and surveyed her cramped living arrangement for the past seven days.

Patrick had locked her into his freaking homemade prison, or "punishment room," as he referred to it. He'd used it a lot over the past two years, and a day or two is a bearable proposition, but his carnal instincts had evolved...like a bored psychopath tired of burning a woman with cigarettes and lighting a blowtorch instead. The cop shows all said the same thing about serial killers—their behavior escalates. She didn't quite believe Patrick capable of murder, but no matter how much she tried to deny it, she had to embrace the truth of her own experiences and the horror of discovering the scrawled phone numbers scratched into the cinder-block walls.

Her desperation grew deeper and wider by the day. *How long would he imprison her this time?*

Hannah pulled the lone chair in the room over to the wall and climbed on it to look out of a small window. Burglar bars had been installed on the inside of the window. She curled her fingers around the despised bars. Patrick had made up a story about a mother with dementia and told her it had been for her safety to do that. She knew now that he'd been lying. The bars sat high on the wall, which put her line of sight even with the front porch steps, the weed-infested lawn that Patrick cut once a year, the mailbox out at the road, and the scruffy bottoms of shrubs she'd planted early in the marriage when he'd still let her go outside. If someone rang the doorbell, the visitor's shoes rested about twenty-four inches from her nose, which gave her a chance to get help. A slim chance, but still.

So far, his soundproofing had prevented anyone from hearing her screams for help through the small window. Not that they had that many visitors. The house sat at the edge of protected wetlands miles from the nearest town. At first, her dreams of rescue had been vivid and realistic. She'd reassured herself over and over that it would happen. The days became months, the months became years, and at this point, she didn't even dream anymore. Her life revolved around doing what Patrick told her to do or getting tossed into the punishment room.

The mail truck arrived.

She gasped. Maybe today would be the day.

Please! Deliver a package to the door!

Her heart sank as she watched the postal worker tuck the mail into the mailbox and pull away. She felt a spark of hope when the truck backed up and parked. Her jaw dropped when the postal worker trotted down the short sidewalk to the front porch. *Do something, Hannah!* Forcing her stick-like arms to move, she pounded on the window and tried to scream, but the pathetic, thin wail that came out was useless. She took a deep breath and tried again.

She almost fell off the chair when the postal worker's feet did not turn around and go back in the other direction toward his truck, but remained pointed toward the door, shifting and uncertain, as if he'd heard something.

Hannah leapt from her perch on the chair, found a metal cup, climbed back on the chair, and raked the cup back and forth across the window bars.

She stroked her throat in a desperate attempt to urge it to release sounds. She watched the black, soft-soled shoes take one step down. The metal cup clanked and clanked across the bars. She shrieked, but nothing came out this time. Her voice had given up.

He took another step down the stairs. A gas-powered blower started. Hannah threw up her hands in despair. How would the postal worker ever hear her with that thing blasting noise? Hopelessness crushed her for a raw, brief moment.

She lifted her chin and kept striking with the metal cup. *Please hear something!*

He stood on the bottom step now. His hands patted his pockets. She blinked. For his phone? *Maybe calling someone about the odd sounds!* He stood on the bottom step, then started walking toward the truck, his cell pressed against his ear. Hannah focused all her energy on him. *Could he hear her thoughts?* She concentrated so hard she imagined a blood vessel popping right out of her temple. The worker turned around, his face puckered, curious. She waved her hands and made faces and plunged her fingers through the bars until they touched the grime-covered window. With a final look at the house, he got in the truck and pulled away.

Hannah slipped off the chair and sank to the floor. She dropped her head into her hands and sobbed. Her stomach grumbled. When had she eaten last? Her throat hurt. It had become unbearable. She walked three paces to the single bed and lay down.

"Hannah?"

She heard the deadbolt slipping away. "It's your lucky day," Patrick called from outside the door, his deceptive, silken voice muffled by the thick wood. Hannah rubbed sleep from her eyes and stared at the door, wondering how many women had come before. How many had Patrick tracked, seduced, and lured into his depravity?

"Lucky day," she muttered with a hoarse chuckle. "Yeah, that's what you call it, asshole." Every bone in her body ached from a recent wrestling match with him that he referred to as "sex," and the mattress might as well be a rock. The thin, stained pillow made her wonder if the stains had been made by the tears of other women. What had happened to them? They'd etched their names underneath the sink, behind the bed, on the ceiling. How had they known someone would need to remember their names?

She glanced at the hash marks she'd carved on the cinder-block wall with the end of a spoon. She made them each time the sun rose. Seven marks. Joining the others in writing her name on the wall seemed...too prophetic, somehow.

"You're going to make it," she growled into the stale air of the room.

The door flew open. Patrick walked in with a delighted grin on his face. "You're free!"

Hannah could not bear to look at him. Rubbing her arms, she mumbled, "Thank you, Patrick."

His lips settled into a firm line. He crossed his arms. "How many times do I have to tell you to look at me when addressing me? And talk louder, for God's sake." His eyes raked her length. "Haven't you been taking showers?"

Hannah stood and looked him in the eyes. "My voice is gone," she croaked. "There's no soap in the shower, and the water is rusty."

His long, muscular legs covered the distance fast. He opened his palm and struck her face. Once. Twice. Her head jerked left, right.

"I saw how you tried to get the postal worker's attention. I came home to give you lunch, for God's sake. How do you think I felt when I saw what you were doing?"

The blower. Patrick had started it. She'd wondered who would possibly be using a blower, since their neighbors lived at least a mile away. She wished he hadn't used God's name. It felt obscene coming from his mouth. God had nothing to do with this.

"Well?" He crossed his arms. "What do you have to say for yourself?"

A thin tickle developed under her nose. She touched it with her fingers and drew them away bloody. She mouthed the words "I'm sorry."

"For that little trick, you'll have to settle for what's in the fridge, which isn't much." He held up a package from a local restaurant. "I'm taking this with me back to the office. You don't deserve it now." He heaved out a sigh. "I'll have to put film on that window. Pity." He glared at her. "The window was an attempt to be *nice!* None of you ever…" his eyelids fluttered.

He's caught himself, Hannah thought. *I knew it. There are others. The man's a psychopath. I have to get out of here.*

"I mean, you've never appreciated my attempts at being nice."

It didn't matter about lunch, she thought, because her stomach had gotten used to being empty, and the hunger pangs would dissipate soon enough.

She followed him out of the basement to the main floor, asking herself for the hundredth time why she'd accepted his response to a pivotal question as a new bride: *Why are locks on the outside of the doors?* A necessary precaution, he'd told her, his mother had dementia and often wandered away. The locks had been for her protection, as well as the bars on the windows.

The fictitious story had become a bitter taste in her mouth.

An uneasy feeling had rolled into her stomach at that point, but she'd shoved it away. Patrick had been handsome, successful, and lived in Florida—a one-way ticket out of single life and into the warm arms of marital bliss.

Or so she'd thought.

She frowned and folded her arms around her thin torso. If she'd paid attention to the nudges that told her to run away from this psycho, none of this would've happened.

She found a pen and paper and jotted a note, resisting the urge to vomit as she did so. She hated herself for what she'd become. *Do you mind if I go take a shower?*

He said he didn't mind.

She went into the bathroom and tended her face. After Patrick returned to work, she'd grab ice from the fridge and watch a little TV. At least he hadn't locked the TV away from her. She chuckled. Small mercies.

She left the bathroom and sat on the bed, the familiar stampede of confusion and fear pounding through her brain. Patrick had driven her so close to the edge of insanity that losing her mind seemed like an inevitable next step.

Her jaw clenched. She whispered the mantra she repeated many times a day: *I can beat this. I will escape.*

Her mind stalled on a memory.

A year ago, she'd tried to call nine-one-one. He'd taken her cell phone six months prior, but she'd tossed the house and found it. Thinking he'd be at the office, she'd connected with nine-one-one when Patrick stormed in, grabbed the phone, and told the operator to disregard, then ground the phone underneath his heel. After that particular brush with death, she laid low. When she tried again, she found his phone while he slept and called Olivia's office number. Sherry's chirpy voice had answered, and after stuttering a few words, she'd ended the call drenched in shame. Patrick walked into the room while she still had the phone in her hand. The broken ribs and bruising on her back had taken six weeks to heal.

"Hang in there," she whispered, "take care of yourself. Even animals in cages try to take care of themselves.

Chapter Four

Olivia

The leaves on the trees had turned a brilliant red overnight.
The lovely, half-mile lane that curled from the highway to my
office and ended at my driveway was bordered on each side with
mature trees that formed a canopy when fully leafed out in the summer. I
sniffed the freshness of a new fall day as I walked to the mailbox and pulled
out the contents. As I returned, Marlowe and Riot watched me with two
anxious sets of eyes. I had to push them out of the way with my foot before
they'd allow me inside. "I know, I know, you're hungry."

As I filled one bowl with cat food and the other with dog food, my eyes
fell on the rather officious-looking five-by-seven envelope that had been
included in today's mail.

I picked up the envelope. "Olivia R. Callahan, Private Investigator,
Watchdog Investigations," I whispered with a smile. I still relished the sound
of my own firm's name. "How far you've come, girl," I told myself in the
privacy of the sunshiny kitchen in my tidy, two-story Maryland farmhouse.
I thought about the days of raising young girls and tending house during my
years with my dirtbag ex—otherwise known as Monty but forever stamped
upon the frontal lobe of my brain as 'dirtbag'. I shook my head in wonder.
What on earth would've happened to me if I hadn't experienced the assault
six years ago? Would I still be the passive, shy wallflower I'd been before my
brain injury flipped me into overdrive? Yes, the attack had been horrible,

and yes, re-learning how to walk and talk and remember things had been a struggle...but without it, I'd not be a successful private investigator, much less opening a piece of mail as the proprietor of my own business. Often, I mused, blessings come disguised as catastrophe.

I popped a K-cup into the Keurig and leaned against the counter, appreciating my wonderful, rebuilt kitchen. How long had it been since the fire? Two years? A highlight reel streamed through my mind. The awful news at Lilly's high school graduation. Clinging to her in the middle of the football field. The terrifying drive down the narrow lane to my house, blinded by haze and ash. Trying to find my cat, Riot, as I batted away the billows of smoke inside. The firefighters screaming at me to get out of the house.

In the end, after the smoke had cleared (so to speak), I got brand-new everything. New front porch to replicate what Monty and I had created before the marriage fell apart; new porch swing, new white, wicker furniture, fresh bead board on the ceiling, and more. My house had been reconstructed better and stronger than before.

Kind of like me.

My mind soared across the last six years. I marveled at how I'd grown as a person.

For one, I'd learned that disaster can lead to a beautiful restoration. Almost a rebirth, if I didn't set up camp in self-pity.

The coffee stopped gurgling. I grabbed cream from the fridge.

I'd made astounding progress, I'd been told. I had my neurologist, Dr. Grayson Sturgis, and Hazel, my former therapist, to thank for that. And God, of course.

I sipped my coffee, closing my eyes in pure bliss. The first cup was always the best. Always.

My rangy half-German Shepherd, half-Lab, Marlowe, had finished his breakfast, and now he noisily slurped his water. When he lifted his drippy muzzle from the water bowl, I reached for the mop. Marlowe considered it his daily responsibility to anoint my kitchen with water and doggie saliva so he could sit on his haunches with his tongue hanging out and watch me mop. I think he found it entertaining.

Riot returned to the kitchen, took a few cautious sniffs, stretched out his body to its full extent, then launched himself like a furry, orange demon onto Marlowe's back.

Marlowe yelped and ran out of the room.

I laughed. Cats liked to prove their dominance every now and then. Often, I'd find Riot curled into Marlowe's stomach, both napping in the afternoon sun.

I considered cats my spirit animal.

Before the brain injury that flipped my personality, my spirit animal would've been a field mouse. Monty had controlled my every move, and I'd let him.

Not anymore.

I pulled out a stool, sat at the breakfast bar, and studied the envelope, which had something hard in it. I tore it open, and when I removed the note inside, a ring dropped out.

I squinted. A ring? What...?

I held it between my thumb and index finger to inspect it. *Monty's wedding ring?* Each time my daughter Lilly visited her father in prison, she told me he still wore his wedding ring. During our twenty-year marriage, he'd been adamant about never taking it off...until he met the bimbo that ended our marriage. Why had he put it in an envelope and mailed it to me? How was that even possible?

The night he'd blindsided me with his intentions to divorce me for another woman, he hadn't been wearing his wedding ring. It didn't occur to me that he'd not worn it on purpose. I thought he'd forgotten it or misplaced it.

Memories began to flood my mind.

Don't go there! Don't go back to the restaurant, the dim, romantic lighting; his face when he told you, vomiting in the toilet, the cold bathroom floor, the long, lost walk back to the table. Just...no.

I dropped the ring on the counter as if it were a rotting piece of flesh. How could this be? The corrections facility secured all jewelry and personal items in a Ziploc. The incarcerated don't get those items back until release.

Did he bribe some wilting, suck-up corrections officer with a thing for studly, lying dirtbags?

I blinked. Re-focused on the page. In Monty's scrawling, disjointed cursive, he'd written:

You made a vow. Remember?

The note fell from my hands.

Though he no longer had the power to turn me into a terrified maniac, stuff like this distracted me from life priorities...like, for instance, making money. Paying bills. Working on client investigations. I stared at the ring. Did this constitute a threat worthy of calling the former investigator assigned to the Mercy's Miracle case? The man responsible for figuring out who and why I'd been assaulted six years ago and had supported and believed in me during my long and convoluted recovery from the brain injury I'd suffered as a result?

I remembered that I should refer to my former investigator as *Sergeant* Hunter Faraday now, instead of detective.

He'd deserved the promotion. I smiled.

Even though he'd been the lead investigator on my assault case and we'd tried to make a relationship work, we'd not spoken in months. It hadn't been a good idea to become involved with the smoking hot detective on my case, but there you have it. I'd become a cliché.

I drank the rest of my coffee.

Monty couldn't hurt me anymore; he got twenty years. How could he be a threat from prison? I glared at the note on my breakfast bar, crumpled it into a ball, put the ring and note in a baggie, and tossed them in a drawer to think about later.

A lot of work waited for me at my office. I needed to get dressed and leave.

Take that, Monty. You're not even a fly on my wall these days.

I raced down the lane in my trusty Land Rover and turned into Watchdog Investigation's parking lot at 8:40 a.m. It took me one minute and thirty seconds to get from my driveway to the parking lot of the office building that sat right on the edge of my five acres of Maryland horse country in

Baltimore County. Beth's little, red Mini Cooper—so clean you could eat food off the tiny floor mats—sat in the lot already.

I exited the Rover and let Marlowe out of the back seat. He marched to the front door like a boss and waited for me. I'd found my wonder dog at the Humane Society. He'd been our official watchdog and namesake of our firm since the day we'd hung the sign. When I opened the door, he loped through the lobby, through the breakroom, and into my office, where he curled himself into his dog bed with a contented sigh. Beyond my office, the builder had outfitted the space with a guest bedroom and private bath, which came in handy if I pulled an all-nighter or had visitors in town.

I strolled inside. "Morning, Beth."

She beamed at me. She *always* beamed at me. It made me a little nervous. I couldn't wait to see her handle a crisis. We exchanged the typical pleasantries, but I didn't want to chat, I wanted to get to work. I told her I'd be in my office.

She followed me into my office. Beth was a spunky fireplug of a woman, her brown, wavy hair worn in a style that would've been all the rage, say…in 1983.

I dropped my purse and shoulder bag on the floor. "I need to get to work. Do you have a question?"

She fidgeted with her hands. "I tried calling Hannah's number all day yesterday. It must be dead. It goes straight to voicemail."

My concern for Hannah ratcheted up about ten points.

"What do you want me to do?" Beth asked.

"I think it's time we think about filing a Missing Person's Report."

Right on cue, Sherry breezed in and walked to my office, fluffing her short, dark crop of ringlets, her expressive blue eyes targeting us. "What? Did someone die?"

I smiled at Beth. "Thanks. We'll take it from here."

Beth returned to her desk, and Sherry plopped into one of the four armchairs we'd arranged around an area rug with a huge, square coffee table in the middle. Instead of the usual two-guest-chairs-in-front-of-desk situation, I preferred to visit with clients in a relaxed way and not pontificate from across a desk.

We sat in the cushy armchairs.

Sherry stared at me with her huge eyes. "What is it? I haven't even had coffee yet."

"It's Hannah. Beth tried all day yesterday to get in touch with her. All of us have tried to contact her for weeks. I think we should file a Missing Persons."

"Well, if that's what you think, then—"

I held up my hand like a stop sign. "I need to know what *you* think. We're a team."

She nodded and went quiet. As I watched her, I appreciated anew the beautiful contrast of her caramel-colored complexion and those deep blue eyes. Since she'd recovered from a disastrous seventeen-year marriage and subsequent divorce, she'd been enjoying the single life. Her exploits had been epic, and many evenings, we'd get together and laugh until our sides hurt. Sherry and I had discovered many advantages to a single life. One…if you're annoyed with a man, you don't have to see him anymore. Two…we had total control of the money. Three…we could do what we damn well wanted to.

Within a few minutes, Sherry made a decision with a slap on each armrest and a bounce in her chair. I half-expected her to get up and start cheerleading. "Let's do it. Why not? It'll cause them to do a well-check visit, right? It'll get the process started, and her description will flood hundreds of databases. I don't see a downside."

"Okay. Ask Beth to set up a Zoom. I'll talk to them."

Sherry started to say something, then clamped her lips together.

I frowned at all the paperwork on my desk and wondered when I'd be able to work on it. "What?"

"Hazel lives close. Do you think she'd do a drive-by to see if Hannah lives there? I mean, how long will it take the cops to act on a Missing Persons?"

I rubbed my chin, thinking. Hazel would do it, of course, but we didn't know the situation. What if we put her in harm's way? What if she had dementia, and we didn't know about it? What if… I sighed. None of these thoughts had a basis in reality, and I needed to stop going down apocalyptic rabbit trails. "Sure, I think that's a plausible idea. Let's look into that before we file."

Sherry flung her purse over her shoulder, hopped up, and walked to her desk. "I'm calling her right now."

Chapter Five

Hunter

Sergeant Hunter Faraday stared blankly at his laptop. His admin had set his calendar to his home page, and the words 'Shiloh in town' hit him in the face like bright, blinking lights that flashed "WARNING. WARNING."

Officer Becker walked in with a cup of coffee and put it on his desk. "Good morning, sir. Detective McPherson called."

"What'd she want?" Hunter barked.

"Just a consult, sir." His face reddened.

Dammit. How am I supposed to handle this? His friend Nick's words came roaring back. 'At least you'll find out if she's *still interested.*' But what if he has a weak moment, they end up in bed, and he lets her down again? He can't let that happen.

Hunter scanned his calendar. "Ask her if she can do three p.m. this afternoon."

"Will do." Officer Becker rushed out, glancing over her shoulder.

Hunter ran both hands through his hair. When he brought his arms down, he knocked over his full cup of coffee.

At three p.m., a knock rapped at his door. Hunter shoved aside the files he'd been working on and folded his hands. "Yes?"

His admin crept into his office like he had a special secret. "She's here, sir."

Hunter felt his eyebrows draw together. "Have you never met Detective McPherson, Becker?"

"No, sir."

Well, that explains the flushed cheeks, the bright eyes, he thought. A young officer just starting out is often stunned into speechlessness at the sight of the tall, gangly Amazonian detective with her shock of wild, blonde hair. Not to mention tattoos out the wazoo. However, according to police regs, she kept them under wraps. He flashed to the first time he discovered them. He hadn't even realized you could ink some of those body parts. "Show her in and close the door."

The poor guy's cheeks flamed scarlet. "Yes, sir." He held the door open for Shiloh. "Y-You can come in now, ma'am…uh…*Detective.*"

"Thanks, Officer Becker." Shiloh trailed two fingers across the young man's chest as she passed. It took him three tries to close the door. Shiloh dropped into a chair in front of Hunter's desk and laughed.

"You enjoy that, don't you?" Hunter asked.

"And you don't?" She smiled.

"How's it going? It's been a while."

"Over a year," she added, putting a hand on her hip and assuming a pose. "How do I look?"

He didn't even hesitate. "Like a million bucks."

Officer Becker brought in coffee, lingering in the background with a wistful expression.

Hunter pointed at the door. "Out."

Shi sat quiet after the young man left, stirring her coffee and studying Hunter. "You're looking older."

Hunter laughed. "Thanks for that."

She moistened her neon-pink lips with her tongue. "It looks good on you."

He couldn't take his eyes off her mouth. His thoughts raced.

God. I'm doomed. Put someone else with her. Put someone else with her. Put someone else with—

She intruded upon his thoughts with the assumptive pronouncement:

"Man. I'm *so* looking forward to finding out if you still have your undercover chops."

And that was that.

He sighed.

Shiloh had asked to meet for dinner at six-thirty, and here he sat, in the parking lot, staring at the restaurant, his jaw set. No matter how hard Shiloh pulled his chain, he limited himself to two hours. Any longer than that, and he didn't know if he could trust himself

Shiloh met him outside the restaurant. The hostess grabbed menus and led them through the dark and intimate interior down a narrow, carpeted hall that culminated at the entrance of a dimly lit room whose main feature seemed to be an excess of faux palms. "Except for your server, you'll be undisturbed," the hostess whispered and slipped away.

"Nice," Hunter remarked as they sat.

"Yeah, they're good people. Almost like family. Met 'em the last couple of times these gangbangers were acting out. I think I might've saved someone's life at one point." She shrugged. "Anyway, they love me now. Always give me privacy and dim the lights."

"Something go down here?"

She nodded. "Out back. There's an alley. Dumpsters. Rats." She chuckled. "The whole deal. Just like in the movies."

Hunter cleared his throat. "I haven't worked undercover for a long time, Shi. I don't know that I'll be an asset."

The server arrived and took drink orders. A Stella Artois for Hunter, a fancy-sounding IPA brew for Shiloh, with a bourbon back. After the server left, Shiloh gazed at Hunter. "You love undercover. I thought you'd jump at the chance."

Hunter felt the furrow between his eyebrows deepen. "You did? Seems like the way things went down last time, you were…"

"Done?" she finished for him. "Well, sure. But this is *work.*"

They sat in silence. Hunter traced figure eights on the table with his index finger.

The server returned with drinks.

Hunter attacked his beer.

Shiloh guzzled hers as well, wiped her mouth, and laughed. "Awkward, huh?"

He grinned. "Maybe not so much in five minutes."

She closed her eyes and leaned back in her chair. "Already feeling it soft and warm in my tummy."

Hunter resisted the images that sprang to mind inspired by "soft and warm." He leaned in on his elbows and threaded his fingers.

"Look. I don't know if we can keep work and our history separate. What do you think?"

"*I* can." She pegged him with her light blue eyes. "Obviously, *you* have an issue."

Hunter sat back and folded his arms. "I don't want to put anyone in danger. End of story."

She sipped the beer and studied his face over the rim of her mug. "What are you afraid of?"

"I am *not* afraid, I'm cautious."

She laughed. "Right."

The server took their meal orders and left.

Shi finished her beer. "Hey. It's okay. Give me a couple of cops you trust, and I'm good with that."

Hunter blinked. Could it be this easy?

Shi waved her hand. "Don't worry. We had a good time, and we've moved on. I just need some warm bodies that know what they're doing. I'm familiar with how you work, that's all. I thought it would be easier than working with people I don't know."

He squinted at her. The woman sitting across the table from him was one of the finest undercovers he'd ever worked with, but she had a fierce temper that she kept under wraps for the most part. This beautiful, exotic creature who reeled in bad guys like hypnotized fish had the capacity to turn into a snake if you crossed her. His trepidation at the thought of the two of them working together again could be construed as rejection. Maybe betrayal.

She gave him the side-eye as she tossed back the bourbon. "You don't believe me?"

"Not sure yet."

She did that slow smile thing of hers. His heart performed the atrial version of a tango.

Their entrees arrived. Hunter unfolded his napkin and put it in his lap. "Let's table the issue for now."

"Tabled," she said, stuffing a huge chunk of red meat into her mouth.

Much, much later, his head spinning and wishing he could get rid of the aftertaste of Tequila, he flopped into bed and hoped to get some sleep, even if it was only a couple of hours. He fell into a troubled dream state.

Gunshots popped off and whizzed so close to his face he could feel the puffs of air. The smell of cordite permeated his senses. He yelled instructions to the one undercover cop left standing. Hunter ducked behind a dumpster. His heart thudded in his chest as he looked at the circle of light underneath a streetlamp in the alley where Shiloh's body lay. He couldn't tell if her chest moved. Had she died? Blood pooled under her head. It didn't look good. Sirens screamed in the distance. Backup on the way, but...he put his hand on his bicep and winced. A shot had caught him in the arm. It needed attention. Poking out from behind the dumpster, he fired once, twice, three times...

Buzzing filled his ears. It stopped, then started again. And again.

Hunter jerked awake and sat up. A stabbing pain shot through his head. He held out his arms, looking for the wound, but found nothing.

"It was a damn *nightmare*," he muttered. The buzzing continued. Hunter pushed the fading imagery of his dream away. He located the phone on the floor beside his bed.

"What is it!" he roared.

A tiny pause greeted him. "Good morning to you, too, sir."

He winced. "Sorry, Becker, I...I had a hard night."

"No problem, sir. Detective McPherson is unhappy with the investigators you assigned to her. She'd like a sit-down."

He clamped his palm across his eyes. How had he slept this long? He glanced at the phone. Almost noon. What had happened last night? They'd relocated to a billiards room, and then they'd…*no*…they hadn't…had they? He concentrated hard, remembering a lot of drinking. He'd gotten stupid drunk, and Shiloh had waltzed away with a smile, not even stumbling. He hoped he'd gotten her a cab or an Uber. Something. But he didn't remember any sex.

"Thank God," he whispered.

"What's that, sir?"

Hunter jumped out of bed and walked into the bathroom. Turned on the shower. "Tell Detective McPherson I'll be able to see her this afternoon. Look at my schedule and pick a time." He ended the call and stepped into the steam.

Chapter Six

Hannah

Hannah's arms ached.

She'd had no warning; he'd just thrown her in there like a sack of potatoes with no explanation. The sound of the deadbolt locking behind him and the clomping of his angry steps up the stairs echoed through her mind on an endless loop.

She'd been locked inside this room for a week now.

A car pulled to the curb and stopped. Hannah perked up. Patrick had left for work...hadn't he? Yes. She'd heard his car leaving early this morning. This one *couldn't* be Patrick. She pulled the chair over to the window and stood on it to look outside. She wiped the glass with her palm in an attempt to get rid of the grime, but the bars kept her from doing much. Still, she could see outside good enough. With a looney grin, she watched the familiar pint-sized woman stare at the house and study the name on the mailbox. Hannah's stomach clenched in desperation.

"You have to get Hazel's attention. No matter what," she whispered to herself.

Hazel, her perpetual Chanel scarf wrapped around her neck, studied the house. Hazel had been Olivia's therapist before she retired and moved to Florida. Someone must've asked her to check in. Tears streaked down Hannah's cheeks as she watched. Hazel would wonder at the shaggy lawn and rusted chairs in the front yard. Hannah had initially tried to keep things tidy, but she learned that Patrick demanded certain things be left undone or she'd end up with a black eye or a punch to the kidneys. Hazel lingered in the street, clearly puzzled.

She reached for the handle of her car as if preparing to leave.

Don't leave! Hannah folded her hands and whispered a quick prayer.

When she dared look out again, she laughed in delight.

Hazel had picked her way through the weeds, dodged the rusty chairs in the grass, and walked to the door. Hannah felt her heart turn over when Hazel knocked. Using all her frail strength, Hannah pounded the window and screamed at the top of her lungs.

She felt the floor vibrations of Patrick's angry footsteps walking inside through the back door. What was he doing home?

"No, no, no!" Hannah cried in despair. The ladder-back chair tumbled, and she fell. She sat cross-legged on the floor, wringing her hands and listening.

Patrick would wrangle his way through Hazel's questions with an airtight story, as usual.

Hannah left the window, ran to the heavy door of her prison, and pressed her ear against the crack. He'd left the door to the basement open in his haste to get to work this morning, because Hannah could feel the slight breeze coming through the cracks around the door.

Her body shimmied with hope. Wine & Whine girls to the rescue! She knew that Hazel had to be here because of their group. She'd managed to get an email to Sherry, Callie, and Olivia with her new address and her new last name before Patrick had closed her email account and taken away her devices. Hannah counted the months on her emaciated fingers. "Ten, eleven, twelve…oh my goodness," she whispered. "It's been two freaking years with this psycho."

During the first few months, Patrick had acted almost normal. He had his quirks, but she'd written them off. When he started locking her in for days on end, she had to face the harsh reality of her situation.

She pressed her ear harder to the slender crack around the door.

"…I am looking for Hannah Delaney, Mr. Somerset. This is the name we have, Patrick Somerset. Are you the Patrick Somerset married to Hannah Delaney?"

Hannah held her breath.

"She's not here right now. I'll tell her you came by."

"Oh. I'm so disappointed. When will she be back?" Hazel asked.

"I'm here! Call the police! I'm here!" Hannah cried, frantic. She needed something to make noise. Patrick had taken everything that she could use...the metal cup, a broom, the bowls. He'd left a plastic fork and butter knife in this room. A plastic cup. Paper plates. Hannah glanced at the bed. Hadn't she hidden something there? Hannah fell to her stomach and reached underneath. Nothing. The squeak of the door told her Patrick had taken the conversation outside instead of inviting Hazel in. She hoped he'd not closed it all the way.

Discouraged, she heaved the mattress off the bed. Her eyes widened. Lo and behold, she'd had the foresight to take a couple of things from his overstuffed garage the last time he'd given her liberty. She hefted an old baseball bat and a single, solid brick. She took them both and started beating the crap out of the door and yelling. She paused briefly to look out the window. Renewed hope bloomed in her chest when she realized that Hazel's car still sat at the curb.

She raced to the door and crammed her ear up against the crack again. Patrick wouldn't risk arousing suspicion, so he'd stay engaged for a while. He must not realize she can hear him when he leaves the front door open and talks to someone on the porch. The voices held a pleasant "getting-to-know-you" vibe, and she heard Patrick tell Hazel he had a large dog that tried to escape his crate.

Hannah gasped. They must've heard her! That's why he had to explain away the noise.

She heard the front door bang shut.

Hannah's hope dipped. Would Hazel believe him? She ran back to the chair and watched through the window, grateful that Patrick hadn't yet fulfilled his threat to black it out.

Hannah strained her neck until she could see waist-high. Patrick's

34

kneecaps and Hazel's waist reached approximately the same height. Hannah watched the tiny, age-spotted hands flutter as she talked with Patrick and the white, bejeweled sandals shift toward the street.

"She's leaving," Hannah murmured into the cold, airless room. In desperation, she took the brick and banged it on the basement window bars as hard as she could. Hazel turned around.

She heard me!

Hannah tried to do it again, but her strength evaporated. The brick slipped from her fingers to the cement floor and broke in two.

Hazel kept walking toward her car.

As Hannah stepped off the chair, heavy, quick steps strode from the front door, back through the hall, and down the stairs to the basement. She clutched her stomach. The fear of Patrick had become so strong that she threw up every time he walked into her room.

She dragged the chair away from the window. Pulled the thin mattress over the bat and brick, then tugged the spread across and fluffed the pillow.

The deadbolt slipped away. The door burst open.

Patrick exploded into the room, his hands tight knots at his sides, his face red and bloated with rage. "Where is it? What do you have in here to make that kind of racket?"

She sat on the bed, her hands folded in her lap.

He bent down until his nose almost touched hers. Hannah smelled garlic on his breath and wondered why he always smelled like garlic. She hated the smell of garlic. He knew that. Maybe he did it on purpose.

She felt her stomach heave and smiled slightly. If she threw up, at least it would be right in his face.

"SAY SOMETHING."

Hannah remained silent. This infuriated him further.

Patrick lifted his arm in a threat and held it there, watching her with his flat, dead fish eyes. His dirty-blond hair fell across his forehead.

"Congratulations," Hannah murmured. "You've reduced me to a permanent state of not caring what you do to me, what you say, or what you threaten me with. I just don't care anymore, Patrick. At this point, I'm more punching bag than woman."

She noted the morning's sun ascent into the sky as faint shadows shifted across the floor.

Patrick pursed his lips. "I don't know why you refuse to give me the respect a husband deserves. That's all I've ever asked."

Hannah said nothing.

"As you wish," he said. "No food until tomorrow morning." He eyed her form. "If you keep this up, you'll be dead soon."

Hannah chuckled. "It'd be preferable to living with you."

The door rattled on its hinges as he slammed it and shoved the deadbolt home.

Hannah smiled a thin smile. He hadn't found the pieces of brick or the bat. "Maybe tomorrow," she whispered. Her body screamed for sleep. She stretched, yawned, and lay her head on the pathetic pillow.

Chapter Seven

Olivia

"Sherry!" I called out as I walked into the lobby. "Do you have a minute?"

"She's not here," Beth answered.

"Where the heck is she?"

Beth changed screens and squinted at her appointment schedule. "Uh, she's at lunch with Curtis Ridgeland? New client."

"I can't even keep up anymore. Who's Curtis Ridgeland?"

Beth chuckled. "You told her to dig up business. A call came in, I gave him to her. I swear, I never knew so many marriages were in trouble until I started working here."

"Can you keep me in the loop on that?" I asked her. "I didn't mean for her to wander off into la-la-land without back-up."

"Of course," Beth said.

I flopped down into one of the lobby's guest chairs. "Have you had any emails or calls from Hazel? I'm hoping we didn't send her on a futile mission."

Beth nodded. "I'm wondering about that, too."

I rubbed the back of my neck. "Hannah has no one. No kids to check in on her, an ex who could care less, and she never talked about her parents, so I don't even know if they're still in her life. Would you tell Sherry to come to my office when she gets here?"

Beth nodded, her eyes glued to her laptop.

"This Curtis guy is a trip," Sherry said as she walked into my office an hour later.

I spread my hands. "I had no idea you were seeing a new client until Beth told me she'd assigned him to you."

Sherry's cheeks turned a polite shade of pink. "Sorry. I thought Beth would've run it by you first."

We took our usual positions in the armchairs. Sherry pulled out a small notebook and flipped pages. "Curtis Ridgeland, age 51, Caucasian, works at the nursery right around the corner from Glyndon in Reisterstown. You know the one. Green Thumb?"

I nodded. "Yep. Continue."

She stared at her notes. "He's also a part-time actor with an agency. His wife is Victoria Ridgeland, age 49. They've been married four years. He thinks she's fooling around and needs ammunition for divorce proceedings. She slapped the notebook closed. "It's that simple. Something about his eyes, though," she said. "He, umm…seemed hesitant. Uncomfortable."

"I hate when that happens," I said. "Hesitant clients always argue about the bill."

"Fun fact: Curtis Ridgeland has a history with Monty."

"What kind of history?"

"Sentenced to six months for insurance fraud. Suspected of setting fire to a rental property he owned for the insurance. Their paths crossed." Sherry fidgeted with her hands. "He was upfront about it. Maybe I shouldn't have taken him. Do we have a rule about that? No ex-cons? He got probation early. That's the only thing in his history that was problematic, but I didn't think it'd be a huge issue. I'm so sorry, I should've talked to you."

"We can't speculate about what you or I want; the important thing is that we agree about the workload. I'd have turned him down the minute he dropped Monty's name and certainly the minute he talked about torching a property for the insurance. He's already paid the deposit, but let's not take any other assignments."

Sherry nodded. "One and done. Promise. Full disclosure, when I showed up for the lunch, I think he assumed he'd be working with you. I bet he had no idea that you had another PI working with you. He probably hired us based on Monty...? Maybe he talked about you."

I laughed. "Yeah, and I can't imagine anything good that he'd say." I bit my lower lip. "Speaking of Monty, he mailed me a letter with his *wedding ring* in it. I mean, the coincidental timing of Curtis's investigation aside, how the heck did he get his hands on that ring? It's supposed to be locked away until he gets out!"

Sherry frowned. "You know, I've read about this. Spouses who can't let go and pursue at all costs. I think his hatred keeps him going."

I let out a long sigh. "Awesome. My life is a Hallmark movie."

"What'd the letter say?"

"Something about wedding vows being permanent." My words poured out in a rush. "Why now? Does he have ears on the outside? Is someone watching me and reporting back to him? Think about the timing, Sherry. The minute my life settles into a normal rhythm and I think I can relax, he emerges from his cave. You'd think a man in a cell wouldn't have so much power."

I sprang from my chair, strode to my desk for Monty's note, and held it out to her.

"*You made a vow, remember?*" she recited, her voice soft. "His writing is bold and slanted. Aggressive." She handed it back to me. "Typical sociopath. They're like spiders. You know how to get rid of spiders, right?"

I waited.

"*Crush* them." Her grin sparkled its way into my increasingly horrible mood. "Splat them into the dirt, and don't look back." She lifted her palms. "My apologies to all the spider-lovers out there."

"I guess the good news is that it didn't freak me out this time. I mean... I'm angry and tired of his weirdness, but I haven't freaked out." I raised one shoulder. "Progress."

"Maybe he was feeling isolated and sad. Thinking of better days."

She had to wait for me to quit laughing.

I held up the note and flapped it in the air. "Monty doesn't get sad; he gets even." I'm hanging onto this in case he shows up somewhere that he shouldn't, and I need evidence of harassment. The connection with Curtis might be an outlier. With my book and everything, he could be a closet fan, like the Foofoos."

"Friends of Olivia? Wow. I haven't heard those words in a long time. Is that group still online?"

"They made the group private, but they're still a thing, I hear."

"You should be flattered," Sherry joked.

I rolled my eyes. The Foofoos had caused madness and mayhem and the near-death of my former therapist, Hazel. Obsession never ended well, and the Foofoos were a strange mix of obsession and hero worship. Two years ago, a demented fan tried to burn down my entire life. Almost succeeded, too.

Sherry tapped her chin. "Two errand boys are better than one." She cocked her head and folded her arms. "Curtis could totally be a straight-up client in need of our help. But what if Curtis, Graham, and Monty are some kind of unholy trinity?"

"Where's he from?" I asked.

"Downtown Baltimore. He grew up in the City."

I nodded. "Rough way to grow up, back in the day."

I shook off my spiraling thoughts. I would *not* let Monty get into my head. Not after six years of freedom from his anger, gambling issues, and sociopathic tendencies. "When does he want you to start?"

"As soon as we can. He gave me a night that his wife is at a dance studio. He suspects she's met someone there."

"Okay. Let's do a little recon first. You free tonight?"

She opened her mouth to respond, but the landline on my desk rang, causing both of us to jump out of our skin. Beth took the call, then sent it to my line.

I hopped out of my chair and rushed to my desk. "I bet it's Hazel. Finally! Let's find out about Hannah." I put the phone on speaker.

"Hazel, this is Olivia. Sherry and I are both here. How'd it go?"

"It's not good news," she said, her voice filled with uncertainty.

"What happened?"

"First, the house is way inland, on the outskirts of Niceville. I couldn't believe the yard…it looked like it hadn't been mowed in six months, and I almost left because it looked like a vacant property. But the name on the mailbox said Patrick Somerset, and how many of those can there be?"

"Good grief, Hazel, if it looked that bad, you should've taken off. We want you safe," Sherry said.

"It's okay. I'm home now, and I have some useful information." We heard the rustling of pages. We smiled at each other. Hazel's therapist background guaranteed meticulous notes.

"Patrick is a large, rather defensive individual, and I could tell he did not want to talk to me. He told me Hannah wasn't at home, so I confirmed that he's the husband and she lives there." She cleared her throat. "He didn't invite me inside and shared too many details about Hannah's location and why. In my opinion, fabrications. He's hiding something. How could our Hannah be attracted to someone like that?"

Sherry and I traded somber expressions. Our suspicions had been correct.

"Some of us take a while to learn the signs. Was he gorgeous?" I asked.

After a short pause, Hazel told us that on a scale of one to ten, he'd be a nine.

I snorted. "All those assholes are gorgeous. I swear. It's disgusting."

"I heard noises, too." Hazel continued. "Something banging around. Like remodeling or…anyway, I thought I heard a voice, but Patrick stood in front of the door like a security guard. No way was I getting inside." Hazel took a breath. "What if Hannah had been trying to signal? What if she's hurt? Or trapped?"

"Wait. Okay. Let's think this through. Did Patrick address the sounds you heard?"

"He told me his dog tries to get out of his crate, then he closed the door and stepped outside onto the porch. What dog tries to escape his crate without barking and whining? And I didn't see any evidence of a dog in the foyer or outside."

I glanced at Sherry. "Don't go back. Promise us."

41

"Okay," she agreed. "But we have to do something."

"Correction," I told her. "Sherry and I have to do something. *Please* try to rest and forget all about it. You didn't give him any personal info, did you?"

She chuckled. "After Pete, do you think I'd do that?"

"Right." I smiled. I doubted anybody could try to scam her after what she went through before she moved to Florida. "We'll take it from here. Thank you for checking on her, Hazel."

I put the receiver back in its cradle and looked at Sherry. "Let's meet at close of business."

My afternoon got sucked into a tangle with a former client who demanded a refund because Sherry and I had decided his request to extract contents from a private home constituted theft and gave him a firm 'no.' This did not sit well with him. I loved taking risks—maybe too much— but as a PI, the risk-taking had to be limited to the boundaries of the law.

Mostly.

If it got personal, we weren't so picky. Take Hannah, for instance. We'd walk across burning coals if it meant saving one of the Wine & Whine girls.

Sherry walked into my office at four-forty-five.

"Ready for our meeting?" Sherry asked. She patted Marlowe on the head when he nudged her leg.

"Sure." I patted the files I'd been working on into a neat pile, left my desk, and joined her in the sitting area.

We sat in our armchairs in silence. The conversation with Hazel had cast a dim glow of unease that seeped out of my pores. My skin even felt clammy. I rubbed my arms.

Sherry lifted her chin. "I think it's a better choice if *you* take the new client assignment."

I nodded, thinking. "Maybe."

"I would like you to consider letting me go check on Hannah by myself. I'm ready. Tom taught me how to pick locks, how to cover my tracks, and keep out of sight. All that time you were taking care of the arson stuff with your house, he was teaching me his tricks. When I wasn't waist-deep in work, he liked to act as my instructor. I'd love to try out what I learned in

42

the field."

"I don't think you realize what you're getting into."

Ignoring me, she continued. "Plus, Beth has three cases waiting for you to review, and traveling to Florida isn't a paid proposition. It's spitballing. I should do it, not you."

My mind raced. We couldn't check on Hannah together, because someone had to tend the firm and keep an eye on the new receptionist. I tapped my fingers on the armrest and looked away. This situation reminded me of dropping off my girls at college...first Serena, then Lilly. Pride with a generous slab of angst. Except, I was dropping Sherry into a possible confrontation with a psycho.

"Ha!" Sherry jumped to her feet. "You're thinking about it."

A tiny pause hovered.

I groaned. "Okay."

"Yeah, baby!" She flung out her arms and in a nod to her ballet background, performed a couple of pirouettes.

"This could be dangerous, Sherry."

She pointed to the firearm in its paddle holster on her belt. "Does this look like a toy to you?"

"It's a different world when you have to shoot to protect yourself."

She frowned. "You think I don't know that? I already had what I'd call a 'baptism by fire.' She laughed. "*Firing,* I mean."

My mind flipped to the horrible afternoon I'd been confronted by an angry spouse in our lobby. Sherry had been our receptionist at the time. When I'd been shot, I'd heard two final shots before I lost consciousness. My last thought had been something like, "I'm too young to die." When I woke up in the hospital two days later, I found out that *Sherry* had fired the final shots...into my assailant, not me.

"True," I admitted, "but you acted on instinct. You were protecting me."

She cocked her head. "Yeah, it was *instinct* that made me sneak away to the safe and get your weapon." She chuckled. "Even I was surprised at the calm I felt under pressure. I'll be fine. Hannah needs help, Olivia."

I couldn't argue with that.

"I'll stay with Hazel." She shrugged. "Maybe he told her the truth and he's just a jerk."

"You don't believe that for one minute," I said, thinking. "Let's surveil the new client for a couple of hours tonight as a precaution, and you can brief me on the way. Can you get a flight to Florida tomorrow?"

We met at the office long after work hours, both clothed in black.

Sherry climbed into the ratty-looking vehicle we'd bought for surveilling—a 1990 Honda Accord that we'd rescued from the salvage yard. I'd gone to great expense to outfit it with a brand-new V8 engine. It could hit 80mph in six seconds, which comes in handy when cops notice Sherry or me hanging out until the wee hours of the morning. The mechanic had offered twice what I had in the car to buy it after he finished the work. He got a little misty-eyed when I turned him down.

Sherry plopped into the passenger seat. I revved the engine.

She rolled her eyes. "You love this stuff, don't you?"

In response, I squealed out of the parking lot like a boss.

"This would be a good time to give me detailed impressions, because we may be here all night," I told Sherry as I parked in a discreet location and grabbed a huge thermos from the back seat. "I have coffee."

Sherry laughed. "Do you have a porta potty, too?"

I reached into the back and produced a magenta funnel with a generous mouth. Sherry's forehead creased. "What the heck is that?"

"Portable female urination device. No splash, quiet, and advertised as foolproof."

Her lips curled into a knot. "Eww."

I tossed it into the back seat. "Easy to use. Crawl into the back, pee, tie up the bag."

"I'll pass on the coffee, but thanks. You use the damn thing."

I smiled.

An hour passed.

Curtis Ridgeland lived in a remote part of Eldersburg, about forty minutes from my office. He worked as a grunt for the State, which made my blood run cold, because Monty's entire career had been with the State of Maryland as a project manager for different software solutions. The more I learned about Curtis, the more it made sense that he and Monty had crossed paths. Through prison, as Sherry had told me, but maybe through work, too.

Sherry started snoring. I poked her in the arm. "Does this guy have any other priors?"

She rubbed her eyes and uncapped a bottle of water. "I brought his file. Here." She tossed it in my lap.

I flipped through. A patrol car passed by. I turned off my iPhone flashlight. Both Sherry and I sank down in our seats until he passed.

"Roll down the windows. It's stuffy in here," Sherry complained.

I cranked the Honda's non-power windows. "You have your own crank. Manual, remember?"

"Oh, yeah." She rolled down her window. "I have to get on a plane at eleven tomorrow, so I'd like a few hours of sleep before I go to the airport. What are you looking for, anyway?"

I scrolled my index finger down the pages. "Forgery, too?" I looked at Sherry in the murky darkness. The wee-hours silence bordered on creepy. Even the tree frogs had stopped croaking. A few sleepless fireflies drifted in front of the windshield. An owl hooted in the distance as the full moon made an appearance. I stared at Curtis's property. A pockmarked driveway scrolling up to the carport, a small, one-story, brick home, a drab shingled roof.

She frowned. "I shouldn't have signed him."

"It's not that, it's just..."

Curtis's door flew open. "Look!" I hissed, pointing.

We slid down in the seats. Curtis strode to his carport, got into a late-model Hyundai, and started backing out of the drive.

"Showtime," I whispered. We left our spot and joined him, keeping a sedate two car-lengths between us.

Sherry gripped the dashboard as I gunned the Honda and skidded around a corner. The light turned red just as I sped through. I glanced uneasily at the bright lights bordering the highway.

"Slow down," Sherry said, her voice calm. "He hasn't made us."

I looked at her. "You know him a little. Where do you think he's going?"

She grabbed the file. Paged through to her notes. "He's a drinker. Does a bit of gambling."

I felt my jaw tighten. "Monty used to be a huge gambler. Maybe *that's* how they bonded. Don't they do it late at night? Like cockroaches?"

Sherry chuckled. "Guess we'll find out."

Fifteen minutes later, I pulled into a packed parking lot in front of a building that nestled between Eldersburg and the quaint town of Sykesville. It had a ten-foot, blinking sign advertising an all-night gentlemen's club. "Oh, crap."

Sherry laughed. "Curtis, you're such a douchebag."

"This is why she's cheating, I guess."

"We don't know that yet," Sherry said.

Another hour slipped by.

I sat there wondering if my gut had been wrong when a chill trailed up my spine and into the base of my skull. My mom was fond of the phrase "Someone just walked across my grave." That's how it felt.

Curtis got out of his vehicle, lit a cigarette, and leaned against the car. Cigarette smoke curled into the night air. My Honda blended in with all the other crappy cars parked in this lot. Although it had its share of Mercedes and Beemers, too.

Sherry drew in her skinny legs, put her feet on the glovebox, and folded her arms around her knees. "I'm about ready to head back."

"A few more minutes," I told her, listening hard to my inner nudges.

A man emerged from the shadows at the far corner of the low-slung building. The parking lot halogen lamps cast shadows on his face as he walked toward Curtis. "Do you recognize that guy?"

She squinted into the dark. "Kind of hard since visibility is zero."

"Wait. He'll walk underneath the light."

And he did. Right under the light and straight into my nightmares.

Sherry gasped. I cursed.

Graham.

My next-door-neighbor Callie's husband and Monty's good buddy. We'd raised our kids together, attended sports events together, monitored field trips. Later in life, after my own marriage fell apart, so did Callie's, and she'd hired me for my first surveillance assignment, which had been to find proof of Graham's affair. My photos of him with his little thing on the side gave her the evidence she needed for a nice, juicy divorce settlement. That had been two years ago, and he still hated me for it. He blamed *me* for the divorce instead of his three-year fling with someone other than his wife. Go figure. He hated me almost as much as Monty did, and it gave me heartburn when they got together.

I exhaled long and slow as a dark foreshadowing drifted through my thoughts. Sherry's hunch had been correct. Curtis, Graham…and *Monty*. An unholy trinity.

Chapter Eight

Hunter

Shiloh shot straight past the admin without a glance and pushed open the door to Hunter's office.

Hunter pushed aside the files he'd been working on and folded his hands. "I heard you're not happy."

She fluffed her wild hair and settled into a chair in front of his desk. With a jab of her index finger, she said, "You, of all people, should know I can't work with idiots! What are you thinking, Faraday?"

"Both of them are excellent investigators. What's the issue?"

"They don't even understand street lingo. Or how to dress! They'd be made at a thousand yards. I need some guys with experience, Hunter."

"Sergeant," Hunter corrected her.

She snapped her lips shut and fumed.

"I'll arrange it. How's that sound?" Hunter said.

She glared. "Don't you train these men?"

This time, Hunter bristled. Sure, they had history, but he outranked her. He remained quiet, studying her.

She slipped in that slow grin of hers. "Look at you, all Sergeant-y. I get it, Sergeant. I apologize. My demeanor is inappropriate."

"Officer Becker will see to it that you have appointments with a couple of different investigators this afternoon or tomorrow. They do have their own assignments, though. Keep that in mind, Detective McPherson. We may or may not be able to shuffle things around."

Shiloh left his office without a word.

On his way home, Hunter stopped at his local bar. He figured after dealing with all the Shiloh fireworks…including how to untangle the thorny threads of their romantic history…he deserved a good IPA. The bartender placed a frosty glass in front of him. He'd just taken the first sip when his cell vibrated.

He dipped into his pocket for his phone while taking another deep, savory taste of his beer. He fumbled for his reading glasses to make out the number. "Dammit," he muttered when he identified the caller as Olivia. "Freakin' ridiculous," he said to himself. "Don't I have enough going on?" he asked with a glance upward. "You have to throw in Olivia, too?"

The vibrating stopped.

She left no voicemail.

He kicked back a long slug of the beer before calling her back. "You called?"

"Hunter! Oh, thank God. I need a professional to talk to about this."

He grunted. "Of course you do."

Olivia cleared her throat. "I apologize. I'm…upset. You know how I get."

He bit back his words. Yeah, he knew how she got. And he never heard from her unless she needed something. "What is it this time?"

Hunter felt her disappointment at his tone through the airwaves and visualized the tiny furrow forming between her brows. He wondered if she'd changed her hair from platinum back to the auburn that he'd loved. He shook his head and re-focused on the conversation.

Olivia remained quiet.

"Cat got your tongue?" He laughed. "Correction, Riot got your tongue? How's the only cat I ever liked, anyway?"

"He's fine. He and Marlowe are best buds now. Marlowe's always at the office with me during the day, so that helps."

"How's Sherry?" he asked, determined to make her work for what she needed to ask him. After all, they hadn't communicated in a year.

"I just put her on a plane this morning for Florida," she barked.

"Huh. That must be the reason for the call."

"I have two emergencies going on at once, Hunter. Can you stop this game you're playing?"

Several smart-ass answers rolled through his mind, but he ignored them. "Okay, okay. What do you need?"

"It involves Monty."

Hunter stiffened. She knew that's all she had to say to get him to sign on. He'd thought they were finished with him. At last count, he still had to serve seventeen of his twenty years.

She explained about Sherry's new client, Hazel's report about Hannah, and that they'd tracked Curtis Ridgeland to a meeting with Graham.

The bartender brought a fresh beer as Hunter listened and removed the empty. "What's your plan, Olivia? You're not a wildflower fresh from the fields anymore. You're a private investigator. Doing pretty well, I hear. You always have a plan."

"Who told you that?"

"I still keep in touch with Sophie and Gray. And once in a while, your daughters. They talk, you know." Hunter wondered how she felt about his close relationship with her mother, Sophie; and Gray, her new husband. Sophie and Gray had met during Olivia's early admission to the hospital after her assault. Gray was Olivia's neurologist and now, her stepfather.

Hunter scowled. He'd tried to be a part of this family until Olivia decided to walk away from his proposal of marriage. At that point, he couldn't continue. Three years to wait for a woman to heal from trauma with nothing to show for it was enough. He'd been satisfied he'd done everything he could, and convinced that she'd never commit.

The last year had been good. He'd leaned into taking on an executive role in the department, and he'd exchanged active involvement in a case for a podium. It had been *good*, he reassured himself. Hadn't it?

"I'm glad you still keep in touch with Mom and the girls. That's nice," Olivia said.

"Well, just because *you* didn't want me around didn't mean they don't. They still like me."

"So. Not. Funny. Stop it."

"You and I both know this is complicated, Olivia. Give me a break."

She sighed. "I need your help, Hunter. Can we push the other stuff out of the way? Please?"

His resolve crumbled. Couldn't he be her friend? Maybe. Maybe not. He could advise, but that's all. As the lead investigator on her assault case in Richmond five years ago, she had every right to contact him. He ran his hand through his hair. Pure and simple, the rejection of his proposal still sat deep in his veins. He'd laid his life bare for her, and she'd wanted nothing to do with it. *Time to put it in perspective, dude.*

"Hunter? You there?"

"I'm here," he said, resigned. "You sure Monty's involved? That's the first thing. If so, what's the motivation? Second thing."

"I...I get that. I've scribbled out a road map, but I thought you might still have connections here? As a cop and former investigator on the original case, I wondered if you could inquire as to Monty's incarceration status."

A thought raced into his mind: *I can do better than that. I can wrap it into a follow-up, get it approved by the Lieutenant, and get the hell out of Richmond while Shiloh's here.*

"Maybe," he agreed. "I'll have to think about it."

"That's all I'm asking, Hunter. Thanks."

"Did you say Sherry's in Florida trying to find Hannah?"

"Hannah's gone underground or something. We've tried to contact for a year now, and no response. She used to text or message us once in a while, but now her phone is shut off, and Hazel went to—"

"Wait," Hunter interrupted. "What does Hazel have to do with anything?"

"Did I leave that out? Hazel moved. She retired to Pensacola. We discovered she's thirty minutes or so from Hannah's address. We asked her to go over and check it out."

Hunter closed his eyes and tilted his head back. Why would anyone in their right mind send an elderly woman to do something like that? He swallowed, hard. "I assume Hazel is okay."

"She's fine. The intel she got from this man helped us understand that finding her is urgent. We filed a Missing Person's."

"I'll check in with the county PD as a courtesy and feel it out."

"That would be great, but unnecessary. Sherry's got it."

Hunter grimaced. Sherry—the equivalent of a mid-life Betty Boop with a shiny, new investigator's license— had barely scratched the surface as a professional investigator. He doubted she "had" much of anything. "Okay. Let me look into Monty, and I'll check back."

They ended the call.

Hunter drained the fresh beer, walked outside, hopped into his Jeep Rubicon, and pointed it toward home. He jabbed the accelerator, deep in thought.

Olivia. Had there ever been a time when she'd *not* complicated his life?

Chapter Nine

Hannah

Hannah's fingers trailed across the kitchen counters she'd scrubbed, the furniture they'd bought as newlyweds, the beautiful desk she'd hoped to use as she grew her fledgling cottage industry. She snorted. "Fat chance that's ever going to happen," she remarked into the musty air. The whole house needed a deep cleaning. She stared at her thin arms, the atrophied muscles, thought about how little physical stamina she had now. She felt too weak to push a vacuum, or mop a floor. She guessed she suffered from severe depression, too, but she knew he'd *never* let her see a therapist. Would Patrick even get her medical attention if she needed it? The possibility of dying alone and forgotten in this wretched house tormented her.

The sun filtered through the barred windows that hadn't had a good cleaning in ten years. Patrick had lied about that, too, and told her that once she moved in, he'd remove all the bars on the windows and deep-clean the house.

How naïve and in love she'd been. She felt the ever-present tears slide down her cheeks. How could she have been so blind? She thought about Hazel, Olivia's therapist. How she'd love to unpack her situation with her and understand how this might have been prevented. But even Hazel had been deceived by a man, hadn't she? NO one was immune to an evil, determined psycho.

With a sigh, she stroked the luscious curtain fabric he'd let her pick out. Patrick had bought her every single thing she'd wanted because unbeknownst to her, the home she'd so fastidiously decorated with all these trappings would become her prison cell, and he wanted it to be a *personalized* prison cell. In his twisted mind, she supposed he thought that made it okay, and she should appreciate his generosity. Besides, what did it matter? From the outside, it looked like a couple of derelict losers lived here.

At least he'd let her out of the basement.

Hannah walked into the kitchen and opened the fridge. She smiled at the bounty there. He must've stuffed it while she'd been sleeping and even left a note. Patrick left lots of notes. They always had smiley faces on them, which Hannah thought ironic when she thought about all the bruises and bloody noses and black eyes he'd given her. Patrick needed his own emoji. It would contain black eyes and a perpetual sneer. For a psychopath, he could be attentive, though. Another thing she needed to ask Hazel. Can psychopaths be bipolar?

"It's such a waste, Patrick. You could've been a wonderful guy," she muttered. She made a sandwich, then pulled out meat from the freezer to set out to thaw for dinner. Patrick expected dinner on the table each night at seven p.m.

She carried her plate to the small table in the kitchen, bowed her head and prayed the prayer she prayed every day. 'God, thank you for keeping me alive one more day. And get me out of here. Please. Amen."

After watching local news on the few channels Patrick allowed, Hannah stood, stretched, and padded to the small guest bedroom at the end of the hall. She glanced at the clock bolted to the wall like a hall monitor. She hated that clock with its loud, infernal ticking and its round, white face that mocked her. The tick sounded with each move of the second hand, a gong sounded on the hour, a mini-gong on the half hour.

"I'm sure you think that's hilarious, Patrick. How many women have you trapped in here, listening to the blasted clock announce the hours and minutes and seconds of our stolen lives? Is this your way of driving us insane?" Hannah looked at her bare, dirty feet, the raggedy sweater she wore, the T-shirt she'd worn for the past week. "I think you might be achieving your goal with me, you creep," she murmured as she fell onto the bed. She hated how much she slept, but it was the only escape allowed.

A knock clattered on the door. She jumped. Raced to the living room window and peered at the front porch. A blurry, tiny person stood at the front door, knocking. The windows had been installed circa 1970 and years of grime had dulled the tiny plates of glass to the point that she could barely see through them. The bars on the doors and windows usually kept people away. But at this very moment, someone other than a package delivery person stood at her front door! She tried to get a read on the vehicle parked out on the street. White, four-door sedan. "It's a rental," Hannah breathed, her heart racing. She rocketed to the front door, banged her fists, and screamed as loud as she could.

Hannah put her ear to the door and held her breath. Had they heard?

A tiny voice called her name. A voice muted by the bars, the thick, solid door, the soundproofing…but she'd heard it! Someone called out *her name!*

Hannah's jaw dropped. Could it be? Could Olivia or Sherry have come looking for her? Her arms trembled from beating on the door, and her chest heaved with the effort, but she had to try. She raced into the kitchen, dragged one of the heavy chairs to the door, put her puny weight behind it, and shoved as hard as she could. "I'm here! I'm here!" she screamed, dragging the chair back a few feet, then pushing it forward with both hands and crashing it into the door. Then again. And again.

A face appeared at one of the grimy windows. Hannah started sobbing with relief. "Sherry!" she screamed. "It's me! I'm trapped!"

She mouthed something through the window, her words unintelligible.

Hannah returned to the door, sat in the chair, and studied the deadbolt. The aging wood had rotted around it. She bent down and put her ear to the door. Could Sherry maneuver through the bars? A grin lit up her face when she heard a slight tinkling and clinking around the lock mechanism. Hannah clapped her hands together and laughed in delight. Lock-picking had been high on Sherry's list of skills a PI should possess; she remembered that much from the Wine & Whine get-togethers. She'd talked about Tom Stark's ability to unlock any door. Hannah choked back a sob. She missed her people. She missed the Wine & Whine group. She missed Maryland. She missed the single life. What on earth had she been thinking, marrying someone within a few months? The Wine & Whine girls had tried to warn her.

The deadbolt slid free. The handle turned. Hannah slipped off the chair and pulled it aside.

The door cracked open a few inches. Sherry peered inside. "Hannah?"

Hannah flung the door open and hurled herself into Sherry's arms.

The two women hung onto each other until Sherry pulled away, leaving her hands on Hannah's scrawny shoulders, her gaze sliding the length of her friend's form. Tears slid down Sherry's cheeks. "My God, honey. "What's he done to you?"

Hannah's laughter bordered on hysteria. "No time. We have to get out of here."

"Do you need to get your—"

"NO." She picked up a small duffel she kept in the coat closet. "I keep a go-bag. It has ID and stuff. It's all I need. Patrick has a way of showing up, and I don't want to wait. Let's go. Now, Sherry. *Now.*"

"Okay. Come on."

"RUN."

They raced to the rental and hopped inside. Sherry's hand trembled as she started the car. After a few tries, the motor turned over, and she screamed down the road in the opposite direction. Five tense minutes of silence later, Sherry handed Hannah a bottle of water. "Are you hungry?"

Hannah uncapped the water and drank. "I don't even know anymore. I'm sure I could eat."

"You're not eating, I can tell that. Do you want to talk about it?"

Hannah looked out the window, one hand fiddling with a lock of her stringy, long hair. "Can we just get out of here, please?"

Sherry stomped the accelerator.

Thirty minutes later, they pulled into a diner. Hannah looked around, eyes wide and staring, biting her fingernails.

"This okay?" Sherry asked.

"I'm not sure where Patrick works. I've been isolated, and I-I don't know how, but every time I've tried to escape, he comes out of nowhere." She looked at the goosebumps that had spread down her arms.

"Hannah. Look." Sherry pulled her light jacket aside to reveal the firearm in a holster on her belt. "He won't have a chance, girl."

Hannah offered a tight smile. "Okay. I know I need to eat."

"Let's do it." Sherry's brow puckered. "Wait...you're barefoot. I have tennis shoes in the back. Let's see if they fit."

Hannah pulled her sweater tighter around herself.

Sherry hopped out, lifted the hatch, dug around in her suitcase. "Size eight. What size are you?"

"They'll work fine," Hannah said, taking the shoes from Sherry and slipping her dirty feet inside.

Sherry put a comforting arm around Hannah's waist as they walked in and sat in a booth. A server bustled to the booth and took their orders. After one glance at Hannah, she put a gentle hand on Hannah's arm and said, "I hope things get better for you soon, honey."

Hannah blushed all the way to her hairline. "She thinks I'm a homeless person. I'll go to the bathroom and splash on a little soap and water, okay?"

"I'll go with you if you want."

Hannah smiled. "I'll be fine."

Hannah returned to the table looking much fresher after a bit of soap and water and her hair pulled back in an elastic. "Maybe now I don't look so much like a charity case."

Sherry pointed at her ear to indicate her earbuds. "I'm giving Olivia an update."

Hannah heard the tiny screech of joy as Olivia answered and heard the news. She smiled.

Sherry glanced at Hannah. "Her husband could be following us."

The server brought their orders. Hannah started eating small bites.

"He had her locked inside that house Hazel told us about," Sherry whispered underneath her hand so Hannah wouldn't hear.

Hannah's hand shook as she lifted the fork to her mouth.

"By some miracle...thank you Tom...I got the stupid lock to open, and when I saw her I couldn't believe it. Dear God. She's a poster child for abuse."

Hannah chewed her food, her eyes darting to every corner of the room.

"Hannah didn't even want to gather her things; we just got the hell outta there. She's like a feral cat, scared out of her mind. She told me that Patrick shows up like a ghost any time she has a chance to escape."

Hannah perked at the sound of Olivia's voice. She put down her fork and leaned in on her elbows.

Olivia continued, "More than likely, that kind of abuser has security cameras all over the place. Did you check?"

Hannah watched Sherry's face go dead white. Of course, Patrick had security cameras. She'd learned to avoid them, but in her haste to get out of that house, she hadn't warned Sherry. How much had Patrick seen? Did he know they were on the road?

Sherry put the phone on FaceTime and pointed it at Hannah. "Say hello, Hannah."

Hannah lifted a hand and waved. "Thank you. I'm so sorry. And Sherry, yes, he has cameras. I forgot to...I didn't think about..." She groaned. "He saw us. I'm sure of it. He checks the app every few minutes, because he's so paranoid."

Sherry flipped the phone camera back around. "Wanted you to see her in the flesh. Gotta go. I'll keep you posted."

She ended the call and slipped the phone back into her purse. "Olivia says you can stay in her guest room."

"We have to leave," Hannah muttered.

Five minutes later, Sherry paid the bill at the checkout counter. As they waited for the receipt, Hannah dropped her head and slid away from the counter into the corner.

"What?" Sherry asked.

Hannah cocked her head at the door.

Sherry turned. A tall man with dark blond hair stood inside the entrance with his hands on his hips and his head on a swivel. "That's him, isn't it?"

Whimpering, Hannah pressed herself further into the wall.

"Is there a back entrance to this place?" Sherry asked the cashier.

She nodded and pointed.

They ran.

Chapter Ten

Olivia

Beth approached my desk with delicate, deer-like steps as if she might startle and leap away any second.

I took my eyes off the screen and fastened them on her face. "What?"

"I know you've got a lot on your mind, Olivia, so I didn't know if you'd want to take a call from Callie or not. She's on line one."

I stared at the blinking button on my landline. "Thanks, Beth. I'll take it." I pressed the button. "Hi, Cal," I answered.

"How's your day going?"

My female radar quivered at Callie's classic "test-the-waters" question before plunging me into the deep end.

I put my pen down and rubbed my eyes. "It's fine. What's going on?"

"I had an interesting conversation with Graham yesterday."

I drummed my fingers on the desk in typical fashion, impatiently waiting for the bottom line.

"You know Graham. He's the king of secrets, and when he mentioned Monty, I paid attention. He told me he's out on work release. I think he wanted this piece of information to get back to you."

I grew dizzy and grabbed the edge of my desk. Marlowe must've sensed a tense moment because he yawned, lifted his head, and wagged his tail at me. I waited for the dizziness to pass before I patted his head. "Good boy," I whispered.

"What?" Callie asked.

"Let me get this straight. The dirtbag is out on work release. I didn't even know his charges allowed for that type of program."

"Yeah, me either. Graham seemed happy about it. *That's* what concerns me."

I picked up a pen and started scribbling on my notepad. "Did he say where Monty is located with this work release thing?"

A tiny pause. "Did you know he got transferred to the prison in Sykesville?"

My heart skipped a couple of beats. *Sykesville is a little too close for comfort. When had that happened?*

"You know I try not to stalk him, right? I stay far, far away from Monty's life as a convict."

"I understand, but he's been assigned to certain private sector facilities in Maryland. He has all those technical skills, and according to Graham, this made him a hero to the warden. Monty's been on his best behavior, I guess. He fixes everyone's computers, and it earned him a work release pass."

After a pregnant pause that could've birthed the baby by now...she cleared her throat. "He's in Westminster."

I gasped.

"He's there once a week, he skips a day, then goes to Owings Mills."

"Is he supervised?"

"I hope so, Olivia. I don't know."

A sinister silence crept between us.

Callie broke in with a hopeful, "Maybe it's no big deal. I wanted you to know, that's all. Should I not have told you?"

"You *should* have, Callie. Thanks. Did Graham say anything more specific about location? I don't know what I'd do if I ran into him somewhere." I frowned. "What are you doing talking to Graham, anyway?"

"I don't know," she moaned. "I'm weak, I guess."

"You know how I feel about that."

"Look at it this way. He keeps us informed. At least you have a head start if he throws something at you."

I nibbled on a fingernail. *Should I tell her about the meeting between Curtis and Graham?*

"I can't believe they're still close friends," I muttered.

"Me either."

We shared a quiet solidarity.

"Olivia, I'd never go back to Graham. I want you to know that. He's my daughter's father, though, and I need to be civil. That's all it is."

Her words reassured me. Maybe Graham would prove to be a better ex, a more appropriate parent; than Monty. "How's Amy doing?"

"She loves it in Richmond, and having your Lilly as a roommate is part of it. She's picked a major, I think. Counseling, Psychiatry, whatever they're calling that major these days. How about Lilly? She enjoying her sophomore year?"

"She tells me she is. Mom gives me the real slant on things, though." A smile spread across my face at the thought of my daughters, Serena and Lilly, one about to graduate with a Poli-Sci degree and the other a sophomore trying to figure out next steps. "Lilly's not sure. She has a boyfriend now though, so I imagine picking a major is the last thing on her mind."

Callie laughed. "I sure hope our daughters have learned to do a better job of picking partners than their mothers."

I twisted a lock of hair around my index finger. "You'd think."

"Sophie had the girls over for dinner last week, did you know?"

"Mom's good about having them over."

"She and Gray still good?"

I groaned. "Isn't it terrible that we think that way now? Since our marriages tanked, we approach marriages with this kind of...oh, I don't know...negative expectation."

"Disaster prevention."

"Maybe," I agreed. "I need to get down to Richmond soon and see Mom and the girls. You want to go?"

"I'll check. I have a lot going on." After a pause, she added, "Your mom invited Hunter to one of their dinners. Isn't that sweet?"

"You're just a wealth of intel this morning, Cal." I sighed. "Hunter and Mom and Gray are big buddies. He bonded with Gray early in my assault investigation, and they've been friends ever since." I laughed. "I still can't believe Mom married my neurologist. Shouldn't surprise me, though. She really is amazing."

"Your trips home must be awkward if he's invited to the family dinners. It's like a fairy tale, he and your mom getting together. I'm glad they have a good marriage; someone needs to," she joked. Callie went quiet...and the persistent and ongoing question hung in the air like a piñata: *When are you and Hunter getting back together?*

"Don't ask," I told her.

"Don't worry, I've learned not to ask. I can *think it,* though."

You have to tell her!

She waited.

"We have this new client, Cal. And..." *have you told her you sent Sherry to check on Hannah yet? Nope. You haven't told her that either.* "And he's Sherry's client, but...anyway. You don't need the backstory. We tracked the guy to a "gentlemen's club" in between Sykesville and Eldersburg where he lives." If ever I needed proof that Monty had linked arms with Graham and Curtis, here it was. It couldn't be a coincidence that we'd tracked Curtis to a bar so close to Monty's new max security prison.

"And...?" she prompted.

I felt compelled to dump the whole sad story. She hadn't asked me to and didn't need to carry such a load of weighty dilemmas, but we *are* best friends, after all. What's the saying about shared sorrows or something? Dividing the grief?

I forged ahead with the story.

As I got deeper into my revelations, her rasping breaths in my ear made me wonder if I'd made the right decision to give it to her all at once. Maybe I should have tried the piecemeal approach. I forget that people who don't look at criminal records or surveil in the wee hours for a living are less tolerant of such information.

"Sherry's got Hannah right now," I said, concluding my synopsis, and she looks like an orphan on the back roads of Calcutta. We have to get her back here."

"Poor Hannah," Callie whispered. "It's just horrible."

"Poor Sherry, too," I added, thinking she'd be calling any minute. "Anyway, that's a very long path to my point…which is *why* I took Sherry's new client. We got busy, and someone had to hold down the fort here." I chuckled. "The brat talked me into letting her go check on Hannah by herself. I had my reservations, but she begged me. She might be more of a risk-taker than I am. Anyway, the latest news you gave me about Monty—"

"Has put more pressure on you," Callie interrupted. "I am *so* sorry."

"No, no…it's good. I needed to know. Now I have an idea of what's going on, and you can pump Graham like no one else can. Try to get a little more, okay? I need to know what Monty's thinking. Maybe we can get this whole work release issue repealed before he realizes what happened."

"What the heck is wrong with him, anyway? My gosh, does he want more years added to his sentence?"

I groaned. "Think about how much he knows his way around software and code. It wouldn't take much to destroy me online." I snorted. "His fondest wish is to destroy anything I've built."

I made a mental note to get Beth to call our tech support and strengthen our software security.

Maybe hire a part-time bodyguard.

"You still there?" Callie asked.

I blinked.

Thinking about Monty always took me down a black hole. I needed to cut the cord once and for all.

"I'm here. Kind of hard to wrap my head around everything."

"You'll figure it out. I'm here if you need me."

Line two popped into a blink.

"Gotta go, Cal. Sherry's calling."

I switched calls. "Hey."

"We're being tailed. I'm trying to lose them."

I heard the screech of tires, the urgency in her tone. "I'm in a rental. It's an SUV and no match for this guy's Mustang…I…I…"

The slam of metal against metal and explosion of airbags hit my ears. Hannah's cries rang out. The terrible screech of tires. Sherry let loose a string of profanity. I imagined her reaching for her weapon. She screamed.

The line went dead.

I stared at my handset, then tried to call back. When she didn't answer, I put it back in its cradle in a fog. I felt my heartbeat at my temples, and everything around me faded into the background. The ache of my inability to help Sherry and Hannah settled in my bones, and I felt myself merry-go-round without the merry-go-round. I jumped out of my chair, promptly lost my balance, and fell to the floor. The familiar TBI-related seizure coping mechanisms sprang into place. I breathed in and held it. "One-two-three-four…" I whispered. Then a long, long exhale. And coffee. I needed coffee. I eased myself over to my side on the floor.

"BETH!"

She scrambled into my office, her eyes as round as dinner plates. Keeping my eyes closed against the vertigo, I mumbled a couple of statements about TBI recovery and seizures and told her gallons of black coffee helped. She dashed into the breakroom and brought back a steaming hot mug of coffee and a couple of bottles of water.

"Do you need help getting it down?" Her soft, plump hand patted my shoulder. "Here. Let me get a pillow." She ran to the guest chairs and returned with a pillow she put underneath my head. "Better?"

I gulped the coffee, keeping my eyes shut against the spinning, tilting world. Sherry needed help, and I needed *not* to have a seizure right now. What if Patrick had rammed them with his car? What if he'd grabbed Hannah and taken her back to his torture chamber? Worse, what if he had a weapon and shot them? What if they'd been in the middle of nowhere, and Hannah and Sherry lay bleeding out on the side of a road? I had to do something!

Eyes still closed, I located the water and kicked it back. Ten minutes passed before my vision began to clear, and the pounding in my head diminished.

Beth helped me to my feet. I opened one eye, then the other. The room had stopped spinning. I took a long, relieved breath. "Thank you, Beth. Sorry, I should've told you about this job hazard."

She grinned. "I worked as an EMT in my younger days."

Could this woman be any more perfect?

My cell vibrated in my pocket. I snatched it. *Sherry.*

I put a palm on my forehead in a vain attempt to staunch the hangover headache that accompanied one of my TBI episodes. "Ohmigod, girl. What happened?" I asked.

Sherry grunted in disgust. "I spun out, trying to lose Patrick, and ran into a freaking Dodge truck. It barely even made a dent in the truck, but my rental is trashed. Thank goodness I took out rental insurance."

I took a second to digest what she said.

"You and Hannah are okay," I stated, in a daze.

"We're fine. It worked out in our favor. A cop pulled over, and Patrick passed on by. We're making a police report now. Do you think I should talk to the cops about Hannah's situation?"

I gave Beth a look of gratitude and told her she didn't have to stay. She left.

I focused on Sherry's predicament. "What does Hannah say about this man? Is he violent? Murderous? What's his MO? Legally, I think her husband would make a case that she's unstable and can't make her own decisions, that we've kidnapped her. I exhaled in frustration. "I'm not sure what to do, and I don't trust cops in small towns." I felt my forehead wrinkle. "Are you sure you two are okay?"

Sherry reiterated that they were, and I kept rummaging for information because Patrick would not let his wife away without a fight. Plus, I'd discovered his family had political ties, which meant deep connections that more than likely extended to the police department. I reeled in my thoughts and continued speaking to Sherry.

"Hannah went with you of her own volition, so I can't see him making a kidnapping case. My issue is with his psychosis. If he's like Monty, he'll craft a believable story that might taint our credibility, and there you go. Hannah is dragged right back to him by court order." I shrugged. "That's how these guys are. They breathe lies like we breathe air."

"I'm listening," Sherry said. "Be right back." I heard her talking to the police. From what I could gather, the cops had a hard time believing that the two of them didn't want to go to the hospital and get checked out. My eyes widened. So, they *did* get hurt. My hand drifted over my eyes. I shouldn't have sent her by herself. "Okay," she said, returning to our call. "The report's finished, and the rental company's on the way with a replacement vehicle, which is awesome. Patrick won't know the car, and I can get her out of the state."

My cell beeped with another call. "Just drive," I told her. "We'll sort out next steps when you get here. Be safe."

Chapter Eleven

Hunter

"Hi there," Hunter began. His fingertips drummed the top of his desk. Calling Olivia after such a long separation made him nervous. He frowned and put his hand in his lap.

"Hey."

"You asked me to use my badge to get intel on Monty. I think I got what you need."

"Let's have it," Olivia muttered.

Hunter felt his forehead crease. He'd gone to a lot of trouble to get this information. Couldn't she at least act pleasant? Grateful, maybe?

"Having a bad day?" he asked.

"Sorry. Things are heating up over here, and I don't know which fire to put out first. Thanks for doing this. I've got my notebook out."

Three seconds passed as he reeled in his irritation. What had he been expecting? She's a busy person. You're no longer a priority in her life. *Get over it.* He returned his attention to his notes.

"Seems like your boy is back to his old tricks, insinuating himself into the corrections officers' good graces, getting the plum assignments, and being the model citizen. Anyway, he's been approved to update some of the prison system software, and he's applied for a work release program."

He heard the scratching of Olivia's pen on her pad.

"This is helpful. Thank you."

Why so formal? He knew her. She had something else on her mind. "I know it's been a while, and we shouldn't expect to slide right into best buds or anything, but…are you okay?"

He imagined the darkening of her hazel eyes, the fidgeting of her hands with the pen, the slight coloring of her cheeks. He still missed every single thing about her. Getting involved in whatever situation she had going on had not been a good idea. Maybe he should hand her off to one of his Maryland contacts.

"Another detail you might not know," he continued. "Monty's friend Dudley is dead."

He heard her pen start scribbling notes again. "No surprise there. Mom told me all about Duds and his…uh…lifestyle choices. So." she continued, thinking aloud, "Duds acted as Monty's go-to and cheerleader. He'll need to replace that relationship. It's got to be tough inside and Monty never could stand isolation. He'll have someone. Maybe that's why he reached out to Graham. What's that phrase from my forensics class?"

Hunter smiled. She was talking like a cop, and he liked it.

"Past behavior predicts future behavior. If he did it before, more than once, it's a pattern," she quoted.

"If Monty's got a psych eval somewhere, my bet is he'd tick a lot of boxes on the psychopath side."

"His first official task in prison five years ago was taking Duds under his wing so he could dig for information to tear my life apart. No telling what Dudley told him about my mother since they dated like…fifty years ago." She chuckled. "Maybe ten percent of what he said might be true."

Hunter listened to her quiet breathing in his ear. It grounded him. "In other news, I had dinner at your mom's place with your girls last week."

"Callie told me. Wasn't her daughter, Amy, there, too?"

He laughed. *"Of course* Callie's daughter would tell her best friend, *your* daughter; that I was there so this information would trickle down to you. I have a feeling those girls want us back together again."

This time, the pause became awkward. Hunter fought the urge to end the call before he said something stupid, like, "I miss you."

Olivia ignored the comment about Callie. "Here's the short version: Monty is working in approved, private-sector businesses in Westminster and Owings Mills a couple of days a week. My concern is the unrestricted access to information, including mine. He'd love to tear my online reputation to shreds and I'm trying to figure out how to go on defense."

"How'd you find out?"

"Graham told Callie about it. When Monty and Graham get together, it's never a good thing, that's all. I'm surprised that he and Graham kept in touch this long since it's been, what, five years? Six? Combine that disturbing piece of news with one of our clients who lives minutes from the Sykesville corrections facility where he is incarcerated. That's not a coincidence. It's a freaking recipe for disaster."

"You'd make a good investigator, you know that?"

Olivia chuckled. *"You're* the one that made me start thinking about it. Remember? Around the same time, we played tag with Monty in the sand dunes on Hilton Head."

"That was the best take-down ever." Hunter felt warmth creep into his chest. Of course, he remembered. That and a thousand other moments. "Look," he muttered, "If you need help, I can talk my lieutenant into a 'follow-up' assignment. A week or two. If that would do any good."

As he waited for her response, he felt a cold sweat break out at his temples and stifled a groan. When would this woman's voice stop making him feel like a puppy starving for affection? He breathed through the silence, the phone pressed against his ear. A visit to Glyndon would solve his Shiloh problem. But, at what cost? How many times would he allow Olivia's rejection into his life? The stress alone was a good reason to avoid her. 'I had to break it off for good,' he'd tell people. 'For health reasons.' He pictured Olivia aiming darts at a dart board with his picture on it, and in the background, his buddy Nick's words playing on a loop: 'I think that bridge is burned, dude.'

Olivia cleared her throat. "Thanks for the offer, Hunter, but I'm good. I have something else I want to talk to you about, though."

Disappointment twisted through his chest like a corkscrew. He bit his lower lip.

Two seconds ticked by. "This isn't going very well, is it?" she asked.

"It's going about as well as it can," he said, his voice brusque. "I've got a few minutes. Go ahead."

"We pulled Hannah out of a terrible situation. Her husband is a mental case, and he'd imprisoned her in that house. She's down to maybe ninety pounds and acting like a zombie. No telling what he did to her. Sherry's driving her home now."

Hunter stared at the wall for a few seconds. How had *that* gone down?

"How'd she manage to get an abused woman away from a psycho?"

"Professional secret," Olivia said, her voice smug.

Hunter grinned. "Cute. Sherry's learned skills, I get that, but the psycho husband *is* going to go ballistic. What then?"

"Thus, my question. We had to get her out of there while she had the chance, but what do you think he'll tell the cops? Kidnapping?"

Hunter thought about that. "She go voluntarily?"

"Yes, but don't you think he'd make a case for mental instability? There are bars on the windows, locks on the outside of doors, that kind of thing. Hannah says he talks his way out of anything." She snorted. "I don't trust small-town cops. It's possible they'd look the other way if his roots go deep in the area."

"The minute she's considered unstable, it's a whole thing. It sounds like you just got her out, so you don't know what you're looking at yet, or if there's tangible proof of harm. She can't help but be unstable after two years in this situation."

Olivia remained quiet.

"Whatever you do, don't put her in a rehab or mental facility. Your chance to get her away from him on a legal basis would go right down the drain. Put her in a shelter unless she's bedridden or in need of medical attention. Does she have a kid with him?"

"Not that we know of."

"Good. Then it should be easy to get a restraining order, and she can proceed from there."

They shared a beat of solemnity in silence.

"This is going to be a lot on you and Sherry," Hunter said.

Olivia chuckled. "Tell me about it."

"Does he have any idea who would've taken her, or where she'd go?"

"I'm sure Hannah talked about us."

Hunter heard the taps of Olivia's pen on her desk.

"At first, Hannah kept in touch. Everything she told us sounded lovely. I'm positive that she'd have talked about her life here and the Wine & Whine group. No reason not to. Odd that she never introduced him to us, though, which should've been her first clue." She sighed. "Water under the bridge. The important thing is that she's out of harm's way. We have to get her settled before we start interrogating her. She's pretty messed up."

Hunter flipped through scenarios in his head. "Has she filed any police reports?"

"How could she? He watched her every move. What I'm thinking is that he started out a good guy, and after a few months, the descent began. I'm grateful he didn't kill her. He feels like a classic predator."

"Give me his details. I'll see what I can find in our system. Often these guys are squeaky clean, though. Not sure how they slide by, but without a documented history of violence the PD's hands'll be tied. If he files charges, a judge has no choice but to look at it. It'll come down to whose word the judge believes."

"I hope you find something on this guy. If he's anything like Monty, he'll dig in and track her to the ends of the earth. We need evidence to present to a judge."

"You could talk to other victims or interview his co-workers. His parents. Does he have family close by? Do they have a good relationship? Why or why not? What kind of trauma is in his background? When Hannah is able, maybe she'll share something that can help her case."

"I'll text you the information I have on Patrick. Thanks for your help."

They ended the call. He swiveled his desk chair so he could look out the window, smiled, and shook his head. Trouble stuck to this woman like a magnet.

A button on his landline started blinking. He grabbed the handset. "Faraday."

"Detective McPherson's here, sir," his admin told him.

Hunter closed his eyes and took a deep breath. Olivia's call had rocked him hard, and now he had to deal with *Shiloh*. It had been a while since he and Shiloh had dated, but the scent of her, the way her body felt…lingered. He ran one of his hands through his hair. Could they collaborate on her undercover operation without issues?

"Sir?"

"Send her in, Becker."

"Yes, sir."

Shiloh burst inside his office like a tsunami.

Hunter wondered why she had to make a show of it. Every. Single. Time.

"Have you thought about who you want to put with me on this? I need a couple of competent people." She shifted her weight, then added, "It's going down *tonight*, Sergeant. Kind of getting urgent, now. Your guys couldn't meet with me on the first dates your admin scheduled."

"Quit calling me Sergeant," he said, his voice irritable. "I was proving a point. And all my people are competent."

"Did not mean to offend."

Hunter threaded his fingers and leaned forward. "You've got an appointment to brief them this afternoon. What's the move?"

"You really want to know?"

"Is that a real question?"

"Very funny. Meth, fentanyl, heroin. Black market firearms. It's a big operation."

"And you're on the hook?"

"You know I can't say any more than that. Let's just say I go big or go home." She jutted a hip.

Hunter laughed. "If you don't like the latest two guys, I don't know what to tell you. Take it or leave it."

She grinned. "I'll take it. Thanks."

Hunter rubbed his palms together. "Do we have your location?"

"You know that old, abandoned brewery downtown? One a.m."

"I've been busy, Shi. Besides, my lieutenant has doubts about us working together. I'll make sure to confirm backup and location, okay? So don't hesitate if you have trouble. We'll be close."

"But not you." She crossed her arms and squinted her eyes at him. "What doubts?"

Hunter struggled with how to respond.

"Ah," she said. "He knows about us." She pushed a wavy lock of blonde hair behind her ear. "That's been over a long time, now."

"I told him that."

She cocked her head. Smiled. Then dashed out the door.

Hunter tried to focus, but he couldn't get past the image of Shiloh all dolled up in her fake persona as a hooker or God-knows-what and just two of his guys as backup. What happens if she's in the middle of a turf war? He cursed. "Becker! Make sure Detective McPherson is confirmed for appointments with Weinstein and Fernandez."

"They've already been confirmed, sir," he answered.

"I need an address for their operation. Okay? Don't text, write it down on a note pad and give it to me."

"Yes, sir."

"I'm out for the day. See you in the morning." He took the note that Becker had written out for him, strode down the carpeted hallway and out the exit.

Sergeant Hunter Faraday's cell phone alarm went off at midnight, at which point, he pulled some tattered clothes out of his closet and put them on over his ballistic vest. After he'd scoped out the old brewery earlier, he had a good idea of the best location to launch his homeless drunk act. As a bonus, the street lamps lit at least two corners of the block. He wouldn't be responding blind. Shiloh didn't have to know he had her back and hopefully the operation would go down as planned, she'd get her man, and everybody'd go home happy.

On the other hand, if he heard gunfire, he'd be a quick sprint away from the entrance.

His lieutenant would crucify him if he found out.

Hunter grabbed his keys and walked out into the night.

The alley beside the abandoned brewery stank of rotting fish and assorted dumpster debris.

Hunter pulled out the collapsible stool he'd brought and a bottle of cheap whiskey. He poured the whiskey over his clothes, his nose wrinkling. If these guys had any doubts about his harmlessness, the smell alone would convince them. Pulling his Indiana Jones hat lower on his forehead, he hunkered down on the stool beside a dumpster and watched a foot-long rat scurry into the shadows.

Twenty minutes later, he heard high-pitched giggling and the sound of footsteps and male voices. He smiled. Shiloh, doing her thing. He counted five different male voices and texted the investigators on his team. A black SUV whispered onto the grounds and parked. Three men in good business suits got out and stood around the vehicle at high alert, their hands inside their coats. Hunter watched their eyes graze him, linger a few seconds, then pass over. As he'd hoped, his presence had been ignored, his personhood voided.

Good.

Hunter watched the bodyguards underneath the brim of his hat, his hands hugging the whiskey bottle to his chest like hundreds of other homeless drunks around the city.

The men circled the SUV, scrutinizing all angles of the building, then urged a tall, thin, well-dressed man out of the vehicle. The guy had to be important, and maybe the big collar Shi had been working for the past three years. She hadn't talked much about it, but he'd felt the unresolved-case-cop-tension hovering in the background whenever they'd been together. If this deal held together, and she got it on a wire, she'd get a big promotion. He smiled. Shiloh was such a great undercover cop, all the way down the line.

The security detail hustled their guy inside. A door squealed open. Hunter did not hear the door close. He lifted his head and looked around. Should he risk a quick look?

Wait.

He settled in, listening hard. If the door had been left open, all the better.

The giggling again. Then a man's deep voice, "You okay, baby?"

"S'long as you're here. I'm okay, I—" More giggling.

"You're loaded," the deep voice boomed. "What did you take?"

Hunter frowned. Did she mean to make the guy mad? Had she planned a distraction? Why? His phone vibrated with a text. He pulled it out. Everyone is in position.

He texted back. All good. Hold.

The bodyguards strode back to the black SUV, started the vehicle, made a tight U-turn, and backed to the door. One of them got out and opened the hatch. They stationed themselves on each side of the door.

Hunter kept one hand on the bottle as the other crawled to the right-hand side of his belt and unsnapped the leather safety strap of his holster. He needed a look inside. He stole across the asphalt to position himself underneath a broken window. Quiet, menacing voices floated out above his head.

He removed his hat and peeked inside. Hunter counted the players…eight in all. Shi had gone all out, sequins, four-inch heels, red lipstick. She looked hot as hell. A *serious* distraction, and he wondered why the man calling the shots had allowed her to come.

Hunter's gut knotted.

Unless they'd made her, and her cover was blown.

A bodyguard's head snapped around to the window.

Hunter shrank back, his heart hammering his chest. "Shit," he whispered.

Chapter Twelve

Hannah

Hannah stepped out of their rental car into the bright sunshine, using her hand as a visor against the sun. The hotel looked as if a light breeze might blow it over, but it had cheap rates and sat a stone's throw from the freeway.

"Over halfway home," Sherry said. "I'll check us in. Stay out of sight, okay? Patrick won't know my name, even if he does check hotels. I'll be back in a sec."

Hannah looked left, then right, then back again. "You think we lost him?"

Sherry put a reassuring hand on Hannah's shoulder, no small feat since Hannah stood six feet tall and Sherry shopped for her clothes in the children's department. Hannah's lips trembled as she stared down into Sherry's earnest blue eyes. "Thank you for all you're doing for me." She put her hands over her face. "I'm sorry...I'm so sorry...I'm so—"

"Stop that," Sherry insisted. "We'll figure it out. I haven't seen his car since the wreck. I can't imagine he'd tail us this far."

A police cruiser drove by at a snail's pace. Sherry's grip on Hannah's shoulder tightened. "Get in the car, and don't look in the direction of the freeway," she said. "I'll be right back."

Hannah got back in the car, locked the doors, and slid down in her seat. She dug into her bag for snacks she'd put inside and frowned at a small, circular device stuck into the interior. She gasped. Her heart dropped like a stone. "Oh, *God*," she cried. A tracking device?

Sherry ran back to the car. "Let's get inside."

Hannah dropped her head. "I think we have a problem."

Sherry blinked when she saw the device. "He found your bag. It makes sense he'd do something like this." She jerked it off the canvas, trotted to the gas station next to the hotel, and stuck it on the bumper of a car in the parking lot.

"It'll be okay. Let's go."

But Hannah had zero confidence that things would be okay. They gathered their bags and went inside. Sherry shoved the deadbolt home and closed the curtains. Hannah stared around the sparsely furnished room. It smelled musty, but it also smelled like freedom.

At least she'd be back in Maryland tomorrow, staying in Olivia's guestroom, protected by the company dog, Marlowe, and looking forward to life without Patrick. Maybe.

She dropped onto one of the single beds and stared at the ceiling.

"Sherry."

"What?" Sherry called from the bathroom.

"I want to get a divorce, first thing. Can we do that?"

Sherry emerged from the bathroom, drying her hands on a towel. "We can help you get all that started, hon'. First, we have to figure out when and where to file a police report about everything that happened to you, and I know you don't want to think about it, but we need a record. I'm not sure how motivated Patrick is to get you back, but if he's as much a sicko as I think he is, he won't be logical about it."

Sherry sat on the other bed, running her fingers through her dark, tight curls. "He may have the cops looking for us right now." She shrugged. "However, he knows he's been a very bad boy, so he might avoid them and…"

"Show up," Hannah finished for her. "That's what he does. It's like…he can walk through walls or something. It's scary."

"The hell with him. He's not watching your every move with security cameras anymore."

Sherry's cell vibrated. "It's Olivia," she told Hannah. She put the phone on speaker.

"What's your status?" Olivia asked.

"In a dive for the night, we're in, uh…" she looked at her phone's map, "…somewhere around Johnson City, Tennessee. I tried to pick an unpopular route."

"Good. Ask Hannah if Monty tried to keep in touch after she got married. And if he *knew* she got married. I need all the intel I can get about what's going on with him."

"I heard," Hannah called out. "He tried several times to call. I didn't respond."

"Why? Is that significant?" Sherry asked.

"Think about it, girls. What does Monty hate more than anything in the world?"

"Women that don't bow to his every wish," Sherry said.

"Women in general," Hannah added.

"Did he write letters, Hannah? Did you give him your address?"

"Of course not. But he found out, somehow. He sent two long, slimy letters. When I received them, I'd just realized what a terrible mistake I'd made with Patrick." She felt tears bubble up. "Patrick would've killed me if he'd known about the letters. I'm serious."

"What'd the letters say, Hannah?" Olivia asked. "And honey, I'm so glad you're safe. We're here for you."

Hannah shook her head. "He said he'd never forgive me for betraying him, that kind of stuff. I'm sure he meant when I went into the prison with a wire. If he could've, he'd have vaporized me on the spot." She winced at the memory. "I'll never forget the way his eyes looked."

"I bet he blames you that all his appeals fell flat, too." Olivia said, her voice thoughtful. "Who could've told him your address, Hannah? Does he even know your new last name?"

Hannah felt her eyebrows draw together. "I'm not sure. But he's a computer genius. He could've found it online. It felt so weird to see the return address of a prison on those letters in my mailbox. Back then, I still had freedom to go outside. I made sure Patrick never knew about the letters."

Sherry's eyes rounded. "What if Patrick *did* know?"

"Patrick always flew me to Florida. I don't think he has any connection to Monty."

After a pause, Olivia asked, "Do you know if he has a criminal record, Hannah?"

"He mentioned jail time once," Hannah said in a tiny voice. "That's one of the reasons I didn't bring him around. I knew you'd be upset." Hannah flung herself facedown on the bed and moaned. "Nothing's going to stop him," she said, her voice muffled by a pillow.

"Jail time is a good thing. It means Hunter will find records we can use in court. We need to be proactive with this. Once we have the records, we'll go to the police."

"One more day, and you'll be home," Sherry said.

Hannah stretched out her arm to the other bed and patted Sherry on the leg. "You have no idea how great that sounds."

"Good," Olivia said. "Sherry, would you take the phone off speaker? I want to talk about our latest client."

Hannah bit her fingernail as she watched Sherry's body language and picked up on bits and pieces of the conversation. When she ended the call, she tossed her phone on the bed with an exasperated sigh.

"Monty's out?" Hannah blinked. "How?"

She snorted. "He's ingratiated himself to the warden. That's what he's best at. Brown-nosing people. They granted him work release, and he's out a day or two a week, working at private prison-related facilities or something."

Hannah gasped. "Where?"

"Westminster and Owings Mills," Sherry said.

Hannah frowned. "That's bad. He's a lot like Patrick. He has to assert his dominance." She glanced at the door. "Is the door locked?"

Sherry nodded. "Of course."

Silence filled the room. A toilet flushed one floor above them. A door slammed outside. Hannah jumped. Sherry put her arm around her.

"Why don't you hop in the shower, Hannah? I'll go get us some greasy hamburgers."

Hannah clutched her stomach. She felt bile climb her throat.

Sherry rushed over. "If you don't want to be alone, I won't go."

"That's not it."

Sherry frowned. "Then what is it?"

Hannah's eyes flicked to the door, the stained carpeting, and the walls painted the same shade of beige as Patrick's "punishment room." Seconds ticked by. She swallowed, hard. "I think I'm pregnant."

Chapter Thirteen

Olivia

I tilted my head back and closed my eyes. What a relief that Sherry and Hannah were safe. I began to gather a few files in preparation to head home. Marlowe lunged around me in excitement. He wanted to get home to his dinner and his buddy, Riot.

Someone kept calling. The blinking on my landline started again. "It's six o'clock," I moaned. "Office hours are over at five, people."

Against my better judgment, I answered. "Watchdog Investigations."

"Well. It's about time. This is Curtis Ridgeland. Who's this?"

"This is Olivia Callahan, Mr. Ridgeland."

"Aren't you supposed to keep me advised or something? I haven't heard from anybody since Sherry went out of town. I've left messages."

I rubbed my eyes. Marlowe sank into his dog bed and gave me a mournful look. "It's been hectic, Mr. Ridgeland. I'm sorry. Sherry filled me in on your case and—"

"It needs to be tonight," he interrupted. "Didn't she tell you that?"

"Mr. Ridgeland, I—"

"Call me Curtis, okay? It's tonight. Eight p.m. Do you have the address of the studio?"

"I'm sure it's in the file."

"And I'm sure that you guys are *not* on top of this." He rattled off an address in Ellicott City. Olivia winced. She'd *so* hoped Sherry would be back in time to take over the case.

She sighed. A long night lay ahead.

"You have photos, her full name and socials, description of her vehicle. Listen. It's tonight, or nothing. The ballroom lessons are once a week, and she's there from seven to nine. Can I expect your cooperation? I don't want to wait another week."

"I'm on it. I'll be there. Forgive us for not communicating better."

He ended the call.

I dragged my feet all the way to the parking lot. Marlowe licked my hand and whined. He didn't understand why my mood had plummeted.

An hour and fifteen minutes later, I'd scarfed down a sandwich, located the dance studio, and backed into a parking space that pointed toward the entrance. I made myself comfortable in my beat-up surveillance vehicle to watch and wait. Every fifteen minutes, I strolled to the back of the building in case his wife slipped under the radar and off to do whatever Curtis thought she was doing. The evening passed in peace, and I'd never seen so many fluffy dresses and tight, shiny pants in my life. The ballroom dancing world must require a uniform.

I stifled a yawn. Nine o'clock had come and gone twenty minutes ago. The life of a PI can be risky and exciting, but much of it is surveilling. Sitting in a car and waiting for someone is boring, and it's hard to stay awake. I yawned again. Rubbed my eyes. Maybe she hadn't come tonight.

My eyes were tired of staring at the door. I checked my texts, answered one, and put the phone down. As I re-focused on the door, I gasped. Was that her? Yep, fluffy ballroom uniform and everything. I fumbled for my phone to verify that she matched the photos I'd been sent.

Bingo.

I picked up my binoculars. Someone had stapled themselves to her. I tried to remember her name. Victoria? That's it. Victoria. It suited her. She wore a knee-length, pink chiffon, flowing dress and sequin-encrusted silver heels. Blonde, wavy hair framed her face, and a dark-haired man wearing shiny, black pants had coiled himself around her body like a snake.

"Huh," I said. Okay. So maybe she *is* stepping out on him.

I clicked off a series of photos, then groped for the binoculars. I'd parked quite a good distance away, but still…I felt exposed. Sliding down in my seat, I propped my elbows on my knees and looked through the binocs. My mouth fell open as I watched Victoria struggle to push the guy away. He looked mad. Victoria walked down the stairs and into the parking lot, the guy right behind her. Her floaty skirt billowed like a pink cloud when she spun around and tried to land a punch. He ducked, then tried to land his own punch.

I blinked in surprise. What was happening here? Should I intervene? I'm just the hired help, right? No additional responsibilities in this situation other than photographing what I see.

My heart rammed my ribcage.

I put the binocs back on my face.

"Wait," I muttered. "What the…" I squinted. Shadows made it hard to see clearly. It looked like the guy had gloves on. Judging by the man's outfit and his black, slipper-like shoes, he could be one of the instructors. But, do dance instructors wear black gloves? Is that a thing?

I grabbed my phone, got a fuzzy shot of his face, and rolled the window down to catch their conversation.

"Get off me, Raul! What are you doing? I told you. It's over."

I sucked in a breath. Okay. It *could've* been an embrace.

"We had a deal," he cried. "You can't back out, you're my partner! There's a lot of money at stake." I watched him gaze around the parking lot into the bushes beyond.

Victoria shoved him with both arms. He stumbled backward.

"It's over! How many times do I need to say it? I can't do this anymore." she declared.

Raul stood there, as still and silent as a rock, his hands clenching and unclenching into fists.

Terror shot up my spine. Does she need help? What would I do, flip out my PI badge? Hold him at gunpoint? I held my breath behind the steering wheel, torn. Visual images of my own assault hit me hard. Memories flooded my mind as if a dam had burst. The next few minutes, I couldn't move.

When I came to myself, he'd grabbed her arm and pulled her across the parking lot and into the bushes. I yanked my phone from the seat and kept clicking off photos.

My mouth stuck in a silent scream, I watched in horror as Raul's left arm shot out in a quick swoop and wrapped around Victoria's neck. She clawed at his eyes. Kicked with her glittery shoes. She grew weaker with every passing second. He was choking the life out of her.

My simple surveillance assignment had turned into a possible homicide.

His free hand shot to the back of his pants. He pulled out a knife and drove it into Victoria's stomach one, two, three, *four* times. She shrieked, but he muffled her mouth with his hand and continued to drive the knife into her body.

"Crap!" I called nine-one-one, and, without thinking, crushed the accelerator, white-knuckled the steering wheel, and headed straight for Raul.

I couldn't breathe.

He watched me coming. At the last minute, he dashed into the darkness. I braked hard and bolted from the car.

She lay on the ground in the grass, the beautiful pink chiffon drenched in blood. Her forearms bore deep cuts from trying to defend herself. Blood pooled in the grass. I couldn't tell where the bleeding ended and her stomach began. He'd eviscerated it. She moaned. I jerked off my black hoodie and pressed it to her stomach. "Hang in there. Help is coming!" I whispered. She couldn't speak. The gurgling sounds broke my heart. I stroked her hair. "Please. Stay with me, Victoria."

Her dulled eyes caught mine. I could read the question on her face: How does she know my name?

I felt sweat gather on my forehead and trickle down my chest. What had she called him? *Raul.* I needed to remember his name. Victoria went limp. Her head rolled to one side. The blood spurting from her stalled to a trickle. Second later, it stopped.

The scream of sirens sounded in the distance.

My beautiful, isolated, tree-lined driveway never looked so good. I turned off the highway and sped the half-mile down my lane, squealed onto the wide space in front of my detached garage, and pulled inside. I sat in my car a few seconds, chest heaving, palms sweaty on the steering wheel. The homicide scene crested, then rolled away, like surf on a beach. I closed my eyes and tried to push the images away. My God. That *poor woman.* After the ambulance left, I'd stayed behind to talk to the police, carefully omitting the part about Watchdog Investigations and the surveillance assignment. I wasn't sure how they'd explain a woman in the parking lot of a dance studio in head-to-toe black sweats, but they hadn't asked, and I hadn't volunteered. Besides, I didn't know the whole story. Had Curtis known she might be killed? If so, who had arranged her murder? From what Sherry told me, his sheet listed white-collar crimes...no violence. An affair wasn't typically a motive for murder, for God's sake. Sane people try to work things out or default to divorce. Something else had happened here, and I'd been on shaky ground as the cops filled out the report. It almost felt like a trap, but *Sherry* was supposed to witness this, not me. Maybe Raul had lost his mind. Maybe the homicide had been the result of an out-of-control temper. It happens.

I rubbed my forehead.

My breathing had returned to normal. I shook my head to flush out the sordid nightmare on a loop in my brain, but it didn't work. Victoria's tragic death would haunt me a long time. I was certain the cops would circle back to me when they discovered what I did for a living, but right now, all I wanted was my bed.

I trudged through the breezeway to the back entrance of my house and into the kitchen, breathing in the sweet, sweet smell of domesticity. Air freshener, the slight scent of a cat box I hadn't had time to clean. Fresh paint from a recent remodel. A hint of coffee from this morning. Marlowe tackled me, and Riot rubbed against my legs. After disentangling myself and patting each head, I went upstairs to my bedroom, tore off my black surveillance outfit, and started the shower. I stepped into the steamy flow and slathered myself in body wash. When I finished, I got out and stared at myself in the mirror. What should I do? I'd taken photos of a freaking murder. I hadn't been very forthcoming with their questions. Cops didn't think much of PIs, so I made up an excuse about why I'd been there. I couldn't tell them I'd been surveilling for a client, and I sure didn't want them to know I was a PI. They bought my stumbling story, but after a few clicks into my background, they'd be knocking on my door. I hoped it wouldn't come to that.

I didn't even want to think about the implications of Raul. Could he ID me? Had he taken a good look at my face?

I put on pajamas and slipped between the covers, adrenaline still rocking along in my veins and my nerves fried to a crisp.

Marlowe lifted his head and pumped his tail. I didn't usually let him sleep in my bedroom…he had a big, comfy dog bed downstairs…but tonight? Tonight, I wanted him with me, and his big, comfy bed had been yanked from the den and transported to my bedroom.

My cell buzzed. I looked at the caller ID. Sherry. A cold sweat slicked my chest. I hit the "answer" button and opened my mouth, but nothing came out.

"Olivia?" She waited a few seconds. "Are you okay?"

I burst into tears. Victoria's nightmare tumbled out.

We talked long into the night.

Chapter Fourteen

Hunter

Hunter edged away from the window. One of the bodyguards had caught him peeking inside. He raced to his spot beside the dumpster and grabbed the gin bottle, slouching against the brick wall. For emphasis, he clutched his stomach and groaned.

Two suits jogged out of the building, and approached.

"What're you doin' buddy?" one of them barked. "We got a problem here?"

Hunter kept his head down. "I don't feel so good. I thought somebody in there might have some water."

The other man pulled out his firearm and stuck it against Hunter's temple. "Nothing happened here tonight, you get me?"

Hunter shrank into the wall. If they decided to do a body search, they'd find his vest and he'd have to pivot. He started working out defensive moves in his head.

A wave of stench from the dumpster drifted up his nose, and he didn't even have to pretend. He threw up all over the guy's shoes.

"Christ!" the man yelped, jumping away. He waved his firearm at his associate. "This guy's wasted. He won't remember a thing tomorrow. Let's get back inside."

Hunter clutched his stomach harder and moaned.

The guy with clean shoes laughed. The guy with the vomit-covered shoes punched him in the stomach and told him to shut his yap. Muttering obscenities, they glared at Hunter and left.

After they returned inside, he circled the building, looking for another entrance. Cigarette smoke curled around the corner. Hunter flattened himself against the wall and deeper into the shadows. He caught a whiff of something sweet. Perfume. *Shiloh.* He approached the corner and peeked around. She had her head down, leaning against the wall, smoking a cigarette. Hunter frowned. Something had unraveled. He inched closer.

When he stepped on a piece of glass, the sound startled her. She whirled around, gave him the once-over, and told him to get the hell out of her space.

Hunter grinned. His outfit must be pretty good. Plus, he smelled like a distillery.

Wait. Was one side of her face red and swollen?

"Shi!" he hissed.

She blinked. "What did you say?"

"It's me," he whispered.

The lighting at each corner of the building cast weird shadows, but Hunter could tell someone had clocked her good. "That's quite the shiner coming on."

"What are you doing here, you idiot? Do you have any idea how much firepower is in there?"

Hunter smiled. "Do you have any idea how many cops are waiting on my command? They're stationed at every corner."

She grunted and tossed her cigarette. "I think I'm made. He had one of his boys crack me on the cheek and take me outside. I told them I needed to smoke, anyway, to cool down. If they find the wire, I'm done." Her face screwed into a knot. "Dammit! I really wanted this!"

Hunter reached out and put his hand on her shoulder. "Would it help if I told you how hot you look?"

She had to smile. "No."

They stared at each other.

Slow and careful, Hunter leaned in until their lips touched. A tear straggled down Shiloh's cheek. "Don't," she whispered. "They're right inside the door."

He passed his fingertips across the swelling. "We're going to make sure you get this collar, Shi."

Shiloh's head jerked at the sound of approaching steps. She gave him a fierce look. "Go!"

Hunter faded into the shadows.

Five minutes later, he found a pull-down staircase hidden by huge, overgrown bushes that he'd missed on his first sweep. The stairs looked substantial enough. He put his weight on the first step. Then another. He made it to the second floor and cracked the door. Voices floated into the space. He smiled. They couldn't see him on the second floor, and the acoustics were pretty good. He went inside and squatted down in a corner, considering his options. He stared at the rotten wood and crumbling planks. Would this old floor hold his weight? From the hushed tones downstairs, negotiations had begun. With Shiloh and her wire out of the picture, the case was screwed. This was a big bust: an international network that imported drugs and firearms and smuggled them into the United States, ostensibly via the Port of Savannah. He had to do something to slow things down until Shiloh was present. He set his phone to record, then snaked his way across the floor to a jagged hole the size of one of his Jeep's jumbo tires and looked down.

Shiloh had returned. The male voices quieted at her presence. She struck a pose and lifted her chin, pursing her perfect lips at the man who seemed in charge.

"Let's all forgive and forget, huh? I'm here to party, boys. Where's the booze, anyway? Whatever we're doing, can you just get it over with?"

A low, sinister response. "Go back outside, Delilah."

Hunter smiled. *Delilah.* She'd never told him her undercover name.

"I'll just stay right over here, okay, Stick? I won't even look. I don't know why you made me go outside, anyway. I'm your girl. You *know* I'm your girl, baby."

Hunter frowned. Stick? This guy had been on the FBI's radar for two decades. This *had* to happen. Stick got tagged with the nickname because he loved Teddy Roosevelt. The "big stick" he carried happened to be an AK-47. Plus, his precise, knife-wielding skills had become legendary. He could throw a knife sixty feet and slice an apple in two. Stick also liked to cut off ears, noses, hands, fingers, tongues...and let his victims survive. If they tried to gaslight him, he'd cut off another appendage until they kept their mouths shut for good.

Hunter closed his eyes and tried to slow his pulse. Lives were on the line.

It all came crashing down without Shi's wire. This bust would make Shiloh a star. A legend. She'd developed and nurtured this case—which included the relationship playing out beneath him— for years, he knew. She needed to convince Stick to let her stay inside.

His ears pricked at a loud and irritated exhale. "Domingo, get it done. We're good. I'm good." He rattled off product details. "They delivered on their promise. Give them the duffel bag." After a pause, he continued. "Gentlemen. A pleasure doing business with you. May we never meet again."

Uneasy laughter all around.

Hunter's eyes widened. *Shiloh had gotten it!* The FBI must be celebrating in their surveillance van right now.

He pumped his fist in the air.

Then he heard Stick say, "Come over here, baby. Let me check your face."

He heard her steps swish across the floor. Soft murmuring. He smiled and shook his head. He had to hand it to her, she played her part well. The murmuring continued, but he couldn't make out the words. Maybe Stick regretted having someone smack her around.

Seconds passed.

Minutes.

Hunter's pulse pounded in his throat as he waited. His palms grew sticky.

After a rip of fabric and the sizzle of tape pulled from Shiloh's chest, Stick wailed, "No. No. No, baby!"

"It's not like that, honey. Give me a second to explain. Stick. *Stick!* Put that thing away."

"I TRUSTED YOU! Do you realize what you've done? I can't..." he cursed. "I can't let it go." After a snap of fingers, footsteps marched across the floor, and he heard the click of firearms being cocked. Her death warrant had just been signed.

The cold finger of fear trailed down Hunter's back. He grabbed his phone, texted GO NOW, and stuck it back in his pocket.

Hunter heard the crunching of bone and Shiloh's long, anguished scream. He winced. Rage streamed through his veins.

Where were his guys?

A silenced shot whispered into the wall. The men laughed. Shiloh shrieked.

His hands raked his hair. He cursed, softly. *They're playing with her before they kill her.* He needed to distract them. He stared at the aging boards beneath his feet and started marching back and forth around the hole, making it sound like an army. Stomp. Stomp. *Stomp.*

All hell broke loose downstairs. Assault rifles launched a firestorm on the remaining pieces of the second floor. Hunter clung to the wall and waited for a pause.

Once the firing stopped, Hunter sprang away from the wall and jumped on a broken, rotting part of the floor with all his weight. Once. Twice.

Stick's men half-heartedly opened fire. When red lights strafed the building, they ran.

The magic jump number three cracked the floor wide open. Hunter landed hard and curled into a tuck–n–roll. Rotting boards plummeted around him. His left shoulder hit the floor so hard he thought he might've broken his clavicle. He pulled his firearm, favoring his left arm. "Where's the damn FBI?" he muttered. On cue, SWAT poured inside.

Hunter pointed his gun at the ceiling and squeezed off three quick rounds. "Richmond PD! I'm a cop!" he yelled. The assault team leader nodded, his men circling low and steady around the space, weapons poised.

More patrol vehicles screamed into the parking lot with sirens wailing. Hunter kept his weapon aimed at Stick, who smirked and calmly watched the process unfold.

One of the SWAT guys motioned for Hunter to approach. Keeping his eyes on Stick, he walked over.

"His crew got a head start." He shrugged. "Or they could be regrouping. If you've got this, we need to head outside and round them up."

Hunter nodded. As they left, he watched five more local patrol vehicles join the party.

"Put your weapons on the floor," he yelled at Stick. "The girl. Where's the girl?"

Stick tugged out two firearms and threw them down. He shook his head. "My God. She's a *cop*. I thought the *Kings* had wired her. A knife joined the firearms on the floor.

Hunter nodded toward a metal chair. Stick sat on it. "I guess congrats are in order. She's accomplished what no one could, the cold, little bitch." He laughed.

The guy's calm unnerved Hunter. An eerie silence unnerved him, too. Every hair on the back of his neck stood at attention. The calm before the storm.

The hush lasted five more seconds before a hand grenade toss from the second floor caused every person in the room to dive for cover. Hunter lunged for the door. The explosion ripped open a wall and took out the rest of the second floor. Pieces of wood planks flew through the air like shrapnel. Smoke made it impossible to see. Stick dropped to his stomach and covered his head with his hands.

Silence fell. Richmond PD cops lay scattered across the floor like human confetti. Groans and soft curses filled the air. The smoke lifted quickly.

Stick lifted himself from the floor to a sitting position. Hunter kept his weapon pointed and glanced around the space, poking at the same shoulder he'd injured in his leap from the second floor. Yep. He'd taken a bullet. Probably when he was glued to the wall waiting to make his grand entrance. He sighed.

"Your guys want me alive. I guarantee you that," Stick said. He pulled his skinny knees to his chest and put his arms around them. His pale, lifeless eyes bored holes all the way to the back of Hunter's skull.

"Shut up," Hunter told him.

He felt blood trickling down his back from the bullet wound. He heard

Shiloh's voice and felt himself go weak with relief that she was alive. He kept his weapon on Stick, tried to ignore the pain, and moved to the door to look outside.

The smell of cordite hung in the air, and little curls of leftover smoke lingered. More sirens wup-wupped toward the building. "I think the good guys won," Hunter told Stick.

The tall, elegant man rose to his feet and dusted himself off. Powdered gray residue slicked his face.

Hunter wiped sweat out of his eyes.

"I'm reaching for a cigarette. You mind?"

"Keep your hands where I can see them!"

Glints of light flared from the silver blade flying directly toward his midsection.

Hunter looked down, perplexed, then realized Stick must've had more than one knife stashed on him. The knife jutted from the soft tissue below the ribs, below his protective vest. Stick performed a little salute and dashed out the back.

Hunter fell to hands and knees. Blood poured out of the knife wound like water from a faucet. He glanced outside, thinking about his lieutenant's admonition to stay away from this investigation as it might compromise both himself and Shiloh. Regret made tears gather in his eyes, and he hoped Shiloh was okay. A tidal wave of dizziness hit him. He rolled onto his back. His eyelids fluttered and closed. The last thing he heard were the EMTs' terse observations as they approached.

Chapter Fifteen

Hannah

S herry burst into the office and draped her backpack and jacket on a coat rack.

"Good morning," Beth said.

Hannah stirred creamer into her coffee and walked into the lobby. "Where's Olivia?"

"She's taking a walk."

"Oh." Hannah sipped from her mug.

"She likes to walk the property with Marlowe to think," Sherry added.

Hannah thought about that. "Is she having second thoughts about bringing me here?"

"Of course not," Sherry said with a smile. "She's happy you're safe. We haven't heard from Patrick, and if he's smart, he'll leave you alone."

"Maybe," she agreed, her voice uncertain. "When can we start divorce proceedings? I want my life back. If I still have one," she muttered, taking stock of the healing bruises on her arms.

Sherry scrutinized the mail on her desk and opened her laptop. "Enjoy the peace for now, Hannah. We just got you back. One thing at a time. We have a shelter on alert, and if anything happens, we'll hustle you over there, and he won't find you. They operate off the grid."

Hannah sat in a guest chair in front of Beth's reception desk and sipped her coffee.

The door opened. Marlowe flew inside and made a beeline for Olivia's office. She walked in behind him, hooking his leash on the coat rack.

Sherry laughed. "That dog! He loves the spot by your desk."

"Do you have time to chat?" Her gaze fell to Hannah, whom she wrapped in a big hug. "Are you still okay in that bedroom? How are you sleeping? We're here if you're ready to talk about him."

Hannah shrugged and looked away.

Sherry gave Olivia a look. "Hazel says we should *not* push," she whispered as she walked her boss through the breakroom and closed them into Olivia's office.

Hannah's lips pressed into a tense line. She heard more than she let on. She knew her situation had put them at risk, and hated to think what might happen if Patrick found her.

Which he would.

She walked from the lobby through the shotgun-style hallway that led to the breakroom and Olivia's office, then culminated in a guest bedroom and bath at the far end of the building. As she passed Olivia's office door, they paused their discussion.

Hannah knew they'd been deep in conversation about the threat of Patrick and anything else they had on their calendars. She went into the bedroom and closed the door. Hannah sat on her bed and looked out the window at the trees, the colorful fall foliage dropping a little hailstorm of leaves outside her window. She traced the window with her fingertips, thinking about falling leaves and the inevitable snowfall, after.

Hannah folded her arms. She hated the cold. She hated snow. This had been one of the reasons she'd married Patrick, to get away from it.

How pathetic.

Her thoughts rambled back over the last five years to the fun "girl talk" group they'd started. Back in the Wine & Whine group days, who would've thought the timid, recovering Olivia would have her own business, and much less their mutual friend, Sherry, as a new associate? It boggled her mind, but helped her cling to hope for her own future, too. If Olivia could survive a traumatic brain injury caused by a vicious assault, *she* could survive a psycho husband.

Hannah startled at a strange noise outside her window. Her hand flew to her throat.

Soft footsteps slid through the brush. Hard knocks assaulted the back door.

She rushed into the corner, dropped to the floor, and curled her body into a ball.

Olivia walked into the bedroom where Hannah was staying. "Nobody tries to come in through the door back here. What the heck...?" With a glance at Hannah, she put her palms against the door and called out. "Who is it?"

"It's me! Callie!"

Olivia opened the door to her friend and neighbor. "You scared us to death!"

The whites of Callie's eyes expanded. "It's Graham. Amy's home early for Thanksgiving and..." She paused to catch her breath. "They're playing video games, so I snuck away to tell you what I found out. I didn't want to risk him seeing me come over here."

Callie caught sight of Hannah crouched in the corner. "Hannah!" She threw a quizzical look at Olivia.

Hannah stood. Briefly raised her hand in greeting. "Hi, Cal."

Callie threw her arms around her friend. "Thank God, Hannah. We've missed you so much. What happened? Where were you?"

Olivia shot Callie a warning look.

Callie released Hannah as if she were made of glass. "I'm glad you're home."

"Olivia," Hannah said, her voice firm. "Callie's a friend, and I'm fine with whatever you want to tell her. I'm going to *have* to talk about it sometime. I know that."

An uneasy silence fell. Callie and Olivia exchanged looks. Their expressions confirmed what Olivia's former therapist had told them— denial had become one of Hannah's coping mechanisms due to the type of depravity she'd endured. It would take time for her to process what happened, and time for her to sift through what his behavior had done to her emotional health.

Olivia put her arm around Hannah. "When Hazel thinks you're ready to share, uh…more intimate details with us, we're here."

"Okay." Hannah swept her hair over her shoulders and sat on the bed. "What's going on with Graham?"

Callie glanced at Olivia.

"Um," Olivia began, "Hannah, it'd be better if Callie and I talked in private."

She frowned, grabbed the remote, and clicked on the TV in the room. "Fine. Can I at least have my phone back?"

She watched Olivia chew on the question, knowing the phone might lead her abuser straight to them, but Patrick had hidden her phone for months. She felt desperate to get her hands on her phone.

"Don't you think it's smarter to leave it inactive for now? Sherry and I will get you a new one."

Hannah frowned, plumped her pillows, and settled in to watch a TV show. She knew that her phone would be handed over to the police the minute she made a police report, and they were still thinking about how to go about keeping everyone safe. Olivia and Callie didn't realize it was only a matter of time before Patrick found her. They didn't know him like she did.

Chapter Sixteen

Olivia

I walked back into my office, thinking *no way* I'm letting Hannah have her phone.

Sherry squinted in confusion at the sight of Callie. "How did you get in here?"

"Back door," Callie said. "Graham's being talkative, and I wanted to share some things with you two while it's fresh on my mind. Once he starts, he can't stop, which works in your favor." She glanced at Beth. "You want to talk in here? Or Olivia's office?"

We voted for the office and settled in the armchairs.

"So," Callie said. "Here it is: Graham said Monty's out a couple days a week on a work release program and that you, Olivia, are going to be good and sorry that you ever..." She paused and tapped her chin. "Trying to remember."

We waited while Callie splashed around in the mud puddle of her brain. My hands tightened on the armrests of my chair. Sherry glanced at me, knowing that Callie's scattered thought patterns irritated me to death. I hoped the information could hold missing puzzle pieces connected to Victoria's homicide and how Monty knew Curtis. Maybe reveal hints about his latest plan to sabotage me.

After what seemed like an eternity, she held up her index finger. "They went to a gentlemen's club!"

I groaned. That much we knew.

Callie's expression grew stern. "Girls. Graham ran across this guy named Curtis, and they discovered they both knew Monty or whatever. Anyway, Curtis and Graham have some kind of collaboration going on, and Monty is involved."

Sherry and I didn't dare look at each other. Callie did not need to know any details about the homicide—*possible* homicide—I'd witnessed.

"Isn't that the kind of stuff you wanted to know?"

I nodded. "Absolutely. Did he say why or describe the collaboration? Any detail could be important."

"Come to think of it, Graham said *she* would be sorry she was ever born. Not Olivia, *she.*" Callie shook her head. "I had a hard time making sense of it, but I have to get back before he misses me." She left.

Sherry and I looked at each other.

"Nothing like learning about an evil plan with no motive, no name, and no plan..." I shook my head.

"Well. Callie doesn't think like we do. Yeah, I wish she'd asked a couple more questions, but now I assume that Monty might be involved. Don't you think the "she" he mentioned is Victoria?"

By mid-afternoon, Sherry and I had pieced together Callie's comments and what we assumed might be true.

I looked at the points scrawled on the whiteboard: One: Graham had proved himself a skillful liar.

Two: Monty and Graham both carried huge grudges against me. Monty blamed me for his homicide conviction, and Graham blamed me for his divorce. Their grudges had no merit, but I still carried them around like a sack of rocks. I cursed under my breath. Would I ever drag myself out from under the consequences of marriage to a psycho? What would it take to get him to leave me alone?

Three: Curtis presented a mystery. How did he even get our firm's contact info? Hiring a PI isn't like putting a finger in the wind and waiting for a direction; it's word-of-mouth and a quiet, intimate selection. So, who told Curtis to give us a call? In large letters, I scrawled on the whiteboard we'd brought into my office: *Possible plant?*

Four: the murder of Victoria could be coincidental. Was she the "she" Monty said would be sorry she was ever born? In parenthesis, I added: *Monty involved? Why?*

Five: Watchdog Investigations does not believe in coincidences.

I stared at our scribblings on the whiteboard. "What's the bottom line?"

"Bottom line is Graham and Monty are gunning for you again."

"Terrible choice of words."

"Sorry. Correction. 'Out for blood.'"

"Still. Terrible."

Sherry threw her arms up in frustration. "We *have* to assume these guys are operating under their usual warped perspectives." She jammed her arms across her chest. "What would be the worst thing that could happen to you?"

The slow drumbeat of my heart thudded to a stall. "Monty would want me in prison. An eye for an eye."

Sherry tapped her chin. "Or smother you in legal proceedings so you can't focus on the firm. Or your family. Or Hunter."

I bristled. "Hunter is out of the picture."

Sherry chuckled. "Like I believe that. Anyway, it's not important what I believe; it's what Monty believes, and he's been jealous of Hunter for years. Callie's husband...uh, I mean ex-husband...Graham, is his errand boy, right? Graham will go along with whatever Monty says. That leaves Curtis. Why would he hire us to surveil his wife if he planned to kill her?"

Olivia stared at Sherry with a solemn expression. "What if Curtis didn't know?"

Sherry put down her marker and dropped into her chair. I studied the whiteboard for long seconds "I guess we wait," I said.

We heard a crash in the guest bedroom.

We raced to the bedroom and pounded on the door. When she didn't respond, we rushed inside. Where was Hannah? I rushed into the small ensuite bath.

My hand rose to my throat. I gagged.

"You don't want to see this."

Her huge, blue eyes rounded. "What is it?"

"Blood," I whispered. "Blood everywhere. Call nine-one-one."

By the time the EMTs arrived, Sherry and I had wrapped Hannah in a blanket and her slit wrists in bandages. Beth hovered like a mama bear, wringing her hands and bringing us whatever we needed. The ambo screeched into the parking lot, red lights throwing crazy patterns across our faces and the floor.

I sat useless and cringing. My Achilles' heel...blood. Brain spatter. I'd seen too many crime scenes, and six years ago, I'd been the star of my own crime scene. Six years and I still experienced flashbacks and emotional impairments from the brain injury. A sudden chill shuddered through me. I told myself to shake it off, that Hannah needed our support now. I could wilt later.

The paramedics rushed in and went to work. I tried to watch but ended up with my head in my hands.

My memories rushed back.

I slid from the passenger side of Detective Faraday's department-issued sedan. Desperate for details, I studied the yellow tape, the forensic techs bustling around, the investigative team going in and out of the hotel room. My hands were clammy. I couldn't focus. The victim's actions had put me in the hospital as a Jane Doe. I almost died, and it had taken a week for my family to find me and five more weeks to regain motor function, or speak my first words. My memory still hadn't filled in all the blanks.

My attacker lay dead in a cheap hotel room thirty feet away from where I stood. Detective Hunter Faraday had told me not to leave his vehicle, but I couldn't help myself.

I had to know what happened to him.

I'd overheard a couple of crime scene technicians chatting.

"The guy's head split wide open, and his brain spilled out the back," I heard the older man tell the younger man. The younger guy vomited into the bushes, then wiped his mouth. The older man laughed. "Trust me, it gets easier. Those yellow globs? In time you won't even see 'em, it'll register and then bounce off."

102

He shrugged. "All part of the job."

Cold sweat had sprouted on my forehead as I pictured my attacker, a tormented man with multiple issues, splayed on the floor inside the grimy hotel, his head busted open like a crushed watermelon.

I shook myself out of the memory.

"Five years ago," I whispered, watching Beth's competent hands tend to Hannah. The bandages around her wrists had already soaked through.

The attack, the crime scene, and my long and torturous recovery had left its mark. Blood was hard for me, but Sherry and I had managed. I blew out a long breath.

When Beth finished, Sherry flipped a towel over Hannah's wrists. "There. Better?"

I nodded. She understood.

The paramedic team slid Hannah onto a bodyboard and lifted her to a gurney.

"She lost a lot of blood." I glanced at Sherry, tears streaming down my face. "What could've driven her to this? I mean, she's got us to lean on, now."

"Living in fear does things to your mind. I had a friend years ago who didn't think she had any other way out. She used pills. I think they need to get far enough away from the situation to find hope again," Sherry said.

We watched them secure Hannah inside.

Sherry took a deep breath. "If Patrick discovers her location, she'll be in danger. Do we need to let them know?"

My mouth fell open. "Yes, of course." I'd skipped over the fact that her name shouldn't be searchable as a result of a police report. I may be useless with blood, but protect her privacy? That I could do. I ran outside.

I approached the driver. "Thanks for responding so fast."

"No problem, ma'am."

I inched closer.

He slitted his eyes.

"I have a bit of an issue."

He opened his mouth to speak, but I butted in before he could say anything. "The person in the ambulance is a victim of abuse and trying to avoid, uh…the spotlight. We have a shelter on alert in case we need to get her out fast."

He folded his arms and cocked his shiny, shaved head.

"That the reason for the suicide attempt?"

I nodded. "If we go to the hospital, this will all be public record, right?"

"We do have protections in place for this type of thing," he said, carefully.

"Great! I hoped you'd understand."

Glyndon PD pulled into the parking lot. Two officers got out and walked toward us. I searched the driver's eyes. "What should I tell the cops?"

"We're trained to be discreet with media in these situations, so we can legit help there, but the PD has their own requirements."

I overheard one of the paramedics radio Hannah's vitals to the hospital. He addressed me. "She got family?"

"*We're* her family," I said.

"We got you," the driver told me. "Don't worry."

Maybe they could admit her as a Jane Doe, I didn't know. But, I got the impression that he knew what to do.

"You going?" one of the paramedics asked. It took a second to realize he was talking to me.

The cops stood around Sherry, filling out the remainder of their report. I waved at her and pointed at the ambo. She flipped me a thumbs-up. I hopped inside.

A couple of hours later, Hannah had been given a spot in the ER and put on a list for the ICU. I was trying to sleep in a stiff, fake leather chair when my cell buzzed with a call from a stressed-out Sherry.

"Maybe this is too much for us," she said.

I let out a slow breath. "We haven't known *what* to do for her. We got her out of there, a necessary first step…but we're not equipped to deal with this much emotional and physical pain and its consequences." I glanced at Hannah. Sedated. I hoped she wouldn't hear my end of this conversation. "How about the shelter?"

"Let's see how her hospital stay goes," she said. "I made sure the records didn't include her real name. They said they'd look into security for her room. We can't stay with her 24/7."

"Okay. I'll cancel Thanksgiving. I'll take Hannah duty, and Beth can take a day, too."

Sherry grunted. *"It's Thanksgiving,* and you have a trip to Richmond planned. You need a break. Beth would agree. Callie's invited me for Thanksgiving, and I'd bet a hundred bucks she'll go with me for Hannah duty. It'll be fine. We'll visit every day."

I hadn't seen my daughters or my mother and my stepfather, Gray, in months. And they were right; the threat of Monty in the background plus Hannah's terrible situation had worn on me, and as Dr. Grayson Sturgis, my neurologist and also my stepdad, kept insisting…due to the TBI I needed to find ways to reduce stress.

A laughable proposition, but necessary. *Mandatory.*

"Okay. I'm convinced. But promise to text me status updates, okay?"

She agreed and continued. "In other news, Curtis Ridgeland called, all freaked out that his wife had gotten attacked. The cops suspect him, and he doesn't know what to do. I'm so sorry I ever took that investigation."

"Tell me the truth. Do you think he had something to do with the attack on Victoria?"

"Oh, Lord," she said. "All we were hired to do was take photos, of a possible liaison. We did that! I can't believe we even have to think about this."

"Have investigators left me a message or anything?" I asked.

"Why would they need to talk to you in the middle of the night?"

"I'm pretty sure they know where I work by now. They'll be subpoenaing us for the photos and interviewing me about my purpose in being there. Then what?"

"Then we throw Monty and Graham under the bus. Hard."

"There's no evidence that they knew Victoria was at risk," I said.

Sherry made a rude noise with her lips. "Have Callie pump Graham. He's the go-between. Ask her to record a conversation."

I laughed. "Oh, yeah, like *that* would go over. I can just see her trying to put her phone on record and Graham staring at her like she's nuts." I rotated my neck in an attempt to work out the stress that had settled there.

"I hope they drag Monty's ass back to jail for Thanksgiving. I can't stand the thought of him out on work release when I'm not here."

"I know for a fact he will *not* be online over the holiday weekend. I confirmed with his corrections facility. His work release assignment is on hold until after the holidays, so I think we're good until next week when you get back. Take the trip. We'll take care of Hannah."

"Maybe it's a good thing Hannah's in the hospital. He'd never think to look there."

Sherry frowned. "Why haven't we gotten a lawsuit? A phone call? A threat? Something from her husband?"

"You know, these creeps wait until their prey lets their guard down. Then they spring the trap," I said.

"Did you run it by Hunter?"

I whipped out my cell. No text. "It's crazy I haven't heard from him about that. He said he'd get back to me."

Sherry shrugged. "He has a life, you know."

I rolled my eyes so hard it should've popped a blood vessel. "Whatever. I *know* he's busy."

"His priorities have shifted, too," she hinted, her voice soft.

"I don't think our personal relationship has anything to do with it!"

Sherry went quiet.

"He's moved on, and so have I," I persisted, like a three-year-old. "It's not like he's on his own. Now, he's responsible for the entire Richmond PD Criminal Investigation Unit."

"You'll know soon enough," Sherry said.

I felt my forehead knot. "What's that mean?"

Sherry rose from her chair. "You're going to *Richmond* for Thanksgiving. Don't you think your mom has already invited him to join?"

Chapter Seventeen

Olivia

The Day Before Thanksgiving

T
he drive to Mom's passed in a pleasant mix of podcast programming and phone calls from my girls and giving Mom updates on my travel status. I felt a cautious peace as I drove. Our plan felt solid, and I'd be back on Monday. I had no doubts about leaving Sherry in charge any longer, as she'd proven her competency. Beth, the perfect neighbor, offered to take care of Riot and Marlowe since she lived next door. Callie's house sat on the other side, right down the road. Between the two of them, I'd know in minutes if something went wrong.

My cell buzzed with a text from Sherry. I listened as my car's read-text program related the text:

Hannah gained consciousness, and her doctor wanted to keep her over the holiday. Fine by me. She'll be safer in the hospital. The doctor is putting her on a high-carb diet; they gave her a blood test. Pregnancy confirmed. I'll keep you posted. Enjoy your family.

I bit my fingernail. No wonder Hannah'd felt nauseous and faint. I hoped they'd feed her gallons of ice cream. She loved ice cream.

Poor Hannah.

Any thought of Patrick sliding out of the picture evaporated with the confirmation of the pregnancy. I'd held onto the slim hope that the pregnancy stick tests had given a false positive.

Whatever we have to do, we must keep this pregnancy to ourselves. Patrick can't know.

I slapped the steering wheel in frustration as I thought about each of the Wine & Whine girls—Callie, Sherry, Hannah, me—and our long, sordid histories with bad choices in men. Why hadn't we seen the red flags before we'd married them? "We need a collective intervention," I muttered into the air-freshened interior of my Land Rover as I drove, writing the scenario in my head.

We'd hire a marital interventionist. It *had* to be an actual specialty somewhere. She'd encourage us that remaining single would be in our best interests. We would all chime in with our personal horror stories, and the interventionist would nod in empathy, take notes on a little pad, and wrap up the intervention session after sixty minutes. We'd go our separate ways, only to pick another loser and do it all over again.

I cackled hysterically and threw another handful of French Burnt Peanuts into my mouth. A road trip always called for a new bag of French Burnt Peanuts.

My car announced an incoming call from Sergeant Hunter Faraday.

My lips parted in surprise. It had been forever since we'd had a real conversation. I pressed my steering wheel button to take the call. "Hi."

The word came out somewhat mangled. I cleared my throat to try again. "Hi there," I managed.

"Hey. Sorry I've been incommunicado."

"I know you're busy."

"I, uh...got detained."

I felt my eyebrows pull together. "Detained?"

"Or, you might call it getting shot in the line of duty."

I almost drove off the road. I jerked the car onto the shoulder and parked. "*Hunter*. My God. Are you okay?"

"I'll be fine, but it's bad timing. I'm not sure the doc'll release me tomorrow. Your mom invited me to Thanksgiving dinner." He chuckled. "I accepted, but with the caveat that you were okay with it."

"Mom never checks with me about that. She loves you. My opinion would *not* keep her from inviting you." Since I'd already gotten used to the idea, I was fine with it. "Besides, it's been a long time. I want you to come, too."

After a two-second pause, he responded. "Good to know."

A burst of compassion detonated in my chest. How bad had it been?

"What happened? Can you talk about it?"

"Short story is a drug deal I shouldn't have gotten in the middle of."

"That's undercover. You aren't undercover anymore; you're the boss."

Hunter remained quiet.

"The only drug war I remember you talking about involved a gorgeous cop, who shall remain nameless."

Hunter laughed. But he didn't deny it.

I poked around in my psyche to see if jealousy had reared its ugly head... nope. I nailed down my emotional state as concern, not jealousy.

He could've died, though.

I frowned. *That* thought put a definite dent in my psyche.

"Is Shiloh okay?"

He laughed. "She was supposed to remain nameless."

I smiled. My pulse raced at the sound of his voice. I didn't want it to, but it did.

Dammit.

"She's still in critical condition."

My hands tightened on the steering wheel. "I'm so sorry, Hunter."

"Yeah. It's hard. She's a great cop."

A couple beats of silence passed.

"Listen, I..."

"Hunter, we..."

Both of us started laughing. Hunter's laughter ended with a fit of coughing.

"Your ribs must've taken a hard enough hit to affect your lungs," I concluded. "Are you sure you're okay?"

"I, uh...made a dramatic entrance from the second floor of an old building. Guess I'm too old to drop and roll like we learned as rookies."

"You did that on purpose, didn't you?"

"How did you know that?"

"I know *you*."

Three blips of silence.

"I'm going to be there tomorrow," he said.

I felt a blush climb from my neck all the way to the top of my head. "I'll have ice packs ready."

I arrived at Mom and Gray's condo on the outskirts of Richmond a few minutes before seven p.m. The girls waited for me in the driveway. I jumped out of my Land Rover and scooped them into my arms. "So good to be here," I murmured into Serena's silky blond hair and Lilly's red, shoulder-length curls. I drank them in as they tugged my luggage out of the back. *How is it possible that I have a college senior and sophomore?* Serena had already arranged an internship in D.C. and applied for the master's degree program in political science with a focus on political institutions, and Lilly's latest swerve into a career path had something to do with state parks. How I wished I could remember more specific memories of them as young girls, but the TBI had changed all that. Dr. Grayson Sturgis had been very clear that no one can predict how a TBI will heal…that it was still possible the memories could return. I hoped so.

Mom threw her arms around me when I walked in the door.

When she released me, she flapped her hand toward the back end of the airy, one-level condo. "Go ahead and put your stuff away."

The girls and I walked into the guest bedroom. Serena plopped onto the bed, and Lilly leaned against the wall. "You look good, Mom. Did you let your hair go back to its natural color?"

"I'm trying," I said, twirling a lock of hair self-consciously. "What do you think?"

"I love it," Lilly said. "Your white-hair phase looked fine, but I love your natural color."

I chuckled. "You mean auburn with streaks of gray?"

Serena frowned and walked over to examine my hair. "Ohmigosh. You're going gray."

"Forty-five this year, girls. It's inevitable a little silver would start to show."

Lilly patted her red curls. "It's a fact that redheads go gray much later in life. Don't worry, Mom. Also, you should get highlights to disguise it. Nobody would think you're forty-five."

I laughed. "I'm *so* not worried about that."

After small talk and sandwiches, Mom, Gray, and I took our glasses of wine out to the back patio, and the girls left to buy some last-minute additions to Thanksgiving dinner for tomorrow. Transfixed by the shimmying flames from the fire pit and endless galaxies in a clear, dark sky, we sat in silence for a while.

"How's life in neurology-world, Gray?" I asked, our meditative silence sliding away with my question.

"Pretty good," he said, averting his eyes.

Mom sipped her wine. Glanced at me.

Uh oh.

"What does 'pretty good' mean, Gray?"

"I need to retire."

"I've been asking him to retire for months," Mom added. "He's stubborn."

"Don't you want to?" I asked.

Gray looked at Mom. Mom looked at me.

"Okay," I muttered. "What's with the subterfuge?"

Gray reached for his wine glass.

"I've gotten a Parkinson's diagnosis," he said, his voice matter-of-fact. "There are good meds now to treat symptoms." He raised both his arms to show me how they trembled, then dropped them into his lap. "It used to be much worse."

Mom smiled at him and took his hand. "We're trusting God in this."

Gray nodded. "Yes, we are."

I felt my lips part in shock. How could he and Mom remain so calm? How long had they kept this news from me? Ever since my assault, the two of them walked on eggshells around me. After all the tragic disappointments Mom had experienced in her life? Now this? *They'd only found each other six years ago*. Our Dr. Grayson Sturgis—the gentle man who'd diagnosed, supported, and strengthened me through a challenging recovery. Tears filled my eyes. I looked at Gray. "How long have you known? I'm so sorry. What can I do?"

"We got three opinions, honey," Mom said. "They all agreed, and we didn't think we needed to burden you with—"

The spontaneous, frustrated fling of my arm shook the patio table beside my chair. My wine glass fell and shattered. Wine streamed across the white concrete patio like blood.

"Burden me? Are you kidding? After what you guys have done for me? After how much Dr. Sturgis has...sorry, I just called him that for so long...I mean, *Gray* has meant to me? It's not a burden! I need to know these things. It's been almost six years! You don't need to treat me as this fragile, breakable piece of humanity anymore. I'm good. Things are *fine!*"

I felt guilt zip up the back of my neck and lodge somewhere within the boundaries of my slightly heaving chest. Maybe I should cut them some slack for not wanting to trouble the waters. I had my own troubled waters. I hadn't told them about it, had I?

I snapped my mouth shut and stared at the sky.

Mom looked at Gray.

"Olivia," Gray began, his voice soft. "We've accepted it."

I stared at him, then Mom. They both had this serene look on their faces. I couldn't believe it.

With a glance at the mess I'd made, I went inside for a cleaning towel and also for a new glass and a refill. Over my shoulder, I called, "Maybe you're fine...but I'm *not.*"

I slammed the door behind me.

Chapter Eighteen

Hunter

Thanksgiving Day

Hunter adjusted the sling on his left arm and the heavy tape around his torso and groin as he walked the corridor in search of Shiloh's room. A nurse strode by. Hunter reached out with his good arm and tapped her shoulder. "Do you know where Shiloh McPherson is? She got out of ICU yesterday."

The nurse spun around with an irritated look, but went to the floor desk and inquired. "Room 435," she snapped, then resumed her brisk steps to her destination.

Hunter couldn't wait to leave this place. He'd seen enough of Richmond's Mercy Hospital to last a lifetime. He shook his head. First Olivia, now Shiloh in this hospital…it must be some kind of payback, he mused. What if it'd been his *wife* in the hospital? If he moved forward with Shiloh, injuries were typical. Expected. On the other hand, Olivia and her investigations hadn't been a cakewalk, either. He groaned. Why couldn't he be attracted to a woman with calm and peaceful pursuits? Someone cloistered in an office instead of immersed in criminal psychopathy and the spray of bullets?

He got out of the elevator on the fourth floor and found her room. He stood outside the door, looking in through the small window. Shiloh's casted, outstretched leg lay on a cloth-covered hammock suspended by ropes.

It'd be months before she could even walk again.

The bruises on her face had ripened, and the swelling of her right cheek had grown to the size of a tomato. Two black eyes, almost swollen shut. She wore a neck brace. A pull-up bar hung over her head. A cast cloaked her right forearm and stopped at the elbow. *Broken wrist.* That had been the cracking sounds he'd heard.

Those bastards must've beaten her half to death. He'd been thirty seconds too late to save her. Where had his guys been? He chewed so hard on his lower lip that he tasted blood. The minute he got back into the office, he'd find out. They'd better have those reports on his desk first thing.

He straightened his shoulders, pushed the door open, and walked inside. Put his hand on her shoulder. "Shi?"

Her eyelids fluttered. She groaned.

"I see you're on recommended bed rest."

Her eyes still closed, she smiled.

Hunter grabbed a chair and pulled it close to the bed. "I've gotten myself discharged, against all professional protocols and wisdom. Wanted to say goodbye and tell you to give 'em hell in here."

Shiloh moved her arm toward him. Hunter reached out for her hand. "Sorry I didn't make it to the party earlier."

A single tear leaked from her eye and trailed down her cheek.

"Hey," Hunter whispered. "You're tough, and you're gonna beat this. You'll be back on the firing range in no time."

Her lips worked, but nothing came out. She turned her head toward him and tried again. "You okay?"

Hunter squeezed her hand. "Took one in the shoulder, and your boy Stick gave me a parting gift."

She frowned.

"He knows how to throw a knife. I'll give him that. Takes good aim to hit someone below the vest and above the belt."

Shiloh rubbed Hunter's hand with her thumb. "Sorry," she whispered.

He bent down closer to her ear. "You got all the credit. I made sure of it in my report."

She grinned, bigger this time. "Got that asshole."

"You did it, Shi."

She yawned. "I need to sleep now."

"Okay."

An hour later, Hunter parked his Jeep on the curb in front of Sophie and Gray's condo. He grinned at the sight of Olivia's familiar Land Rover. If he still had any pull with her, he'd recommend she trade it in. Maybe Gray had already suggested it, he thought as he approached the door.

His jaw clenched. Why did he still feel he should insert himself into this woman's life?

He *shouldn't*. He walked to the porch and knocked.

Steps approached. Olivia opened the door.

He blinked at the sight of her non-platinum hair. "You're back."

"This feels more like me." She laughed. "Still working on who that is."

Hunter fought through the memories of his first sight of her after she'd been released from the hospital. She'd opened the door, looked up at him, and taken his breath away. The first few months after weeks of recovery in the hospital were hard for her. She'd been confused by her memory loss, sad that she had little recollection of raising her girls, lost without more memories of her vivacious mother, and to make matters even more confusing, her healing brain had flipped her personality. She wasn't even sure who she'd *been*, much less who she was now. He'd been drawn to her so hard that every time he had to question her for the assault investigation and later a homicide, he could barely keep his hands to himself.

Hunter pushed the thoughts aside and managed a smile. "You're doing a good job of putting that together." He put his nose in the air like a bloodhound. "Sure smells delicious in here."

They walked into Sophie and Gray's combo den and kitchen. Serena and Lilly rose from the couch and hugged him. Gray walked over and in his typical booming voice, told Hunter it had been too damn long since they'd seen him.

Hunter smiled. He loved this family. The ache in his chest that they'd not become *his* family never seemed to go away. He'd been wrong about Olivia. He'd miscalculated the depth of her wounds—both physical and emotional—from the assault. Her life lay in two pieces: BA and PA. Before assault and post-assault. Some things couldn't be changed, and he had to accept it.

"Wine or beer, Hunter?" Sophie asked.

"A beer's good."

"Still Stella?"

He nodded. Sophie handed him a frosty bottle. "Glad you could come."

"Me, too," he said, with a glance at Olivia. She'd curled into the huge sectional in the living room with the girls to chat. Gray walked over to the gas fireplace and turned it on. Flames whooshed to life. Soft jazz floated from the speakers, and outside, snowflakes drifted to the ground. Hunter gaped at the spectacle happening outside the window. It *never* snowed in Richmond on Thanksgiving.

"Look outside, everybody," he called, sipping his beer.

Sophie walked to the front window. Serena and Lilly raced to her side. "It's snowing!" Lilly declared a huge smile on her face. "I'm going out."

"Me, too," Serena said.

The girls grabbed coats and launched themselves into the postage-stamp-size front yard.

Olivia watched them through the window. "It'll be gone in five minutes," she said.

"The last time it snowed on Thanksgiving in Richmond was 1989," Sophie called from the kitchen.

Gray leaned against the counter, watching his wife. Hunter noticed his hand shaking as he held his wine glass. "We should think positive, honey," he said.

She gave him a warm smile. "You're right. Yes, we should. I hope we have a big snowstorm." She kissed him on the cheek. Her hand drifted to his shaky one and held it still.

Hunter noticed Olivia staring at them with sad eyes. She turned back to the window.

"Snow is coming down harder," Olivia murmured as Hunter joined her.

"I believe in miracles, now," Hunter said, staring at the snow flurry.

"I've believed in miracles a long time," she whispered, sneaking a glance at him. She moved three millimeters away, lest they touch.

He frowned, drained his beer.

"I'm going to get my coat and go outside!" She glanced at his sling, noted the stiffness in his torso. "You up to coming out with us?"

He snorted. "As if."

Outside, snow had begun to dust the sidewalk, the grass, the bushes. Hunter laughed as he watched the girls try to make snowballs out of the tiny amount of snow on the ground before it melted. Olivia was bundled in a pillowy jacket, her hands stuck deep into her pockets. She sat on a bench in the front yard. "It's freezing out here!"

Hunter walked over and sat beside her. "That means it'll stick. I've never seen snow this early here." Her scent hadn't changed. He resisted moving closer, just so he could inhale the perfume. With a sigh and an irritated jerk of his sling, he turned his attention to Lilly and Serena.

Shrieking like two-year-olds, they chased each other around the yard with tiny clumps of snow in their hands.

"Put on gloves!" Olivia cried.

Hunter laughed. "Where are they? I'll get them."

"I don't even know if they brought any."

"I'll go ask Sophie. Back in a sec."

Hunter walked inside, his nose twitching with the smells of stuffing, pecan pie in the oven, the golden-brown turkey on the counter. Sophie and Gray sat at the kitchen table talking, and he caught pieces of the conversation as he walked down the hall to the coat closet.

"...we have to be making some decisions..."

"...I can't think about it. I don't want to! This is Thanksgiving. I know you're worried about us, but we'll be fine."

Hunter felt his forehead tighten. Worried about what?

"...the tremors are getting worse. It's just a matter of time and..."

"...uncertain science at best. They can't tell you how long you have! They have no idea."

Hunter's throat closed. Gray? Oh, no. Hunter calculated his age around seventy. Olivia's mother, a few years younger. Should he ask? He'd best let them know that he could hear them.

He walked into the kitchen. They stopped talking and smiled. "Snow still coming down?" Gray asked.

"Olivia wants gloves for the girls. Any ideas, Sophie?"

"I've got some in the bedroom. I'll get them and take them out."

Hunter sat at the table. The two men remained quiet until Hunter said, "I couldn't help but hear."

Gray exhaled. "I'll let 'er rip, then. You have no idea how hard it is to control the tremors."

"What's going on, Gray?"

"Parkinson's." He placed his arms on the table. "It's early yet. So, nobody should freak out."

Hunter didn't trust himself to speak.

Gray shot out a shaky arm and put his hand on Hunter's shoulder. "I'm good, bud. Just look at what I've got, here. Women who love me; who are strong when I'm weak. I could be alone, y'know?"

"Does Olivia know?"

"We told her yesterday."

So *that's* what the expression had been a few minutes ago...sadness. Helplessness. He felt the same way. "I'm around," Hunter said. "You guys call on me if you need anything, okay?"

Gray nodded. "We know that. And I appreciate the offer." He moved from the chair and had trouble keeping his balance. He shot Hunter an apologetic look and asked, "Would you get my coat for me out of the closet? I'd like to enjoy the snow while it lasts. It's the gray puffer."

Hunter returned with the coat and helped Gray into it. They walked outside and into a fluffy, gusty snowfall. Gray laughed, stumbled, and held onto Hunter.

Olivia spun around in concern. "Are you okay?"

Gray waved his hands. "Of course. Hunter's got me. This is incredible."

He tilted his head and held out his arms. "I love this. We haven't seen snow in a long time."

"I'm going to go back inside and help Mom." She stepped closer to Hunter and whispered in his ear. "I guess you know now. Stay close, okay?"

The two men sat on the bench. "My affairs are in order," Gray told Hunter, his voice gruff.

"I wouldn't think anything else."

He shrugged. "Don't want you worrying about Sophie and the girls. I know you're as much family as anyone, and you being you…" Gray smiled. "You'd be over here picking up the pieces. Don't worry. Final will and everything, investments, even a gravesite. I'm all set."

"Good to know. But we're not planning a funeral yet. Don't get ahead of yourself. You could outlive us all."

The men watched the girls cavorting in the snow like a couple of nymphs. "They're so beautiful, aren't they?" Gray smiled. "They are a joy."

"Indeed."

Gray held Hunter's gaze. "Go after her."

Hunter blinked. "You mean Olivia?"

Gray grabbed the back of his neck and winced. "Damn. Neck is stiff. I can't even nod. Yes, Olivia, who else would I mean? That girl is wandering around like a lost pigeon, and you're sitting here in Richmond, letting her get away. She needs you. Don't let frustration get the best of you. Brain injury patients have a hard time recognizing a good decision. It's a result of all that rewiring. Both of you are stubborn as the ole' mule my father used to have." Gray laughed. "Sometimes it takes convincing. I used to walk out with a bunch of carrots behind my back, and the minute that mule saw them, he'd follow me all the way into the barn."

"You think a bunch of carrots would convince her?" Hunter grinned.

"If they don't believe the words, show them by your actions. Take her on a trip or something. I know she's missing her daughters. Suggest something that includes them. She'd love that."

Hunter looked unconvinced. "She's got a hectic job."

"She works for herself," Gray countered. "She can take time off anytime she wants."

Hunter sat quiet.

"I know it's tough," he said, his voice soft.

His brow wrinkled. He hadn't expected such transparency from a man like Dr. Grayson Sturgis. He guessed the diagnosis had him thinking deep thoughts. Things he needed to say before it was too late. He pinched the bridge of his nose to keep the tears at bay. "What's tough?"

"The rejection. Man, I've been there. Half the time, people are just scared to commit. Find out what her objection is and overcome it."

He filed this away to think about later. The snow had already morphed into rain. "Why are we sitting here getting soaking wet?"

Sophie opened the door. "Dinner's ready!"

"That was a fantastic meal, Mom," Olivia said as she emptied the last of the dishes from the dishwasher three hours later. Wiping her hands on a tea towel, she threw it on the counter and sat at the kitchen table with Hunter.

"That's an understatement," he added. "Delicious, Sophie."

"Glad you approve," she said with a smile. "I'll be back. I'm going to check on Gray."

She left.

Olivia and Hunter looked at each other.

After a few awkward seconds, Hunter asked, "How's life in your world?"

"Confusing."

He nodded. "I can imagine. Monty behaving himself?"

She grinned. "Boy. Have I ever heard that question before."

"We have history," Hunter replied in mock seriousness.

"Yes, we do."

The conversation stalled. Olivia cleared her throat. "I told you we got Hannah, right?"

"I assumed you did since I hadn't heard any more. How's she doing?"

Olivia shook her head. "That nut job she married left some deep scars."

He grunted. "Lot of 'em out there."

"This one's a psychopath." Olivia filled the next ten minutes with Hannah's

120

dilemma and Patrick's behavior.

"Doesn't surprise me since his sheet pointed to bigger and better crimes. It's a type."

"How can you know that?"

Hunter shrugged. "A profile. You had to have researched him when Hannah got involved."

"It was small stuff," Olivia muttered.

"Yeah, well, some of the small stuff leads to bigger stuff. He didn't just bonk a kid on the head; he bragged about it. His other priors were misdemeanors, but if I'd been that boy's parent, I'd have him in counseling. There's a heartlessness to his juvie record. Takes time and experience to learn to read between the lines."

Olivia exhaled. "It's been a long day."

"No calls?"

"No calls, no crisis to manage. I'm going to bed...unless you wanted to talk or...?

Hunter shook his head. "I'm headed home. Tell your family goodbye for me."

Olivia reached for her coat. "I'll walk you out."

They heard the soft burble of a rom-com from the TV as they walked to the door. Lilly and Serena lay sleeping in the den, one in a recliner and the other wrapped in a comforter on the floor. When they walked outside, their steps crunched over a crust of ice.

"This is incredible," Olivia said, spreading her arms at what passed for "snow" in Richmond.

"*You're* incredible," Hunter blurted.

Olivia stared at him, her lips parted, a question in her eyes.

Hunter pulled her into his arms and kissed her. Soft and easy. An exploratory exercise.

A "how we used to be" kiss.

When the kiss ended, Olivia wrapped her arms around him and held his gaze. Hunter thought her even more beautiful than when they'd first met. Her hazel eyes held the same warmth he remembered from the first moment she'd opened the door to let him into her home for an interview, conflict etching her features, the lit candles casting shadows across her face.

It hadn't been the easiest investigation, but they found a way through it...*together.*

Hunter cursed softly. "Why can't I get over you?"

Olivia smiled. "I've missed you, too."

He kissed her again. When common sense kicked in, he removed his lips from hers. "I better go."

Backing away, she nodded. "You better."

"Can we get together and talk tomorrow?"

"I need to see what the girls and Mom have planned. I'll text."

"Okay." With one last look, he got into his Jeep and rumbled off into the night.

Chapter Nineteen

Olivia

The Day After Thanksgiving

"Mom!" Serena called.

I tossed off the comforter. "I'm up, come on in."

Serena and Lilly flew into my room and jumped onto the bed.

"So…" I rubbed sleep out of my eyes. "What do you two want to do today?

"Lily wants you to meet Buddy."

"Okay. Who's Buddy?"

"Her boy-friieeennnddd," Serena sing-songed.

Lilly frowned. "He's *not* my boyfriend. We haven't even talked about it."

"Would he join us for lunch?" I asked.

She whipped out her phone and texted him.

"He asked where."

"Isn't there a deli or something close?"

"Patty's," Serena said. "It's great."

"Patty's it is," I agreed.

They bounced out of my room. Had I ever had that much energy?

With a sigh, I went into the bathroom and turned on the shower.

An hour later, I sat at the kitchen table chatting with Gray and Mom. We tried to avoid talking about the elephant in the room, but Gray's diagnosis whispered from the walls, dripped from the ceiling, and stomped across the floor. It lingered in silent pauses over our coffee and muddied our words with fear.

When I couldn't stand it any longer, I spoke out. "I feel like my chest is caving in, and there's...there's this big *hole* in our conversation. Shouldn't we talk about it?" I folded my hands on the table. Gray and Mom couldn't meet my eyes. I looked at Gray. "Can you at least give me more details about your condition?"

Gray had put on a brave front, but now he looked about a hundred years old. I figured if we talked about it as family, he'd feel better. We'd help carry the load. Or something.

He sighed. "The Parkinson's is progressing fast, and they tell me that's the norm for my age group." He rolled his eyes. "I'm an age group now."

"You're ageless, Gray," I told him, reaching for his hand. "We are all interested and want to know. You carried us for years with all my brain injury issues. Now it's our turn to carry you. I hope you'll let us."

"They're managing it with meds, of course, but I'm having a heck of a time keeping my balance." He took Sophie's hand. "Sophie's been a champ, but I don't want her to have to..." He looked away.

"Gray, don't you dare be upset or thinking we don't want to take care of you! We love you," I declared. My thoughts raced. He meant *so much* to all of us. "We are with you one hundred percent."

Gray laughed. "Man. Do you know how good it makes me feel to see that spark? When I think about when I first laid eyes on you... a Jane Doe left in the bushes outside Mercy Hospital...and how we thought you might not make it..." He shook his head. "I still think about what a miracle it was."

"Does Sarah know about your diagnosis?" I asked, remembering my wonderful, kind nurse.

He said nothing.

"You need to tell her," I insisted. "She'd want to know."

He averted his eyes. I registered the slight tremor of his hands and tried to control my frustration. This couldn't be happening. Not to Gray!

He'd been my rock through the long road to recovery, and when he and

Mom had announced their engagement, I'd been thrilled. I couldn't bear to think of our family without him. My frantic eyes searched out Mom's calmer ones. I noticed that she wore subdued colors instead of her typical tie-dye skirts and hundreds of bangle bracelets. She had no earrings on, either. I frowned. How long had they been handling Gray's diagnosis alone?

"I'm going to take him to our bedroom," she said, helping him out of his chair. "You go ahead with the girls. It's important to have time with them."

I watched them walk down the hall as Serena and Lilly bounced into the kitchen. "Mom! Are you ready to go?"

With one last glance at Mom and Gray, I focused on the expectant, dear faces of my daughters. The next three hours belonged to them.

First stop, lunch at a wonderful, sunny café where I got to meet Lilly's boyfriend, and second, third, and fourth stops, women's clothing boutiques. I sat in lounge areas as they tried on clothes, where they'd come out at intervals and ask me what I thought. Lilly burst from her dressing room in a sleeveless, Boho-style sundress and pirouetted for me. High on her arm, I noticed a series of small fingertip bruises that made my heart stop. Monty had given me plenty of similar bruises. I felt adrenaline pump through my veins as I walked over to her. She stood in front of a three-way mirror, and it looked like we were holding a meeting in triplicate. "That's a great dress, honey," I said. Lowering my voice, I slid my fingers along her arm. "What are these from, Lilly?"

Her cheeks colored. She tugged her arm away. "It's nothing.

She started to walk away, but I held my ground. "It's not nothing. Is it Buddy?"

She glared. "People aren't perfect, Mom!" She stalked back into the dressing room.

Lilly walked out in a summer jumper. "I love this! What do you think?"

"Cute," I said, but my thoughts were on the bruises on Lilly's arm.

"Mom, I can't believe we found all this stuff!" Serena cried as we drove back to their grandmother's condo. "Thank you so much."

"Yeah, Mom. Thank you," Lilly said, her voice subdued. "Buddy says he appreciated you paying for his lunch, too."

I said nothing. My opinion of Buddy had taken a nose dive. I'd need to schedule a serious conversation with my daughter.

I turned into the driveway with a smile. "I'm glad I got to meet him."

"He was nervous," Lilly added.

"Understandable," I said, thinking how he'd focused on Lilly to the point of awkwardness, and more than once, she'd caught our eyes and shrugged it off as if to say, "he's a lot, but I put up with it." Now, I'm wondering exactly how much she puts up with.

My phone buzzed. I pulled it out of my purse. "Just a sec," I said. "You guys go on in. I'll be there in a minute." I sat in the car, staring at my phone.

Serena and Lilly grabbed the stuffed shopping bags and walked toward the door. My gaze lingered on Lilly, her soft, auburn curls so like mine, her athletic, strong body. I thought about the consequences of staying married to Monty, a man who modeled inappropriate and controlling behavior for twenty years. *Of course,* she'd think bruises on her arm were normal. I'd start a conversation, then get her into counseling. I'd do anything to keep her from marrying a man like her father. I re-focused on my phone. The call was from Sherry.

She had promised she'd only contact me in an emergency. A dread-shaped bowling ball rolled through my stomach. I let the call go to voicemail, got out of my car, and sat on Mom's bench between two large, winter-naked Crepe Myrtles.

A happy sigh escaped my lips. Today had been such a gift with its balmy temps in the sixties and sunshine after the unprecedented snow of yesterday. The girls and I had pounced on the downtown shops like kittens with a ball of string, and it had been fun to watch Lilly try to compose herself as I chatted with Buddy in the restaurant over lunch. I thought about Serena's sparkling eyes as she tried on outfits and paraded around for my approval…the hats that looked so silly we'd laughed and laughed. Oh, yes. It had been a good day.

Except for the bruises.

I took a deep breath. I had to take this call. Which of the locked compartments in my brain would the voicemail address? How much stress and chaos would tumble out? I had so hoped for a few stress-free days where I could focus on family without a bunch of complex issues blocking out the sun.

My jaw tightened. I clicked on the voicemail.

"Let me start with an apology...I tried to figure it out myself, but..."

The connection faded in and out. Her voice returned.

"It's Patrick. Callie went over to your house to feed Riot this morning and saw a car in front of your garage. She got some photos before she confronted him."

She confronted him? I held my breath as I continued listening.

"He got out and asked about Hannah. Callie BS'd her way through and told him the last thing she knew, Hannah had gotten married and moved to Florida."

I started to breathe again. Good girl, Callie.

"Anyway. Call me."

The three-hour drive back to Glyndon felt more like six. I'd resorted to pummeling my dashboard in frustration once in a while.

"C'mon!" I sputtered at the impossible traffic on I-95. I'd made it through the DC beltway's post-Thanksgiving traffic when the cars in front of me staggered to a complete stop.

I called Sherry.

She answered. "How's it going?"

"Right now, about an inch at a time."

"How's Hannah?"

"She's numb, but fine. Her wrists are better."

"She's making it, though?"

"Yes, but after an evaluation from one of their psychiatric staff, she refused to say anything else and demanded to be released, so we went to the hospital, made all sorts of promises, and put her in Callie's guest room. Did you talk to Hunter about her situation? Don't you think it's time to get the cops involved? Also, the hospital has a spot for her in the psychiatric wing. Callie and I had to promise to get her in somewhere. What do you want me to do?"

I took a second to register that the Hannah-shaped compartment had burst open and shaken out its contents all over me. So much for a "stress-free" vacation.

"I tried to get my mind off everything so I could reconnect with Lilly and Serena, and as an added bonus, I found out Gray has Parkinson's." I rubbed my eyes wearily. "I didn't have room in my brain to think about work or Hannah. Give me some time to catch up."

Three seconds of dead air drifted between us before she spoke. "Did you at least talk to Hunter about it? He was at your mom's house for Thanksgiving, right?"

"I-I…didn't."

"Why not?" Sherry asked.

I didn't know. My Hunter-status screamed uncertainty. And the spontaneous bout of passion? Awkward didn't even begin to cover it.

Sherry sighed. "I know you guys are going through a weird space, but come on, Olivia, this is life or death. Get your feelings out of it." Sherry grunted. "If you don't call him, I will."

She ended the call. I told my Bluetooth to call him.

"Good morning," he answered, oblivious to the fact that I'd left. I'd gotten up early, explained to Gray and Mom and the girls, stuffed my belongings in my duffel, and walked out the door, my mind on Hannah.

"I hoped you'd call earlier, but maybe we can do dinner? When are you leaving?" he asked.

I pinched the bridge of my nose, thinking about what an idiot I am sometimes. *All* the time.

Whatever.

I took a breath. "I'm already gone, and I'm so sorry I didn't let you know."

An incredibly long pause commenced.

Did his phone die?

Had he ended the call?

My finger hovered over the "end call" button on my steering wheel.

"Okay," he said. "You must've had a reason for that."

Immediate tears sprang to my eyes. Why did Hunter Faraday have to be so darn understanding? "Hannah," I muttered.

"What about her?"

"Her husband knows where I live. He came to my house."

She listened to Hunter's breathing. Heard him scrawling notes with the ever-present pen and notepad he kept on him. "Let's assume he's got a room somewhere in town. That would be Reisterstown or Westminster, right?"

"Yeah, I'd think so. He has a rental car, Callie said. It's white."

"I've got his full name, social, his juvie record, so I'll just add this info into my report for Baltimore PD. Did he approach?"

"Callie noticed the car when she was over there to feed Riot, and after taking a few photos, she decided to approach. Like a friendly neighbor."

"Smart. He doesn't know you guys have Hannah, right?"

"I'm not sure." I exhaled. "Hannah slit her wrists, and we rushed her to the hospital. They kept her for a few days, and wanted to put her in a psych ward. I mean, I get it, but we have to think about protecting her from Patrick. She demanded to be released, and they couldn't keep her. She's at Callie's now. Callie has been briefed. She's watching Hannah like a hawk."

"Did he ask about Hannah?" After a pause, he said, "She tried to commit *suicide?*"

"She told him all she knew was that Hannah had gotten married and moved to Florida." Olivia sighed. "I didn't tell you about the suicide attempt."

"Hm." Hunter lapsed into silence.

"What?" I blurted after his pause, which went on longer than I wanted it to.

"Interesting that he didn't pose as someone else. All these guys want initially is information. For him to come right out and state his purpose is an outlier for this psychopathy, that's all."

"Profiling isn't always accurate."

"Nine out of ten," he murmured.

"I don't know what to do."

"Are you home?"

"An hour out."

His exhale floated through the connection. "Chances are he waited and watched Callie. He knows where she lives."

"She *walks* to my house. On the path out back. She wouldn't have taken her car."

"We need to anticipate that he parked, doubled back, and followed her. I bet he knows about that path now."

The "we" gave me pause. Maybe I needed to embrace it instead of freezing out the word every time he said it. He's perfect. Why can't I commit?

The words "followed her home" rang in my head like a gong. *Followed her home Followed her home Followed her home.* I lost my breath for a minute.

"Olivia?"

I gulped. "I'm an hour away and..."

"Sherry and her gun are on-site. Correct?" Hunter finished for me.

"Correct. We need to warn her."

"I'll call her. You focus on getting there. Is Marlowe with them?"

"He is."

"Good. I'll contact Callie and then Baltimore PD. They still know me; they'll get right over there with patrols. Breathe. Okay? *Olivia.*"

I kept nodding until I realized I was stuck on bobble-head mode. It took me a minute to realize Hunter would be concerned about stress that might throw me into a TBI-related seizure. It warmed my heart to realize he still worried about me. "I'm fine."

"Keep it that way," he muttered before ending the call.

I stared at the road. Traffic had cleared.

Chapter Twenty

Hannah

Sherry knocked on the bedroom door of Callie's guest bedroom a second time. Then a third.

"Hannah, can you let Marlowe out now? He'd bark his head off if anyone was around. It's safe to come out, and you need to eat something."

She didn't want to intrude, but she had no choice. She opened the door and walked inside.

Hannah sat cross-legged on the bed, rocking back and forth. Her arms were entwined around herself. Her eyes were closed.

Sherry sat and put an arm around her.

Hannah stared at her in surprise. "Oh, gosh." She wiped sweat off her face. Took deep breaths. "I was back there," she whispered.

"Tell me about it."

"In the, uh…the room. The basement room with one tiny window. Like a prison cell. Like a *prison*," she repeated, her voice robotic. She turned to Sherry. "Look." She stretched out her arms.

She scrutinized Hannah's bandaged wrists and her arms. "What am I looking for, honey?"

She jabbed her index finger. "The bruises. See them? They're always there. It hurts all the time. *It hurts.*"

Sherry shook her head. "The bruises are gone. They've healed. He's gone, Hannah."

"He's never gone," she muttered.

"He doesn't have a choice, hon'. Olivia and I will take care of it. Amy, Callie, and I are about to have lunch, and we want you to join us."

"When's Olivia getting here?"

"Any minute."

Hannah followed Sherry into the kitchen, scrutinizing each window. Marlowe strode along beside them, his tail at half-mast. Even Marlowe sensed the disquiet. They joined Callie and her daughter, Amy, at the table in her huge kitchen.

Callie bustled to the miles-long countertops and asked Hannah if she could get her a sandwich. Hannah shrugged. Callie cut her eyes at Sherry, who also shrugged.

"I'm fixing you a turkey and cheese on rye, Hannah. You like those, remember?"

Hannah looked at the items on the countertop. "I do?"

"Of course you do!" Callie exclaimed, as if Hannah were joking.

She wasn't.

"Patrick starved me, you know."

Sherry and Callie stared at each other. Amy stopped chewing and looked at her mother, who shook her head and put her index finger to her lips. Hannah needed to get it out, and they'd been waiting for her to feel comfortable enough.

Hannah yawned and stretched her arms overhead, as if she'd awakened from a long nap. "His parents starved him, too, he told me." Hannah stared at her feet, then raised her head. "Patrick seemed perfect. Courteous, kind. Handsome. Made plenty of money. We were happy at first."

"I remember," Sherry said. "We were thrilled for you."

Hannah stared blankly. "I tried. I really tried."

A quiet hush sucked the air from the room. Marlowe wandered over to sit beside Hannah.

She shivered. "He didn't have friends and didn't want people over. Ever. I was so bored, and it seemed like my car had countless repairs." Hannah cranked out a laugh. "I found out he'd hidden it on his property, so I couldn't

132

go anywhere when he was gone. One day, I found a file in his closet—it had a psychiatric evaluation from the time he'd been in juvenile detention as a kid." She wiped a tear away. "That's the first time I realized I'd made a horrible mistake."

Callie looked at her daughter and cocked her head at the hallway. Amy left the room. Her bedroom door closed seconds later.

"I-I guess I shouldn't have asked him about it. He got upset and…" Tears tumbled down her cheeks. She let them fall. "He told me I didn't respect his privacy. After that, I couldn't think about anything else but that report. It talked about his behavior patterns exhibiting sociopathic tendencies, that his parents had trapped him in closets and withheld food as punishment." She raised her head and looked at them with sad eyes. "The report concluded his behavior pointed to violence in the future."

She rocked in her chair, a self-soothing motion she couldn't seem to stop. "The room. That was the end of it."

"The end of what?" Sherry asked, breathless.

Callie put the sandwich in front of Hannah.

"The end of the marriage. The end of my dream to live in Florida with a good man. The end of living a fantasy, I guess." She stared at her bandaged wrists as she chewed and swallowed. "He started locking me in right after that. If I didn't want to have sex, it didn't matter. He raped me. If I even looked at him the wrong way, he threw me in that room." Hannah lowered her head and closed her eyes. "He had locks on the *outside* of the doors, and I bought his story about why."

Callie put her hand on Hannah's shoulder. "You'll get your dreams back, hon'. Give yourself time to heal."

Hannah shot Callie a look. The whites of her eyes were visible all the way around. "You don't know him."

Marlowe growled and moved to the front door.

Sherry left the table and walked to the foyer. Hannah scurried behind.

The same white car that had been in the photos sat in the driveway. When the doorbell chimed, it felt like a bomb exploding.

"It's him!" Hannah cried.

"Get down! Find a wall." Sherry ordered. "And stay quiet."

Sherry pulled her weapon and kept a low profile beside the window.

Marlowe's frantic barking echoed through the home.

The doorbell rang again. When that didn't work, he knocked, waited, and knocked again. Harder.

Sherry stiffened.

Callie crept out of the kitchen. "What's going on?"

"Get back!" Sherry hissed. "Go to Amy's bedroom and lock yourselves in. Now, please."

Callie ran down the hall and into Amy's bedroom. Hannah crouched on the floor beside her, flattening herself against the wall.

Steps crackled through the dry grass. Sherry crammed herself into a corner alongside Hannah. Patrick's face appeared at one of the front windows, his huge hands hooding his eyes as he looked inside.

Nausea climbed Hannah's throat. She closed her eyes.

He moved to another window.

Sherry raced down the hall. "He doesn't know anyone's here yet. I want to keep it that way," she told Hannah. "Stay out of sight against the wall."

Hannah remembered the way she'd felt a blind panic when Patrick duct-taped her to the bed. She had the identical feeling now.

Marlowe's claws click-clacked on the flooring as he raced back and forth between windows. Hannah breathed a prayer of thanks for the dog. Patrick had an aversion to dogs. Maybe the barking would discourage his efforts.

Patrick's face materialized at another window. Sherry jerked back, but too late—he'd seen her. "I just want to talk," he called, his face shapeshifting through the glass.

She glanced at Hannah. "He hasn't seen you yet. Stay still."

Marlowe's barking took on a different tone. His tail wagged. He whined and ran to the front door.

Olivia's here, Hannah thought as she watched Sherry dig out her cell and start texting.

Sherry showed Hannah the answering text from Olivia. *Let Marlowe out.*

Sherry wiped the sweat off her forehead and texted again, showing the phone to Hannah. *He knows I'm in here. Hasn't seen Hannah.*

Voices rose and fell from the driveway. Sherry inched closer to a window to try to hear.

"Patrick will act like the most charming human she's ever met," Hannah whispered.

"Olivia knows what's going on," she said.

Another text came through. Sherry read it to Hannah. *He doesn't know Hannah's in there. I told him the same thing that Callie told him. Let Marlowe out.*

Sherry peeked out the window, then signaled Hannah to let Marlowe out the back. Hannah grabbed Marlowe's collar. "Okay, boy. Here we go," she whispered.

Quiet and slow, she opened the back door, let out the dog, and ran back to her spot beside Sherry. Marlowe loped into the front yard and dropped into a crouch at the sight of Patrick. He snarled. The hackles on the back of his neck rose. Olivia put a hand on Marlowe's back.

"Nice dog," Patrick said, with a tentative step backward as the growling grew more intense.

Marlowe fought against Olivia's hold on his collar and twisted himself loose. He leapt into the air. Patrick screamed, a high-pitched wail like a little girl, and lifted his forearm in a defensive move. Marlowe's intimidating teeth sank into Patrick's arm and clamped down tight. The kicks and curses didn't loosen the dog's jaws a bit, and meanwhile, Olivia fluttered her hands and pretended she didn't know what to do. One of Patrick's kicks landed a solid shot to the ribs that made Marlowe yelp and let go. Patrick jerked his bloody arm to his chest and ran, a trail of blood following him down the driveway to his car.

Olivia gave Sherry a thumbs-up behind her back as she voiced apologies to Patrick.

At the sound of Olivia's sharp whistle and subsequent hand command, Marlowe returned to her side and sat.

Patrick powered down his window. "Get a handle on that damn dog!"

"Sorry about that," Olivia called, smiling and waving as he pulled away.

She patted Marlowe on the head and walked inside.

Sherry opened the front door. "Perfect timing, partner."

Olivia laughed. "He bought my story, I think." Marlowe trotted toward Callie and Amy as they came out of the bedroom.

"Are you guys okay?" Olivia asked. "We sure didn't mean to put you in this position, Cal."

She kept one arm around her daughter and reached out to hug Olivia with the other. "Crazy times," she muttered.

Hannah scowled. "You guys don't need this." She pushed her hair out of her eyes and stared at Olivia. "Maybe he doesn't know about the guest bedroom in your office. I'll be less, um, discoverable there."

Olivia scratched her chin. "Sherry, did Patrick see you when you took Hannah? You think he can ID you?"

She looked at Hannah. "You know where the security cameras are. You think he got a good look at me? I'm so short maybe the cameras didn't catch me."

Hannah thought about it. "Could be. I learned to stay away from them, but I can't remember much about when you came. I didn't have time to think." She rubbed her eyes. "But it's possible. You weren't in the house that long."

Olivia waved one of her hands in dismissal. "Your face is all over our website. I'm sure he knows who you are, but I wanted to find out if he knows *you're* the one who drove her across the state line." She shrugged and looked at her watch. "Callie, I can't thank you enough." She gathered Callie and her daughter in a group hug. "He won't bother you anymore. I said something about your huge, rather weird husband, and he thinks the dog belongs to you, so…"

Callie laughed.

Chapter Twenty-One

Hunter

The flesh wound didn't bother him as much anymore, but the effort of pulling himself into the driver's seat caused him to break a sweat. He raised his shirt to look at the bandage over the stab wound. Blood had seeped through. He jerked his shirt back down.

"Why'd you have to go and play the white knight again?" he mumbled to himself as he roared down the street and onto I-95 North. His buddy Nick's number appeared on the screen. "Hey," Hunter answered.

"What's up, dog?" his friend chided. "Where've you been? I had to hear it from an admin in the DA's office…you get shot?"

"Shot, yeah. Also used as a target for knife-throwing practice."

Nick cursed. "Maybe you should look for another line of work. I thought you'd distanced yourself from all that. What happened?"

Hunter waited.

Nick groaned. "I know what happened. I remember you tellin' me. *Shiloh* happened, didn't she?"

"Yeah."

"So, you got involved after all."

"Good thing I did," Hunter said as he navigated the ramp onto I-95 toward Glyndon, Maryland.

"You in the car?"

"Yeah."

"Why aren't you at home healing?"

"Supposed to be," Hunter admitted.

"Have a good Thanksgiving? Mine consisted of your basic family drama, eating too much, and reinforcing my hatred of life in the suburbs."

Hunter laughed. "My Thanksgiving was good."

"What's the emergency that you can't stay in bed a few days?"

"I'm headed north."

"Uh oh. North? That means Olivia." He chuckled. "There's a limit to madness, dude."

"I know."

"Which one will it be, then?"

Hunter smiled. Nick was the master of the bottom line. "I'm leaning toward Maryland."

"Damn! I had a pot goin' at the office."

"Wait...what?"

Nick laughed. "You're such a freaking flip-flopper. I bet on Shiloh this time. You're going to get shot by that babe, Shiloh, if you're not careful. She's dangerous."

"She is," Hunter agreed. "Case is over, though, and she got hurt real bad. I think our status is on permanent hold."

"Always thought she'd make a better friend. That's a tough kind of female to figure out. Those desperado junkies, y'know? Not for me."

"Let's get together after I'm back. I'll help Olivia with a few things, then be back for the last two weeks of my medical leave."

"You got it."

Three hours stretched out before him. With a yawn, he focused on the road and tried to forget the ache in his shoulder from the gunshot wound and the gash in his stomach still bleeding.

The familiar main drag of Glyndon looked threadbare and sad. The trees had lost most of their leaves, and a hint of snow lurked in the air.

He passed the tidy stores and centuries-old homes and picket fences of historic Glyndon until he arrived at the bottom of a hill with an overlarge mailbox at the street. He turned left onto Olivia's lane and pulled into Watchdog Investigation's parking lot.

He sat a minute, took in the "Watchdog Investigations" sign that he hadn't seen before, and listened to her dog barking. "Marlowe, buddy, it's me," he murmured with a smile. In the parking lot, he counted three vehicles… Olivia's Rover, a Prius, and maybe Sherry's car. He looked at the time. Five p.m.

The door opened. Olivia waved from the small stoop, and Marlowe burst outside and spun in excited circles.

Olivia trotted out to his Jeep. "Marlowe! Sit. Stay."

He sat, but his tail continued thumping the pavement.

"Thanks for savin' me from this vicious dog," Hunter joked, pulling his bag from the back of the Jeep. "Where am I staying'?"

"You're still hurting, aren't you?" she asked, her eyes grazing his shoulder, his belly. He lifted his shirt. "You got another band-aid? A big one?"

She stared at the bleeding and nodded. "After all the mishaps that we've experienced at this office, I have every possible resource that one might need if bleeding is involved."

Marlowe whined.

"Come on, you big baby," Olivia told Marlowe, her arm sweeping toward the door. He raced inside. "He's so happy to see you," Olivia said.

"I'm glad one of you is," Hunter said."

"Oh, good grief, I'm glad to see you, too. Stop it."

"About time you got back here," Sherry said as she left her desk and threw her arms around him, then noticed him wince. "Are you hurt?"

"His shoulder and stomach," Olivia told her.

Beth frowned. "His shoulder and stomach, what?"

"Hunter, meet Beth, our new receptionist."

She studied Hunter's shoulder. "Injuries in the line of duty?"

"Yep," Hunter said, dropping his bag on the floor. "I'm out of commission for a while. Thought I might as well see if I can be of use here while I'm recuperating." Hunter walked over to Beth's desk and extended his hand. "Good to meet you, Beth."

She shook his hand. "Same. Can I get you coffee or water or anything?"

"I know where everything is. I'll get it." He looked at Olivia and pointed toward the back of the building. "Am I in here?"

"Yes. We've got Hannah at Callie's until a space opens for her in the hospital."

"Hospital?" Hunter shook his head. "No. Don't do that. It'll play into his...what's his name? *Patrick.* It'll play into Patrick's hands. Legally, you won't be able to save her if you do that. He can declare her incompetent."

Olivia glanced at Sherry. "They want her to be observed for a while."

"Where is she now?"

"At Callie's."

Hunter stroked his cheek, thinking. "In light of the circumstances, we might put her in your house, and I should stay in your other spare bedroom. That okay? We'll all be in one place, and Marlowe will let us know if anyone's snooping around outside. And do *not* tell the medical professionals that you agree with their assessment that she needs admission to the psych ward. Put them off, do whatever, but don't put her in there. Believe me, this guy will find a way to get her charts and use the information if the situation winds up in court. He's still her husband."

Sherry shot Olivia a "told you so" look. "Sounds good to me."

"Okay, then. Let's get you settled, and we can talk about what's going on."

"I'm heading home," Sherry said. "See you all tomorrow." She left.

Beth pulled her purse from a desk drawer and put on a quilted jacket. "I got to meet the famous Detective Faraday from your Mercy's Miracle days! Imagine that." She fluffed her hair. "I can't wait to tell my friends."

Olivia's smile vanished. "Don't do that! He supposed to be—"

"Under the radar," he finished. "I'd appreciate it if you didn't spread it around."

Beth flipped a thumbs-up. "Got it. See you tomorrow."

Hunter watched out the window as she drove away. "I never knew anyone who drives a Prius."

Olivia laughed. "Lots of people have them."

He shook his head. "Not the ones I know."

Olivia and Hunter looked at each other.

"Let's go into my..."

"I thought we could..."

Hunter lifted his hands. "You first."

"My office is more comfortable than out here."

They walked through the breakroom and into the office.

"I remember this," Hunter announced as he sat in one of the comfortable chairs. "New rug?"

"I can't believe you noticed. Yeah, it is. You haven't been here since we tackled the arsonist situation. It's been a while."

Hunter took a swig of his water. "How's Hazel?"

"She retired and moved to Florida."

He chuckled. "Don't blame her, after that madness with...what's his name?"

"Pete."

Hunter spent a few seconds studying Olivia. Faint lines had developed around her mouth and her eyes. When she moved her head, the gentle lighting from the end table lamps caught a glint of silver in her hair.

She tapped her fingers on the armrest. "What are you doing?"

Hunter smiled and held up his palms.

"Looking at you. You look great."

"Stop."

"Can't a man give a friend a compliment? Don't worry about an agenda, okay?"

"Thanks for clarifying," she said, a hint of sarcasm in her tone.

Hunter refused to pussy-foot around this woman anymore. He would speak his mind and not worry about her reaction. "Okay. So, let's start with Monty. What's going on?"

"Speaking of agendas." She smiled. "He's still in touch with Graham and Sherry, and I think they're colluding with a new client we brought in."

"New client?"

"A man named Curtis requested we surveil his spouse. An easy job, or so we thought."

Marlowe grunted and sighed from his dog bed beside Olivia's desk. She laughed. "He's dreaming."

"I've missed that dog," Hunter said.

"He's missed you, too," she said.

After a beat, she pushed her bangs off her forehead and leaned in. "When we had the brilliant idea to check on Hannah, we decided I should stay, and she should go. I had my doubts, but she convinced me she could do it on her own, so I agreed. But things got dicey, and I started to wonder if it had been planned that way."

Hunter's forehead creased. "Why?"

Olivia blew out an exasperated breath. "Before Sherry left, I wanted to know more about Curtis, and we tailed him to a gentlemen's club on the outskirts of Eldersburg. I thought, well, the guy's a jerk for surveilling his girlfriend if he does stuff like this, but what do I know? It's a job. We wait a while, and then it gets interesting. Callie's husband…remember Graham? Of course, you do. Anyway, he meets our new client there. I don't think that was a coincidence, and on top of all that, I find out Monty's ingratiated himself to the warden, and he's in a work release program." She groaned. "It's like…close. Just around the corner from me."

"Makes sense. Monty doing what he's always done. He's making sure you feel his iron fist." Hunter put down his pen and folded his arms. "No wonder you were distracted at Thanksgiving. Gray's news couldn't have been easy, either. It's a lot," he said, his voice soft.

He felt the urge to take Olivia in his arms. Tell her everything would be fine.

But he didn't know that for sure, did he?

"Yes, I had a break over Thanksgiving, but Gray's news put me in a tailspin. I can't believe how well they're handling it."

Hunter smiled. "Your mom's faith. It's infectious."

Seconds passed.

Olivia's jaw clenched. "It was supposed to be a simple surveillance assignment. I'm thinking Curtis, Graham, and Monty are connected, and the work release plays into it."

CHAPTER TWENTY-ONE

"How do you think they're connected?"

Olivia eyed him. "You, above all people, should know that Monty hasn't changed. He's furious that he's still in prison, that all his manipulations and appeals fell flat, and now he's out for blood. *My* blood." She sighed. "Again. The man never quits."

Hunter stared at the ceiling and tapped his fingertips together as he digested the information. "Tell me what happened next."

"Sherry traveled to Florida and found Hannah. I kept tabs on them by phone, and in the midst of it, Curtis freaks out that I'm not on the way to the job he hired us to do at a dance studio in Eldersburg. I guess Sherry forgot to mention a *specific* date for his job. I hoped he'd wait on Sherry, but he insisted. I had no choice but to go."

Hunter picked up his pen. "Dance studio?"

"She goes to ballroom dance once a week. Takes lessons or something. I did the whole thing, you know…disguise, parked facing the entrance from the darkest corner of the parking lot. I sat there, bored out of my mind. Then she appears like a diva from a movie, all dressed in this pink, fairy-tale, floaty dress." Olivia shook her head. "I didn't know ballroom dancing had a uniform. Anyway, I started clicking off photos. Then a younger guy joins her, also in ballroom attire. I took a thousand pictures, and realized they'd started throwing punches at each other. I kept taking pictures and freaked out when he pulled a knife."

Olivia rubbed her eyes. "I didn't know what to do. I froze. When I came to my senses, I stomped the accelerator. It just…happened. He ran away but…*God.* I almost ran over Victoria."

His fingers trailed across the bandaged knife wound in his belly. "Is the victim deceased?"

"Last time I checked, she was on life support."

Olivia started pacing back and forth. Hunter went into the breakroom and returned with a cup of coffee.

"Here. It'll make you feel better." He slid her hair out of her face with his fingers. "You're crushing it, you know."

She sipped her coffee, thoughtful. "You think?"

"I do."

He watched her wrestle with her emotions. This time, he thought, it had to be her move. It would happen, or it wouldn't. Her call. His thoughts flew to Shiloh in the hospital, and his gunshot shoulder started to throb. He tapped his fingers on the armrest of his chair. He'd been through a lot with *both* these women, and if he had any sense at all, he'd walk away and find someone with a nice, normal life and a kid or two, maybe. Some women had *manageable* baggage, unlike Shiloh and Olivia, who dragged around baggage that could result in shortening his life span. Or theirs.

"Maybe I'm coming into my own," Olivia said. "I feel grounded."

"You called nine-one-one, I'm thinking."

Olivia nodded. "But they didn't ask why I was there, and I didn't tell them."

"Weird they didn't ask."

"I thought so too, but hey. Maybe I got lucky."

He nodded. "You got a file on Curtis you can share with me?"

Olivia walked to her desk and opened her laptop, pecked at it for a few minutes, and returned. "I emailed you the details."

"I assume you agree that Hannah and I should stay at your place?"

"Oh! That's right. Forgot you're not staying here. Yep, let's head down the lane, and I'll order pizza. Is that okay? I'll pick up Hannah and move her to my house."

He sprang from his chair and strode to the door. "Let's go."

Chapter Twenty-Two

Olivia

I t had felt strangely familiar to settle Hunter inside my home last night. Flashes of him in different rooms scrabbled through my mind. I counted the years we'd known each other. Six. "He's almost fifty," I whispered in wonder. It made me sad. Had I shot down any chance at a permanent relationship with him? Should I have accepted his proposal when I had the chance?

Lost in thought, I walked downstairs. Hannah was already up and doing things in the kitchen.

I walked to the breakfast bar and sat on one of the three stools.

Hannah grabbed a tea towel and wiped her hands. "I found bacon and eggs in the fridge. Is that okay to make for breakfast?"

"Sounds good to me."

I watched her rummage through my pantry, my elbow on the counter and my chin resting in my palm. "How're you feeling?"

She rubbed her stomach. "Okay, I guess. I was tired all day and threw up this morning." She lifted a shoulder. "Morning sickness."

My cell buzzed with a text. I ignored it.

"I've been pregnant twice, you know. You can ask me anything."

She cracked eggs into a frying pan and slapped slices of bacon into another one. Then she gripped the edge of the counter and held on, her arms rigid, her head lowered. "What am I going to do?" she whispered.

I straightened. "What do you mean?"

"If I have this baby, it'll have his genetics. And he'll have parental rights." Her eyes darted around my kitchen. "He *can't* find out."

"Hannah, look at me."

Her head stopped swiveling.

"This child has a right to be born. That's what I believe. But I'm not you. What do *you* want?"

Her eyes hardened. "I don't want anything of his in my body."

I'd expected as much. I bit my lip.

"Nine months of this, of waiting for him to find out, and my rights fly right out the window. Nine months of torture, wondering if this infant inside me will turn out like the father. How do people handle this?"

"They keep the child, get an abortion, or work with an adoption agency."

Hannah put both hands on her stomach. "I want to love this child. I do." She looked at me with sad eyes. "I can't," she whispered.

I slid off the stool and put my arms around her. "We'll figure it out. Give it a few days."

Hannah flipped the eggs and poked the bacon with a fork. "As a therapist, Hazel says it's my decision, that she can't give me advice or anything."

"You can tell her you're struggling, though. Sometimes, we arrive at our decisions once the air clears around the trauma. I don't think you're there yet, but you will be."

The bacon sizzled and hissed. "I thought I heard someone walking around last night."

I froze. "Where?"

"In your yard."

Hunter's steps clunked down the stairs and into the kitchen. "Something smells great," he announced, leaning against the kitchen door frame.

Hannah smiled at him. He walked to my Keurig and fixed himself coffee.

"She heard someone last night," I said.

"You did?" He looked at Hannah. "Here?"

Hannah pointed. "Outside."

"Show me," Hunter said.

"I'll take over breakfast," I told her.

They walked out of the kitchen. I heard my red screen door snap shut, their steps on the porch and beyond.

Fifteen minutes later, they returned.

"Help yourself," I said, cocking my head at the plates and silverware and food.

"I think she's right. Someone was here," Hunter told me when Hannah had gotten her breakfast and sat out of earshot.

"Where?"

"I saw tire tracks at the edge of the property, and it looks like someone walked into the undergrowth to surveil. We found a flattened area, busted sticks and vines, and a tree limb about waist high they could prop their arms on. If someone had good binoculars, they'd see straight into the kitchen."

The floor slipped away from me.

"I have a test for you, now that you are an official PI with experience," he continued.

I blinked. "Okay."

"What would your next steps be? If I weren't here?"

My lips squiggled themselves into various shapes as I thought it through.

"Loaded firearms in strategic places. Close all blinds and windows. Keep exterior lights blazing."

"Good."

"Marlowe remains loose in the house at night."

"Yep."

"Police report as soon as possible."

"Big one," he agreed. "Tomorrow," he emphasized. "Why?"

"So she can get a restraining order."

He pointed his index finger. "You passed my test. I'll call the PD and ask them to come out."

My heart slowed down. I took a breath. The warmth filling my chest had everything to do with him sitting here with me, quizzing me on defensive moves. I couldn't think of anything more reassuring. "Thank you, Hunter."

Hannah peered through the screen door. "Breakfast is getting cold," she said.

After breakfast, I took Hannah back to Callie's and went to work. Hunter and Sherry put their heads together while I took care of more mundane matters. Beth sat in and, as she put it, "tried to learn everything she could." I gave her diligence points for effort. The day passed without incident.

Later that night, I lay in bed and remembered all the times Hunter had slept one wall away, while I wilted in my own bed, longing for his touch.

I groaned and rolled over.

A knock sounded on the wall.

I felt my eyes widen. I scrunched the covers against my mouth.

The knock rapped again. Then a muffled, "You up?" Through the wall.

No, no. You are not up.

My eyes cut to the other side of the room, the wall that separated my bedroom from Hannah's.

On one side, Hannah's situation lurked slick and mean, and I needed to conserve all my energy to stay alert. On the other side, Hunter's many attributes pulled me like a magnet, and I knew I couldn't give in to them right now. A trouble sandwich.

"You made a promise to yourself," I hissed underneath the covers.

"Did you say something?"

No. No. Shh. No!

After a few minutes I heard him shift in his bed. Then he said, "I know you heard me."

I giggled.

Then I rolled over and tried to fall asleep.

Chapter Twenty-Three

Hannah

L ike most mornings, she woke early. Today, she gasped when her eyes flew open, struggling for air.

You're safe. Remember? It's okay.

The deafening voices stalked her each night. Patrick would *find her and kill her.* Then the spin cycle began: the whirling of his words, threats, accusations. The crazy-making. To stop the cycle meant getting out of bed.

She stepped over to the mirror above the dresser. Her hair had started falling out. Hannah looked at her fingernails. Once so long and healthy, stress had made them soft and prone to peel, so she had to keep them short. She couldn't remember the last time she'd had a manicure. Her undereye shadows refused to go away due to her chronic sleeplessness. She held her arms out to each side and smiled.

"At least you've filled out a little."

She pictured Olivia and Sherry's expressions when she'd asked for her phone. They were right, though. If she powered it on, Patrick would find her and break down the door in to get to her. Plus, he had a way of wearing down her defenses, making her think she'd betrayed his poor, wounded soul. She had to remember the evil in him.

Head cocked back, eyes closed, she sighed.

"Those crazy bitches. They have no idea what he's capable of." She crept downstairs and made sure all the windows and doors remained locked. She

149

frowned. The familiar clatter of Marlowe's paws and his friendly nose-bumps were absent this morning.

"Marlowe?" she called. "Here, boy!"

Nothing.

Hannah yawned and walked into the kitchen for something to eat. Sounds of scratching tickled the door. She frowned. A squirrel? Raccoon? She peered out the window. Marlowe lay on the porch, weakly lifting his paw. She jerked open the door, her head swiveling in all directions, and tugged the dog inside. Hannah squatted and looked into his eyes. "What's wrong, Marlowe?" she whispered. He whined.

She raced upstairs and pounded on Olivia's bedroom door. "We have to take Marlowe to the vet!"

After a few seconds, Olivia's sleepy face appeared as she cracked the door. "Something's wrong with him!"

They ran downstairs into the kitchen. Olivia fell to her knees and stroked Marlowe gently as he lay twitching on the floor. "Let's get him into my car."

Hannah and Olivia muscled him into the backseat.

They left him with the vet, who told them he'd be in touch. Olivia asked Hannah if she'd go with her to the office, but Hannah begged off, promising to stay inside. Olivia told her she wouldn't be gone long.

Three hours later, she regretted not going. She'd straightened her room and downed three cups of coffee. The nervous energy from all that caffeine made her crazy. She grabbed one of Olivia's jackets, walked outside into the sunshine, and sat on Olivia's front porch swing for a little while.

She glanced down the lane that ended at Olivia's office building and realized she had time to search for her phone. It would give her hints about Patrick's plans, and against her better judgment, she began a search. Kitchen cabinets. Dresser drawers. Sideboard drawers. Foyer table drawers.

Nothing.

She went upstairs and searched Olivia's bedroom.

She found her phone in Olivia's bedside table drawer, along with the charger. She rolled her eyes. Olivia had always been the organized one, but still. Her nightstand drawer? How unimaginative. She took the phone into her bedroom and charged it.

What would she find on her phone? Had Olivia blocked Patrick's number? Or worse, erased her contacts? Taken it back to factory defaults? What if she'd changed the password and she couldn't access anything? Her forehead felt sweaty; her heart pounded in her chest. Discovering what was on the phone wouldn't end well, but she couldn't help herself. Patrick had kept it from her for so long that she couldn't be without it again. Sherry and Olivia had unwittingly continued the cycle of isolation and fear with their incessant insulation. She felt like a trapped animal.

After a few minutes, the phone sprang to life.

Notifications popped up, one after the other, dating back months. Olivia hadn't paid any attention to this phone, just tossed it in a drawer. The texts from Patrick sounded too polite and bordered on creepy, and yet, she felt the stirrings of regret. The three long texts from Monty curdled in her gut like spoiled milk, but she texted him back anyway. He'd had a magnetic pull on her ever since she'd first visited him in prison. Did he know she'd fled from her marriage in an attempt at a normal life? Memories of how close they'd been ran through her mind. Not that she wanted a relationship with him now—she'd learned not to trust him—but he could be useful. With a sigh, she checked her emails and messages, powered off the phone, and put it back into the nightstand, along with the charger. Olivia didn't need to know she'd found the phone, and now she had a better sense of her situation.

Steps pattered onto the porch. The front door squealed open. "Hannah! Marlowe's ready to pick up. Please go with me."

Hannah jumped off Olivia's bed, smoothed the spread, and trotted downstairs.

"The vet said his blood panel and symptoms point to poison."

She gasped.

"He could've eaten something, I guess," Olivia said. "But I don't think it was random."

Olivia stared at Hannah for a few seconds. "Let's go get my dog."

When they returned, Hannah and Olivia settled Marlowe in his dog bed. Olivia insisted she accompany her to her office, but Hannah refused, told her someone needed to keep an eye on Marlowe. "Fine, I'll work from home," Olivia told her. "I'm going to pick up my laptop and a few files and come right back."

"No need," Hannah insisted.

"I don't mean to state the obvious, but you *do* remember why you're here, right?"

Hannah folded her arms. "I'm fine."

"You will be, eventually," Olivia relented, "but please. I need you to stay put for half an hour, tops."

Olivia surrounded Marlowe with every doggie comfort available and left.

Hannah squatted beside him and felt his neck. A nice, strong pulse. A tear straggled down her cheek. She felt so bad about it, and she had to do *something.* No one else needed to suffer because of her choices.

She paced through the house, thinking that once again, she'd put herself in a prison, although a much nicer one than Patrick's had been. She pulled a jacket from Olivia's coat closet and, with silent apologies to Olivia, exited through the back door for a quick walk. The sunny weather would do her good. She speed-walked the back path with a smile, planning to turn around at mid-point and go back inside. A cardinal dropped from the sky and swept so close she felt the brush of its wings on her cheek. She laughed.

From the line of bushes that bordered the path, a voice interrupted her thoughts.

"You really love cardinals, don't you, my love?"

Chapter Twenty-Four

Hunter

Hunter shot out of bed with a muttered profanity. Why had he slept so late?

He remembered some ruckus about the dog this morning, but Olivia had told him to go back to sleep, so he had. Now, the house seemed as quiet as a tomb. He took a quick shower and got dressed, then trotted downstairs. The quietness felt suffocating. His damn gut again, nudging him to keep his eyes and ears open. He walked through each room and found Marlowe in the den. On the side table close to Marlowe's bed lay a piece of paper with typed instructions. And a bottle of pills. He connected the dots—someone had poisoned the dog. He exhaled, rubbed his eyes, and bent down to pet the sleeping dog. Olivia's cat, Riot, had curled himself into a ball beside the dog bed. "You've got good company, bud," he told Marlowe and reached out to give Riot a pat on the head, too.

"Hannah?" he called, checking each room.

Nothing.

"Hannah!" he called, striding through the kitchen and into the backyard.

He heard the faint sound of a woman's shriek from the direction of the lane between Olivia and Callie's houses. He ran inside for his firearm, then rushed down the lane and arrived at her front porch in six minutes. Callie opened the door to his urgent knocking.

"What's going on?"

"Have you seen Hannah?"

She took note of the heavy breathing, the brusque tone. Her hand rose to her throat. "No," she whispered. "Should I have?"

"Stay inside and lock the doors," he told her and ran back the way he'd come.

He juggled his phone out of his pocket and paused, scanning the perimeter as he waited for Olivia to answer.

"Wondered if I'd hear from you sometime today. You must've needed the sleep."

"Is Hannah there?" he blurted.

A slight pause. "She's supposed to be there with you."

"She isn't in the house."

"She's not with me. Did you try Callie?"

Hunter groaned. "I heard a woman's voice a few minutes ago. As in, a *scared* woman's voice. I already asked Callie. Hannah hasn't been there this morning. The police are supposed to come by and get her report, but I can't find her."

Hunter shoved the phone back in his pocket. He took note of the undergrowth on one side of the path and the privacy fencing on the other. His gaze landed on the bushes, perfect ambush cover. Muttering to himself, he swept aside foliage and branches as he searched. Memories flooded his mind. Three years ago, he'd awakened in surroundings exactly like this with a crushing headache from a whack on the head outside Olivia's office building, and here he was again. Déjà vu. He rubbed his shoulder, his belly wound. The unhealthy prospect of staring down the wrong end of someone's firearm did not sit well. He could've at least waited until he'd healed from the last time.

He crept carefully through the space and found three cigarette butts and footprints. He punched in the number to Westminster PD to get the crime scene folks out here.

Two hours later, Olivia and Hunter watched the patrol vehicle pull out of Watchdog Investigation's parking lot.

"Dammit," Hunter sputtered in frustration.

Olivia rubbed his arm. "Don't beat yourself up. She's been like a monk. We never expected her to go off on her own like that."

They walked into the lobby.

Sherry looked up from her desk, her brow rutted with concern. "So, do they think he took her?"

Hunter lifted his good shoulder in what passed for a shrug. "Can't hurt to put it on Westminster PD's radar. They have his information and it'll get dispersed to all patrol units. The thing is, we know he's here, but he probably used an alias. I can drive around and see if I can spot a white rental SUV, but how many hotels are in the area?"

Olivia groaned. "I shouldn't have left her alone."

"You didn't! I was there. It's on me." He shook his head and frowned. "She probably got tired of staying in and decided to go over to Callie's. Like I mentioned before, Patrick could've known about the path back there."

Olivia trained her gaze on Sherry. "Can you audit the rental services within a fifty-mile radius? Let's see if we can find that rental. Hunter? What else?"

"Do you have her phone?"

Olivia nodded. "I do. I made sure it's powered off and the locator is disabled, then hid it."

They piled into the Rover and sped to her house. Olivia ran upstairs, found the phone, raced back into the den, and powered it on. "It's got a charge. Hannah must've found it and powered it on." She stared at him. "Now what?"

"We assume Patrick surveilled both houses when you saw the guy the first time." Hunter cocked his head toward Marlowe, who'd lifted his head and wagged his tail. "I'm glad he's going to be all right."

Olivia shook her head. "I couldn't believe it. I don't think Monty or Graham would be capable of something so cruel. It had to be Patrick."

"It's great you have her phone, but it won't do any good without a password."

"I got her passwords when she was in the hospital," Olivia told him with a lift of her eyebrows. "She doesn't remember. The meds made her sleepy."

Hunter grinned. "Good job. Well then, let's see what we've got."

Olivia scrolled through. "What a creep," she whispered as she read text after text, pausing. She looked at Hunter. "She's recently texted Monty. It's like, a generic touch-base kind of text, but why would she do that?"

Riot sauntered through the den, his tail brushing both their legs. Olivia smiled at him. "I need to feed my cat. Back in a sec."

Hunter reached for the phone when she returned. "Let's hand this over to the cops and…"

"Now, hold on a minute." Olivia frowned. "They're not going to jump on this immediately, you know, and *we can*. They've still got to verify her as missing and do their research. They have those cigarette butts, right? Are they sending them out for DNA? Which takes forever." She wagged the phone in the air. "Let's not send the phone yet. Let's play Patrick's game."

"Let me see." Hunter read the texts, then switched to emails.

He pointed. "The one I left open. Read that. It's from Monty. Are they still in touch after she told you she'd learned her lesson? What's it been, five years since she developed a crush on him in prison? I thought you guys had this big discussion about better choices. Remember?"

Olivia grunted in disgust. "Of course, I remember! How could I forget? I'm just as mystified as you are. I did a sweep of her phone. I didn't think I should delete anything."

Hunter frowned. "Could Monty know the husband?"

"I have no idea." She started reading the email aloud: 'I've done a lot of thinking about the last time you visited me, and I've forgiven you. I know you thought you were doing the right thing. I want to talk. We can start fresh. I need you on my side, Hannah. I miss you'.

"Ew." Olivia held out the phone to him. "Take it back. How did I miss that one?"

"Manipulators. Like you said, it's a game. She fell for it once."

Olivia tapped her chin. "She's so vulnerable right now, too. I don't think she understands that it'll take months, maybe years, to get her bearings."

"If Monty knows she's been in that situation, he'll use it."

Olivia dropped her head. "When will he finally cut ties? I mean, how long can he maintain this insanity? I don't feel like I should have *any* friends. He gets to all of them!"

Hunter held the phone up and pointed it at Olivia. "We need to back up all these texts before we hand it over to the authorities."

Olivia took the phone. "Okay. I'll get Beth to take care of it."

"We can't afford to have them cut off service to this phone. Would you ask that she also check on who's paying the bill?"

"Yep. I should've already done that. It's been hard to focus."

Hunter hesitated, then reached out and put his hand on her shoulder. "We'll find her."

Olivia reached up and placed her hand on his. "Thank you. I'm so glad you're here."

His grip tightened on her shoulder. She held his gaze. He put his hand on her cheek and drank her in a few seconds. "I've missed you so much."

She lifted her face. It took him a second to realize that she actually *wanted* him to kiss her. So, he did. For a long time. Afterward, her flushed face and warm, hazel eyes held the promise of more. Sort of. He'd been wrong before.

"Let's find her," he said, his arms sliding away. "You ready?"

"I'm ready," she said quietly.

Chapter Twenty-Five

Olivia

The house without Hannah felt cold and empty and terrible. I walked around muttering all the things I should've done or should *not* have done. In a surge of emotion, I bundled up and plopped myself onto my loveseat on the front porch, in spite of the freezing temps. I always thought better on my front porch. I surveyed my yard. The birds had migrated, and my lonesome bird feeders hung bedraggled and empty from their hooks. Sunshine peeked out from behind winter clouds, making my eyes water. I closed my eyes and tried to think. He'd take her straight back to Florida, his own turf. I looked up into the sky, trying my best to channel my late mentor, whom I missed with everything within me. "What did you use to say, Tom? That the simplest path to a solution is also the most overlooked?" The heavens remained silent, but in my heart, I felt a solid conclusion. We'd be making a trip to Niceville, Florida.

My cell vibrated. I pulled it from my pocket. Beth. "Morning."

"Are you coming in today?"

I looked at the time and bit my lower lip. Oops. "Sorry. Lost track of time. I'll be there in a few."

She chuckled. "I didn't want someone else disappearing on us."

I flinched.

"Sorry," Beth said. "Bad joke."

You think?

"Here's some good news. Sherry found Patrick's rental car. He turned it in last night."

I felt a shot of adrenaline shoot straight up my back. "Did she get the alias?"

"Pat Samuels."

"Close to his real name. A hotel front desk clerk wouldn't even blink at his driver's license."

"Yep. He didn't leave an address or a card. He paid in cash."

I frowned. "Of course he did."

The cold had seeped into my skin through my coat. Ice lingered on the doorframe from last night's freeze. The warmth and smell of coffee inside my cozy farmhouse embraced me like a hug. Hunter walked out holding a mug in one hand and extending another to me.

"Cream and sugar, right?"

The mug felt warm in my hands. "Thanks." I sipped. "Sherry found Patrick's rental."

He nodded. "She texted me. Also, his alias. I followed up with the rental desk and they confirmed he had a woman with him that fit Hannah's description."

"You've been busy."

"What's the plan?"

"A trip to Florida?" I asked, gauging his reaction.

He nodded. "Already called Niceville PD. Small department, but they're on it and sending someone out to check on Patrick's place."

I sighed. "Wish I could hire you."

"Why? You get me for free." He grinned. "We all going?"

"Let me get Beth or Callie to take care of my boys and throw a few things into a duffel." I ran upstairs, fear for Hannah heavy in my chest. I felt my teeth clamp down, my jaw clench. One way or another, Patrick would no longer enjoy life as a free citizen.

My cell lit up with a call. *Unknown.* After a blip of hesitation, I took the call.

"I saw you."

The sucker punch worked. Victoria's pink chiffon swam before my eyes. I almost fell to my knees. "Who is this?"

He laughed.

I felt my forehead constrict. "What do you want?"

But only dead air responded. With a long exhale, I ended the call and continued getting ready for the Florida trip. The timing seemed too perfect. Had I told Callie what had happened with Victoria? Had she inadvertently told Graham? Why would a caller dump a threat on me just before I leave? I looked around the room, holding a folded T-shirt and pair of jeans to my chest. Had someone put up cameras in my house? Secreted a microphone, somewhere?

"Stop it," I commanded myself, and threw the clothes in my duffel.

I yanked my packed duffel over my shoulder and strode into Hannah's room to gather what she might need when we found her. If the cops found out I had pictures of the actual homicide, I was toast. Is that what someone saw? Me taking pictures?

Sherry greeted me the minute I walked in the door. "I made reservations."

I blinked. "Wait..."

"You didn't think I'd fool around with this, did you? We *have* to go. I figured you and Hunter would come to the same conclusion."

Hunter walked inside behind me. "You were right on the money," he said. "Who's car?"

I lifted my arm like a student in a classroom, waiting for permission to answer. It boggled my mind that Sherry could now *predict* my behaviors. Was it possible to know each other too well? "We can take the Rover to the airport." I looked at Beth, who sat there watching us, unblinking and still.

"We'll be at least two or three days, Beth. Put people off, make up something about where we went, and we'll get them when we come back. Can you watch Marlowe and Riot?"

She nodded, folding her plump arms like a disapproving granny. "Are you sure you guys want to do this?"

Something in her eyes gave me pause. "Yes. But you need to keep it quiet."

"Beth, if you're worried, don't be," Hunter said. "I have some ideas that'll get us inside that asshole's house. Bam. Game over. The police can't enter without a warrant, and unless there's a friendly judge, we don't have enough evidence for one. We're going to get it."

Beth's jaw dropped. She looked at Hunter. "Aren't you worried about losing your job? An off-duty cop isn't supposed to aid in an investigation, right?"

Hunter shrugged. "It's a risk, I know. I'll be careful." He winked. "It's not an official investigation."

Sherry threw out her arms. "Let's go!"

The minute we deplaned and got our luggage, we scouted car rental places until we found a Rent-A-Wreck. We didn't want to stick out like a sore thumb in his neighborhood, so we chose a slightly abused Chevy Impala that had thug-tinted windows. We sped down Highway 10 like lunatics. We had to crack the windows due to the stench of cigarette smoke.

"There it is," Sherry said, pointing at Patrick's house as we rolled by.

To me, it looked vacant. A dump for squatters.

"I know," she agreed. "It's awful. I only saw the interior a few minutes because we had to hurry, but I noticed he has bars on the windows. *Inside.*"

"I didn't even know that was a thing," I said.

Hunter drove us past the house. I watched in the rear-view. The backyard had a fence around it, and as Sherry had indicated, bars had been installed on each window and door. "I guess Patrick doesn't like to mow the yard."

Sherry grunted. "We all know what Patrick likes to do."

We made a U-turn, then headed back the other way. "That's where he parks, but there's no car. They might not be here yet," she said, pointing at the backyard. "Hannah would never accept a trashy yard like that. Remember how beautiful her flowers were in the spring at her place in Maryland?"

I couldn't think about it. All I wanted to think about was the end result: forcing the smug grin off his face and holding him at gunpoint until the Niceville cops put him in handcuffs. I wanted it so bad I'd visualized the scene the entire trip.

We passed his one-story, circa 1960 home again as we drove the other way.

Sherry squealed. "That's it! See that little window beside the front steps? It's coated with dirt, but that's where he keeps her. That's his 'punishment room.' Poor thing watched people come to the front door. She could only see their legs from that angle, but she made her hands bleed, bashing the window and trying to rip out the bars. He must've installed insulated glass and soundproofed the room. Remember? Hazel told us she'd heard muted sounds, and Patrick explained them away."

"He's got it locked down tighter than a prison," Hunter said.

Sherry and I stared at each other.

"She can't be dead," Sherry said, putting a voice to our thoughts.

"This is what I think," Hunter said, tightening his grip on the steering wheel. "Hannah would've been hysterical. It wouldn't have taken much to get her to quiet down, though; she's been there before. She knows what happened, and now he's got her in a locked car. An abused woman is conditioned by the abuser's emotional and physical violence. Hannah wouldn't try to escape until she's taken his pulse, so to speak. Find out where his head's at." He turned and looked at our stricken faces. "That's the sad truth, ladies."

I closed my eyes, feeling a symbiotic pain for Hannah that I could not explain with words. Sneaking a peek at Sherry, I could tell she felt the same. I reached for her hand. She grabbed it. We hung onto each other a few seconds.

"Okay, gang, let's go," Hunter concluded as the stars began to pop out. "We can't let him see us driving back and forth, and it's obvious they're not here yet. Let's find a nice, quiet diner and make a plan."

"I have a better idea," I said. "Hazel offered her house overnight and invited us to dinner."

"A much better option," he said.

We drove to Pensacola along the coast with the windows down, watching the night sky and listening to the waves pound the beach, hoping Hannah would survive the night.

Chapter Twenty-Six

Hannah

She regained consciousness in Atlanta.

With careful fingers, she explored her scalp. The pounding in her head felt like someone had taken a hammer to it. Little rainbows floated in front of her eyes when she tried to sit up. She couldn't remember what happened. An upright position made her so dizzy that she threw up the scant contents of her stomach.

Patrick cursed. "Now I have to stop and clean out the freaking back seat. There's a plastic bag back there. Use it."

Hannah's heart stopped. Patrick? The last thing she remembered had been walking to Callie's…Olivia's house had begun to remind her of being trapped in Patrick's house…so she wanted to shake off that feeling and took the bold step to go outside. It had been wonderful…the sun on her face, the crunch of last night's frost underfoot, the chilly breeze. She'd enjoyed watching the birds. Nausea hit her stomach again, and she dry-heaved for several seconds. She eased down on the seat to her back. She stared at the headliner of the car, the backs of the front seats, the treetops scrolling past the windows as they drove. The big sign that told her they'd just crossed into Atlanta.

She cleared her throat. "What did you use this time?"

Patrick laughed. "The gold standard. Rohypnol. You can't remember anything, can you?"

"My head is killing me. Please. Get me something."

He threw a plastic bottle of water in the back seat, followed by a container of ibuprofen. "That should fix it. Take four."

"I would if I could open my eyes. I can't move, or I'll get sick again."

"For Christ's sake," he fumed. The car slowed; she heard the tires grind over gravel, then stop. Hannah felt the car shudder as other vehicles sped by. He'd parked on the shoulder of a major highway. When she felt more human, perhaps she could find a way into the trunk and kick out a brake light so a cop would pull them over. She doubted she'd survive another onslaught of Patrick's abuse. The easy way out taunted her, seducing her like a lovely fantasy. She'd had plenty of time to think about ending her life. She stared at the bandages on her wrists. "Why didn't I die?" she whispered.

Patrick opened the back door of the sedan, reached to the floorboard and retrieved the water. Grabbing a fistful of hair, he lifted her head and put the bottle to her lips. She drank. "Better," he said, popping the lid of the ibuprofen and pouring four of them into his hand. "Open," he whispered. Hannah opened. He lifted her, gentler this time, and helped her get the pills down. It amazed her how gentle and kind he could be when he wanted to.

Patrick slid onto the seat, put her head in his lap, and shut the door. "You're going home, sweetheart." He stroked her hair. Hannah flinched at his touch, but the old helplessness vanquished any resolve to fight. Struggling against him led to bouts of torment she didn't want to think about. Patrick put his arms around her and held her close when she started to cry. Hannah cried even harder, his smell reminding her of all the things he could do to make her life a living hell. How she despised the smell of him, his touch, his breath, his darting eyes, never still.

Patrick kissed her on the forehead. "I'd kiss you on the mouth, but I'd rather not partake of the uh...you know." He laughed. "You'll feel better in a few minutes," he said. He slid her head off his lap and returned to the driver's seat.

When a siren wailed in the distance, Patrick let out a string of profanities and remained parked on the shoulder to wait it out. Hannah struggled to the door's armrest and used it to push herself upright and put her face against the window. She groped for the back console's window controls. A quiet squeak of excitement burst from her lips when she found the window control. The siren wail grew louder.

She peeked out the window.

Patrick pounded the steering wheel and muttered something under his breath, his focus rock-solid on the cop's approach. He jerked on sunglasses and a ball cap.

The patrol vehicle would pass them any second. Hannah pushed the control. The window powered down. With a glance at Patrick, Hannah plunged her arms out of the window and whipped them back and forth.

It took a few seconds before he noticed. He spun around. "What are you...?" His face reddened. He rammed a fist into her cheekbone. Hannah's head jerked, she felt blood in her mouth; but she kept moving her arms. "Stop!" Patrick yelled, fumbling for the window controls. The back window rose. She gasped and snatched her arms back inside, but it caught her underneath her chin. The screaming siren passed them. Patrick reversed the window.

Thirty seconds later, a patrol vehicle eased in behind the car on the shallow bit of shoulder, parking at an angle. A young cop in uniform exited the vehicle and walked to the driver's side, his eyes flicking to Hannah lying in the back seat. He asked for license and registration and told Patrick to step outside and move away from the car. Patrick got out, explained who he was, and told him Hannah had fallen because she'd been nauseous and they were on their way to an urgent care facility. Patrick made a joke about her attempts at signaling for help and downplayed it. Hannah stared blankly at the ceiling liner.

The officer inquired of Hannah, who tried to communicate distress with her eyes. The young officer told them the location of the closest medical facility and offered a police escort. As he talked into the mic on his shoulder and walked back to the car, Patrick scooted into the driver's seat and opened the glove compartment. He pulled out his firearm. Hannah watched his head and shoulders from her prone position in the back. She heard the metallic click of the safety release. She watched the back of his head turn left and right as he scanned their surroundings and the position of the police cruiser on the shoulder of the highway. Hannah felt her vision blur; her mind clawing back from a sudden hysteria. Patrick was checking the dashcam angle! *NO! Patrick, don't!*

Patrick eased from the car, barely opening the door, and slid to the ground. She heard his body rake across the gravel and his soft curses as he crawled underneath the rental car, bumping his head.

The pop-pop of two shots made her scream. She felt the bounce of the car as he rolled out from underneath and jumped inside.

Hannah propped herself up on her arms and looked out the back window.

The young patrol officer lay on the ground beside his vehicle, blood pooling around his body. A sob stuck in her throat. He'd been more worried about getting her to the ER than keeping an eye on Patrick. He hadn't had a chance.

Her eyelids fluttered, a swirling vertigo overwhelmed her, and she lost consciousness.

Hannah's eyes flew open. She felt the stiffness of the fake leather upholstery and realized she hadn't died as she'd hoped. How long had she been unconscious? Hours, apparently. Dying had been nice to think about, but she was still in the damn car.

Patrick made a hard turn.

She blinked and pushed herself up. The world had stopped spinning, and her head felt better.

"I hope you're happy," Patrick said.

"I'm *so* happy," she responded, her voice dripping sarcasm.

He frowned. "That cop back there? He'd still be alive if you hadn't drawn attention to us."

She blinked. What? The memory opened like a parachute and made its descent. Hannah moaned in despair. Why hadn't *she* died instead of the nice, young police officer who tried to help her?

"You've forgotten what your husband is capable of, sweetheart." Patrick laughed.

The loathing she felt for this man climbed up her windpipe. "I haven't forgotten. *You're* the one who's forgotten how determined my friends are. Your days are numbered, asshole. I don't care anymore what happens to me."

His arm whipped over the seats. She dodged his grabs for her hair, her throat, anything he could touch. "Let me out!" she screamed. "Let me out!" she screamed again, falling over in a heap, the sobs coming thick and fast and choking her. "Let me out..." she whispered.

Twenty minutes later, Patrick turned off the engine after he'd parked behind the house. "I'm bone-tired," he announced, with a wry glance at Hannah. "Not that you'd care. C'mon. We're home."

Hannah glared at the back of the house, lurking like a demonic presence in the darkness: the barred windows, the overgrown grass, the rotting trash. He opened the sedan's back door. She felt her lips pull back in a snarl. Fear erupted from her throat in a primal scream. She lunged, her thumbs digging into his eyes. Patrick howled in anguish and tried to throw her off, but adrenaline had turned her into a machine. Her fingers a vise around his temples and eye sockets, she head-butted his chest and focused all her strength into keeping her thumbs in place. Patrick howled in pain, stumbled backward, and tried to unseat his wife's vise-like grip on his eye sockets. When she felt the time was right, she ducked beneath his arms, and scrambled away. Patrick stood beside the car, shouting profanities. Screaming threats and rubbing his eyes. Hannah considered her options: go back to the hellhole or disappear into the Florida wetlands.

Her legs felt like rubber and her vision swam, but she stumbled forward toward the marshes. She exhaled hard, closed her eyes, and mouthed a quick prayer. Then she ran.

Chapter Twenty-Seven

Olivia

Hazel opened the blinds in the bedroom with a hard tug that sounded like a buzz saw.

I threw off the comforter and lurched from the bed. "What is it?"

Hazel chuckled. "There you are! Figured I'd better wake you as you have things to do and places to be."

I exhaled the breath I'd been holding. "I forgot for a minute."

"I can see that." Her eyes twinkled. "It's wonderful to have the three of you here. Breakfast is ready, so come on in when you can."

After Hazel left, I took a quick shower, flicked a comb through my wet hair, swiped on a few minutes' worth of makeup, and walked into the kitchen. Hunter and Sherry sat at the kitchen table, eating bacon and eggs and drinking coffee.

"Are we all refreshed and ready for battle, ladies?" He looked at me. "Grab something to eat, and let's get started. It's going to be a long day."

"Give me ten minutes," I told him. "What did Niceville PD say?"

"They verified her husband's workplace and that he is supposed to be in today, but that's about all they'd say. They are definitely not going overboard to help. He'd been on 'a short vacation', I was told. They've been keeping an eye on his property, though, so that tells me they might be taking this thing seriously. He got home around three a.m."

I scarfed down the food on the plate Hazel sat before me, mumbling my thanks through chewing my food as fast as possible. I knew we needed the strength. No telling what we were looking at today. We'd sat at Hazel's kitchen table last night, weighing every option until our brains wouldn't work anymore.

Hunter placed his elbows on the kitchen table, lacing his fingers. "They drove it in one day. He's at work, at least for now, and we need to proceed with extreme caution. Our perp is operating with lack of sleep, stress, and the assumption that a police report has been filed. Anyway, he confronted one of the patrols assigned to his area this morning before he went to work, and the officer fabricated a story about feral boars or something. We've got a window."

I nodded, and accepted a water bottle from Hazel. "I sure hope we have time to drag Hannah through that window."

Within five minutes, we'd hugged Hazel goodbye, promised we'd try to come by one more time before we left, and sped off to Patrick's house. I hated to think what his house looked like in the light of day. It had looked bad enough in the gray fog of twilight yesterday.

I'd talked Hunter into letting me drive. I wanted him to focus on our getaway plan for Hannah instead of the road. He sat in the front passenger seat, studying his phone. Every time it buzzed, I tensed. My shoulders had gotten so knotted and hard it would take a pickaxe to get them back to normal.

"Niceville PD is not going to do anything without a warrant to search Patrick's place," Hunter said. "That's why we're here. If they won't move on this, we'll have to poke around."

His cell buzzed. I flinched. He aimed a chuckle in my direction, and answered his call.

Sherry watched the Florida landscape roll by from the back seat. I flew down Highway 10, well above the limit. I made a conscious decision to slow down because we did *not* need a speeding ticket.

"Dammit!" His voice thundered through the car after the call. My hands tightened on the steering wheel.

I glanced at him. "What?"

"A highway stop yesterday, outside Atlanta. A woman that fits Hannah's description signaled for help from the back window of a rental vehicle."

I grew light-headed. I took a deep breath and focused on the road.

"The patrol officer's bodycam captured the stop. One problem, though."

"What kind of problem?" Sherry asked from the back seat.

"The patrol officer that checked on them took two shots to the back. They found him by his vehicle. The driver wore sunglasses and a cap, and the bodycam captured what appeared to be a friendly conversation, so the kid dropped his guard. Rookie cop. The footage is compromised...the cameras didn't capture the shooting as he walked back to the cruiser." His jaw clenched. "An attorney will tear it apart, but the good thing is the whole county is going to be looking for Patrick now." Hunter stared out the window. "The young guy didn't survive. The jerk killed a cop. No coming back from that."

Silent seconds passed.

"Do we have vests?" I asked Hunter, with a glance at Sherry. She looked pale.

He shook his head. "I didn't think to bring them, but I should have, I guess. I don't have any authority to arrest anyone in a different state, and I'm not collaborating on a case, so I didn't think we'd need them."

I bit a fingernail. "We're not collaborating, we're finding evidence."

Hunter chuckled. "Yeah. *That's* what we're doing. We're finding something, but anything we find there cannot be used in court, it would be ruled an illegal search and seizure."

"Then what are we doing?" Sherry asked.

"Let's not get ahead of ourselves. If she's in that house, we'll grab her and get outta there. I'll loop in Niceville PD, tell them we felt imminent danger, blah blah. They'll extend me courtesy, I can already tell they're on our side, but it's tricky. Patrick is from a political family with deep roots in the area. They have to handle this with discretion."

He twisted toward the back. "Sherry?"

She edged closer.

CHAPTER TWENTY-SEVEN

"How'd you get in the first time?" he asked.

"I picked the lock."

He nodded, thinking. "He might've changed them to combination locks."

"Those aren't pickable?"

"You can, but it's a lot of trouble. It takes time."

"We can try the back door."

"You said that lower window in the front is the room where he keeps her?"

"Sometimes," Sherry said. "When she's done something he considers an infraction, he sticks her in there."

"I didn't see any cameras outside," he continued.

"They're inside," Sherry said. "One at the front door."

"We'll know what to do when we get there," I said with a confidence I didn't feel.

We lapsed into silence and watched the Florida landscape scroll by. Ten minutes later, we arrived. I drove past the house at fifteen miles per hour.

Patrick's home sat behind a chain link fence with a padlocked gate at the front sidewalk.

Sherry snorted in disgust. "He's added the padlock. That gate was open when I was here."

"I don't see a vehicle," Hunter said. "Which story did we decide on?"

I took note of Sherry's long-sleeved T-shirt, jeans, and athletic shoes. "We're handing out flyers for a window washing service."

She flapped the stack of flyers in the air. "Got 'em right here."

"Okay. Who wants to go first?"

"I will," I told Sherry. "You've done all the hard work so far. My turn."

I drove another mile down the road, turned around, and parked in front of the house.

My heart raced. My hands slipped from the steering wheel, slick with sweat. I wiped them on my jeans. "Here I go."

Sherry handed me the flyers.

I put on my baseball cap, walked through the tall weeds, had a little trouble climbing over the fence, and strode to the porch. Hunter and Sherry watched from the car.

I rapped on the front door.

Nothing.

Rapped again.

Silence.

Sherry and Hunter exited the car and walked around back, signaling me to join. With a glance up and down the deserted road, I realized we really *were* in the middle of nowhere. We'd discussed terrain and figured out escape routes since Patrick's house was surrounded by scrubby trees, pines, marshlands, and bayous. None of us had any expertise in navigating the land of palmetto bugs and alligators, and we hoped our explorations wouldn't result in a flat-out foot race. With a sigh, I slapped at a mosquito as I walked around back.

"I don't think anyone's here," Hunter said, peeking inside the kitchen window from the backyard.

"I'm going to check the window by the porch," Sherry said and left. A few minutes later, she returned. "I kept close to the wall to avoid the security camera. The window's filthy. I tried to get a look, but I couldn't tell."

"Let's get inside," I said.

We all started checking windows.

"Found one!" Sherry stage-whispered. "The bars look loose at the bottom."

"The security cam in the front can pick up audio." I put my index finger to my lips. "Shh."

She nodded, and moved away from the front porch. She held up a can of spray paint and a pair of scissors. "For the inside cameras. I'll black out the video, then find the source. If it's not wireless, I'll cut the cord."

I laughed. "You thought of everything."

"I consulted a talented friend of mine." She smiled.

Hunter found a shovel in the back yard and used the handle as a lever. The window fought the good fight but succumbed to his efforts. Tiny Sherry was elected to go inside and get rid of the surveillance cameras. The sound of her light footsteps scampering through the house and the hiss of spray paint made me nervous. I glanced at Hunter.

Hunter patted his firearm. "I'll be security. I'm going into the front. Look for my texts. If you don't find Hannah, at least get us some evidence she's been there. Put on the gloves."

"Got it," I said, hoisting myself over the windowsill. "I'm too big."

After five minutes of grunting and effort, he bent the bars even more. "My hero," I said with a grin as I pulled the nitrile gloves into place. "Here I go."

"Sherry!" I called, feeling my nose twitch at the ungodly smell of the place. "Where are you?"

"Down here," she responded. Her voice echoed eerily up the stairs. "We don't have to worry about the security cams anymore. They weren't wireless. I found the source and cut the cord."

I trotted down the stairs to a basement room floored with concrete and found an open door. My gut churned. This was it. *The room where he'd imprisoned Hannah.*

Sherry stood inside, one hand on her hip, the other on the butt of her firearm at her waist. "Look at that excuse for a bathroom. It's maybe three feet by three feet. How would someone even use the toilet?" She pointed at the small window. "That's where she looked out to see people coming and tried to get their attention. It's above her head, so she'd have pulled over the bed or something to stand on. Sherry illustrated. "But the window's covered with a film of dirt, so I don't know how she saw anything." She stretched as high as she could reach and touched the bars on the windows. "We have to get this guy."

"Did you find anything of hers in here?"

Sherry shook her head. "Nothing significant. If they got in late last night, and he's at work now..." She lifted her shoulders. "Where is Hannah?"

I nodded, thinking. Where would he put her? Did he have more torture chambers scattered throughout the property?

I looked at the twin bed, its dirty sheets, and the threadbare oval rug in the room. A single ladder-back chair. An old-fashioned gooseneck lamp. Sherry and I spent quiet minutes searching and found only a few ragged pieces of clothing, a washcloth, a broken bat, and a plastic knife and spoon. "This is giving me the creeps. Let's go upstairs."

"Wait. Look at this," Sherry said. She yanked out her phone and clicked a photo.

I followed the direction of her gaze on the ceiling.

"Yep. Someone else has been here. And another one…" She squatted, pointed underneath the sink, and clicked another photo.

The almost illegible letters had been tediously scratched into the cinderblock walls. I laid my hand on my breastbone. "He's had other women in here."

"We'll check our databases and see if they've been missing. At least we have something to show the cops now."

We closed the door to the room as we left. I rubbed my eyes in disbelief and pointed to the unassailable deadbolt on the outside of the door.

Sherry's eyes darted around the space. "Where's Hunter?"

I wrenched my phone from my pocket. Two texts. All caps. "Oh, no," I whispered.

Sherry's eyes narrowed. "What?"

"Don't look back. Go upstairs and out the window…and *run*. I'm right behind you."

"My God," she whispered, her eyes round as saucers.

"Go!"

We bolted into the kitchen and wedged ourselves out of the back window. We hopped the chain link fence and raced into the brush. The parched grass and bushes in the arid bottomlands proved useless as hiding places. We dropped to the ground on our stomachs.

"Hunter's using our cover story. He's great at this, don't worry. He'll handle it."

Sherry squinted at our surroundings. "Yeah, I can't wait to see how he explains those bent bars on that window." She exhaled. Rubbed her eyes. "Do you think Hannah got away?"

I was riveted on Patrick's backyard. Maybe our ruse worked. I'd left the flyers with Hunter when I'd gone through the window to join Sherry inside. "I don't know if she was in any shape to run."

"She could've been. Right? He had her in his car. She wouldn't go with him unless he drugged her, and that's easy. Pour chloroform or an inhalational anesthetic on a cloth and immobilize her. Get her in the car, follow up with something to put her to sleep for several hours. He's an expert at the art of the roofie, and we didn't think to check his medicine cabinet?" She groaned.

"The cops will get a warrant to search the place eventually, and they'll find stuff like that. We couldn't risk it, Sherry. We didn't have time."

"It's possible whatever he gave her wore off." She stared at me as she developed her scenario in her mind. "She could be out in this godforsaken wilderness somewhere. Think about it—she gets home and discovers what happened, he says 'honey, we're home' and she goes ballistic. I would, wouldn't you? I'd take off like a jackrabbit into the wild rather than go back in that house with him."

I locked eyes with her. "It's possible," I admitted. "With that drug in her system, she'd still be weak. Maybe even sick."

Sherry picked up a handful of sandy soil and let it cascade through her fingers. "And lest we forget, she's pregnant."

"We *have* to find her."

With a last glance at the house, we kept low as we trekked further into the Florida wetlands. My heart pounded and sweat poured off me due to the unfamiliar level of humidity. We avoided sticker bushes, a snake, and a bayou. We almost walked right into the damn bayou, and I felt sure I saw an alligator in there, licking his chops and waiting.

Performing sweeps with our eyes, we kept a distance of six feet or so between us. Flies attacked. We batted at them with our arms, but they came right back. I glanced at my phone. No text. What happened with Hunter?

"Is he okay?" Sherry asked.

"Got nothing," I mumbled. The phone vibrated in my hand, and I almost dropped it. A text! *He's gone*

I tilted my head back, closed my eyes, and sent a brief prayer of gratitude into the sky.

Another buzz. The next text read: *Where are you?*

I told him what we were doing and to meet us down the road. He agreed.

Ten minutes later, we'd found nothing that indicated Hannah had passed this way, however, in this type of terrain we couldn't even find footprints much less a scrap of material on a bush. Sherry and I pushed through the trees, fought our way through boggy marshland, and emerged on the road to meet Hunter. I texted him that we'd arrived. We sat on the lower branches of a sprawling live oak to watch the road and wait.

Our thug-tinted rental car approached and parked. We hopped off the branches and jogged toward the car. Sherry gasped. "There's two people! You think he found her?"

We ran faster. I laughed. "It can't be this easy."

And it wasn't.

As we approached, our steps dragged. We stared at our rental in various degrees of shock. We could barely make them out through the darkly tinted windows, but Patrick sat in the driver's seat, and Hunter sat in the front passenger seat. We watched in horror as he slid from view.

"He must've overpowered Hunter," Sherry whispered.

My hands were blocks of ice. "Don't move," I whispered.

Patrick got out of the car, smiled, and spread his arms. In one of his hands, he held a big, black Glock, which meant, at minimum, seventeen rounds.

"Oops. Guess the seatbelt didn't hold him up." He wagged the Glock toward the car. "Get in."

"Over my dead body," I called across the thirty feet that separated us.

He shrugged. "Have it your way." The shot whizzed by an inch over my head.

Sherry ducked, pulled her weapon, and remained in a squat. "He's serious. What do you want to do?"

"Remember how to get away from an active shooter?"

Sherry's jaw clenched. "Shoot back, then zigzag."

"Did you bring extra rounds?"

"Yes. You?"

I sighed. "Between us, we have more rounds than he does unless he's got an extra cartridge on him. Make every shot count. Ready?"

She nodded.

"NOW!" I hissed.

We jumped up with double war cries, took aim, and fired several rounds.

Patrick ducked behind the rental car. His return fire hit trees, dirt, and air as we zigged and zagged for ten minutes, then slumped beside a bayou, breathing hard and watching through the trees. The undergrowth had become more tangled and less sparse. Good for us, bad for him. I hoped Hunter had survived whatever Patrick had done, but I couldn't think too hard about that right now. With trembling hands, I notified nine-one-one, blurted out a brief synopsis, described the vehicle, and shared the location.

I licked my dry lips. Put a hand on Sherry's shoulder. "Let's find Hannah."

"Yeah, well. Let's shake Patrick first."

"I think we have," I said, rising from the dirt and dusting off my jeans. "My gut tells me he doesn't have her, or he wouldn't have tried this. Holding onto one of us means leverage with the cops. He doesn't have her." I tried to slow my breathing. "Now he knows we're armed. He's not going to do anything stupid."

Sherry squinted at me. "He has *Hunter.* And Hannah doesn't have her phone."

"I know, but if she made it this far, she's smart enough to go to a house and get help."

A shot zipped past us and hit a tree. "We need to split up." I pointed. "I'll go this way; you go the other. Maybe one of us will find her. Have you got a signal?"

She jerked out her phone. "Yeah."

"Be safe."

She rolled her eyes at me and took off.

Chapter Twenty-Eight

Hannah

Hannah fell over an exposed root and landed on her stomach. She cursed, shoved her hair over her shoulders, and rubbed sweat out of her eyes. Ahead, miles and miles of undeveloped, marshy Florida terrain; behind her, life as a slave servicing Patrick's every need. She'd take the Florida wilds over Patrick any day.

"There's nothing out here," she whispered, growing as hopeless and desolate as the spartan landscape. A snake slithered through the grass, its tongue flicking in and out. She jumped away and clapped her hands over her mouth to stifle a scream. Its diamond-shaped head lashed out, barely missing her leg.

Patrick could be close. She'd heard shots. A lot of shots, but couldn't tell which direction they'd come from, and didn't care. The single mantra she repeated to herself as she ran echoed through her mind and sighed from her lips: *Keep going and don't look back. Keep going, and don't look back. Keep going, and don't look back.*

She hoped it was enough.

Her throat scratchy and raw, she knew she wouldn't last long without water. Struggling with the blisters on her feet and shoes that threatened to come apart, she wondered how long she could hold out. Last night, she'd run until her lungs felt like they would explode, and when she found a decent-sized tree, she climbed it and folded herself into its thick branches.

Her stomach ached with hunger, and her throat felt desert-dry. "Water," she croaked. "That's the goal for today." She shuffled forward, hoping the soles of her flimsy tennis shoes would hold out.

An hour later, she stumbled across a clearing that held a sheet attached to a makeshift clothesline, an ax resting against a stump, a fire pit with a thick bed of ash. A sliver of hope nicked her heart. She scanned the area for something to drink. A search revealed nothing but a discarded black garbage bag filled with refuse. Those prepper shows that she'd watched with Patrick might be worth something, after all. Her jaw worked as she concentrated, trying to remember water purification methods. The clothesline caught her attention as it flapped with the breeze. That's it, she thought. A piece of cloth can filter and purify water. "It'd be better than dying out here," she whispered. With a sigh, she grasped the cloth and felt it between her thumb and fingers. Cotton, not a polyester blend. Cotton could sift out the muck. She tore off a couple of pieces and put them in her pocket. Next, she pounced on the garbage bag. An empty milk carton lay right on top. Laughing, she picked it up and held it in the air like a trophy. She also found a box of Chik-fil-A scraps and scarfed them down. She dug out discarded napkins and wiped her face, her neck, and her mosquito-bitten arms. The trash bag yielded little else, but at the next bayou she came across, she'd try the purification technique with the milk carton and layers of fabric. The small ax she slid into her back pocket, head-first.

Her grim thoughts scattered like baby spiders. She had little chance of spending many more nights out here without food or water, and Patrick had taken her phone. She stared at the landscape with a growing sense of desolation. She'd fought through miles of swampy bayous, boggy marshland, and undergrowth that snatched at her legs. And the cold! At night, the temperature dropped, and she couldn't sleep. At least the gnats and flies gave her a break during the night, but the minute the sun rose, they attacked. Who owned this property? She'd thought by now she'd have run into a community or a house. Sweat trickled into her eyebrows. She wiped her forehead. Without a GPS, she felt helpless and lost.

The fire pit held an opportunity for warmth, but building a fire without matches or a lighter? Impossible.

Hannah stared into the wide, blue sky and wondered whether to leave the campsite, or stay and see if someone might come back to it.

She decided to stay. The odds of someone returning and leading her to civilization were better than going it alone in the swamplands. The tree stump provided a seat as she pondered her fate, glancing at her watch every few seconds. Fifteen minutes, she told herself. She'd give it fifteen minutes before she left. Her eyes grazed the clothesline. A note! She'd leave a note explaining the circumstances pinned to the clothesline with instructions to call the cops. Hannah jumped off the stump and returned to the trash bag, this time looking for a piece of paper, something to write with, and something to hang the note on the line. When her fingers touched a broken crayon in the bag, she cried in relief. The Chik-fil-A sack provided paper, and she scrawled a note with the crayon and attached it to the clothesline with one of the clips holding the sheet to the line.

After that, she re-seated herself on the stump to wait. Her eyelids drooped, and soon, she discarded her timeline, yanked the sheet off the line, and wrapped herself in it.

Later, Hannah's eyes flew open. She winced at the crick in her neck and the sandy soil she'd used as a bed.

It took her a second.

"Crap," she whispered, trembling. She'd slept the afternoon away. Long shadows draped the clearing. She shivered. The temperature had dropped. "It's still better than being a captive in his house," she muttered, tugging the sheet around her shoulders. She let out a long exhale and stared at the fire pit. "Keep going? Or stay?" she whispered into the stillness.

Wait. What was that sound?

Stealthy footsteps through the brush?

She discarded the sheet and crept behind a tree.

The steps grew less stealthy, more confident. Sherry emerged from the shadows and assumed a firing stance. "Show yourself," she declared.

Hannah started blubbering in relief. Big, fat tears rolled down her cheeks.

"Who's there?" Sherry demanded.

CHAPTER TWENTY-EIGHT

"It's me," Hannah cried. "Sherry, it's Hannah."

"Ohmigod!" Sherry jogged across the campsite and threw her arms around her friend.

"Shhh," Hannah whispered. Her eyes darted around the space. "Where's Patrick?"

Sherry holstered her weapon. "It's a long story. When I get service again, we'll figure it out."

Hannah showed Sherry her ax, milk carton, and fabric. "Those prepper shows Patrick made me watch with him came in handy." She smiled. "I can purify my own water."

"Maybe it won't come to that."

Hannah wiped her cheeks with her palms. "What are you doing out here?"

"We," she corrected. "Hunter, Olivia, and me. The three musketeers." She chuckled. "We're here to take you back."

Hannah's head whipped around, looking for them. "Are they with you?"

"Olivia's out here somewhere, and Patrick apprehended Hunter. We think." She swallowed hard, then lifted her chin. "He can take care of himself."

Hannah shrugged. "A few seconds, that's all it takes to immobilize a person with a cloth soaked in chloroform or paint thinner. Whatever the hell that asshole uses."

Sherry raked Hannah with her eyes. "That what he did to you?"

She nodded. "He threw me in the back seat. I didn't wake up until we were halfway back to Niceville. I tried to get help." She squeezed her eyes shut, remembering. "A cop saw my distress signals and stopped, but..." Her shoulders slumped. Her head dropped to her chest. "Patrick shot him."

"We know about it. Hunter's been in touch with the local police." She gave Hannah's arm an affectionate squeeze. "It terrified us, but we were determined to get into his house and find something incriminating."

Hannah tossed her head. "Let me guess. He appeared out of nowhere."

"Olivia and I barely got away."

Hannah's laughter bordered on hysteria. "I told you guys. He walks through walls. You never know when he'll appear." Her gaze sliced left, right. "Like now."

"Right," Sherry agreed, studying her phone. "Let's get going. The minute I get a signal, I'll contact Olivia, and we'll meet."

The ground vibrated. Branches snapped. Startled birds burst from the trees and flew away as the gray-blue of twilight seeped in like smoke. Hannah gripped Sherry's hand. "Run!" Sherry whispered. "Follow me!"

Bullets strafed the campsite. Chunks of bark flew off the trees around them.

Sherry rabbited through the undergrowth. Hannah tried her best to keep up.

Chapter Twenty-Nine

Olivia

One of Patrick's shots had creased my scalp.

I wiped the blood out of my eyes.

With a sigh, I huddled into the trees, watching and waiting for this bastard who had decided on a free-for-all with no chance of compromise. I imagined at this point he'd be fine with suicide-by-cop since he'd backed himself into a corner. No way out for this guy, but he seemed determined to take Hannah, or me, or Sherry—and especially Hunter—down with him.

The mist clung to me like a wet blanket. I gently probed my wound. My fingertips dripped with fresh blood when I drew my hand away. "Great," I muttered. "What would Dr. Sturgis say about this?" Thinking about my neurologist's horror at a fresh head wound made me laugh. It had taken me six years to recover from the last one.

My phone buzzed. I felt my bloody eyebrows rocket up into my equally bloody hairline. I stared at the number. Sherry! We had a signal!

"Hey!"

"I've got her. I found Hannah!"

I blinked. It took a minute for my voice to catch up to the words. "That's wonderful. How is she?"

"Good. Send me your location. Patrick's closing in, it's like, he has nothing to lose or something. I didn't tag him as a killer, but he's gone complete nutso."

"Shoot to kill," I said, my voice matter-of-fact.

"Roger."

"How's Hannah?"

"Scared. Tired. Can't believe she's here with me."

I smiled. "Me either. Good job."

"A fluke."

I shook my head even though she couldn't see me. "Not a fluke. An answer to a prayer."

I felt Sherry's smile through the phone. "Have you heard from Hunter?"

"No," I whispered, scanning the perimeter and listening, hard. "Patrick must've snagged Hunter's phone. The texts that came in that I thought were from Hunter were bogus."

"Yeah," she muttered. "I figured that out. Asshole. What if he still has Hunter's phone?"

I stared at my phone's map. "We're five miles apart. I see a road in the middle." I sent the address. "We're close to Highway 85, and there's an airport about three miles away. I hope we can hang onto this signal."

"I vote for the airport. I think we'd be more protected there."

"Okay. I'm calling nine-one-one and letting them know. Be safe."

"You, too," she whispered. "Wait." She gasped. "He's here."

The connection went dead.

I rearranged my route to head straight toward the pin Sherry had sent. Adrenaline gushed through my bloodstream. My mind cleared. My legs received fresh strength. I checked how many shots I had left, secured my firearm in my holster, and ran like the wind.

When the adrenaline spike dropped off, I'd covered three miles. I figured I'd best slow it down or risk a cardiac event. Within thirty minutes, it'd be pitch-black outside. Then what? My lace-up boots served me well as I trudged through the sloppy terrain, dodged vines with inch-long stickers, and kept an eye out for alligators or rats. Five minutes passed. The low hum of insects and frogs began. I had fifteen percent battery life left on my phone. I leaned against a tree to think.

A scorpion inching down the tree tried to hitch a ride on my shoulder. I yelped and jerked away in shock. Florida had scorpions? I watched it perch on its skinny, little legs at full attention and curl its deadly tail. I kept my distance. Perfect. Now, I couldn't even trust the trees.

When I heard the faint sound of a woman's voice, hope surged through my chest. I wrenched my phone from my pocket, and to my great relief, the GPS showed that I'd reach my destination sooner than I'd thought. I kept walking. The breeze picked up, and a half-moon slid above the tree line. The insect sounds intensified, creepy and nightmarish; a Hitchcock movie. This can't be happening, I thought, my teeth gritted, my fingers tight around the butt of my firearm. Blood had ceased its trickle into my eyes, which helped. I walked faster toward the female voice whimpering and moaning. Every few seconds I stopped to listen, making sure a male voice hadn't inserted itself into the mix. What if Patrick had set a trap using the injured woman as bait?

I held my weapon with both hands and kept walking. At the sight of a clearing, I paused.

A person lay on the ground. I slid my gaze from one end of the clearing to the other, looking for Patrick within the perimeter or the glint of a gun barrel poking from behind a tree. Nothing. I left my hiding spot and approached. *Sherry.* My fingers shook as I placed them on her throat and found her pulse. Erratic. I cursed. Where had my nine-one-one call gone? Why didn't I hear sirens? We weren't that far from the highway. Were we?

I bent toward her ear. "Sherry, can you hear me?"

She groped for me, her eyes closed. "I'm shot. He took Hannah. I've lost a lot of blood, and I..."

One final exhale, and she passed out.

"Sherry!" I ripped off a piece of my shirt and tied it as best I could around the wound in her shoulder. The moon cast an eerie glow around us, the breeze making the trees dance, the shadows pulsate. I looked around for something to put her head on and made her a pillow of leaves and moss.

I'd never felt so alone in my life. I stared at the twinkle of fireflies deep in the woods and tried to fight the strands of hopelessness winding around my ribcage, pressing. Crushing. "Work, dammit!" I commanded my phone. "Work!"

A signal flickered. I yelped with joy when several texts appeared that told me help had been summoned. How would they find me? I checked my settings and sat on the ground beside Sherry. Would the signal hold?

I wiped sweat and grime off my face.

Five minutes passed.

Ten.

My phone died. Fear clogged my throat.

I put my hand on Sherry and my weapon in my lap.

Later, something touched my leg, causing me to startle awake. I made sure Sherry's chest still moved up and down before I jumped up and stomped around to get rid of whatever had flicked across my leg. Little scuttling sounds moved away, assuring me I'd scared them more than they'd scared me. It had grown so dark I couldn't see two feet in front of me. A groggy Sherry propped herself up on an elbow. My heart soared with joy.

"What's going on?" she asked.

I let out a long breath. She hadn't died on my watch. How could I have lived with that? I couldn't. I gave her a hard squeeze on her good shoulder. "Good to have you back."

"Where are we?"

"My phone died."

"My pocket," she said, indicating the location with her chin. "Get my phone."

I slid it out. "You have service! And battery life."

"Why isn't someone saving us?"

I croaked out a laugh. "That's the question, isn't it?"

"Call Hunter."

I bobbed my head and put in his number. "It's ringing."

Sherry swiveled her head. "I hear it, too."

We flinched at the sound of branches being pushed aside and stumbling footsteps heading toward us. Hunter burst into the clearing on shaky legs, the white of his smile visible in the murky dark. "Found you," he said before

186

he collapsed.

After a thorough search, I'd found no bullet wounds and concluded that Hunter had been drugged but powered through its effects to find us. I put his head in my lap and stroked his forehead as he slept. Sherry had fallen asleep again and dozed a few feet away.

I tried to sleep sitting against the tree with Hunter's head in my lap. I forced myself not to think about night scuttlers feasting on my body while I slept.

As dawn broke, Hunter regained consciousness.

"What happened?" I asked, watching him shake off sleep and arrange himself cross-legged on the ground in front of me.

"When I tried the window-washing pitch, he jumped me. I didn't expect it at all. One minute he appeared interested in what I had to say, and the next, he damn near smothered me in whatever he'd soaked into a towel." He studied my face. "It was almost like he knew we'd be here."

Tears filled my eyes. "He's been hunting us like animals. We had to separate when he started shooting at us. Our phones didn't have consistent service, and it's a miracle I ran across Sherry and another miracle that she found Hannah." I looked at the sky turning pink above the trees. "But then he shot Sherry and took Hannah," I whispered. "I don't know if we can do this."

"So much for Niceville PD," Hunter snapped. "I knew there'd be a lag time before they could get a warrant to search Patrick's place, but I impressed upon them the urgency of her situation."

I shrugged. "Small-town cops. They have a network. You've experienced Patrick, he's slick. The guy next door."

"Yeah. And now he's got my firearm. It's a wonder he didn't take my phone; something must've spooked him. I woke up in the rental car, and he was gone."

I looked at his grimy face, and the thick eyebrows knotted over angry eyes. "I only have one clip, but at least I have my firearm. He probably left the phone with you to track you. What do you want to do?"

Hunter stretched out his legs and slapped at the dried mud on his jeans.

"What we came to do. Find Hannah and get her away from that jerk."

I edged closer to him. "I'm grateful you're still alive."

He pulled me into his arms. He smelled like sweat, dirt, and Florida marsh, but I didn't care. I kissed him hard. "Don't you scare me like that again."

He traced the shape of my jaw with his finger. "Okay."

Hunter stood, stretched, and offered his hand to help me up.

"Let's get out of here," he said, powering off his phone. "Can Sherry walk?"

Chapter Thirty

Hannah

"What'd you tell them?" Hannah demanded, tears cascading down her cheeks. She watched through the small window in the basement room as the police cruiser rolled away from the house. Patrick looked as pleased as punch as he responded to her question in pantomime:

"I have no idea what you're talking about, Officer. Someone got misinformation. My wife is right here, and she's fine, see?" He laughed. "Good job acting like the faithful wife when they asked to see you, by the way." He lifted a shoulder, nonchalant. "My family has lived here for three generations. My father is a U.S. Representative for Florida's First Congressional District. You think they're going to believe a private investigator from Baltimore?" He laughed. "Florida is where people come to *escape* Baltimore."

Hannah watched in horror as the patrol cars sped away, their red and white lights no longer striping the sky, all sirens silenced. She stared into the dark, vile eyes that she'd grown to hate, the face she'd once thought so attractive.

"Let's get you upstairs. Patrick prompted her out of the punishment room and up the stairs with a shove to her lower back. He walked into the kitchen and broke out a bottle of Johnny Walker Red. His eyes shiny with anticipation, he announced, "I think this calls for a celebration, don't you?"

Hannah tilted her head toward the floor. She didn't dare challenge him when he had the upper hand. She had no idea what he'd do if she resisted, and his behavior felt odd. Manic. The calm before the storm. And a storm was on the way, she knew.

Patrick strode down a narrow hallway and opened a closet. When he returned, he asked her to extend her arms. Hannah frowned. "Why?"

"I've got a present for you. Hold out your hands."

The cruel set of his mouth scared her. She held out her bony arms. Quick as a lightning strike, he snapped handcuffs on her wrists. Hannah stared at them, the last spark of hope draining away.

Patrick laughed. "That's how I treat a woman who doesn't appreciate me. You'll get used to it." He slid the glass of Johnny Walker across the table in her direction. "Now drink."

With both hands, she lifted the glass and drained it.

"That's what I'm talkin' about! We're going to enjoy ourselves tonight."

Hannah felt something die inside her. How could she bring a child into this madman's world? She almost wished the poor child *would* die and wondered if she could miscarry through sheer force of will. Once he discovered the pregnancy, she knew she'd never be rid of him, and neither would her child. Patrick grabbed her hair and tilted her head back in order to pour two more glasses of whiskey down her throat. She sputtered and coughed and tried to spit it out, but he just laughed and held her lips together until she swallowed. When he carried her into their bedroom, she forced her mind back to Olivia's house, to Hunter's kind, concerned expression, and Sherry's comforting presence. As she'd done many times before, she removed herself to a better place and insulated herself within the memory. So much so that she barely felt Patrick drop her on the bed and strip off her clothes. Instead, she heard the soft reassurance of Olivia's voice and the clatter of Marlowe's claws on hardwood; smelled the nutty aroma of morning coffee, and felt the sunshine streaming into Olivia's kitchen.

The awareness of Patrick's movements faded, and when she blessedly passed out, she was smiling.

Hours later, Hannah woke. Like a terrified, beaten dog in a cage, her first

190

thought centered on survival. She struggled to get her arms and legs to work. Tears straggled down her cheeks when she realized he'd moved her to the punishment room and trussed her naked body like a turkey. Fresh bruises bloomed on her chest, between her legs, her thighs. Her arms had been secured to the metal headboard of the twin bed, and her ankles tied to the bed frame. Her hands and feet had no feeling in them, and were useless. Hannah cleared her throat a couple of times before she got out a good, hard scream. "PATRICK! PATRICK!" she cried, wrenching her arms. A final effort rewarded her with the squeal of metal. She blinked. "You can do this," she whispered. Closing her eyes, she took a deep breath and focused. A primal groan exploded from her mouth as she almost pulled her arms from their sockets. The flimsy metal detached from its moorings and fell apart. She slipped her restraints from the headboard and eased her arms down, examining her raw wrists underneath the tight handcuffs. She rotated her shoulders and studied the way he'd tied her ankles. Her fingers worked feverishly until the knots gave way. Wincing in pain, she dangled her feet from the edge of the bed to get the blood back in them. After a few minutes, she attempted standing. Every part of her body ached. She fought through the dizziness until she felt stable. She struggled to drag the ladderback chair beneath the small window. After she got it there, it took her five minutes to catch her breath and gather enough strength to step up onto it and look out the window into the front yard.

Her jaw dropped at the blurry images she saw. She rubbed her eyes to make sure it wasn't a mirage. Through the grimy window, she watched uniformed people swarm the yard. A man with a battering device stood to one side of the porch, waiting. Someone yelled, "Niceville PD. Open up!" She watched one of the uniforms give a hand signal.

BANG. BANG. BANG.

Hannah whooped in delight. A flurry of footsteps above her head turned into a stampede. She screamed. The footsteps paused before they rushed down the stairs to the basement. The battering ram shattered the door to the basement room, and four uniforms rushed inside. Hannah crumpled to the floor, sobbing. "Thank God," she whispered. "Oh, thank you, God."

By the time Hannah had been tucked into a bed in the ER and hooked up to an IV at Twin Cities Hospital, Hunter, Sherry, and Olivia had been transported as well. Through her haze, she listened to hospital personnel speculating in hushed, somber tones about the Somerset family, how Patrick had been a black sheep all along, and the recent admissions were stone-cold proof. In short order, Hannah learned that Olivia and Sherry arranged a sit-down with the criminal investigation unit and explained each detail, camping out on the unsavory fact that not obtaining a warrant to search Patrick's house earlier could have resulted in unnecessary homicides. Niceville's investigative unit had the good grace to apologize and thank Watchdog Investigations for their efforts. Hunter stayed out of the limelight, hoping his lieutenant wouldn't find out about another foray into unauthorized waters that could result in suspension, at best—termination, at worst.

Patrick, however, had gone missing.

Which surprised everyone but Hannah.

A rotund, gum-smacking man stood beside Hannah's bed with a notepad. "Where do you think your husband could be, Mrs. Somerset?"

Hannah stared at him. She crossed her arms, the IV drip pole rolling with the movement. "Please don't call me that. Call me Hannah. I don't want to hear his name again. Ever."

He cracked his gum. "Got it. Have any ideas?"

"He kept me on tight lockdown. For two years. I never met his family."

The man frowned. "You never met Congressman Somerset? His father?"

Hannah chuckled and rubbed her wrists. The nurse had applied ointment on her wrists, and they felt smooth and slick. Much better. She sighed. "That's hysterical. He's a politician's son?"

The man stopped scribbling. "The Somersets are well regarded around here. They're no joke."

"Well. I'd give up on that if I were you. Have you read the report?"

He resumed his scribbling. "Not yet."

"Are you a reporter or a cop?"

"Thomas Linkletter, Mid Bay News."

She nodded. "Press. Okay. Take a quote. Victim says it is imperative to search the property for graves of additional victims." Hannah recited the women's names she'd found scrawled on the cinderblock walls.

The man's expression brightened. "You tell anyone else this?"

"You're the first."

He grinned. "Thanks!"

He sped off to get his piece in by deadline, she supposed. Olivia walked in sporting a bandage on her scalp, and pulled a guest chair beside Hannah's bed. "They gonna let you get out of here tonight?"

"I sure hope so," she muttered. "What happened to your head?"

"It's just a graze, no worries. It bled a lot, though."

Hannah felt tears fill her eyes. "I'm sorry about all of this."

Olivia waved her hands. "We're fine. The important thing is Patrick *is done.* Sherry's out of surgery and squawking to go home, but they're going to keep her a couple of days."

Hannah gripped the sides of her bed. "What happened to Sherry?"

"Shot in the shoulder and waist. One's a nick; the other had to be dug out. She'll be fine."

Hannah dropped her head back on the pillow and closed her eyes.

"They're watching Patrick's place, and there's a BOLO out for him. It's just a matter of time, and he'll be locked away for good. What do you want us to get for you from his house?"

She frowned. "If it's a crime scene, can I take stuff?"

Olivia shrugged. "They'll be done with the crime scene by four today. We're heading to Hazel's in Pensacola tonight, so we'll get whatever you need before we go. Unless they're going to release you to go with us."

"Where's Hunter?"

"Keeping a low profile. He's not supposed to be helping. He's supposed to be recuperating."

"Oh. Right," she said, her voice thoughtful. "He's amazing, isn't he?"

Olivia nodded. "He is."

Hannah reached out. "Would you just go ahead and marry him? Please?"

Olivia swiped at sudden tears and laughed. "Maybe."

Hannah groaned.

Hunter knocked and walked in. His grin indicated that he'd heard them talking. "I'll take a 'maybe'."

Olivia's cell buzzed. She looked at the screen. "I need to take this," she told them and left Hannah's room.

Chapter Thirty-One

Olivia

The hallway bustled with activity. Nurses in scrubs studying charts, MDs trotting down the hall, rubbing their hands with sanitizer. I couldn't help but flash back to my own prolonged hospital stay six years ago. I breathed deep of the antiseptic smell and told myself to soft-pedal the call with Mom. She had no idea what we'd been doing the last few days.

I put my phone to my ear. "Hi, Mom."

"Hi, honey. How's your day going?"

I stifled a bout of sarcastic responses. "Fine. I'm sorry I've been out of touch."

"That's okay. You know if I don't hear from you, I'll call."

I thought about how to return to "normal." Did I have a "normal"? Ever? *No.* With a roll of my eyes, I re-focused on the conversation. "I'm glad you called, Mom. How are the girls? Have they been by?"

"We got together last week. You've raised such wonderful daughters. I'm so proud of them."

I stared at the polished linoleum beneath my feet as I leaned against the wall outside Hannah's room. Routine conversation didn't rest properly on my tongue yet, but I didn't want Mom to worry. She had enough going on with Gray's health issues. I scraped the edges of my brain for a safe topic.

"Is Serena still liking her Poli-Sci major?"

Mom laughed. "She loves it. I think she'll go the distance. She got that internship."

I smiled. "That's great news."

"She called you first, but you didn't answer."

I felt warmth begin to crawl up my neck. "I've, uh…been busy."

A heartbeat pause. "Doing what?"

In a desperate attempt to divert, I blurted, "How's Gray doing?"

"Remarkably well. He's responding to the meds. I'm more interested in how *you're* doing." Two-heartbeat pause. "What's all that noise in the background? Where are you?"

I cursed under my breath. How did she always know? "In Florida."

"Let me guess," she stated flatly. "It's not a vacation."

"We're staying with Hazel. She moved."

"Didn't Hannah move out that way, too?"

I swallowed, hard. Sometimes, my loved ones did not need to know the whole truth. Did that constitute a sin of omission? Maybe. I didn't care.

"She did, but she's had some issues. We're here to support her."

"Who's with you?"

"Sherry and, uhh, Hunter."

Mom laughed. "Okay. I'm not asking any more questions because I'm pretty sure what's going on will keep me up at night."

I let out the breath I'd been holding.

"When are you getting home?"

"Tomorrow or the next day."

"I love you, honey."

My heart constricted in my chest. "I love you, too, Mom."

"I'm praying for you. Always." She ended the call.

I slid my phone back into my pocket, thinking about Patrick in the wind, whatever nefarious plot Monty had hatched, and how grateful I was for a mother's prayers. "Thanks, Mom," I whispered.

Hunter stuck his head out into the hall. "Tell her hi for me."

"Too late, we're off the call. Are they keeping Hannah?"

"I talked them out of it. I can be quite persuasive, you know."

"Tell me about it." I entered Hannah's room and asked if she needed help getting ready to go, and she told me no, so I continued on to Sherry's room.

She raised her head from the pillow and frowned. "They're keeping me until tomorrow afternoon."

"That's for the best, Sherry. Your body's had a shock."

She stared at the bandage covering most of her shoulder. I could see the edge of it peeking out from her hospital gown. "They want to make sure it won't start bleeding again or get infected." Her eyes slid around the room. Her voice dropped to a whisper. "Do you think I'm safe in here? With that Patrick creep out there somewhere?"

"Niceville PD has it handled. You'll have security outside your room." I chuckled. "They're covering *all* their bases. I think they're worried about a civil suit."

"Okay."

We sat in silence for a few seconds.

I cleared my throat. "I can stay if you want."

She shook her head. "You've been through enough. You guys go on over to Hazel's and get a good meal and a decent night's sleep. I'll be fine."

I leaned down and gave her a gentle embrace. "We'll be back right after lunch tomorrow to get you."

"Sounds good." She rolled over and plumped her pillow.

We completed our release paperwork and walked outside to the car. It seemed surreal that Hannah's debacle might be over. Something nagged at me, though. I peeked over my shoulder at her. Something in Hannah's manner didn't sit right. Hunter fobbed open our rental. I sat in the front with him, and Hannah sat in the back, rigid and staring.

The weight of what had happened over the past few days created a formidable presence in the car—a thick, sticky miasma rife with bayou muck and slithering snakes. I felt it down to my bones and wondered if they did, too, but nobody spoke a word for twenty minutes. I'd never think of Florida in the same way again and couldn't wait to get back to the rolling hills and gentrified landscape of Maryland horse country. I closed my eyes. *And my house.* My charming, historic, Maryland farmhouse. Hunter reached over and grabbed my hand. We stayed like that for the next five miles.

"You okay?" he asked, negotiating a four-way stop. He looked in the back. "She's fast asleep."

I laughed. "I bet. Poor thing."

"You're a hero, Olivia."

"I'm tired and pissed-off and sick of sickos."

He chuckled. "You've had a glut of them, for sure. What's waiting for you when you get back?"

"Well, I haven't wanted to think about it, but Beth should be checking in any minute." I pulled out my cell, scanned it, and bobbed my head. "Sure enough."

He frowned. "Don't respond."

"Whatever. I can't do that."

"Constant stress is a major cause of stroke. Don't say you weren't warned."

I laughed and returned Beth's text.

After I read her response, I stuck my phone in the side pocket of the door, folded my arms, and looked out the window.

"What?" Hunter asked.

I sliced my eyes at him. His curiosity and teasing smile made him look twelve years old. In spite of the advancing years and the crinkles around his eyes, he kept sailing along in his manhood, getting more and more attractive. Like most men.

"Curtis Ridgeland continues his weird hold on me. The strange thing is that he was *Sherry's* client. I wasn't even supposed to be involved, and now..."

"Now, what?"

I bit on a fingernail. Had I told him I'd witnessed and photographed Victoria's murder? No. Should I tell him I had? NO. What good would that do? He should return to Richmond and heal. He only had another week of leave before he needed to get back to work, and I refused to put anything else on his plate.

Beth's text said Curtis had talked to the police. A prickle of concern started at the base of my neck and worked itself into my brain. What had he said? Should I worry?

"Nothing," I told Hunter, keeping my voice light and airy. "She's concerned. I told her we'd be home tomorrow night."

Hunter flicked his eyes at me, then back at the highway. Although he knew me well enough to pick up on a dodge, he respected my privacy. I loved that about him. He didn't pry. His cop brain had intuitive perceptions that scared me sometimes, but I knew he'd never use those insights to dig something out of me that I didn't want to share.

I reclined my seat, closed my eyes, and pretended to sleep, but all I could think of were Monty's stupid agendas. Had Monty's warped mind come up with a plan to involve me? Why? Graham and Curtis "just happened" to be friends with Monty, and the timing of Curtis's request to surveil Victoria seemed suspicious. My thoughts flipped over to Hannah. Monty's texts to her had been a big surprise. Why would she stay in touch with Monty? I focused all my mental faculties on remembering how she'd reacted when I asked her about it. She'd downplayed the texts, acted disgusted by them, but if that had been the case, why had she saved them? I'd have trashed the texts and blocked that person.

"No," I whispered. "It can't be."

Hunter glanced at me, concerned. "Are you okay?"

I reached out. He took my hand.

"Fine. I had a nightmare."

After we made a quick and uneventful drive-by to Patrick's house to pick up clothes and personal items for Hannah, we sped to Pensacola. Hazel greeted us with her typical cheer. I could tell our visit to her new home in Pensacola was a bright spot in her life, and she'd hate it when we told her we'd have to return to Maryland tomorrow. I bounded out of the car into her hug. Now that we hadn't had a professional relationship for two years, we could drop all pretense and become best friends. Or big sister, little sister. Whatever. The last couple years of therapy had been hard. Those professional boundaries had become a wall neither of us wanted, but it had demanded respect.

Two years later, we'd smashed the wall to pieces.

"Come on in," she said, taking stock of Hannah. "It's so good to see you, dear. It's been a few years, hasn't it?"

Hannah gave her a wan smile. "A lifetime. That's what it feels like. Thanks for letting me stay here, Hazel."

"Of course. Anyone want coffee?"

We all trooped into her coastal-themed kitchen and sat around the table. Hannah remained silent while we chattered like a bunch of old coots on the golf course. And, we *were* actually on a golf course, as Hazel lived in a retirement community full of them. Right outside her back door, two men played the tenth hole. Hunter lifted his mug of coffee, winked at me, and followed my gaze outside. The thunk of his mug crashing down on the table made half the coffee splash out.

Hazel jumped. I frowned at him.

Hunter popped from his chair, struggled with the lock on the patio door, and ran outside, cutting through manicured hedges to get to the putting green. The men yelled at him to get out of the way, and Hunter showed his badge as he ran. A familiar figure streaked by. Hunter raced after him.

I gasped.

Hannah sat in her chair as pale and still as a marble statue.

"Where did he go?" Hazel fluttered around the kitchen in confusion. "What happened?"

I couldn't speak. Had we put Hazel in danger? What should I tell her?

I cleared my throat. "He's tying up loose ends. He'll be back."

Hazel stared at me with a look that reminded me of my ex-husband on a bad day. She fisted her hands on her tiny hips. "I'm going to check doors and windows and make sure they're locked. You stay here with Hannah. It's Patrick Somerset, isn't it?"

The emotion felt like a stone in my throat. "I'm so sorry," I whispered.

She waved one of her hands. "Poof. I'm an old woman. I'm not worried about me. I'm concerned about…" She poked her index finger at me, then Hannah. "You two." She swept out of the kitchen to take care of business.

I slumped in my chair. "How on earth did he find Hazel's house?"

Hannah stuck out her lower lip. "Patrick had me wrapped around his little finger before his inner monster appeared. I talked about you guys all the time. I'm sure I mentioned Hazel and a quick Google search would tell him where Hazel lived. I think he spends his whole life gathering ammunition to protect his perverted lifestyle."

"He can't do any more damage. Hunter's already contacted back-up, I'm sure. They'll pick him up any minute."

She chuckled and shook her head.

I said nothing.

Hazel returned and dropped into a chair. "My loaded firearm is in that drawer." She pointed. "I have pepper spray right there." She pointed again. "My fire extinguisher...which makes a great deterrent, by the way, is underneath the sink. Any questions?"

My nervous laugh felt inappropriate.

Hannah yawned. "Where do you have me sleeping, Hazel? I need to lie down."

Hazel walked with Hannah to one of her guest bedrooms, closed the door, and returned to the kitchen, and sat in a chair next to me. "That one? She's in shock."

"She's been through a lot," I said. "And she's pregnant."

Hazel's eyes rounded. "I didn't know."

Hunter knocked on the patio glass. Hazel scurried over to the door to let him inside. "I handed it off to nine-one-one and gave them enough to pick him up."

"Hannah says he's a ghost."

"If he is, he's a stupid ghost," Hunter quipped, wiping sweat off his face. "Gave me a run for my money, and I lost him around the clubhouse." He grimaced. "What's he doing showing up here?"

"The act of a deranged man. A desperate man." Hazel stared out the window. "Unpredictable."

"A criminal whose time has come," Hunter finished for her. "I checked in with Niceville PD, too. They're still watching his house. He'll have to come home sometime."

None of us had slept very well, and after breakfast, we bid Hazel a teary adieu and piled into the rental. We made it to the hospital by early afternoon and hustled to Sherry's room, Hannah in tow. We formed a protective semicircle around her as she signed the release forms. She protested riding in the wheelchair, but I insisted.

I deposited her in the front seat with Hunter, where she could recline if needed.

Hannah remained silent. I wondered what she could be thinking, but I'd grown weary of trying to figure things out hours ago. Hunter drove us to the airport while Sherry nattered on about her hospital stay and anything else that dropped into her mind. Her voice provided a welcome distraction from the tension that infected us all.

We landed in Baltimore without any issues, got our luggage, returned the rental and picked up my vehicle, our breath making little vapor clouds in the chilly air as we walked outside to the parking deck. I heaved a sigh of relief once I started driving the familiar highway toward home.

I glanced into the back seat. Sherry and Hannah had nodded off. In the passenger seat beside me, Hunter rubbed his face wearily. The beard stubble had become ragged, the dark shadows underneath his eyes darker.

"How are you?" I asked him.

He patted his stomach and shoulder. "I guess the older I get, the longer it takes to heal," he joked. "Sore, that's all."

"Once we get to my house, I'll find pain relievers and make tea, and you can go to bed and watch mindless TV."

"I'll take you up on that."

The silence became unbearable. I turned on music.

"So. Did you mean it?" he asked.

I grinned. "Which part?"

He rolled his eyes. "You know what I'm asking."

I glanced at him, then returned my attention to the traffic in front of me. "I meant it, Hunter."

"It was a 'maybe.'"

"I've missed you."

CHAPTER THIRTY-ONE

He put out his hand. I slapped mine into it and held on tight.

"Let's do it," he said.

I felt my chin jerk in surprise. "Are you proposing?"

"Already did. Two years ago, by my calculations."

Little rainbows flared around the street, lighting with the fog we'd been driving through. A light mist turned into erratic drops, and within minutes, a hard, driving rain slammed my windshield. The wipers worked so hard I thought they might fly right off.

"Better pull over and wait it out," Hunter said.

With a glance at my sleeping passengers in the back, I edged off the highway onto the shoulder. We listened to the insistent hammering of the rain on the roof of my Land Rover and looked at each other in surprise when it sputtered to a stall. Both of us watched, our eyes wide, as huge snowflakes drifted from the sky and veiled my windshield in white. A hushed and holy moment. Hunter's warm, brown eyes shimmered. He put his hand on my arm. "What are you feeling?"

"It's a sign," I whispered.

"I agree."

He leaned in for a kiss, and I melted into the quiet, white grace of snowfall and his warm lips.

"I'm ready," I whispered.

"It's about damn time," he whispered back.

A giggle from the backseat shattered the moment. With a sigh, I twisted around.

"Congratulations," Sherry said.

Chapter Thirty-Two

Hunter

"I hate to go, but I'm pushing it as it is…" Hunter pulled Olivia in for a long hug. "As always, it's been an adventure." He looked at her hand. "Let me see it again."

Olivia laughed and held out her left hand. A three-carat, rectangular emerald framed by diamonds glinted in the morning sun.

"Looks great on your hand." His gaze ping-ponged between the ring and Olivia's face. "You like it, don't you?"

"It's perfect."

He cleared his throat. "I thought an emerald fit you better than a diamond. An emerald matches your eyes."

Olivia studied her ring, then put her palm on his cheek. "I love it."

"Glad I held onto it," he said, surveying the ring on its intended destination with a pleased expression. "I had it on me any time we were together. I knew you'd come around." His eyes twinkled. "Last night was pretty fabulous, by the way."

"Right." Swatting him playfully, she blushed.

He planted a kiss on her forehead. "Gotta go. Talk later, okay?"

She nodded.

He got in his Jeep and wrapped his fingers around the well-worn, leather-encased steering wheel. "It'll be good to be back in Richmond. Think about what we talked about."

"I will," she promised.

He rammed the Jeep into gear and drove toward the highway. He looked up at the arching branches that twined across the lane, which would soon create a leafy canopy. He remembered the many times they'd argued over one thing or another, and he'd screamed out of her driveway, spurting gravel underneath the tires.

"Things change, bud," he told himself. "No more dramatic exits." He turned right, sped through Glyndon, accelerated onto I-795, and eventually, I-95 South toward Richmond. The highway unfurled before him, and this time, when he thought of Olivia, he would refer to her as his "fiancée." With a smile, he tried the word out loud. "My fiancée lives in Maryland right now, but she's moving to Richmond."

He chuckled. If he said it enough times, would it become true? He hoped so, and furthermore, he'd start looking at the real estate market as a gesture of good faith.

An hour outside of Richmond, his cell informed him of a waiting call from Shiloh. He felt his jaw tighten. How would he tell her about the engagement? He stared at the screen in his car and the waiting call. His lips a tight line, he accepted the call. "Hey, soldier."

Shiloh laughed. "Soldier? That's one way of putting it, I guess. I definitely feel like the walking wounded."

Hunter smiled. "I take it you're out of the hospital?"

"Not yet. Two more weeks. I'm feeling good, though, and grateful the breaks are on opposite sides. Right wrist, left leg. At least the injuries are balanced." She chuckled.

He swallowed. "How long...will you...um..."

"Until I walk again? They tell me I'll be in a cast up to eight months, so I'll be on a desk, but that's okay. I could use a break. Ha-ha. No pun intended. The wrist cast will come off in four weeks."

"I'm glad, Shi."

The silence stretched.

"You're pretty quiet. You in the car?" Shi asked.

"Can you tell?"

"Sounds echo-y. You're on your vehicle connection. I can always tell. How are you, anyway? Why haven't you been in to see me?"

Hunter gripped the steering wheel until his knuckles turned white. Thoughts raced through his mind: *Because I've been busy saving an idiot of a woman who married a psychopath? Because I convinced the woman, I couldn't get out of my head to marry me? Because the ring I've had in my possession for two years now rests on her finger? Because I've bounced back and forth between two women, and it doesn't feel right to tell the one I consider the best cop-friend a man could have that I've made the choice to marry someone else?*

The thoughts reduced him to the days of adolescence when he hadn't been able to string two words together in the presence of a pretty girl. "I'll be in to see you tomorrow."

He frowned as he ended the call. The reprieve only prolonged the agony of telling her. Why did he care so much about her reaction? Maybe she wouldn't even *have* one, which would be worse. Maybe she'd cut ties and walk away.

He rubbed the back of his neck, then slapped the steering wheel in frustration. "You've made your choice," he hissed. "Be happy about it. Shi will do what Shi will do. It'll be fine."

Twenty minutes later, he pulled the Jeep into his garage and stalked into the house. His cell buzzed in his pocket. He jerked it out. Olivia's mother, Sophie. He exhaled in pure relief. Maybe she'd invite him to dinner. He needed a good meal and a change of focus after the last few days.

"Hi, Sophie."

"Congratulations!" she squealed.

Hunter grinned. "Thank you."

"I know you've been driving, but I have a big roast I'm about to take out of the crockpot, and we'd love to see you and celebrate."

His tension began to creep away. "Give me thirty minutes."

He walked inside his condo with a lighter heart. The relationship with his own estranged family had lapsed into the occasional phone call on holidays. And now, Olivia's family would soon become *his* family. Maybe his life had come full circle—a nice, round, predictable circle. Not oblong. Not oval. A circle, dammit. *A full and satisfying circle.*

Whistling, he dropped his oversized duffel on his bed, stepped out of his clothes, and started the shower. Relaxing with Sophie and Gray sounded great.

The following morning, he walked outside into the bright sunshine and put on his sunglasses. The follow-up appointment had gone well, and two ibuprofen had eclipsed the throbbing in his gunshot shoulder. The knife wound in his gut took time, his physician had told him, and it looked fine. He walked away from the medical complex, through the parking lot, and across the street to the hospital to visit Shiloh.

He started to get on the elevator, but walked into the waiting room and dropped into an armchair instead. He needed to think about what he'd say. He couldn't predict or control Shiloh's response to his engagement, that much he knew. What he didn't know was how to tell her that their friendship—if she still wanted one after his news—would move to platonic. Full stop.

With a determined lift of his chin, he walked to the elevator.

His knock on her door sounded like grenades exploding in his ears.

"Come in," she called, her voice curt.

She sat upright in bed, holding a black remote pointed at the TV. Her expression brightened when she saw him. "Hi! Welcome to hell. This damn thing won't work."

"Let me see it," he said, extending his arm.

She slapped the remote into his palm and folded her arms across her chest. "I've tried the nurse's station. My buzzer must not work this morning."

A young nurse walked into her room, eyeing her with an air of long-suffering. "Oh, it works. It's just not supposed to go off every ten minutes."

Hunter handed the remote to the nurse. "It may need batteries."

"I'll see to it," she said, lingering.

He stuck his hands in his pockets and cocked his head toward Shiloh. "Difficult patient?"

She tittered. "Not difficult. *Insistent.* Most cops are that way."

Shi rolled her eyes. "He's a cop, too."

Her cheeks reddened. "Oh. Sorry." She wagged the remote. "I'll get batteries." She left.

Shiloh laughed.

He frowned. "What's funny?"

"The way she looked at you…you're downright mesmerizing, Sergeant."

"Right," he cracked, amused. He slid a chair over and sat. "How's it going?"

"Terrible," she said. "I need to get out of here. My leg is…well, who knows, but they can fit me with one of those wheelie things, and I'll be fine. I don't know why they're keeping me this long."

He shrugged. "She said you're insistent. Insist on getting out."

"Yeah." She sighed and looked away. "They say I'll need help." She focused her intelligent, blue eyes on him. "I don't have anyone to help me."

Hunter stared at the floor. He'd almost blurted the magic words "You have me" before he stopped himself, cold. God. He couldn't say that. She *didn't* have him. Not anymore. Instead, he said, "You must have a ton of cop buds in Savannah. You'll figure it out."

She nodded. "I will," she whispered. "I'm getting tired of this, that's all. Not my usual, sunny self."

Hunter smiled. "Is that what you call it?"

She laughed. "Jerk."

"No argument here."

They enjoyed a companionable silence, listening to the sounds of hurried footsteps in the hall, rolling carts, snips of conversation, authoritative, deep voices. A baby's squall from the waiting room.

Shiloh turned a dreamy expression on Hunter. "You want kids, Faraday?"

His back got as rigid as the cast around Shiloh's leg. "Not at this point," he said, his voice cautious. *Where was she going with this?* Oh. NO.

"I've had a lot of time to think," she said, her voice quiet and thoughtful. "Why am I doing this? I almost died with this assignment. And for what?" Her thick, wavy blonde hair flew in every direction as she shook her head. "I want a *family*. I don't think when I'm dying I'm going to say 'hey look at all the bad guys that got arrested because of me.'"

CHAPTER THIRTY-TWO

Hunter didn't say anything.

She eyed him. "I'm a *lot* younger than you."

He smiled. "So you've told me. Many times."

She sighed. "Hunter, I can't do it anymore. You don't want kids, and I don't think my future is with you."

The relief acted on him like a muscle relaxant. He felt so boneless he almost slid out of his chair. "I understand." He forced a somber expression.

"I enjoy you. I enjoy *us.* But it's not a forever thing. I've never pictured us married. Have you?"

Hunter stared at the floor. Actually, he *had* thought about it.

Shiloh jumped in before he could answer. "I'm sorry if I've offended you."

"No worries. We have different objectives, and it's all good." He stuck out his hand. "Friends?"

She took his hand and gave it a firm shake. "Forever."

When he left, he felt lighter than air. He couldn't wait to tell his buddy, Nick. Who said former lovers couldn't be friends? He'd just gamed the whole system.

Chapter Thirty-Three

Olivia

The sun blinded me.

My head throbbed from a lack of rest, a lack of coffee or tea, and the stress of trying to stay alive the last seventy-two hours. I stumbled out of bed and took a couple of pain relievers. Marlowe's barking had awakened me far too early, and I'd yelled at him to shut up with no success.

I stomped downstairs, making a list in my head of things I needed to do at home and at work. I glared at Marlowe, who wagged his tail and pointed his nose at the door in response. Oh. I rubbed my eyes. That's why he'd been barking—someone is at the door. Fine.

The scowl on my face deepened. I yanked the door open.

My next-door neighbor, Callie, said good morning and thrust a basket of fresh-from-the-oven biscuits, jelly, and butter at me. She quickly surmised my bad mood, my rumpled attire and bed hair, then told me she'd leave so I could go back to bed.

I opened the door all the way. "Get in here. Thanks for the biscuits. I'm starving."

We walked down the hall and into the kitchen, and I gasped at the mess, rushing around like a nut job collecting food cartons and used paper plates and tossing them in the waste basket. Callie sat at the breakfast bar. "Don't do that on my account. I know you've had a lot going on."

I put the homemade biscuits on a nice plate and tried to act civilized. As I started on my second butter-and-jelly-slathered biscuit, her mouth dropped open. She stared at my hand, then at me, with wonder writ large.

Warmth crept up my neck. I felt like a kid with her hand stuck in the cookie jar. After years of Callie, Sherry, and Hannah's jokes about my unwillingness to move forward with Hunter, I didn't know what to say.

"If that's NOT an engagement ring, it'd be on the other hand," she concluded.

I stuffed the rest of the biscuit in my mouth and chewed.

Callie leapt from her stool and squashed me in a hug accompanied by shrieks of delight and congratulations.

"It's very fresh. I haven't processed." I gently untangled myself from her embrace.

Callie threw out her arms to each side. "What's to process? Olivia, he is perfect! We've all been holding our breath that he'd still be around after you turned him down a thousand times." She tightened her ponytail and paced around the kitchen, her fingers punctuating the words. "He's a saint to wait this long on you. And you've found your, y'know…your *groove*. Your *calling*. So it's time." She frowned, fisted her hips. "Beyond time!" She jutted her index finger at my nose. She'd painted her nails neon pink. "You better keep this guy. He. Is. A. GIFT."

I sighed. The weight of her frantic excitement could crush my more subtle feelings about accepting Hunter's proposal. It had seemed inevitable and meant to be, the intimate moment in the car, the ring. The snow. But Callie's glee made it Hallmark-movie-surreal. I'd given over my identity once before—to Monty—and the horrible consequences still tormented me. What if I'm doing the same thing now? What if Hannah's situation with Patrick is a harbinger? A warning?

I stopped my spiraling thoughts and tuned back in to Callie, who hadn't stopped talking.

"…and I think that old, historic church about five miles from here? You know, the one with all those big rocks and a grassy hill where we could set up an arch and set up chairs." She clapped her hands together. "It'd be beautiful. A spring wedding, you think?"

So. We're on to the wedding, now.

"Callie."

Her glee retreated. "What?"

"I get it. I'm glad you're excited for me. It *just* happened, and in the middle of an investigation that involves Monty, and add to that, figuring out Hannah's situation. It's too much. I can't think that far ahead. I just can't!" I let out a strangled sound and laid my head on the counter of the breakfast bar. I had to push the plate of biscuits out of the way to do so.

I felt Callie's gentle palm on my back. "Sorry. I know you're exhausted, but I'm *so excited*," she squeaked. I prayed silently that she'd give my ears a break. "I'm leaving now," she said.

My head still cradled in my arms, I lifted one hand and waved.

I heard the back door slam shut and her steps through my yard back to the little path between our houses. Marlowe rushed to the door and whined. Marlowe loved Callie. With a tired sigh, I lifted my head from the counter and saw Riot giving himself a bath at the foot of my stool, the way cats do when they feel their humans need support.

I stared at my left hand. "You picked out such a gorgeous ring, babe."

I'd just called him 'babe.' I'd never called him that before. Not once.

With a smile, I went upstairs to get ready for work.

I regained some bounce in my step after checking on Hannah and downing two more cups of coffee. No telling how much work awaited me, but since I'd faced the rage of the Florida beast and slayed him with my spear, catching up on work didn't have the power to intimidate that it once had.

However, I was still nervous to leave Hannah alone.

I would quit looking over my shoulder when Patrick got locked up. Which should be any minute, according to Hunter. I didn't think Hannah had the strength to move, much less go anywhere, and she promised me she wouldn't leave my house. Besides, Marlowe would rip out a throat if someone tried to come inside. I'd make sure the doors were all locked, check in at lunchtime, and keep in touch via text.

Beth greeted me with a big smile when I walked in and told me things had been pretty calm on her end. "Good," I responded, thinking I could catch up on my emails. Maybe I'd spend the *whole day* with my emails. Emails do not include conversation unless I make it happen, which I wouldn't. "Where's Sherry?"

"Running late. You guys must've worn yourselves out down there."

I chuckled. "Not a fan of Florida anymore, that's for sure."

"Oh," Beth said, lifting a finger. She gave me a sticky note. "I wrote this down for you. It's about Hannah. They have a place for her at the shelter. They said you should decide today. They can't hold it any longer than that."

I felt an immediate confirmation in my soul. One big, glaring issue crossed off my to-do list. No waffling, no waiting, no wringing of hands; the decision had been made for me. "Awesome. I'll call them first thing."

Beth had not said anything about my ring. Good.

"I'm engaged," I muttered to myself. "It's fine." When I powered on my laptop, I got the dreaded black screen of death. I rebooted. Rebooted again. Checked the drivers. Checked for missed updates. Started the process all over again. When my screen remained stubbornly black, I gave up.

An hour later, Beth had me set up with a different laptop and called someone to fix the other one. With a sigh and a mumbled curse about technology, I logged into my email.

"Sorry, this username does not exist," the error message informed me.

A prickle of fear crawled into my stomach.

I tried at least ten more times, thinking I'd not put in the correct email address or password. After a while, I had to admit that someone had hacked into my business email account.

Three guesses who, and they all began with "M."

Later that afternoon, we were informed that someone had, indeed, hacked the account. I needed to sign out of all my accounts, change my password to a two-factor verification, and make sure my security had been updated. Furthermore, I had to make sure the email addresses on the resurrected accounts contained the same information I'd originally put there. What a mess.

It took me a couple of hours to straighten out my business accounts, and for good measure, I changed the passwords on all my personal accounts as well. Fortunately, they hadn't tapped into my bank accounts. I'd made those passwords super complicated and two-factor deep. After I shot Beth a back-up list of my new passwords, I pushed away from my desk and stalked to the breakroom for more coffee.

"All done?" Beth called from the lobby. She wiggled her fingers at me.

"Was our internet server okay when we were in Florida?" I asked, stirring creamer into my coffee.

"Fine. No issues." She put a finger on her chin. "Wait. Some emails bounced back to me. I didn't think anything of it at the time." She gave me a mournful look.

I picked up my mug and walked into the lobby. "You wouldn't have suspected anything. All good now."

She stared at me a few seconds. "Thanks."

The landline on her desk rang. With her gaze still on me, she answered. "Watchdog Investigations." I watched her forehead crinkle, her eyebrows draw together. "I understand. Of course. Can I have Olivia call you back?" She cocked her head as she listened. Her fingers played with the cord. "No problem. Thank you." She replaced the receiver. "Paul Wright told me to let you know their firm will no longer be doing business with us."

"That can't be true; they love us," I said in a small, strangled voice that didn't sound like me at all.

Beth drummed her fingers on her desk. "I'm not sure how this hack could've happened. I should've told him that we fixed it."

"I'll call them," I muttered and stalked into my office. I punched their number into the landline on my desk and put it on speaker. I leaned forward on my elbows, ready for battle. *Aching* for battle. I wanted to kill someone. Monty, in particular. This had to be his fault.

"No need to call, Olivia," the smooth, polished voice of the managing partner of Wright, Lewes, and Moore purred into the phone. "I told your receptionist—"

"I know you did," I interrupted. "But there are mitigating circumstances.

214

My business accounts were hacked over the last few days. I've spent all day reworking them. I'm wondering if you got anything strange from my office and if that's the reason for your decision. Apologies if I'm overstepping, but the hacker could've flooded my whole customer base with false information."

I heard him pecking at his keys. "Okay. Let me look. I think it's in here somewhere…with a special code."

I winced and put my hand over my eyes. What had been sent out?

My client, uhh, *former* client, spent a few quiet minutes tapping. I didn't want to lose this account! Working for a legal firm guaranteed steady business and a dependable paycheck. "Ah! Found it. I'll forward."

My heart jackhammered in my chest as I watched my email. Within seconds, it appeared. After a deep breath, I opened the email and scanned it as my client waited.

My jaw dropped. *"Paul.* You know I wouldn't do this!" Staring at the long, tedious email in horror. It listed clients, phone numbers, addresses, and details about each case I'd worked on with his firm. Scope of assignment. Outcome details. Photos attached. In short, this had become priority number one on Watchdog Investigation's workflow chart.

"It doesn't matter, Olivia," he said, his voice kind. "I can't risk it happening again. I knew it had to be an oversight, but your security must have holes in it, and my board is furious. This affects two years of work. Thirty assignments. And this information didn't come under attorney-client privilege, as you know, though our clients trusted us when we told them working with our own investigator limited the chances of the information being used in litigation." He sighed. "This opens the door for our clients to re-litigate in some cases, and we won't get that business back, and worst case? They'll sue the pants off us. I'm sorry, Olivia. I hope you recover from this."

I replaced the handset in its cradle and allowed myself two full minutes of horrified paralysis, then yelled at Beth to print out a spreadsheet of every client we had and include their numbers. I popped up from my chair and ran into the lobby. "Where's Sherry?"

Beth's head bobbled in confusion. I watched her try to function, thinking that this woman was *not* good in a crisis.

"It'll be fine," I assured her. "But we should act fast, and I need Sherry. Please try to get her on the phone and tell her it's urgent."

Fifteen minutes later, Sherry appeared, looking tattered around the edges. She walked to the desk, which sat fifteen paces across from Beth's in a corner of the lobby that she'd made her own— private and tasteful, with original pottery on a bookshelf and local Maryland art on the walls. She sank into her chair and opened her laptop before she noticed us staring at her. "What the hell is going on?"

Chapter Thirty-Four

Hannah

Hannah had trouble shaking off dreams of Patrick's leering expression and the thick, saturated cloth he'd smashed over her face. She hadn't had a full night's sleep in months.

His silky voice slithered through her brain on repeat: *"You really love cardinals, don't you, my love?"*

The minute she'd identified his voice, she should've taken off running. But she'd frozen in place like a startled deer.

She got out of bed and walked into the hallway. Olivia's home felt warm and comforting. Marlowe bounded up the staircase to join her. She squatted to give him a hug, considering the carefully preserved, turn-of-century staircase; its authenticity, its original steepness.

It would be easy to take a tumble down these stairs and break her neck. But with her luck, she'd probably survive, and someone would have to take care of her. She didn't want to be a burden to Olivia and Sherry.

She choked back a sob. Put her hands over her face, remembering the poor patrol cop, dying on the side of the highway in a pool of his own blood.

A buzz vibrated from her pocket. She gasped. She'd forgotten to put it back in Olivia's hiding place. The caller was "Unknown." After a pause, she answered.

"Who is this?" she asked.

"I've been worried about you."

She had trouble breathing. "Monty?"

"Back from the dead, you might say. I'm on work release a couple of days a week. Where are you?"

Hannah blinked. "I shouldn't be talking to you."

"Why not? I've forgiven you. Prison's been good for me that way. I've learned a lot about forgiveness."

Hannah swallowed. Her hand tightened on the phone. She thought about the letters he'd sent to Florida. The texts. What did he want from her?

He chuckled. "I'm surprised you still have this number."

"Olivia doesn't know I have it," she blurted before she realized now he'd know her location.

"Graham told me you'd had problems with your new husband. Patrick, right? Patrick Somerset. I'm sorry it didn't work out for you."

Her mind flipped back to walking into the waiting room in the Hagerstown incarceration unit after his conviction five years ago. Listening to him blather on and showering her with compliments, insisting that Olivia had never understood him. She remembered how he'd looked at her with such admiration and longing that she'd been unable to resist the attention. He'd sucked her in with his charm, the dimples, the dark, twinkling eyes… and caused her to betray Olivia in the worst way. She felt her back straighten. That would *not* happen again, but she could cash in on his narcissistic tendencies. He might prove useful. It wouldn't hurt to have a conversation. Would it?

Later that afternoon, the golden-brown, fried chicken lay in a pretty bowl on the table, and homemade hash browns sat in a matching bowl beside the chicken. Hannah folded her arms and considered the dining room table arrangement. She'd put out plates, silverware, napkins, glasses, and a candle centerpiece.

After talking with Monty, in a burst of energy, she'd plundered Olivia's fridge to make dinner and have it ready when she walked in the door. Riot had laid in the doorway the entire time, watching her scurry about the kitchen, flour flying everywhere. She'd left the kitchen spotless, too.

She smiled and surveyed her efforts. Taper candles shimmered in the center of the table, and a decanted bottle of wine sat on the sideboard.

She heard tires speed down the lane and stop. The garage door powered open. Olivia's brisk steps tapped through the breezeway from the detached garage and into the kitchen door. She heard the slap of Olivia's purse as she slung it on the counter, and clunk of her leather carryall dropped to the floor. "Hannah?" she called.

Hannah felt a zing of excitement for the first time in years. "In here."

Olivia walked into the dining room. Her eyes widened. "Wow. Did Callie bring dinner?"

"I did it," Hannah announced. She spread her arms. "Ta-daaaa."

Olivia laughed. "This is a great surprise after a horrible, terrible, stupid day."

Hannah poured the wine. "I have news that'll make you feel even better. But you first."

Olivia pulled out a chair and sat. She leaned back, folded her arms, and took in the dim lighting, the flicker of candles, the delectable smell of hash browns and fried chicken. "Thank you so much for this."

"What happened today?" Hannah asked, seating herself.

"Monty happened," she muttered. "He's in a work release program doing his technology thing and hacked into my computer. He found my emails and private folders and disclosed details about Watchdog's investigations to my mailing list." She shrugged. "And I'm sure he sent it out to any other group that has the power to put me out of business."

"That's all?" Hannah teased.

Olivia laughed. "You're in a good mood."

"Have you decided how you're going to handle it?"

Olivia nodded, took a bite, and dabbed her mouth with a napkin. "Chicken's perfect. Sherry and I called all our clients and explained the situation. He didn't have all the intended targets' emails, thank God...so much of it entailed emailing the clients with what they already knew, and the others had trashed the email, considering it a mistake. Our bigger accounts took the hit." Olivia paused to chew and swallow. She used her fork as a pointer and emphasized the words as she spoke with it. "Attorneys don't like it when their clients' investigation results get blasted to the local neighborhood websites and show up on social media. We have no idea yet how deep it goes, but at least my clients know what happened now."

"I'm sorry," Hannah said. "Speaking of hacking events..." With a guilty look at me, she reached into her pocket, drew out her phone, and put it on the table.

Olivia frowned. "You found it?"

She grinned. "You're terrible at hiding things."

Olivia jabbed her fork into the hashbrowns a bit harder than necessary.

"Monty called me this afternoon," Hannah said.

"Oh, great. And how did he try to use you to make my life miserable this time?"

"I turned it around. Every time he wanted to talk about you, I talked about something else." She grunted. "Monty and Patrick should've been brothers."

Olivia's eyebrow rose. "Did you learn anything I should know?"

Hannah settled back in her chair and folded her arms. "Graham hangs around with him on these work release things. Monty thinks he is using *me* to get information about you. Which...I did share some stuff. Bogus stuff."

Olivia put down her fork and fanned herself with her hands to stop her eyes from watering. "Is this day ever going to end?"

"No...no...you don't understand. I'm misdirecting him. You and Callie and Sherry think I'm in a coma or whatever, but I've been listening. Thinking. I've been through a lot with Patrick, but I'm feeling more like myself every day. However, I got up this morning so depressed I wanted to...well, you don't want to know. But then Monty called, and I felt *useful*. Like I had a purpose or something." She pushed her shoulders back and set her jaw "It's a way I can pay you back. I'll use that bastard the way he's used me. I'll twist him like a pretzel until he doesn't know what happened, and he'll go back to prison with additional charges. Slander and fraud, to name a couple. Hacking email is a crime." She slitted her ocean-blue eyes. "Maybe you and Sherry can put me in the loop."

Olivia smiled, but remained quiet as they clinked their wine glasses in a toast.

Hannah sipped her wine. "What?"

"Sherry and I feel the best place to put you right now is not in our loop, but in a women's shelter. They have a spot for you, and I need to get you over there tonight."

The rolling hills and twisty curves of the back roads between Glyndon and Gettysburg, Pennsylvania, made Hannah's stomach do flip-flops. The trip took an hour. The nondescript, two-story, weathered-wood house sat off the road at a distance.

"This is definitely in the middle of nowhere," she said as she tugged her duffel out of the back.

"It's for your protection, honey," Olivia said. "Patrick's still out there, and you'll be safe here." She held out her hand. "I'll need the phone."

Hannah groaned, but handed over the phone. "How am I going to help you with Monty, then?"

Olivia put the phone in her purse. "Let him simmer for a while. He'll think you're ignoring him, which drives him nuts. Once Patrick's in a cell, I'll give it back. Okay?"

Hannah hugged Olivia. "I love you guys."

"You too. Stay safe. No bending the rules. Promise me."

Hannah held up three fingers like a girl scout. "Cross my heart."

They hugged again. Hannah walked to the woman waiting at the door, who glanced right, left, ushered Hannah inside, then slammed and locked the door behind them.

Chapter Thirty-Five

Olivia

"Are you convinced that Hannah's safe there?" Sherry asked, sitting at her desk with her gaze fastened on her laptop screen and her hands cradling a mug of morning coffee.

"That's the best option we had, don't you think?" I responded.

"I agree," Beth chirped from her desk. "I tried to find them online. There's nothing. I think it'll be a safe place."

I glanced at Sherry. The look between us expressed our mutual bewilderment that Beth had chimed in. Why had she tried to find the shelter online? She had no relationship with Hannah at all, until we'd brought her here. I wrote it off to her becoming more comfortable with our business, but I needed her to stay in her administrative silo.

"You have a minute?" I asked Sherry, with a nod toward my office.

She logged off and closed her laptop. "Sure."

We settled into our respective places on the corner armchairs with an end table between us. The flea-market lamp on the table cast a warm glow. Marlowe wagged his tail from his dog bed beside my desk. I'd made sure to close my office door.

Sherry frowned. "You okay?"

"I don't think Beth needs to know details, that's all."

Sherry nodded slowly. She sipped her coffee. "Hannah's situation kind of makes you realize."

"Realize what?"

"The stuff we should keep to ourselves."

I laughed. "So true. Be careful what you say and how you say it."

Sherry rubbed her healing, gunshot shoulder, winced, and folded her arms. "I agree we should be careful what and how we say things but... also *who* we tell."

I nodded. "How's new business looking?"

"Not so good. Monty's latest plan to kill you is working." She sipped more coffee. "Metaphorically speaking."

"I called everyone I could yesterday."

"Me, too. Sorry to say, but the assignments we had on the books? Most of them dropped out."

"We stopped the bleeding, though."

"Hope so."

A gloomy silence settled. I walked into the breakroom to warm up my coffee in the microwave. I heard Beth talking in lowered tones and giggling. I'd never heard her giggle —not once. Maybe she was talking to one of her kids. I returned to my office.

"I can tell you're frustrated," Sherry said.

I plopped down into the chair. "You should know. You've had a lot of experience with my frustration. It never ends well."

"But it does end. You have a gift for making that happen." She grabbed her notepad and pen, waiting expectantly. "What's the plan this time?"

I smiled. "Let's meet at Eddie's in an hour."

I had an itchy, uncomfortable feeling about Curtis, and a possible civil suit against my firm ticking out there like a woodpecker on a dead tree.

Staring out the window, I watched Sherry wave at me from the sidewalk.

She walked in and sat across from me at "our" table. The Wine & Whine girls had shared many a tale at this table over the years. "It's twelve-thirty. Too early to drink, I guess," she joked.

I shook my head. "I'm not in the mood to drink, anyway. I wanted privacy."

We ordered lunch by memory before the server even had a chance to give us menus.

I folded my hands on the table. "Before we left to get Hannah—"

"Which seems like just a few days ago…oh wait. It was." Sherry interrupted with a smile.

"This job is like a hate crime that never ends," I muttered.

Sherry's dark eyebrows gathered together. She'd let her dark, tight curls grow out, and it resembled a poufy Afro from the seventies. She'd worn a bright yellow fabric headband in an attempt to tame it, which looked adorable.

"I mean, yeah, we have this internet thing going on, but it's handled, and we have to find new clients to replace what we lost, but…" Sherry tapped her fingers on the table. "Anyway, it's not the job that's a problem; it's our personal relationships. Hannah. Monty. We need to break the mold."

"I got a phone call," I blurted.

She stopped tapping and waited.

"I didn't want to think about it right before we left to go to Florida. I had to pack, book a flight, and leave. I pushed the call to the back of my mind to think about after I got back." I paused to let the server give us our drink orders. When he left, I continued. "A guy said, 'I saw you.'"

Sherry frowned. "Victoria's homicide?"

I nodded.

"Do you have any ideas about who it could be?"

I shook my head. "None. But I'm concerned about the implication behind the words. Did the person see me take photos of the whole event? Am I looking at a withholding evidence charge? Should I tell the investigators and pre-empt the whole situation?" I felt sweat pop out on my forehead. "Think about it. Should I have held the guy at gunpoint the minute he started becoming hostile to her? I wasn't even supposed to be there! I mean, it's no excuse, but I seriously could not move. All I could think about was my own assault."

Sherry's hand shot across the table to pat my arm. "Don't think about that. Six years is a long time. Refuse to take it into your brain. It's over. Done. You're not that person anymore. You tried to help. You *did* help."

CHAPTER THIRTY-FIVE

My heart raced. I drank some water. "Not soon enough."

The server approached with our lunch and set the plates before us, pursing his lips and sliding away as he registered our tension.

Sherry forked a bite of her quiche. "I love quiche," she said as she chewed. "Okay. Let's do bullet points."

"Bullet points," I repeated with a smile. A joke between us. "We don't have a whiteboard."

"*Virtual* whiteboard, then. Bullet point one: You were the hero, and the cops don't suspect you."

"So far," I added.

Sherry made a face. "Quit catastrophizing. Point two: Victoria didn't survive, her attacker, Raul, ran...my bet is that all he'll want is to disappear. But there might be a connection to Monty, and Monty is a brat."

"That's four bullet points, Sherry. Maybe five."

"Efficiency is a virtue."

My resultant chuckle—anemic though it was—acted as a stress reliever. I sucked in a breath and blew it out. "All I could see was the glint of his knife and his arm going up and down. The screaming didn't register at first, and I checked out for several seconds with a flashback. I woke up when I realized he was staring at me. That's when I rammed my car into gear and headed straight for him." I thought for a few seconds, tapping my finger on my chin. "What if I was *supposed* to be there?"

Sherry shook her head. "They couldn't have known that I'd be running off to Florida to save our damsel in distress. They had to think I was the one that would be there. How would they have gotten that information? The trip to Florida was a last-minute decision."

I started ticking off the names. "Monty. Graham. Raul. Curtis. What's the connection?"

"Curtis," Sherry whispered, thinking. "I'm trying to remember his initial call and our discussion."

"We record all those calls, right?"

She nodded. "I can get it on my phone. Wait a sec."

I focused on my food while she scrolled through calls. "Here." She thrust her phone at me. I put it to my ear.

I listened to his raspy, hesitant words three times. Sherry's voice, competent and confident; Curtis's voice...not so much.

"He sounds nervous," I told her, giving the phone back. "But it could've been the first time he talked with a PI, y'know? People get nervous hiring someone to spy on a partner."

"Of course they do, but not that nervous. I had to dig to get information out of him." Her fingers thrummed the tabletop. "Let's check his financials. Can we do that?"

I lifted a shoulder. "Not legally."

She signaled for the check. "Tom would be so proud of your inability to keep the law."

"Tom would call it payback. A hack for a hack." We spent a few seconds toasting my former mentor. He was missed. "We know someone that can, um...hack, don't we?"

"Of course we do," she said, pulling out her company credit card for the server.

Sherry called her contact. "He's at his office. I'm sending you his contact info and address. He's available now. It's just five minutes from here."

When I arrived at the three-story, redbrick building sandwiched between other versions of the same, I wondered what kind of business Sherry's had with this guy. I parked behind the building, got out of the car, my nose wrinkling at the weeds, trash, and general unkempt feeling of the place. Three concrete stairs led to a door with a glass window in the top half upon which the words "Computer Service" had been applied. I watched as Sherry pulled into the tiny parking lot and finagled her car into a slot.

"How do you know this dude?" I asked as we walked toward a door that once upon a time, had been white.

"My dating life is like panning for gold, as you know. And, often I meet men that don't pan out, but keep in my back pocket for special moments like this. Remember the "talented" friend that told me how to take care of the security cameras? This is the guy. After you," she said, opening the door, which squealed like a cat with a stepped-on tail.

Walking down a linoleum hallway that smelled of antiseptic cleaning agents, we arrived at an office. Sherry knocked. We entered. "Olivia, meet Cosmo."

A lanky, red-haired, bespectacled man rose and extended his hand. I shook it. "Nice to meet you."

"You too," he said, distracted, returning his focus to a battery of laptops and monitors strewn across two desks that spanned the length of two walls.

"Cosmo is gifted with uh, computers."

Still studying his screens, he tossed words over his shoulder. "So, you guys need someone's financial information? Are we talking Feds? CDC? Government officials?"

"Nothing like that," Sherry assured him. "It's a regular guy, Curtis Ridgeland. I texted you his contact info. He's uh…" she patted her cheek, trying to remember. "He's in landscape design. Family business."

Cosmo twirled his chair around. "Piece of cake. Five grand. Half now, half after you're satisfied with what I find. Deal?"

"Wait," I said, feeling off balance. "This needs to be…"

"Kept quiet," he finished for me. "I know. That's what I do. He'll never know. I go in, get copies, and get out. How far back do you need?"

I stared at Sherry.

"Six months?"

"Sure. No problem. When do you need it?"

"Tomorrow."

He dipped his head. "I'll do my best. If there are no unforeseen situations, I'll text one word when I have it."

Sherry glanced at me. "What's the word?"

"Dipshit," he said, totally deadpan. "Write this down, do not put it in your phone." He gave us a number. "If I run into problems, I'll text another word, and we'll need to talk on a secure line, which is the number I gave you. If I have issues, I'll text the word Butterfly."

"Got it," Sherry said. "Good to see you, Cosmo."

"You too, Bodacious."

We walked outside. Down the steps. In the cracked and crumbling parking lot, I stopped her. "Bodacious?"

She waved her delicate, childlike hands. "He gives nicknames to everybody."

"But Bodacious?"

She grinned. "Don't ask."

Chapter Thirty-Six

Hunter

On his way to work, he found himself whistling a tune.

His Jeep announced a call, which he took. "Nick. I'm whistling."

After a two-second pause, Nick blurted, "No way!"

"Huh. You remember"

"How could I forget? Lydia."

Hunter groaned. "The infamous 'Lydia.'"

"Dude. You must have it bad."

In response, Hunter whistled a few measures of "My Girl".

"Stop," Nick said. "You're not even a *good* whistler."

"I'll spare you. So. What's on your mind?"

"The Chief of Police got an email about your involvement with a situation in Maryland."

Hunter slapped his steering wheel. "You have got to be kidding."

"It'll be okay. Listen, I know you were helping her, and I think they'll understand. But I wanted you to be aware so you can figure out how to frame it."

"Thanks. You don't happen to know who ratted me out, do you?"

"Wouldn't tell you if I did. I'm sure you have strings you can pull. Congrats again, dude."

Hunter smiled and ended the call.

Puckering his lips, he resumed his whistling.

An hour later, his lieutenant called him to his office. When initial pleasantries had been exchanged, the lieutenant pinched the bridge of his nose for a second, then looked at him. "What's this I hear about Maryland? And in particular, Olivia Callahan?"

"A support role, sir."

"You don't have to call me sir." He leaned back in his chair, folded his hands across his stomach. "Faraday, you should think about getting married. First, the Shiloh McPherson debacle, and now this." He rubbed his droopy cheeks, shook his head. "What kind of support role?"

Hunter lifted a palm. "She had a friend in trouble who needed someone who knew how to handle a gun and navigate an abuse victim situation. A friend helping a friend."

"My concern is collaboration with a private investigator. Can you look at me and tell me you did *not* do that?"

"Depends upon perspective. I'd call it a security detail."

The lieutenant stared out his window for a few seconds. "Fine line, you know."

"I do."

The two men stared at each other. "I'd never have had to dig into this if someone hadn't called the Chief. You have any idea who would've done that?"

"Do you want me to look into it?"

"Don't you think it's relevant?" The lieutenant raised his eyebrows at Hunter.

"Depends upon per—"

"Perspective," the lieutenant finished for him. "Whatever it is...was...it needs to stop."

"Understood. And under the circumstances, you'll be glad to know that I'm engaged."

The lieutenant smiled and extended his hand across the desk. Hunter shook it. "That's great news, Faraday. Who's the lucky gal?"

"Olivia Callahan," he said.

The lieutenant blinked, then roared with laughter. "Of course it is." He pointed at the door. "You can go. I don't want any further collaborating, Faraday. I'd hate to bust you all the way back to patrol, and we'll need to have a sit-down about how you plan to navigate married life in light of your news. Dismissed."

Hunter's cell vibrated. "Thank you, Lieutenant," he said and left.

"Faraday," he answered.

Olivia's voice. "Hey. Good morning."

"Morning." He grinned. "How's it going?"

"I wanted you to experience a call from me that doesn't beg you to help me through a crisis."

He chuckled. "Much appreciated." He told her about his meeting with his lieutenant.

"We knew that might happen," she said.

Hunter paused. She'd said "we." He couldn't remember Olivia ever referring to them as a unit. He liked it.

"I wanted to pass along that Serena and Lilly both love the ring you chose. Next time they see you, expect group hugs or a cake and a mariachi band or something." She laughed.

"I'll look forward to it."

A tiny pause hovered before she spoke. He walked inside his office and sat behind his desk.

"How did Shiloh take the news?" Olivia asked.

He felt his forehead crunch. "What?"

She repeated the question.

"She-she…" he stammered, then tried again. "How did you know?"

"She's still in the hospital, and I know you'd want to check on her because you think you're responsible for her injuries or whatever. Plus, you'd be anxious to settle that part of your life."

Welcome to the process of becoming one, he told himself silently.

"The injuries put her on a life-change trajectory," he said. "It worked out. An easy transition."

A pause lingered. He pictured Olivia's hazel eyes turning more brown than green, like they did when she thought something through. "You *didn't* tell her."

"I…uhh…"

Olivia laughed. "You *bailed* on that part."

"She'll find out soon enough. I didn't want to, um, cause her any pressure."

"Life-change trajectory," Olivia repeated, her tone speculative. "So, she broke it off with *you?*"

He frowned. "Does that even matter?"

"What matters is that I should get the truth. The *absolute* truth, without leaving out an important detail like that."

He frowned. First his lieutenant, now this. He'd been trying to be thoughtful with Shiloh and hadn't meant to avoid details. The way it had turned out had been a damn miracle, period, whether Olivia felt he'd "omitted" something important or not. "And what matters to me, is that you *trust* me."

Her silence irritated him. "I need to get to work."

"Me, too." She ended the call.

He stared at his cell. "Fine," he muttered.

Chapter Thirty-Seven

Olivia

I tossed my cell on my desk and folded my arms.

So much for our *personal* calls. We'd have to work into them. Our relationship had been built on desperate crisis at one end and white-hot, forbidden passion at the other. On one side, I'd not been able to breathe without him. On the other, I'd gotten into the habit of pushing him away. The in-between stuff needed work. Lots of it. What had gotten under my skin, anyway—the fact that he'd gone to see her, or the fact that he had dodged telling her about our engagement?

Both.

"You'd never have to deal with this if you hadn't asked the question, dork. You had a mental checkpoint before you asked, remember? You should've paid attention to that inner signal. He would've told Shiloh about our engagement in time."

Maybe.

Sherry knocked on my office door. "You available?"

"Come on in."

She stood in front of my desk, not quite meeting my eyes. "What's going on?" I asked.

"Cosmo got the financials."

I refreshed my newly encrypted email. Her email appeared.

"Before you take a look, let me prepare you, okay?"

I lifted my hands from the keyboard.

She took a breath.

My hand drifted to my throat. "What is it?"

"As a bonus, he hacked into Curtis's phone records."

I blinked. "He can do that?"

"He's amazing. We wouldn't want to be on the wrong side of the guy, that's for sure. Curtis had, like...*five* calls with Graham. Two with Monty. Monty is Graham's go-to, so I'd love to know what they talked about." She raised her eyebrows up and down. "But that would be crazy illegal to hack into their phones. We could, though."

I gave her a look.

She shrugged. "As far as financials, Curtis had two big payouts within the last six months from Graham's bank account. She lifted her chin and fisted her hands on her hips, which made her look like Hallie Berry, the miniature version. "It has to be Monty! He can't access a bank account as a locked-up felon. He has to be funneling money to Graham. Maybe he put him his accounts as a signatory."

"That's right. Cosmo found that information. Graham is linked to Monty's financials."

I walked to my desk and unplugged my laptop, putting it on the coffee table where we could both see the screen and opened the attachments. We studied them in silence. Cosmo had annotated improprieties or certain deposits or calls he'd felt expedient. "This guy is a valuable resource."

"I agree," Sherry whispered. "Why are we whispering?"

"Oh." I laughed. "I forget that Hannah's not sleeping in the back anymore. It feels good to know she's somewhere safe."

Sherry tapped her chin. "I know it's early, but have you heard if they apprehended Patrick?"

"I've been texting with the investigator assigned to her case. Patrick's been interviewed and is out on a million-dollar bond. A judge granted a search warrant for his property. They're taking cadaver dogs out to his place."

Sherry paled. "You mean...?"

"Three other women have gone missing in the last eight years in that area. Based on Hannah's allegations, I expect them to excavate his lot and tear his house apart."

"Thank God we got her out of there. I hope they find something," Sherry said.

"So. Back to Victoria. Are you thinking Monty's using Graham as the "money launderer" for lack of a better term?"

Sherry pointed at one of the payments. "This one is big enough to be a contract on someone. So yeah, Curtis might've been motivated to consider murder." Sherry slumped in her chair. "He paid *us* in cash, too. He could've used the payout to pay someone like Raul. I would never have thought that about him."

I made a face. "Wouldn't Monty love it if I was indicted as withholding evidence in a homicide?" I rubbed my hands together, feeling a chill. "They believe the photos we gave Curtis are all I took, don't they?"

She lifted a shoulder. "I hope so."

I took a few seconds to think about how much I appreciated having Sherry as a colleague. "I knew you'd make a good PI."

She shot me a tired smile. "It sure wears you down, though."

"Indeed," I said, my mind riveted on the homicide, trying to piece together their plan. "She tried to break it off with him. It was civil until he started grabbing her. She got mad. Scared. They struggled. He wouldn't leave her alone. After it seemed like he would walk away, the scorned lover...he stopped fighting with her. I thought it was over." I closed my eyes and put myself back there. "Within the next couple of minutes, he went total psychopath."

We sat in silence.

I pursed my lips, thinking. "Do you think Curtis was there? Would someone crazy enough to hire a hit want to watch?"

"Hold that thought," Sherry said, grabbing her mug and walking into the breakroom for a refill.

"Is Beth here yet?" I called.

"She's not at her desk, and her car's not here either," she told me as she walked back to my office and sat.

"Since when does she not come in to work without telling us?"

"Private business? Something that couldn't wait?"

I jerked out my phone and texted her to let me know if she was running late. I needed to be able to depend on her. "Maybe it's getting into the groove of a full-time job again."

"Anyway. Curtis is about as smart as a rock, and I don't think he could've brainstormed this. I believe it was about proof of cheating. Did you see all the creditors on his statements? A ton of them. And, who knows? Maybe Victoria had spending issues, or he needed proof in court to sue for damages. Maybe Raul has evil urges. Maybe it's a random act of violence."

I stared at Sherry, could feel my eyes bug. "Who *are* you?"

She chuckled. "Too many crime shows, I guess. These are all plausible, though."

"We should find out soon enough. Hunter has the photos, and he's trying to locate Raul. The problem is that we don't know if that's his real name. He's running everything through facial recognition, but he has to be careful. He has a buddy at Baltimore PD who's doing him a favor.

"Is Victoria going to make it?" Sherry asked.

"They took her off life support yesterday."

Sherry dipped her head. "Poor thing. Rest in peace, Victoria."

We engaged in a moment of silence for the departed. "Could happen to any one of us," I murmured.

"We *don't* have affairs, and we carry firearms," Sherry quipped. "Chances are slim."

I smiled. "True. You were saying about Monty...?"

"He seems determined to screw with your life. What better way than to create chaos around the work you do? Can't you just hear the two of them yukking it up, talking about the fallout and the problem it'll make for us? Maybe it's as simple and as horrible as that."

A knot of fear tightened my stomach. "Why does he still feel mandated to wreck my life?" I asked her. "People move on. People don't cling to the past like this and expect to extract their own special brand of vengeance.

CHAPTER THIRTY-SEVEN

Do they?"

"The ones that have mental problems do. Sorry, but Monty is a world-class psycho."

I took a potty break and went into the breakroom for a bottle of water. The fridge revealed its normal contents: twenty or so bottles of water, various soft drinks, plastic-wrapped sandwiches, the occasional apple or banana. In the back, nestled between the Hershey's chocolate syrup and a half-quart of milk, sat a crumpled paper sack. I pulled it out and looked inside, winkling my nose, expecting a sour smell to burst from the sack. Instead, a half-eaten package of Mallomars lay inside. Hannah had been the one person I knew who ate Mallomars. She hoarded them, because they were a seasonal cookie. I stared at the package in confusion. The expiration date stamped on the package told me the purchase had been recent. I grabbed my water and raced back to my office.

"Do you eat Mallomars?"

Sherry shook her head. "Hannah loves those things. I don't like them."

"Does Beth?"

Sherry lifted a shoulder. "How should I know?"

I thrust the bag at her. "Just found these."

She looked inside. "Sooooo...?"

"Wait."

I rushed into the guest bedroom. The bed had been made up, but not in the typical way. The throw pillows sat in a straight row, not in layers, like I'd arranged them.

I sat on the bed and ran my palm across the comforter, thinking. Sherry walked in. "What is it?"

"Someone's been here."

"Who?" She gasped. "You think Hannah left the shelter?"

"Remember? I gave Hannah a key to the back door of the office, so it's a possibility." I frowned. "Which raises a lot of other questions and could explain why Beth's been weird."

Sherry shot me a puzzled look.

"Tonight, I'll work late. Don't worry, I'll keep Marlowe with me."

"I'll stay, too."

"You don't have to."

She rolled her eyes.

"Okay. Fine. I'll order takeout for us. And there's white wine in the fridge."

Sherry grinned. "A surveillance party!"

The rest of the day passed in a nice mix of reaching out to attorneys or small businesses in the area in an attempt to replace the business we'd lost. Sherry and I made a side bet on who could bring in the first account. I won. Fifty bucks.

My reputation as Mercy's Miracle continued to reap benefits. In one afternoon, I'd snagged four new clients.

Take that, Monty Callahan.

My book about the whole "Mercy's Miracle" experience had been released four years ago, but people still talked about it and loved the story. A small percentage hated it, but that's expected. So much has happened since then that I could write a sequel, but in spite of my agent's protests and desperate attempts to get me to write one, I turned her down. You might say my former agent, Agatha, went down in flames. Quite spectacularly, in fact, and I'd closed the door on that chapter of my life.

I'd replaced Agatha with Catherine March. Catherine helped me re-work the book as a screenplay, and she's hawking it to producers. Of course, the media coverage about this development catapulted Watchdog Investigations into the public eye. I had to smile when I thought about the old adage "the best revenge is success." I liked to imagine the look on my dirtbag ex's face as Watchdog Investigations zoomed to success in a matter of months, many thanks to inheriting Tom Stark's clients, of course. But for him, I'd never have become a PI at all. The book had also experienced success, which made Monty crazy. His sins had been splashed all over the world.

However.

I'm sure Monty fantasized about the look on *my* face when the full onslaught of hacking my information hit me. The labor pains of rebuilding my client base had become torturous, and I tried to breathe my way through it. As Sherry and I cold-called prospects, many had already heard about the breach of security and declined to talk further. Each rejection was a slap in the face, which made me more determined than ever to crush Monty and his bizarre hold on my life. He would *not* steal my livelihood, my reputation, or my success. The long and winding cord Monty kept wrapped around my neck had turned into a leash he pulled at his pleasure.

Sherry lifted her head when I walked into the lobby. "Wow. What happened?"

I uncurled my fists, shook out my hands. "We have to figure out how to stop this. I can't take it anymore."

"I can tell. You look like you want to punch someone."

"Whatever it takes to get him the hell out of my life!"

She called another potential client and put the handset to her ear. "Yeah, well, try to stay out of prison. We need you." A voice answered her call, and she began her spiel extolling the virtues of Watchdog Investigations and list of services.

I took Marlowe's leash and my coat off the rack. "I'm taking Marlowe for a walk. Back in thirty minutes." I whispered. She nodded, not missing a beat in her conversation. Sherry was much better at cold calls than me.

As I walked outside, I breathed deep of the wood-burning fireplaces, the smell of pine trees, and a hint of snow in the air. Marlowe stiffened and let out a couple of soft woofs.

My hand flew to my side for my weapon, but I'd left my gun belt on the coat rack. "What is it, boy? Show me."

Chapter Thirty-Eight

Olivia

Marlowe tugged on his leash, and I followed. We walked off the parking lot, past the office, and into the untamed wildness of my five-acre slice of Maryland—the bare-bones winter skeletons and dense thatches of sticks clinging to the promise of spring. A thick fog had rolled in on the heels of last night's rain.

The heavy, lurking fog filled me with dread.

I flopped Marlowe's leash in frustration. "What are you after?"

He assumed a dog-show pose, looking every handsome inch of his combination breed—German Shepherd and Labrador Retriever.

My gaze followed the point of his nose. I squatted down to his level, wishing the fog would lift. I heard a rustling. The wind in the trees? I couldn't quite identify it, but then the obvious whoosh-whoosh of steps through dry winter weeds drew closer. Marlowe whined and started wagging his tail. My shoulders relaxed.

"Hannah! I saw that the bedroom had been used. Let's talk about this," I called into the fog, assuming it must be her, though I couldn't really tell.

The steps drew closer.

My mouth dropped open when not one, but *two* women emerged from the fog. Beth in front, wearing a deep scowl; Hannah behind, pointing a gun at Beth's back.

My heart stopped. A gun?

I yanked my cell from my pocket, sent a quick text to Sherry. Marlowe's whole body wiggled with joy. He strained against the leash. He loved them both, and in this situation, he'd be no help at all.

Twenty-five feet.

Fifteen.

Ten.

My shirt grew damp with sweat. I had no idea how to handle any of this. I hung onto Marlowe's leash with a firm grip, an anchor attached to a boat tilting wildly on a stormy sea.

"You'll never believe what she's been doing," Hannah said, prodding Beth with the gun barrel.

The fog that floated around us put my mind in a dream state. I knew one thing, though...Hannah didn't have any business swinging around a weapon. I held out my hand. "Give me the gun."

"Y'know, at that damn shelter, they cut us off from the outside world, but I snagged an iPad off a desk when they weren't looking."

Out of the corner of my eye, I glimpsed movement. *Sherry.*

Beth remained silent, her expression unreadable.

She laughed. "It wasn't even password-protected, so I logged into my socials to see if Patrick had tried to contact me, and of course, he had, but then I thought I'd check Beth's. She's a big Foofoo. I thought your groupies had disbanded, but no. Friends of Olivia is alive, and Beth is right in the middle of it."

My lips parted in surprise. I tried to make sense of the words, but the scene playing out in front of me seemed more like a dream sequence than reality. Marlowe sat quiet and patient beside me. Hannah's arm shook from holding the gun in place. Her face bloomed a bright red. Perspiration dotted her forehead. The *pregnancy!* I glanced at her growing stomach. "Give me the gun, Hannah."

She ignored me a second time.

"I messaged Monty, too. He went on and on about Beth. *That* set off big, freaking alarms in my head." Hannah gave Beth a hard stare. "Tell her!"

If looks could kill, Beth's would've incinerated me right on the spot. A total departure from her typical "Aunt Bea" approach. When had this shift happened? How?

Beth pressed her lips together so hard they'd disappeared. Her round face was slick with sweat. Hannah dropped her arm but held onto the gun. Beth let out a long exhale and jammed her arms across her generous bosom.

"I read your *book*," Beth said, glaring at me. "I can't believe people bought the story...the poor, pathetic victim of such an..." she paused to think about the right word, "...*idiotic* choice to drive to Richmond and spend a weekend with a man you didn't even know. What kind of example is that to your daughters? What did you *think* would happen?"

The words hurt. How many times had I already condemned myself for that decision? I clung to Marlowe's leash as every hideous decision I'd ever made flashed through my mind, including hiring her to work for me.

I heard subtle movements behind me. Sherry getting closer.

"Monty loved you! Passion for a wife is not a crime."

I felt my eyebrows jerk together. "Have you been talking to Monty?"

She drew herself up to her full five-foot-three. "Poor man needs *someone* to talk to."

"It started with a lonely prisoners' website," Hannah said "She's been talking to Monty for years and I thought you needed to know. Did you realize websites like that existed?" She snorted her derision. "I thought prison was supposed to *change* people." She poked Beth again with the firearm. "You're the one that's an idiot, Beth. Monty is a master manipulator, and you fell for it."

My focus riveted on Beth. "What did he ask you to do?"

She spread her hands. "I didn't know what would happen; I mean...he said he misses you so much, and in some small way, he wanted to help. He is *proud* of your success. We were co-conspirators, you know?" Her beady eyes shone with...something. Not warmth, but something.

The depth of Monty's deceptive charm never ceased to amaze. I felt the full brunt of this poor woman's brainwashing, because he'd done it to me, too, and almost won over Hannah.

Beth clutched her hands together like a penitent nun. All she needed to complete the image was a rosary. "I didn't think it would go this far. I don't know that much about email lists and social media."

"The hell you don't!" Hannah blurted, waving the gun around. "You fed him passwords, links, everything. I heard you!"

I groaned. "Hannah. Please. Give me the gun before you hurt someone."

She handed it to me. I slid out the cartridge and rolled my eyes. "It's not even loaded."

Hannah smiled. "I took the bullets out, but she didn't know that. You should've seen the look on her face when I confronted her in the office this morning."

Beth worked her jaw and stared at the ground. Sherry gave up her stealth approach.

"You sure hid it well, Beth," I said, sticking the gun in the waistband of my pants.

She frowned. "Hid what?"

I stared at her. "Why on earth did you accept the job offer if you hated me so much?"

She lifted her chin. "You ruined your husband's life. He has nothing." She snorted. "You've internalized the word "victim" so long you can't even tell the difference between right and wrong anymore. I saw an opportunity to do some good in the world."

I felt immense compassion for this misguided, aging woman who had arranged her life around a mutual hatred. The intensity of my murderous thoughts toward Monty increased accordingly. She must've skimmed over the part in my book about how hard it had been to juggle two recoveries...the physical one from the brain injury and —different but just as traumatic—the emotional pain of marriage to a man like Monty.

I let go of Marlowe's leash and rubbed the cramp out of my hand.

I'd heard about "prison passion." My mind pieced together what must have happened: Monty had paid a small fee to join a "meet-a-prisoner" website and Beth had been looking for him there. These vulnerable, bored women look for men they can control. Men in a cage, or in some cases, the women have histories of abuse and want relationships with men who are unable to hurt them. In Beth's case, she'd developed an emotional attachment to someone she thought had been wronged, which made me wonder about her own marriage.

"He used you, Beth," I said. "Just like he used Hannah. It isn't possible to trust him."

"I tried to tell you," Hannah interjected, her gaze on Beth.

I glanced at Hannah in surprise. "How long have you known?"

"A while." She averted her eyes.

I frowned. What was that about?

She continued. "But I thought it was harmless. She's spouting off. The book can be polarizing. Some people think Monty should've gotten a lighter sentence; some think you're a hero." She shrugged. "But after I talked to Monty, the weirdness increased. You know how he gets, all giddy and everything, and he can't keep his mouth shut. When he told me about all the women he'd met through a prison dating website, I had to say something." She turned to Beth. "You weren't the only one, you know. And he played you like a fiddle."

Beth stared at her. Hannah's cheeks had become beet-red. "I need..." she gave me a funny look, then crumpled to the ground.

Even pregnant, she felt light as a feather. Between the three of us, we carried her back to the office. Marlowe followed, his leash trailing through the brush. The fog began to lift.

We fixed Hannah a peanut butter and jelly sandwich, and got her a bottle of water. We told her to rest, and put Marlowe in the bedroom with her.

Which left the issue with Beth. Her air of defiance stunned me. The woman was convinced that she'd acted with impunity. I asked her to join us in my office.

Sherry and I sat beside each other in our regular spots, and Beth sat in the chair on the other side of the coffee table. The end table lamps cast a cozy glow. Beth studied the faded rose, boho pattern of the carpet, her hands clutched in her lap.

I cleared my throat.

Sherry gave me a tight nod of encouragement.

CHAPTER THIRTY-EIGHT

"Beth. Do you see that we have a conundrum here?"

She glared. "If I'm guilty of anything, it's that I care too much about people."

"Collaborating with a felon? Causing great harm to a local business? Libel issues? Privacy issues?" Sherry frowned. "Give me a break, Beth."

Beth pushed a sweaty curl off her forehead. "I thought he wanted to help you." The fire had gone out of her.

I flicked my eyes at Sherry. "Are you admitting that perhaps you were a *victim?*" I asked, thinking about how she'd mocked me earlier.

"Yes! Yes, I was a..."

I could almost hear the gears grinding in her head about tables turning or karma or whatever you want to call it.

"I guess I need a lawyer." Her shoulders slumped.

I gave her a curt nod. "It goes without saying that you should pack your things and leave, Beth. I'm filing a police report, so you should stay in the area. I'm sure Baltimore PD will want a word."

Beth flounced from her chair and stalked to her desk.

"Will you supervise? "I asked Sherry. "Get her office keys and make sure she's not taking anything proprietary? Walk her to her car? No flash drives."

"Yep." She jogged through the break room to the lobby. I heard Beth's voice, once so comforting, now shrill and insistent that she didn't need a babysitter.

The weight of every single one of my forty-five years pinned me to my chair. Would she still communicate with Monty? Would the police find it necessary to track her calls? Would they even bother with this? Sometimes it surprised me what our local PD wouldn't pursue.

I heard Beth throwing things into a box and muttering at Sherry. Within the next five minutes, Beth and her belongings walked out the door. I heard the purr of her Mini Cooper's baby engine leaving the parking lot.

I went into the lobby to wait for a report.

She entered, closed the door, and leaned against it. "What? You didn't want to say goodbye?" she asked, a teasing glint in her eyes.

Chapter Thirty-Nine

Olivia

The morning dawned with the faint chirp of birds waking and a winter sun peeking through the trees. I sat in the porch swing with a heavy coat on, one foot on the whitewashed, wood-plank flooring, moving the swing back and forth.

I had little hope that Baltimore PD would do much about Beth's transgressions, but they *would* send out someone to take my complaint. I didn't know if I had it in me to gather the evidence they'd need to prosecute.

I had to think about it.

Sherry walked outside, holding two steaming mugs of coffee.

I stopped moving the swing and accepted one of them.

"I'm not used to all-nighters anymore," she said, sitting in one of my white, wicker porch chairs.

"It's freezing out here," I said.

"It's a cleansing cold."

I laughed. "Like the "dry heat" Arizonans talk about?

She shrugged. "Whatever. It clears my head."

My cell buzzed with a text from Hunter. I read it and smiled.

"Your fiancée?"

I snuggled further into the comforting thickness of an oversized coat Gray had left at my house when he and Mom visited. I wore it at times like these, as he'd become more of a dad to me than my own. Its presence around my shoulders reminded me that I had a tribe. Family. People who cared.

"He's worried and wants to come. I'm not letting him."

Sherry snickered. "Told you."

I stared at my left hand. The emerald and surrounding diamonds sparkled in the sun. I put the ring on every morning right after I got dressed. "I know. He's one of the good ones."

"Absolutely."

We enjoyed a comfortable silence.

The sun rose higher, warming us. "I don't know what to do." After a tiny pause, I continued. "Thanks for staying with me last night."

"One of the perks of being single is that I can do what I want." She scratched her cheek, then cupped it in her palm, thinking. "We wait, that's all. Trust that the cops are doing their job and Beth's learned a lesson. We may want to think about a civil suit for damages. Are we taking Hannah back to the shelter today?"

I slitted my eyes at her. "Do you think she'll stay there?"

"Is she awake yet?"

Marlowe whined inside the door. Riot stared at us with his golden eyes. They both sat there, watching us through the screen. Two reminders that once upon a time life had been predictable, even enjoyable. "Those two will let us know when she gets up, so I'd say no."

I finished my coffee. Looked at my cell. My jaw dropped. How had I missed a text? I'd been looking for them all night long.

"The cops have something. They want us to come in." I said, the words punctuated by little breath clouds. "I'm Hannah's emergency contact now. They want to talk to Hannah."

"You go wake up Hannah. I'll fix a quick breakfast."

I followed her inside.

It took us forty-five minutes to drive to the police station, and the traffic stalled a couple of times, so when we got there, we were not in the best of moods. We were ushered into a small waiting room floored with black-and-white linoleum and adorned with circa-70s landscape art. My mind spun with possibilities: Did they have Patrick in a cell? Did they run into extradition problems? Did they need Hannah in Florida to testify?

I rubbed my forehead in frustration.

"Stop," Sherry said.

My head jerked up. "Stop what?"

"That thing you do…let your mind go crazy. Don't think the worst. We don't know anything yet. Hang in there, hon." Sherry was exhausted, too, judging by the starkness of the bags under her eyes.

"Thanks for your support. Whatever's happened, I'm glad you're my partner in all this."

She smiled. "Wine & Whine girls forever, right?"

"Right."

"Right," Hannah echoed, looking forlorn. We sat in a row on the same side of a metal, rectangular table. Someone had brought each of us a mini bottle of water.

A door shot open. A somber-looking plainclothes cop in a blue sport coat and open-collared dress shirt walked in with a file under his arm. "We've had an unfortunate development," he said.

My heart sank.

"I'm Sergeant Matthews. We got a call from Florida about a body." He whipped a photo out of the file and put it on the table in front of her. "You know this man?"

She pulled the photo closer and looked at it. "How can I tell? Looks like someone shot his face off."

She pushed it back to him.

"He's been identified as Patrick Somerset of Niceville, Florida. Your husband, correct?"

Hannah started fanning herself. "Are you sure that's him?"

I glanced at Sherry, who bit her lower lip. I looked past her at Hannah. "How are you doing?"

She looked pale.

Turning to the sergeant, I added, "She's pregnant. Do you have crackers or something?"

"Sure." He left the room.

"Hannah," I hissed. "Do you think he committed suicide?"

She turned weepy eyes on me and said nothing.

Sherry mouthed, "They're recording us."

Sergeant Matthews returned, put a pile of Saltine packets in front of Hannah, and re-opened the file. "Where were you day before yesterday?"

"A women's shelter."

He paused. Put his pen down and leaned forward on his elbows. "Mr. Somerset was abusive?"

Hannah nodded. "There should be a report."

He flipped through. "Doesn't look like it."

Hannah glared. "If you're looking for hysterical screaming and tears, that's not going to happen. The world is a better place without him, but let me be clear: I did not kill my husband."

"So. You left the shelter? Where did you go?"

She pointed at Sherry and me. "Their office."

My back stiffened. Had she been there two nights? We could account for one night at the office. Not two. Sherry nudged me with her elbow, which meant: remember the "Wine & Whine" credo. We'd have Hannah's back. Always. "I have a guest room in my office building. We are both investigators in my firm, Watchdog Investigations. We've been trying to help Hannah, as her husband had become dangerous. A report was filed with the Niceville Police Department, and I don't know why you don't have access."

Sergeant Matthews' eyes slid from one of us to the other. He folded his arms. "You can corroborate Ms. Somerset's whereabouts at the time of the homicide, then?"

We nodded in unison.

He returned to his file. "Okay."

I stifled a sigh of relief.

"Ms. Somerset, can you take a closer look? A distinguishing mark, a tattoo you recognize?"

He slid the photo across.

She closed her eyes, exhaled, and looked again. "His wedding ring. I recognize his wedding ring."

Holding her stomach, she rose from her chair. "Where's the ladies' room?" He told her. She left.

His hard eyes raked our faces. "Where were you two nights ago?"

Sherry and I wrinkled our foreheads at each other. "Company business," she said.

"Working an investigation," I added.

He tapped the table with his fingers. "Didn't you guys have a big security issue?"

"It's taken care of," I mumbled.

"Glad to hear it," he said. "Those damn hackers. We get so many calls these days, and it's not easy to trace those guys."

Sherry stared at the floor.

The door squeaked open, and Hannah returned.

Sergeant Matthews stuck the pages and photo back in the folder. "Okay, ladies. We'll be in touch if we need anything else. Ms. Somerset, my sympathies on your loss."

We said nothing until we got back into my Land Rover and pulled away from the parking lot.

Sherry sat in the front passenger seat, and Hannah sat in the back.

"Just tell us," Sherry said.

"Tell you what?" Hannah gazed out the window.

"That couldn't have been random."

"Why not?" Hannah replied.

"Maybe we don't want to know." I said. "Let's leave it alone."

"Okay."

Hannah leaned in from the back seat. "I can live my life now," she said. "It was fate."

"This 'fate' have a name?" Sherry persisted.

I cautioned her to stop asking questions.

"I guess I need to go back to Florida," Hannah said, her voice on the dreamy side. I looked at her more closely. Enlarged pupils, rapid breathing.

CHAPTER THIRTY-NINE

Sweating.

"Her blood pressure's dropping. We need to get her to an ER or something," I said.

"I'm still his wife," Hannah continued. "I'll take care of the house, get him buried...did we ever find out what they found in the yard?" Her voice had become lethargic, sluggish. "He made me his beneficiary."

Sherry ran her hands through her curls and gave me a look. "This is horrifying."

"He's gone," Hannah said. "That's all that matters." With a sigh, she told us she wanted to sleep and lie down. I floored the accelerator and drove to the closest medical facility I could find.

Chapter Forty

Hannah

A week later

Hannah woke early.

Where was her damn phone? She groped underneath the covers, scanned the tops of dressers, end tables. The burner she'd bought when she left the shelter had to be here, somewhere. She showered and got dressed, then got down on her hands and knees and looked under the bed in Olivia's guest room. "Thank God," she said, slid the phone into her pocket, and went downstairs.

The phone pressed against her ear, she paced back and forth in the den trying to reason with the man on the other end of the call. She had to pull the phone away from her ear when he started screaming obscenities.

She cast a worried glance at the second floor. Olivia's bedroom door remained closed. Good.

"Listen to me. You'll get your money," she whispered. "I have to get back to Florida first. There's paperwork to fill out. But, I promise, you'll get every penny. In cash, okay? Don't worry. The cops down there have no leads at all."

A door opened. She heard the click of Marlowe's claws on the hardwood floor. Hannah put the phone away and jogged into the kitchen.

Olivia walked in, rubbing her eyes and yawning. "The girls will be here

252

sometime today. I'm *so* looking forward to it." She walked to the Keurig and put a K-cup in. "How'd you sleep, Hannah?"

"Not good. I have a lot on my mind."

Olivia nodded. "I'd imagine so. How are you feeling?"

Hannah's hand fell to her stomach. "I have things to take care of, but with Patrick out of my life, at least I *have* a life."

Olivia sipped her coffee. "Want to help me put up a tree?"

Hannah laughed. "Sure. Patrick didn't let me put up a Christmas tree. He never liked Christmas."

Olivia made a face. "That's terrible. I don't want this to happen again, so busy that I can't focus on Christmas. I'm decorating a tree for my girls and planning a whirlwind shopping trip this afternoon in Westminster. You're going with me."

"Okay," Hannah said. What else could she say? She had no car and very little cash. At this point, she depended on Olivia, Sherry, and Callie to hold her head above water until she figured things out.

Hannah sat at the kitchen table, her mind spinning with all she needed to get done. She watched Olivia fix a quick breakfast. Her stomach rumbled at the smell of eggs and toast.

"I need to get a cheap flight to Florida," she said. "They're releasing his body, and I have to arrange a funeral and meet with the attorney about his will. I never even met the family, and I don't know if they kept in touch, so it's clear that I'm the person to do all this stuff. Do you think you could loan me the money? I'll pay you back as soon as I can."

Olivia spun around, her eyebrows arched in surprise. "But you have to be with us for Christmas!"

She dug out her phone and started scrolling. "I have to get back and settle things, Olivia. You understand, right? It has to be *over*." She glued her eyes to her phone so she wouldn't have to face Olivia's scrutiny. If she wasn't careful, Olivia would guess. For all she knew, maybe she'd already guessed what had happened to Patrick.

"Found one," she announced. "Tomorrow at two-thirty. Maybe I can get back by Christmas Eve." She put the phone down. "Why aren't you going to

Richmond, anyway?"

"Gray's not up to it," Olivia said as she flipped eggs in a skillet.

Olivia pulled out a couple of plates and put eggs and toast on each. "Why don't you tell me what's really going on, Hannah?"

She busied herself with the eggs. "Nothing."

Olivia cocked her head. "How long have we known each other?"

"What does that have to do with anything?"

"Hannah, I can help you."

Her chin quivered. "Help me what?"

Olivia raised her hands in frustration. "Okay. Have it your way. I hope you know what you're doing."

"Me, too," she responded, her voice soft.

A car rolled into the driveway. Two doors slammed. "Girls are here," Olivia said, with a smile.

Hannah followed Olivia outside to greet them and watched the joyful reunion with a wistful expression on her face. It had been good to go shopping with Olivia, to enjoy the sound and feel of Christmas again. It troubled her how Patrick's insistence on isolating her made it scary to mingle with regular people now. She'd enjoyed watching the kids, the toddlers, and babies, but parents had whisked the kids away from her with mean expressions. It had hurt her feelings. Had she become so strange that doting on a child felt creepy to the parents? Had Patrick made her into something to avoid?

"Miss Hannah! It's good to see you," Lilly exclaimed, and gave her a quick hug, too. "Didn't you move to Florida?" She watched Hannah rubbing her tummy. "Wait. Are you...?"

"I am," Hannah said. "Merry Christmas to me," she joked.

Both girls squealed their congratulations, and Olivia hustled the two of them inside before they could ask questions.

"Aw. You put up a tree! Mom..." Serena flashed her eyes at her mother, "That's so nice! I know you've been going crazy with everything. And presents? Wow, Mom. Thank you."

"I'm not doing anything this week but enjoying you two," Olivia said.

"There's hot apple cider on the stove. Go get some. It's so nice today. Hannah and I will be on the porch, okay? Bring us some."

"I love your cat," Hannah said as she walked outside. "I wish I could have a pet."

Olivia searched her face. "You can do anything you want, Hannah. First, though, you need to heal from the ordeal. Give it a year or so to settle into a rhythm. Maybe Hazel will give you free consultations until you get back on your feet. It'd be good for you, maybe for her too. I bet she'd love it."

Hannah stared out into the yard. The bird feeders had been re-stocked, and winter birds had pounced on them.

Olivia followed Hannah's gaze. "Most of the birds return in April. This time of year, it's mainly chickadees and wrens."

Hannah nodded, studying her. "I wish I had your serenity."

The girls exploded out the screen door, which slapped closed behind them, leaving Riot's expression more disgruntled than usual. Hannah laughed. "That cat!"

"He's a good one," Olivia said, accepting the hot cider from her daughters. They sat on the porch swing, chattering about school, boys, their majors, and extra-curricular activities. Hannah sank into the warmth, relishing the feel of a family. A *real* family.

Maybe she'd have one someday.

"Mom!" Lilly cried.

Olivia flinched. "My ears aren't used to "loud.""

She laughed. "Sorry, mom," she said in a lower tone. "We haven't seen your ring in person."

Olivia took it off and handed it to them.

"I don't even know if I've congratulated you, Olivia," Hannah said.

"You've had other things on your mind."

"The ring is beautiful. I'm happy for you." After a pause, she continued. "We all knew it'd happen sooner or later."

Olivia laughed. "Well. Someone should've told me."

"We did. You didn't believe us."

Hannah lapsed into silence, thinking. Would she ever feel happy again?

Right now, she felt numb, hopeless, and exhausted all the time. How would she raise a child?

She rubbed her forehead. *Stay in the moment.*

Tires rumbled onto the driveway. A door slammed. Hunter waved and walked into the yard.

Olivia snatched her engagement ring back from the girls and slid it on her finger before she walked out to meet him.

Lilly started giggling. Serena told her sister to shut up.

Olivia walked into his outstretched arms. The hug lasted a long time. An intimate, forever kind of hug.

She looked at her watch. Twelve-thirty. With a gasp, she shot upstairs. It would be a miracle if she reached the airport in time to make it to the gate.

As she jogged down the stairs with her suitcase, Olivia glanced at her watch. "Is it time?"

She nodded. "I'm late. I gotta run. Thanks for everything, and I'll call."

Olivia hugged her. "I'll hold you to that. We love you, Hannah."

The girls said their goodbyes. Hunter hugged her and told her to stay in touch.

"I'm so happy for you guys," Hannah whispered. She ran down the porch stairs, through the yard, and hopped into the waiting Uber.

Chapter Forty-One

Olivia

Callie sat in my kitchen eating a Croissant with jam and butter. I wiped down my kitchen counters and washed the rest of the dishes as I waited for Lilly and Serena to get out of bed.

"So, how are your Christmas plans coming along?" Callie asked.

"Rushed. Fine. I'm determined to find a work-life balance, though." Olivia said.

"Lover-boy upstairs?"

Olivia blushed. "He is. He's still on medical leave."

"Will the next earth-shattering news I hear from you be about moving to Richmond?"

"Who told you that?" I slung my tea towel over my shoulder. It slipped off. I bent down and yanked it from the floor.

"No one. I just figured. You guys are getting married. You can't do marriage long distance."

I muttered a few choice words under my breath.

"What?" Callie eyed me.

"We have to talk about it."

"I get it."

"No, you don't!"

"Wow. Why are you upset?" Callie asked, licking jelly off her fingertips. "Do you have coffee?"

"Help yourself," I told her, flicking my tea towel toward the Keurig. "You know where it is."

"What happened with Beth?" Callie asked. "I've seen her in her yard, passed by and waved, she doesn't wave back anymore. You guys have a falling out?"

I laughed. "You could say that. I had to let her go."

Callie's face fell. "Aw. That's too bad. I thought she'd do a great job."

My jaw worked. Should I tell her?

Callie's face screwed into a knot. "What am I missing?"

I used the tea towel to rub a spot on the counter. "You know, when something seems too good to be true, it probably is." I cleared my throat. "Beth and Monty found each other through a prison dating site. And— adding insult to injury—she was the *president* of the stupid Foofoos."

Callie gasped. "You have got to be kidding me!"

"Guess I haven't had time to fill you in on the exciting details of my life."

She frowned and tapped her chin. "That's what Graham must've been talking about," she whispered, almost to herself.

My ears perked. "What did he say?"

"Graham's getting tired of Monty. I've seen that coming. But this time, he's carrying around something heavy."

"Like an indictment, maybe?" Even as the words fell from my mouth, I regretted saying them. Callie didn't know that Graham had already crossed the line performing Monty's "errands." Many times.

As if reading my mind, she continued. "I think it's too late for Graham. I know for a fact he's involved in some illegal stuff, and sure, I hope he doesn't get caught... but part of me hopes he does." She shook her head sadly. "How else is he going to change?"

I reached for her hand. "We can't depend on them to change, hon'. We can hope and pray, but we also have to be smart and keep our distance. Some men are users." I bit my lower lip. Should I tell her? Should I tell my best friend about Curtis and Victoria? What if Graham knew something that would help me get to Monty's bottom-line agenda?

I closed my eyes and took a breath. "There's something I need to tell you."

An hour later, Callie paced my kitchen, circling around the breakfast bar until I felt dizzy. "Sit, Callie. Let's think about this. Tell me again what Graham told you."

She plunked herself down on one of the bar stools, and her perpetual ponytail swung left, right, left, right as she fumed. "How stupid does he think I am? That's why he was talking about doubling up on my alimony checks...he got a windfall from being an accessory to *murder!*" She slapped her palm on her forehead and kept it there. "Good Lord, Olivia. Am I implicated, too? What if the cops think I knew about it?"

"The cops haven't even checked back with me after the fact. They have to know by now I'm an investigator and had been in the studio's parking lot in some official capacity, but I haven't been questioned at all. You're not even a blip on their radar, okay? You're fine."

"Okay." She exhaled. "Let me think."

I smiled. Callie's brain worked like a Rubik's Cube, and mine worked like a...well, since the injury, like a shattered mirror I put back together, piece by piece.

I waited.

"I have to filter what he said through all this," she explained, her forehead furrowing. "As I mentioned, something's weighing him down, and it must involve what you told me."

My cell buzzed. Callie ducked like someone had tossed a lit firecracker at us.

"I have to take this. Keep thinking. I'll just be a minute." I walked into the den.

"Hey. Good morning, gorgeous."

I smiled. "It couldn't wait until you came downstairs for breakfast?"

"We got a hit," Hunter said.

"On what?"

"Raul. We finally got a clean close-up from those photos you took to work with facial recognition software. Raul Zambrano is an undocumented immigrant from Venezuela...a gang member with a record as long as my arm. He should've been turned away at the border. He's managed to cross through without incident three times with a sheet that includes rape, attempted murder, manslaughter, kidnapping. Assorted petty theft."

I blinked. So. Someone like that might *enjoy* killing. I said as much to Hunter.

"You can bet on that," Hunter stated, his voice somber. "The lifestyle over there can be ruthless. If Victoria pushed back, he'd shut her up for good without a second thought. It's likely he got his back up over a female Anglo who rejected him, and his temper got out of hand. It's imperative that they find this guy."

I felt the inevitable puzzle piece slide into place with that "click" I could feel in my bones.

"That makes total sense."

"That's it, babe. I thought you'd want to know right away."

I felt my cheeks burn and wondered when he'd stop having that effect on me. Never, I hoped. "I love you."

"Love you, too. I'll be down in a few minutes."

We ended the call. I ran into the kitchen. "Cal! Guess what I found out?"

Callie watched me tug out a stool and sit. "Must be good."

"Raul is undocumented and a gang member from Venezuela," I told her. "With a long and violent history of crime."

"And that's good news because…?"

"Raul's a killer, the real deal. It means that it's possible that *rage* and a murderous frenzy killed her. Victoria tried to break it off, and you don't break it off with those guys, y'know? Maybe all Monty did was hack into my system and try to put a major hit on my business." I shrugged. "I guess even Monty's not dumb enough to help someone kill his wife. If that were the case, he'd *never* get out of prison."

Callie put her elbows on the breakfast bar, and plopped her chin into her hands. "Okay. That's a good point. Still, what about the money dumped into Graham's account?"

I noticed the sharp twist in my gut that happens when something so impossible…so *ridiculous*…sizzles through my brain like a zap from hell. For once, I'd pay attention.

CHAPTER FORTY-ONE

I sighed. "Did Graham say anything about Hannah talking to Monty?"

"He mentioned her in passing, then gave me a look and changed the subject." Her fingers drummed the counter. She'd had her nails painted white with tips of black. The woman seriously had a manicure fetish.

Serena and Lilly jogged down the stairs and into the kitchen. They told us they were going over to Callie's house to see Amy, slung their backpacks across their shoulders, and left.

Callie and I watched them leave out the back door of my kitchen and head to the lane behind our homes. "At least we don't have to worry about anyone being snatched on our path again," I said.

Callie lifted her mug of coffee. "Amen, sister."

We clinked mugs. "Back to Graham. He got uncomfortable about...?"

"Monty's conversations with Hannah." Her lips pursed as she concentrated. "Yeah, I'm sure. He avoided talking about it."

All the hair on my arms stood at attention. I heard Hannah's voice in my head: *he thinks I'm helping him, but really, I'm helping you...*

"Callie," I began, "when Hannah stayed at your house, did she ever mention talking with Monty?"

Callie nodded. "She told me you knew about it."

"She mention anything about Patrick?"

Callie laughed. "She had plenty to say about him. I was happy to see her animated like that."

"Animated?"

Callie tilted her head. "All ex-wives think about getting even from time to time, right? Hannah mentioned her fantasies about getting rid of Patrick. We talked about different ways to do it. It was funny."

I felt my eyebrows get so high on my forehead that it hurt. "And you didn't think to tell me about this? You thought it was *funny?*"

The giggling stopped. "What? She wasn't serious. It was her way of venting." Her leg jiggled with nerves. "She couldn't be serious. Right?"

Chapter Forty-Two

Hannah

Hannah watched Hazel putter around her open, airy condo. Her canaries warbled their little lungs out, providing a merry backdrop to an otherwise dark and muddled conundrum.

Hannah finished her eggs, rinsed the plate, and put the dish into the dishwasher. "Thanks for letting me stay here last night, Hazel. I thought I'd never make it to Pensacola; the flight got delayed twice."

The tiny octogenarian appeared in the kitchen doorway. "You're welcome anytime. I'm happy your situation is coming to a close, dear."

If Hazel knew what she'd done, would she feel the same way? Olivia had suggested that she ask Hazel for counseling, but Hannah no longer thought she was fixable.

"The birds are loud this morning. Are they bothering you?"

"Of course not. They're wonderful."

"Will you be back tonight?"

"Maybe. I'll let you know."

Hazel raised an index finger. "Let me check my phone to see if I have your information."

"You do. I texted you yesterday, remember?"

"Okay," she said, her voice uncertain.

"I'll send it again," Hannah said.

"I know this won't be easy for you. When is Patrick's funeral, again?"

Hazel asked.

Hannah felt her chest tighten. His family had taken care of everything. They hadn't even known he'd remarried. They'd been shocked by what the police had discovered. Hannah hadn't made any efforts to reach out, and she had no intention of attending the funeral. "I'm not sure yet, but seriously. You don't need to come."

If it had been me, I would've cremated his ass and been done with it. He didn't deserve a funeral.

Hazel studied her. "I'm offering support."

Guilt pricked her conscience. "Thanks, Hazel."

The crime scene investigator told her it had taken only forty-five minutes to find the first victim.

Hannah parked on the road in front of the house. She couldn't feel the tips of her fingers or her feet. She forced herself to get out of the car.

The circa-Sixties brick ranch home looked much the same, except for the big holes that pockmarked the front and sides and copious derogatory slurs spray-painted across the front. The investigative team had told her that Patrick's victims had been buried in shallow graves in a neat row. She got out of the rental and walked into the yard, studying the rectangular, corpse-shaped holes in the earth. One, two, three...one after the other, in various stages of decomposition and meticulously dressed, complete with jewelry. Hannah felt a raw pain radiate through her chest. *The jewelry he'd gifted her.* He had been so happy when she'd worn it. Now she knew why. It had belonged to his victims. She wondered how he'd chosen which jewelry to leave on them and which to give to her. She groaned. Her hand went to her throat and touched a necklace he'd gifted her right before their wedding, a delicate silver cross. She'd worn it so long, she often forgot she had it on. Her fingers wrapped around the chain and jerked. It snapped and fell to the ground. She picked it up and dropped it into one of the holes, then moved to each makeshift grave and prayed, tears streaming down her cheeks.

Her hand faltered when she tried to put the key into the lock of the door. Hannah had counted his victims as her friends. She'd carried on full conversations with the names she'd found scratched into the walls of the punishment room, and she'd kept her promise to them—that he'd never hurt anyone else.

The police tried to prepare her for the way the house looked inside after being torn apart by the crime scene unit, but it didn't matter. Nothing mattered, except the fact that he was gone. Entering the house at this point, no matter what shape it was in, held no terror for her. She read the graffiti with a tight smile, noticed the many floral arrangements that had been placed beside the graves and plugged into the chain-link fencing.

She tried again to insert the key in the lock. The deadbolt slid away.

"I will never set foot in this place again after this. I swear," she murmured to herself, thinking about the will he'd told her about. She had no idea if he'd been telling the truth about making her his beneficiary. She'd emailed the attorney about it, who promised he'd call soon. Also, she knew he'd kept a lot of cash hidden in various places around the house. She needed to find it. Then, she planned to go far, far away.

She pushed open the door.

Filled her lungs with air, and blew it out.

Stepped across the threshold.

The smell of rancid food and mustiness curled up her nose. The contents of the home had been tossed. Drawers upturned and thrown aside, pictures ripped from the walls, bookshelves emptied. The incredible havoc she observed slaked a deep wrath within her. She laughed. "I hope you can see this, you bastard," she yelled at the ceiling. Patrick would've *hated* having his things touched. She picked her way across the broken pottery, table lamps, and faux plants flung across the rug. Her chest felt as if someone had spiked a football into it, and she lost her breath for a few seconds. The desire to slam the door on this nightmare grew intolerable.

"Where would you hide cash?" she whispered to herself as she glided through the rooms like a wraith. The master bedroom lay at the end of a short hall on the main floor. She'd search that room, then the kitchen; after that, she'd go to the basement.

Straightening her shoulders, she entered the master bedroom, where the marital bed had been slashed and hollowed out and cast aside. "How fitting," she said, even as she recognized that the police had been looking for keepsakes from victims as evidence. She tapped her chin with her index finger. Her gaze fell to the closet.

Patrick had been picky about his closet. He'd never let her go through his clothes, organize the closet, or use it for her own clothes. She grabbed her long hair and swept it off her neck with an elastic before she began a methodical search.

Most of his clothing had already been removed. She clicked on the closet light and cleared out the remaining items. A careful study of the walls revealed a section that didn't quite match the rest of the paint. She placed her palm on the area and pushed. Cracks appeared in the paint at the edges. Hannah pounded on it with her fists until it fell behind the sheetrock, leaving a square hole large enough to put her arm through, but she couldn't see to the bottom.

She sped to the laundry room and opened all the cabinets. There! After a few clicks, one of the flashlights she found sprang to life. She raced back to the bedroom, stepping across the clothes, shoes, belts, and socks, wrinkling her nose. His cologne must have imprinted on everything he wore. She forced down the bile rising in her throat.

Hannah stepped inside the small closet, clicked on the flashlight, and peered into the tight space between the sheetrock and the framing lumber. A dark green, zippered duffel bag had been wedged inside.

She plunged her arm down the hole she'd made and poked at the duffel with her fingertips until she grabbed a good handful of canvas and eased it out. The bag's weight surprised her.

The doorbell rang.

Her eyes darted to the duffel. "I'll be back," she whispered, dropping it on the floor of the closet and closing the door.

Her steps quiet on the worn, hardwood flooring, she peeked out the dining room window at the front porch. A man with dark hair and a wide set of shoulders stood there with his back to the door, his hands in his pockets. Hoping she wouldn't regret it, she opened the door.

"Good morning. Can I help you?" Hannah smiled.

Quick as a wink, he slipped a ski mask over his head and turned around. "You *can* help me. *Hannah*." He pushed past her into the house and slammed the door behind him. He gripped her arm above the elbow. "Where's my money?"

As always, her hand fell to her stomach, her first thought to protect the child she carried. "Are you...are you...?"

"Monty says hello. And you're welcome. Okay? No need to know my name. You'll never see me again after I get my money. He said he gave you the payment."

Hannah felt the floor give way beneath her feet. Monty had told her *Graham* had the money, he'd give her the cash, but Olivia had put someone with her 24/7 and secreted her off to the women's shelter with no notice. She didn't have any money yet, and she sure didn't know where to find Graham. However. The duffel. "Things got twisted around. If you can just give me a second..."

He scowled. "We're joined at the hip, sweetie, until you produce twenty big ones." He held out his large, upraised palm. "In my hand. Cash."

"There's money stashed in this house. I just have to find it."

The man rolled his eyes and pulled out a firearm. "We better get to it, then."

"I-I..." she pointed down the hall toward the master. "I found something, I think."

Hannah led him into the bedroom. She opened the closet, got the duffel out, and unzipped it. She blinked at the piles of cash and zippered it shut again with shaky hands.

The man pushed her aside, yanked the bag from her hands, and almost tore it apart with an angry rake of the zipper. "There must be two hundred grand in this bag," he whispered.

"The deal was twenty thousand!" she cried.

He laughed and hoisted the bag strap over his shoulder. "This is my money now, bitch." He left her in the bedroom. When she heard the front door close, she raced to the window, logged the color and make of his car, and memorized the license plate number.

She rubbed her face wearily. Fat lot of good it would do.

Getting the police to track him would not end well. She'd hired him through a felon, which would have Monty breathing fire and the cops all over him. She didn't have the strength or desire to lie for him or anyone else.

The cell in her pocket vibrated. She tugged it out and looked at it. Olivia. "Yeah?"

"What's wrong?" Olivia asked, her voice radiating worry at the abrupt response. "I *knew* you shouldn't have gone down there by yourself."

"What do you want?"

A few silent seconds drifted through the connection.

"What's going on, Hannah?"

Nothing you need to know, and I don't want you involved in my life anymore and...

And nothing.

She ended the call and muted the notifications.

The plan had been to conclude things in Niceville, figure out what was left of his estate, and disappear. Now what? His family didn't want anything to do with her, much less a baby on the way. She dropped her head into her hands. If his family knew about the baby, they'd get involved. She didn't want that.

Patrick's voice filtered into her mind. *You need rest, Hannah. A few days in the room to shut out all the distractions and remember to be...what? What have I told you over and over again?*

"Grateful. I should be grateful."

He'd nodded in satisfaction. "That's my girl. You'll remember better next time. Won't you, my love?"

With robotic steps, she approached the staircase and walked down the stairs. She wrapped her arms around herself, lowered her head, and walked to the punishment room. The same thin, lumpy mattress lay on the floor. The flimsy, metal headboard she'd mangled when she freed herself mere weeks before sat against the wall in two pieces. The names of the women they'd found in the yard hadn't been removed. She ran her fingers across each name. Lifted the mattress from the floor where the cops had discarded it and placed it on the box springs. Then she lay on the mattress and slept.

Chapter Forty-Three

Olivia

The joyful explosion of fireworks in New York's Times Square erupted from the flat screen in my living room.

I heard a few firecrackers in the neighborhood. Maryland frowned on the use of private fireworks, but certain intrepid neighbors insisted on shooting them off every year, anyway.

"You still there?" Hunter asked.

"How long have we been talking?" I asked, my eyelids drooping. They'd had a "phone date" for New Year's Eve.

"Two hours or so. You getting sleepy?"

"I've *been* sleepy," Olivia said, yawning.

"Happy New Year, babe."

"Same to you, future husband."

I still had a hard time thinking about moving, but someone had to make a choice if we wanted to be together. "Wish you were here."

"I offered. You turned me down. Did you ever hear from Hannah?"

Olivia grunted. "Last time we talked, she made it crystal clear that she wanted to be left alone, and furthermore, she cut me off and ended the call. There's a time to let someone go.

He laughed. "I tried very hard to do that with you."

"I guess you weren't supposed to," I said with a stupid grin on my face.

We spent a few seconds breathing at each other.

"I miss you," Hunter whispered in a husky voice.

"Me, too. Want to sleep with me tonight? I'll leave the phone on. I hope you don't snore, though."

"I don't."

"All men say that." I thought about how Monty had snored like a freight train, but insisted he didn't. I'd always meant to record him to prove it. Oh, well.

"I don't. I sleep on my side. I may snore once in a while, but..."

"Why are we talking about this?"

"I don't know, but I'm going to bed. I love you, wish I was there, too."

We ended the call. Even though we couldn't be together, my heart felt full. My girls had returned to their dorm, Sherry's dating life had taken a turn for the better when she'd met Duncan a couple of weeks ago, and except for work, I didn't see her much. Callie had the flu, and her daughter, Amy, was taking care of her. I hadn't heard a thing from the Carroll County Sheriff's Office Major Crimes Unit, which had jurisdiction over Victoria's homicide. Last I heard, someone had called in with an anonymous tip, and I didn't want to know any more than that. I wanted to stay as far away from that investigation as possible. They'd tracked down Raul and had him in custody, but someone had paid his bail, and he'd skipped. None of us could believe he'd gotten bail in the first place. What was wrong with our justice system?

I had the faint flicker of hope that Monty had gotten scorched by Watchdog Investigation's civil suit for damages naming both him and his overseers on the work release program. Maybe he wouldn't bother me anymore.

A faint flicker of hope is better than no flicker at all.

Investigators had combed through Curtis's phone and bank records, found the connection to Graham, and both men had been interviewed to death. Curtis had popped right out of the gate, dumping everything he knew. The investigators poked around awhile, but they didn't have enough evidence for an indictment. Sherry and I weren't sure how Graham's interrogation had fared, but Callie would fill us in when it suited.

It had been an immense relief to realize Monty had *not* facilitated Victoria's death. Curtis had been so frantic and broken up about it that I couldn't believe he had anything to do with it, either. Her lover was a bad guy, end of story. Bad guys do bad things.

I never had to tell them I had actual photos of the homicide, and they didn't ask. Raul had a long and checkered criminal history. I was the witness that placed him at the scene, but I didn't tell them I'd actually seen the whole thing, or been working an investigation. Plus, they had a body, and the cops found the murder weapon on him. What kind of idiot keeps the murder weapon? That had been the final straw that cleared Curtis of the murder, but they'd hung onto accessory charges like a pit bull with a bone and told him not to leave the county.

The county had assigned Raul a public defender.

Good luck with that, you creep. I doubted Raul would even show up for his indictment.

In short, I no longer ran on crushing anxiety and adrenaline. Hannah didn't have to worry about Patrick anymore, and we still had a decent client list. My daughters had spent seven days with me for Christmas, Gray's meds had started working, and...I stared at my ring for the millionth time. I was engaged! A rosy optimism had begun to creep into my life.

I smiled at Marlowe and Riot tucked into their beds beside me. The two glasses of red wine I'd drunk in honor of a new year had infused me with more rosy optimism than necessary, but I deserved it.

Monty's work release had been pulled out from under him. I'm not sure if the civil suit and allegations had an impact or what, but it didn't matter. Hunter had subtly inquired, and Monty's privileges had been stripped. Extra charges tacked on, too.

I'd been sleeping better.

The delicate light of a full moon shimmered through my window. I lay in bed with my head propped on two pillows, rotating my empty wine glass and watching the light dance through the glass.

A nice send-off to the past year and toast to the next should include a final glass of wine on my porch, I decided. I wanted to enjoy my tipsy glow in the moonlight, accompanied by a nice fire in the gas fire pit I'd gifted myself for Christmas. I looked at my watch. The baby new year was only thirty minutes old.

My slippers made little shushing sounds as I padded downstairs.

An hour later, clouds had drifted across the moon, and a breeze whistled through the trees. With a contented sigh, I walked down the porch steps into the center of my yard and considered the stars. The night grew still. An occasional hoot of an owl or creak of branches interrupted the quiet.

I gazed around the perimeter of my white, picket-fenced front yard from my position beside a large holly bush. A moving shadow caught my attention. A deer? We had *so* many deer, but in the winter, they found a place to sleep long before this.

I jumped when I heard the sound of rushed steps through the bushes, expecting a buck or doe to walk into view any minute.

The shadow moved through the trees. The steps grew louder. I watched in horror as the shadow morphed into a short, chunky person and approached the gate into my yard. A strangled, squeaky sound died in my throat. I dropped into a crouch behind the holly bush. As the person entered the gate and tip-toed toward the far side of my house, I peeked out. *Beth?* I sucked in a quick breath. She skulked through my yard in head-to-toe black, the same type of clothing I used to surveil.

I tugged out my phone and pressed nine-one-one and whispered "intruder" and my address, then put the phone on record. This woman did not deserve any second chances. I made sure she didn't hear me approach.

"Beth, what do you think you're doing?"

She froze momentarily, then turned an inch at a time.

Caught.

"Why are you here?" I asked.

That's when I saw the baggie in her hand with a piece of meat in it.

A flash of realization hit. "You're the one poisoning my dog?" I held out my hand. "Give me that!"

She reared back like winding up for a pitch and let the bag fly. It splatted on the driveway in front of my garage. I rolled my eyes. "Very mature."

CHAPTER FORTY-THREE

She glared and fisted her hands. I half-expected her to stomp her feet as well.

My mind went into overdrive: Beth's connection with Monty and all her claims that she hadn't known what she was doing with my online security breech clumped into a huge mud ball at the front of my brain. It hadn't been Curtis. It hadn't been Graham.

"It's always been *you*," I whispered into the night, a breeze snatching my words away.

She folded her arms and rotated to face me with a smirk. "It's been such fun, you know. You didn't even do a deep background check." She shrugged. "I held my breath over that, but you're so darn naïve. Didn't you learn anything from what you went through at Mercy Hospital? It's survival of the fittest. Surely you know that. You cannot be that stupid."

I blinked. We'd done background, but it must not have been comprehensive enough.

"I had priors, but since it was juvie, the records were sealed. It would've raised flags if you'd checked." She grunted. "And Graham. Wow. Such a gift. He's Monty's lapdog, of course, but more than that, he's unintelligent. He has *zero* instincts. Monty and I..." She smiled a tight smile. "We have a transcendent connection. It's unearthly and beautiful and..." She made a rude noise with her lips. "You wouldn't understand."

I thought about the phone doing its job in my pocket. I had to get her to talk. "You're right. I don't understand."

Clouds raced across the sky. I could see the setting moon reflected in Beth's dark eyes. She pushed the hood of her hoodie down.

"Monty and I had it all worked out, how I'd move into the house next door, how you missed your mom, that ridiculous woman with all her bracelets and homilies; how you'd be primed to trust a surrogate. It worked. You trusted me."

I nodded. "You did a good job."

Sirens sounded in the distance. Beth didn't bat an eyelash, because she had no idea I'd called nine-one-one.

"The set-up with Curtis was genius," she said. "In the beginning, Monty and I suggested Curtis hire your firm for simple surveillance with the intention of office time with you." She cocked her head. "We paid him a lot of money to help us get access to your computer, but when Victoria got herself killed, he was a mess. Useless. He had all he could handle trying to maintain his innocence." She exhaled and broke eye contact. She scraped one of her pudgy hands through her hair. "Unforeseen consequences. They're a bitch."

"You collaborated with Curtis from the beginning. *That's* why you didn't tell me about the new client."

Beth's eyelids dropped to half-mast. "You're catching on, aren't you?"

"It was supposed to be Sherry." I frowned. "I don't understand."

"All Monty wanted to do was discredit your firm, okay? Deepfakes, misinformation. All the things. Cause you to shut the doors. Easy. It could've been either one of you. A surveillance assignment that blew up and started people talking. We only needed to place you onsite, and he did that for us. Curtis took photos of you in your car when you were in the parking lot that night." She shook her head. "But I saw an opportunity to *cripple* you permanently." She lifted a shoulder. "I thought the attack on Victoria could be leveraged."

The strange light in her eyes made me shrink back a step.

She groaned. "But the cops wouldn't take the bait. You had to go all "commando" and try to save her. They didn't even look in your direction, much less question you. I thought at least you'd get tagged with a withholding charge. That "Mercy's Miracle" reputation still serves you well, doesn't it?"

We stared at each other.

"The cherry on top was Hannah, you know."

Ice water poured through my veins. My hand floated nervously to my collarbone and stayed there. "Hannah?"

"An abuse victim? Sooo easy to manipulate."

My mind flew back to the times when Hannah had stayed in the office guest bedroom and Beth had been at her desk in the lobby. Hannah's bruised mind would've been fertile ground for brainwashing. Beth had insisted she'd keep an eye on her if I couldn't be there, and I'd thought I could trust

Beth. I stared at her, amazed. Where was the gentle, grandmotherly persona she'd used to get the job? The persona I'd come to trust as the best neighbor, ever? I'd even asked her to babysit my pets.

I shuddered. Beth, oblivious, kept talking.

"In the end, I felt sorry for her, the stupid cow. It took a slight nudge to convince her to talk to Monty about hiring Raul, who, in the end, proved very useful to us until he got arrested."

I felt my eyebrows draw together. "Wait. She's the one who found out *you'd* been talking to Monty."

"Right, well, that was unfortunate. I let Hannah think she'd "caught" me. Marching through your property with all that fog. Quite dramatic, don't you think?" She laughed. "Monty and I have a connection that transcends the ordinary. Surely, you realize that job you put me in served as a vehicle for what he wanted to happen. It didn't matter if I kept the job or not, what mattered is that we were in close proximity to one another." She smoothed her hair and touched her lips, staring at the moon. "The goal has always been the perfect symmetry of justice."

I glanced at the glare of headlights turning off onto my lane from the highway. The sirens had stopped chattering. Headlight beams sliced through the darkness, into the trees, around each curve of my lane.

Two patrol vehicles quietly rolled to a stop and parked in front of my garage. I caught the stunned look in Beth's eyes, but before she could run, I head-butted her stomach. She stumbled backward. I elbowed her in the jaw with a hard strike and twisted her arm behind her back. After such a pompous speech, I expected her to retaliate, but she didn't. I forced her to the ground and held her there until the patrol cops could cuff her.

"How about this for justice?" I muttered as the Baltimore PD uniforms got out of their vehicles and ran toward us. I released her to them and sat on the pavement, my arms around my knees, watching Beth get cuffed, read her rights, and plopped into a cruiser. I gave a polite, young patrol cop an embellished version of what happened, including poisoning my dog. I prayed she'd get her own damn "transcendent connection" in the holding cell tonight.

Chapter Forty-Four

Olivia

Ten days later

Sherry strolled into the office, going through the mail. I watched her from the break room and called out. "Good morning! Find anything interesting in the mail?"

She dumped her purse and shoulder bag on Beth's old desk and walked into the breakroom to hand me a couple of envelopes. "Not that I can see. We used to say this, remember: 'Boring is good. Boring is fantastic'?"

I laughed, thinking about all the Wine & Whine adventures we'd shared across the table at Eddie's Bistro. "I'm still a fan."

"Me, too," she murmured as she got out her favorite mug and stuck it in the Keurig. "The less drama, the better."

"Speaking of..." I said, "How's Duncan these days?"

I couldn't quite tell under her mocha-colored complexion and perfect makeup, but I think she blushed.

"He's good. Boring."

I laughed. "Fabulous."

She nodded. "I never appreciated good, old dependability and responsibility before. Just the fact that he hasn't *lied to* me about anything goes a long way."

"I'm sure you did a background on him?"

She sniffed in disdain as she walked to the reception desk and sat behind it. "As if. Have *you* done a background on him?"

I shook my head. "After all the crap we've endured at the hands of fools, I didn't think I needed to do that. I decided to trust you."

Sherry paused to take in my words, then pinned me with a sincere gaze. "Thank you. That means a lot." She sipped her coffee. "By the way, he's clean as a whistle."

I cop-nodded my approval. "I'm screening new receptionists. You won't have to work that desk much longer. I appreciate you stepping in."

"No problem," she said, opening her laptop. "What's Beth's status?"

"She lawyered up, and I hear she's having trouble convincing anyone of her innocence. She's out on bail. I've been putting them off, but I guess I have a sit-down with the investigation team in a few days. They think there's more to it than my initial report."

"Well," she said, her tone pragmatic, "there always is."

I looked at the envelopes she'd handed me as I walked through the break room and into my office. The corrections unit address made my skin crawl. I never wanted to hear from Monty Callahan again, but we were linked by our daughters. It wouldn't be long, they'd be on their own, and they could negotiate their own relationship with him. I hoped their careers would take them away from the ability to visit him often or at all. He had the habit of poisoning minds, and his daughters were no exception.

I felt my lips draw down at the corners as I opened the envelope with a pearl-handled letter opener I kept on my desk in honor of my former attorney, Earl Sorenson. May he rest in peace. With a sigh, I unfolded the letter.

Olivia:

My work release has been revoked for perpetuity, and they've tacked new charges onto my sentence. I may never get out of here, thanks to you. The warden had a meltdown over your lawsuit and threw me in solitary for two weeks. Such fun. Graham has his own charges to deal with, and I understand Callie's trying to get his parental rights revoked.

I've come to the conclusion that seeing Serena and Lilly are worth more than playing these games with you.

I paused, held the letter to my chest, and laughed. Games? Is that how he rationalized his dangerous anger and jealousy? His God-complex? His out-of-control rage when I confronted his lies and abuse after my brain injury flipped me into a person with a backbone? And what about the pathological use of someone as miserable and emotionally crippled as Beth to crush me?

In retrospect, Beth had been too perfect. Too helpful. Too available.

I wondered if her marriage was even legit, or if they'd been on Monty's payroll. There had been quite a lot of payments to Graham, who had been funneling money for Monty. Perhaps the money had been for Beth. I made a quick note to suggest the possibility to Baltimore PD. I smirked. How ironic if she'd been conning Monty. Nobody on the planet deserved it more.

My cell had been buzzing like a horsefly the last few seconds. I snatched it and answered.

"Hey, gorgeous. How's your day?"

I walked to my office door and shut it.

"Could be better," I said, dropping into an armchair.

"Huh. I thought you'd had a few days of peace."

"I have, but then I got a letter from dirtbag."

Two seconds of silence passed. "Maybe you should return to sender."

"Maybe," I agreed. "But I need to know what he's doing. I read them to protect myself, but whatever, he says he's dropping the swordfight. That we're even."

"Is that good news?"

"I don't trust him."

"You'll never trust him. However, you have me, a man you *can* trust."

I laughed.

"Can I do anything to ease your struggle with this ongoing nightmare that takes up way too much headspace?"

"You already have," I told him with a smile. "On the bright side, it's made me realize that I still have this tidal wave of support from the Mercy's

Miracle experience. It's a good feeling to know that people believe in you. Anyway, he told me he's stripped of privileges and spent some time in solitary. I told you we sued the prison facility, right?"

"You did. It was the right thing to do," Hunter said.

I sighed. "Which leaves Hannah."

He groaned.

"I know we've worn ourselves out, but could you do a quick check? As far as I know, she's still in Florida."

I heard voices in the background. "I'll look into it. Gotta go," he said.

I turned to the rest of Monty's letter.

I need you to know something. Since they threw me in a mandatory recovery group and I'm supposed to make amends, here it is: Hannah and I have been involved ever since you guys brought her back here, and she is one messed-up individual. You worked so hard to keep her safe, and she still found a way to schedule visits. I didn't invite her; she just showed up. The whole sad story about her marriage has made her a little kinky. I wouldn't trust her if I were you. Watch your back. Monty

I stuffed the letter into the envelope and put it in a file labeled "Dirtbag."

I ran my hands through my hair in frustration. First Beth. Now Hannah. Surprise, surprise. Backstabbers everywhere.

I looked at the ceiling, opened my mouth to give God a piece of my mind, but my phone buzzed.

"Hi, honey. We haven't talked in a while. How are you?"

I laughed. God sent Mom instead.

"Your timing is amazing."

"Of course it is. You're my daughter."

Tears fell, then, and I poured out a condensed version of what had been happening the past few weeks. She interrupted halfway through, stopping a long spiral down a dark tunnel.

"We need to pray," she said.

I couldn't agree more.

She spent the next five minutes praying for me and anything else she could think of.

As I wiped the snot-storm and tears off my face with a tissue, I told her how much I appreciated her. After we ended the call, I thought about how sometimes we need God to give us a hug in human form.

Sherry knocked on my door and leaned in the doorway. "Sounds like some intense stuff going on in here, girl."

"You'd be right," I quipped, blowing my nose a final time. "Sit with me. I have information."

Two hours later, I sat at my desk reading through my emails when Hunter's call came in.

"You sitting down?"

My mouth pressed itself into a line. Someone says that, it's never good news. "What is it?"

He took a deep breath. "Hannah's in a holding cell until they decide what to do with her."

It took me a minute. "Wait..."

He continued in a gentler tone. "She's being held on suspicion of manslaughter, a second-degree felony. It's pretty clear-cut that Patrick didn't kill himself, and after questioning her, they arrested her. She'd made an appointment to view the body, and they mentioned they had a few questions for her after. She skipped the viewing and the questions. They couldn't get her on her phone. A uniform went out to the house and found Hannah in that "torture" room you told me about. It appears she's been living there and sleeping in that room."

I winced. Poor Hannah.

"There's more. The DA is looking at leniency because of mental instability. They're operating on the premise that your ex pushed her into a hit-for-hire situation."

I thought about Monty's letter. "I just found out the whole time we were rescuing her, *she* was figuring out a way to go see him." I spread my arms in frustration. "What *is* that?"

"It's another nail in Monty's coffin."

"Shocker," I muttered.

"Victims like Hannah feel both affection and hatred for the abuser. They're brainwashed through deprivation, punishment, isolation, and rape. They're full of guilt, shame, and…"

"Rage," I finished for him."

Silence stretched. The seconds ticked past.

"You've done as much as you can to help Hannah, and now it's up to the court. Trust the process," he said.

I snorted. "You're kidding, right?"

Chapter Forty-Five

Olivia

Mid-January

I'd just gotten home when Sherry called and asked me to take a new client.

"Who is it?" I asked, my phone clamped against my ear as I walked through the breezeway to my kitchen door.

Marlowe barked.

Sherry laughed. "Aw. He's happy to see Mom."

"Tell me about the client. Does it have to be tonight? Can't you take it?"

"I can't," she assured me. "Or I would. I didn't want you to have to do it but I have an important situation with Bill. You remember him?"

I rolled my eyes. "The repeat client who never quite gets what he wants."

"Yeah, but he pays on time. Anyway, it's his daughter. He needs me to crash a party she's attending tonight and make sure she doesn't get into trouble. I'm headed there now."

"Okay. So…"

"The client wants a meet in Hunt Valley, in the outdoor shopping mall by the bench in the middle. You know which one I mean? The one with all the sidewalks leading to it?"

"Yep," I said, not bothering to keep the irritation out of my voice.

"His name is Curt. He'll meet you there and explain."

"Do you have background on this man?"

"He is a client of the new law firm that put us on retainer. I cleared it with them."

"What time?"

"Tonight, at nine."

"Everything'll be closed."

"That's the idea. Call if you need me."

She ended the call.

I stared at my phone. "Whatever," I muttered. I'd looked forward to a night alone with my animals, a glass of wine, and my latest binge-worthy series.

Since I'd be out in the open, instead of my customary head-to-toe black, I wore darkish jeans, canvas shoes, sweatshirt, no hoodie. I didn't want to stand out like a thug on a street corner selling drugs. Hunt Valley was an upscale area.

I pulled on my gloves, zipped up my coat, folded my arms, and wished for an outdoor space heater.

At nine-ten, a lone man strolled toward me. I ran my hand to my waist for reassurance that my Glock still rested in my holster, which it did. I rose from the bench as he approached. How had I allowed myself to accept an appointment *outside* during the freaking coldest cold snap of the year? The man kept walking toward me, his head down. When he got within a couple of feet, he raised his head.

"Curtis?" I squeaked.

"Here," he said and pushed a hundred-dollar bill into my palm. I looked at him like he was crazy. "What are you doing?"

"That's for your time. I wanted to speak to you. I'm represented by that law firm you guys work for a lot. Ward & Ward. I wanted to see you in private and off the record."

I nodded. "Okay."

He tugged on his ear and bit his lip. "Look, when I hired you guys to surveil Victoria, I was paid to do it. Graham acted as go-between." He sighed. "I'm an actor now, not a criminal. I wish I'd never taken the job. My God. What a nightmare."

His voice sounded different. I believed him. I motioned him to sit beside me on the bench.

He sat on the other side of the bench and continued. "The pictures you took of Victoria and the guy…I gave them to Graham to hand off to Monty." He frowned. "What are they, joined at the hip or something?"

"They've known each other since our kids were young, so yeah. They are."

"I came clean with the cops and told them I'd been hired to do an acting job that went wrong. I was paid to hire you for the assignment to watch my wife, and the original job was to have a sit-down with you and look around a little, you know, act the part of a wronged man and try to grab your passwords, or files." He shrugged. "I know my way around computers, and I guess my method acting experience was a bonus. My wife and I were already on track to divorce anyway, so I was fine with the surveillance. It'd go better for me in court if I had photos of an affair. They paid me a lot of money to act as a new client, then take photos of you doing your thing." He looked in the other direction, unwilling to look me in the eye. "Not saying I was proud of what I did, I want you to understand that. I didn't know the extent of things." He sighed. "It was real brave, what you did. Gunning your car like that."

"It was reflex. Why were you taking pictures of *me?*"

"You ruined everything when you tried to ram the guy with your car." He laughed. "They didn't take *that* news well. They figured you'd high-tail it outta there."

I thought about Beth's strange expression when she'd learned what had happened. She'd overheard us talking and mentioned it afterward. She'd seemed off-balance and almost mad. I'd cut her off from our communication because I'd had a feeling, even back then, that she couldn't be trusted. Now I knew why. She'd been disappointed that I'd intervened. Upset that I talked to the police about what happened. I was supposed to do the job and leave, not use my car like a battering ram and make a police report. They'd wanted to use Curtis to get me to the scene and implicate me in a conspiracy to commit a homicide with his photos. Which was ridiculous, but would've kept me in the public eye and scorched my reputation. I hadn't revealed that I'd been at the crime scene on a job; they thought I'd "just happened" to see a woman in distress. The cops could've made a case against me. Not to mention, until I fought off the frivolous charges, I'd be unable to work.

I re-focused on Curtis.

"I should've known," Curtis muttered. "All those shady meetups at that titty bar. The whole thing had a weird vibe from the beginning. But now I'm pretty much in the clear. However, they still…" He sighed. "I just want it to be over." His eyes watered. "All I wanted was a paycheck. I never expected to watch her die." He wiped his eyes, rubbed his hands together, and stood. "I can't forgive myself for being part of that."

"That had nothing to do with you. Raul's a murderer. He's an illegal with a criminal history that shouldn't be here in the first place." I folded my arms. "You should've never seen your own wife being stabbed. Nobody expected it." Even as the words came out of my mouth, I wondered. Had Monty known Raul was capable of murder? He must have. He steered Hannah to Raul. Raul killed Patrick for a fee and Victoria in cold blood. A chill shot through me, and not as a result of the freezing temps. Maybe Monty's *true* ambition had been to make sure I was in Raul's deadly path, too.

Curtis's eyebrows pulled together. "He has a record?"

I nodded. "Sherry and I both realize that they used you. I hope your attorneys succeed with your case."

He swallowed, hard, swiping at the tears on his cheeks. I wondered if he'd even had time to grieve his loss, since he'd gotten so wrapped up in alleged accomplice charges. He sniffed and stuck his hands in his pockets. "Anyway. I wanted to make sure you heard the facts from me. Thanks for meeting me." He walked away.

My drive home was contemplative. Before I went to bed, I called Sherry.

"Wow," she breathed. "Curtis is just a normal schlub with a record who happened to be looking for work. Poor guy. I'm glad he's hired Ward & Ward. They'll do a good job."

"He was *there.* He saw the whole thing."

"So? Coming to you is an act of good faith. Don't you think?"

"Maybe. I never told him I have photos of the homicide."

"I don't think you have to worry. They've got the assailant, right? Did you print them out?"

"No, but they're still on my phone."

"Get rid of them! Wow. Dangerous."

"I'll do it right now." My fingers shook as I pressed "delete" six times. But in my heart, I knew they could be retrieved if necessary. Has anything ever really been deleted in web-based technology? I'd have to talk to Cosmo about that.

"I told you about Raul, that someone paid his bail? He's probably in Mexico by now," I said.

"I'm sure he is," she said.

My cell clicked in with another call. I put Sherry on hold and took it.

Hannah's teary voice stuttered through the airwaves. I texted Sherry that I would conference her in and told her to put her phone on mute. She agreed.

"Hello? Hello? Olivia, are you there?"

When I was sure Sherry got on the line, I answered. "I'm here. How are you, Hannah?"

"I'm fine, considering I'm in a cell waiting for them to let me go," she said. Her voice sounded like a dull knife slicing through canvas. "Some guy took advantage of me and stole all the cash I found in the house. I'm broke and homeless. Patrick never made me his beneficiary, after all. Any money went to his parents. That cash was all I had."

"That's terrible," I said. My cold lack of emotion helped me realize that I'd never trust anything she said again. With a pang of regret, I realized this would be our final conversation.

"Did it go okay? Packing up and getting him buried and everything?" I asked, stringing her along to see what she'd say. Hoping for the truth, or a confession, or *anything* that hinted at contrition.

"It went fine. Very sad. I'm looking forward to coming back to Maryland."

I resisted a snort of derision. Hannah should be indicted and sentenced within weeks, and I knew for a fact she hadn't lifted a finger to get Patrick buried. His family had made arrangements. She was looking for bail money. Her bail had probably been set in the hundreds of thousands.

The connection went eerily silent. "Why haven't you called?"

"I figured you had lots to do."

"Aren't you worried about me?" she asked in a tiny, pitiful voice.

"We'll always be concerned about you, Hannah, but we also know you've got to make your own way."

"Sure," she said.

The conversation dwindled. "It's late. I need to sleep. Thanks for calling Hannah."

I ended the call.

"She's off," I said.

Sherry unmuted her phone. I heard reggae playing in the background, happy and soothing with its promise that "everything's gonna be all right." "She's wanting money, isn't she?"

"Yep."

"We're not going to help her, are we?"

"Nope."

As I waited for her response, I thought about the last couple of years. The havoc scattered across weeks and months like an ongoing nightmare; the traps I should've avoided, the desperate race through Florida wetlands in order to keep breathing. The betrayal I'd experienced from a woman I counted as my neighbor and friend. Tom Stark, my mentor who died, special to me in so many ways. My wonderful stepdad's Parkinson's diagnosis. My dirtbag ex that never tired of haunting me. Hannah's final betrayal.

I rubbed my forehead wearily.

A new season lay ahead. I decided that the lessons learned from persevering through the hard stuff carries with it a sober maturity that cannot be learned any other way. My mother says that God uses everything, even the hard stuff, to enrich our lives. I believe that. I *have* to believe that.

Sherry broke into my reverie with a similar sentiment.

"I think we're learning when to let go of something and when to hang on."

After a pause, I added: "When to lift up and when to tear down."

"When to hold 'em and when to fold 'em," she added, giggling.

"When to reconcile and when to crush a threat into freaking oblivion," I declared.

"Oooh," she enthused. "That one's my favorite."

I smiled. "Mine, too. Good night. See you tomorrow."

Riot walked into the bedroom, leaped on the bed, and curled himself into a furry, golden ball beside me. I reached over and turned off the light.

A Note from the Author

I've had several early readers tell me that it was hard to read this book. And it should be...the grueling and gritty content is earth-shattering and happening all around us. *The Crushing* is meant as a metaphor that embraces both the crushing of a woman's spirit and the crushing of her enemies. However, "crushing" is also the reason that grapes experience rebirth as a fine wine, or flower petals emerge as a lovely fragrance. When a person is crushed emotionally, spiritually, or physically, this may act as a catalyst for positive change and evolution or be received as punishment and result in depression or worse. It's certainly possible to let crushing experiences prune us and make us wiser. More resilient. The characters in my story have all been crushed. It was interesting to write this story and discover how each individual handled their personal journeys. My hope is that this book will inspire the reader to explore their own thoughts about "crushing" experiences and make the choice to use them to create a life-giving and hope-filled fragrance.

Acknowledgements

From the bottom of my heart, I want to thank Level Best Books and the whole team for giving me a chance back in 2020. It's been a merry-go-round of plots and ZOOM meetings and printing issues and in short, it's been the very best growing and learning experience available. I also want to give a shout-out to my critique group, James Mallory, Eddy Hoyle, Hiyaguha Cohen, and Richard Wright of Island Writers Network for their insightful critiques. Without you guys, the book would've fallen short. Thank you. I especially want to thank my Navy photo-journalist daughter, Bonnie Miller, for her constant discerning eye as one of my faithful beta readers, and Brian Thiem, an ever-present source of cop-wisdom. Also, my "Besties" author family from Level Best Books as well as the late Dawn Dowdle's family of authors with Blue Ridge Literary Agency have been a great help in the overall business of marketing and selling books, as well as sharing information about becoming a better, more skillful writer. These authors are definitely my "tribe," and I'm proud to be counted among them. And most importantly, a huge thank you to my readers! Without your support, reviews, and encouragement, none of this would be possible.

About the Author

Kerry Peresta is the author of the Olivia Callahan Suspense series, Level Best Books, and *Back Before Dawn*, a standalone suspense, Level Best Books. Kerry spent thirty years in advertising as an account manager, creative director, copywriter, and editor. She began writing full-time in 2009 as a humor columnist for a daily newspaper before she decided to take the plunge and begin writing novels. Kerry was chapter president of Maryland Writers Association when she lived in Maryland, and currently is a member of the Island Writers Network, the Sisters in Crime organization, South Carolina Writers Association, International Thriller Writers, and is a popular presenter and speaker for the Pat Conroy Literary Center in Beaufort, SC. Kerry and her husband are originally from Little Rock, Arkansas, and moved to Hilton Head Island, SC, in 2015. She and her husband enjoy kayaking, road trips, their grandkids, their three cats, and the scenic vistas of the Lowcountry. Discover more at kerryperesta.com.

AUTHOR WEBSITE: https://www.kerryperesta.com

SOCIAL MEDIA HANDLES:

Instagram: https://www.instagram.com/kerryperesta
Facebook Personal Page: https://www.facebook.com/klperesta
Facebook Author Page: https://www.facebook.com/kerry.peresta
Twitter/X: https://www.twitter.com/kerryperesta
Bookbub: https://www.bookbub.com/profile/kerry-peresta
Goodreads: https://www.goodreads.com/kerryperesta

Also by Kerry Peresta

Back Before Dawn, Standalone suspense, 2023

The Torching, Book 3, Olivia Callahan Suspense, 2023

The Rising, Book 2, Olivia Callahan Suspense, 2022

The Deadening, Book 1, Olivia Callahan Suspense, 2021

Short stories:
  "The Toad Lady," Carroll County Chapter MWA Anthology, *That One Left Shoe*, 2012
  "The Day the Migraine Died," Anthology, *Rock, Roll, and Ruin*, Triangle Sisters In Crime, 2022

www.ingramcontent.com/pod-product-compliance
Lightning Source LLC
Chambersburg PA
CBHW021505110726
47899CB00001BA/298